THE WINDS OF FATE

To purchase these titles in e-book form, please go to www.baen.com.

THE WINDS OF FATE

S.M. STIRLING

THE WINDS OF FATE

This is a work of fiction. All the characters and events portrayed in this book are fictional, and any resemblance to real people or incidents is purely coincidental.

A Baen Books Original

Baen Publishing Enterprises
P.O. Box 1403
Riverdale, NY 10471
www.baen.com

ISBN: 978-1-6680-7272-1

Cover art by Sam R. Kennedy

First printing, July 2025

Distributed by Simon & Schuster
1230 Avenue of the Americas
New York, NY 10020

Library of Congress Cataloging-in-Publication Data

Names: Stirling, S. M., author.
Title: The winds of fate / S.M. Stirling.
Description: Riverdale, NY : Baen Publishing Enterprises, 2025. | Series:
    Make the darkness bright ; 2
Identifiers: LCCN 2025001594 (print) | LCCN 2025001595 (ebook) | ISBN
    9781668072721 (hardcover) | ISBN 9781964856278 (ebook)
Subjects: LCGFT: Time-travel fiction. | Science fiction. | Novels.
Classification: LCC PS3569.T543 W56 2025 (print) | LCC PS3569.T543
    (ebook) | DDC 813/.54—dc23/eng/20250228
LC record available at https://lccn.loc.gov/2025001594
LC ebook record available at https://lccn.loc.gov/2025001595

Printed in the United States of America

10 9 8 7 6 5 4 3 2 1

To Janet Cathryn Stirling, 1950–2021, dearest of all.

Thanks to—

To Esther Friesner, good friend and talented author, for checking something out for me.

To Bill Fawcett, for numerous valuable suggestions in this series.

To Kier Salmon, longtime close friend and valued advisor, to whom I have always listened carefully. And for things like managing the beta-reader stuff. I owe her greatly for everything I've written since 1998.

To Markus Baur, for help with the German language and as a first reader, and for being my native guide to Pannonia Superior, which provided valuable help with *To Turn the Tide* and *The Winds of Fate*.

To Dr. Donald Ringe, author of many insightful volumes on linguistic history, for a single piece of advice on Proto-Germanic chronology. All mistakes are mine!

To my first readers: Pete Sartucci, Markus Baur, Steve Brady, Ara Sedaka, Mike Ralls, Diane Porter, Margaret Carter, Kier Salmon, Romaine Spence, Jade Cheung, Sandy Michaud, and Emily Sedaka.

To Patricia Finney (aka P.F. Chisholm), for friendship and her own wonderful books, starting with *A Shadow of Gulls* (which she wrote when she was in her teens, at which point I was still doing Edgar Rice Burroughs pastiche fanfic) and going on from there. One of the best historical novelists of our generation!

And to Joe's Dining (http://joesdining.com/), and its splendid proprietor, Roland Richter, for his help with German stuff, and the servers for running relays with my Diet Coke.

Also Tribes Coffee House, (https://www.tribescoffeehouse.net/) here in Santa Fe.

To both institutions and their staff for putting up with my interminable presence and my habit of making faces and muttering dialogue as I write.

Also, they don't have attention-demanding cats walking on the keyboard. A cat sleeps more than fourteen hours a day, yet somehow manages to interrupt you continuously—feline magic.

⇒ PROLOGUE ⇐

Outside Vindobonum
Provincia Pannonia Superior
Imperium Romanum
September 5th, 167 CE

Imperator Caesar Marcus Aurelius Antoninus Augustus stepped up to the edge of the purple-draped wooden platform on a cool bright autumn morning, standing tall. At five-eight he was several inches above average by Roman standards, and looked imposing in his gold-embossed, muscled bronze cuirass, with an Imperial purple sash about his waist and a cloak of the same hanging from his shoulders.

A wreath of gold-wrought laurel leaves rested on hair a dark brown that verged on black; that and his close-cut curled beard showed a few threads of gray.

The platform was ten feet above ground level, which added to the effect. But the eyes that looked out from that very Roman face were deep brown pools where thoughts moved glinting, like fish in the depths. Those who knew him well would have remarked that his stance was easier than it had been last year, as if some internal pain—which his Stoic training let him mostly ignore—had gone.

Stretching in front of the silk-draped square plank dais to both sides were units from all five of the legions that had crossed the Danube this May past, and from the auxiliaries who'd accompanied them and fought beside them... or at times in front of

1

them. The rest were still in the north, consolidating and clearing up, building forts and roads, and nailing the victory down.

They looked splendid in their ordered ranks with the unit banners bright in front of each infantry cohort or cavalry *ala*, but the cool wind from the north also brought the rancid-oil-sweat-iron-brass-dirty-socks smell massed Imperial troops had in this age. Even the new legions raised three years ago—II and III Italica—now had the look of veterans, and their gear was well-kept but also showed hard use.

It all combined with the familiar scent of horses and what horses did, copiously, whenever the impulse moved them. Tribune Lucius Triarius Artorius—born Arthur Vandenberg in West Texas just a few days before Christmas in the year 1999 CE—had spent much of his childhood and adolescence on the family ranch there, and found that part a bit nostalgic.

Behind the Emperor at the rear of the square platform was a giant banner hanging from a crossbar; the pole that supported it was topped by a spread-winged golden eagle with its claws on silver thunderbolts. Embroidered on the rippling crimson silk below was a golden wreath with the letters SPQR inside it in *capitalis monumentalis*.

For *Senatus Populusque Romanus*.

Also behind the ruler and in front of the banner were a collection of bigwigs, the provincial governor of Pannonia Superior, Marcus Iallius Bassus, the legionary commanders, and *Legatus Augusti pro praetore* Marcus Claudius Fronto—officially second-in-command for this campaign, unofficially its general under the Emperor's overall direction. A round dozen of the ruler's *comites*, his closest advisors and the functional equivalent of a Cabinet, filled out the roster; some were in military garb, some in civilian togas with the broad or narrow purple strips of a senator or *eques*.

And five former Americans, here via a one-way trip in a very temporary time machine, Artorius thought.

The Emperor nodded to his court physician, Aelius Galenus, and extended his left arm in a graceful quasi-rhetorical gesture. Public speaking was at the core of Roman upper-class education, and he'd been drilled in it since childhood.

Galenus was the Latin form of Galenos, something which showed his Roman citizenship though he was born a Greek in the great city of Pergamum, in Roman Asia Minor. He was a spare man in his late thirties, wiry-slim with a high brow beneath his thick black hair and short-cropped beard.

Now his hand raised a vial of glass for the audience below the platform to see. He knocked the stem off with a deft blow from the handle of a surgical scalpel, and wiped the Emperor's shoulder with a swatch of damp cloth that had been boiled and allowed to cool in a covered container. Then he used the point of the blade to make a deep scratch. Into that he poured a little of the liquid inside the vial, rubbed it in with another clean swatch, handed the vial and scalpel to an assistant, then deftly bandaged the slight wound.

Tribune Artorius watched it all from the rear of the temporary dais. He was thirty-four and a bit now biologically, which made him a few years younger than the Greek . . . as well as over eighteen hundred years younger, in another sense.

He was also six feet tall—which was towering by Roman standards and well above average even for the barbarian Germanii—broad-shouldered and leanly muscular. His sun-streaked fair hair and beard were cropped close and his skin deeply tanned, which made his slightly tilted blue eyes stand out vividly.

What he wore was unexceptional in this exalted company: a bleached-white tunic of fine wool with two narrow purple stripes running down from the shoulder to the hem, marking his elevation to the status of *eques*, a member of the Equestrian Order, the lower ninety-plus percent of the Roman aristocracy. It had often been rendered in English as "knight" and literally meant *horse-rider*.

Far in the past that had been meant literally, describing those who came to early Rome's war levy on horseback. Most later European languages had had some equivalent that meant *gentleman* too, chevalier or caballero or the like.

As opposed to cowboy *in Texan,* he thought with a hidden whimsical smile.

That elevation to the Equestrian Order had been made by Marcus Aurelius himself, and on this very spot, a little more than a year ago. Along with enough *land* to make him quite respectable, gifted from the *res privata,* the Emperor's private estates. All four of his American companions . . . once graduate students . . . had gotten lesser but substantial rewards then too.

Back from June 2032 CE to June 165 CE in an instant, unconscious, then two years plus three months forward at normal living pace, he thought. *We started slow, but things have sped up lately . . . since we showed up at that first battle here last May and turned things around. Nine months to get ready for that, on our own. Birthing a biggish baby . . . We've sure done a lot more since, but it helps to have the Big Boss grateful and helpful.* Per ardua ad astra!

The hem of the tunic came to his knees, because the garment was bloused up through his *balteus*—the military belt and baldric that held his sword and dagger—of red-dyed leather mostly covered in worked silver plaques. That and the *caligae* on his feet, the strapped hobnailed sandal-boot of the Roman army, were rank markers too: they showed he was a soldier, and the whole ensemble said *tribunus angusticlavius* to Roman eyes—literally a tribune of the narrow stripe.

None of them would blink at the white scars on his legs, though they might find their shape unusual . . . because they'd been made by an improvised bomb, eighteen hundred years from now in a future that probably no longer existed. Though he'd never know for sure, which was one of the many reasons he thought about that future as little as he could. Particularly not about the personal parts, which still gave him nightmares now and then.

He was also a Tribune attached to the *Imperial* headquarters; in American terms he was a high-ranking general staff officer. Lively rumor made him much more, that and the fact that the Emperor obviously paid his counsel close attention.

Which had brought an embarrassment of bribe offers, too, from people who wanted to buy their way to the Emperor's notice. Learning to turn those down tactfully and without giving mortal offense had been . . .

A steep learning curve.

The troops before them had won a crushing victory over the coalition of barbarian tribes led by the Marcomanni and Quadi. They were still feeling cocky about beating what Romans called the *Magna Coniuratio Barbarae*—the Great Barbarian Conspiracy. For that matter, those who'd fought the fight would boast about it all their lives, and on their inscribed tombstones too.

And they were feeling very, very well-inclined toward Tribune Artorius and his clients, who they all knew had drastically reduced the *cost* of that victory with his *new things* aka "the Pannonian gear."

Artorius the War-Wise was their nickname for him.

Though they don't *know the Marcomannic Wars would have lasted for* fourteen years *without us Americans. That's an accomplishment, soldier! From fourteen years of mutual slaughter and burning and wasting from here to Italy . . . all scaled down to one campaigning season on a successful defensive and then one more on the* highly *successful* offensive. *With a fair bit of slaughter, granted; the first battle here, that Quadi night attack on Carnuntum that I called . . .*

That still made him sweat in retrospect. He'd made an educated guess and it had vastly increased his reputation. If it *hadn't* worked out, though . . .

. . . then vastatio *north of the Danube until the enemy were desperate enough to stop retreating and fight the final biggie this summer. . . . But not year after year of* mutual *slaughter this time, and the* Roman *territories aren't devastated. And it's over for good, and the Marcomanni and Quadi and a lot of others are* under the wings of the Eagles . . . *also for good.*

Which Roman phrase meant the Marcomanni and Quadi were now obedient subjects of the Empire and beneficiaries of the *Pax Romana*, whether they liked it or not.

Probably every second free man of military age in those great tribal confederations was dead, or crippled and fumbling at tasks that had once been easy, or in chains heading south to the slave markets and the Imperial mines and the gladiatorial arenas. With a much *higher* casualty rate among the tribal elites, because they were the closest thing to professional fighters their people had and had been in the front lines from the beginning.

The survivors were not eager for a rematch.

Their few living chiefs . . . or the minor-age sons of their *dead* chiefs, represented by their mothers . . . were scrambling to accept the terms offered, harsh though they were. They knew full well that the Romans could kill or enslave them all . . . and were perfectly willing and able to do just that if they caused serious trouble.

And by the time a new generation had grown up and could start thinking about revenge for dead fathers, with gunpowder weapons no longer so supernatural seeming . . . By then the new provinces would be webbed with Roman roads—done macadamized style as helpfully suggested by Artorius and his four followers. And tacked down with forts, newly founded cities and veteran colonies, and heavily salted with civilian settlers from the older, more Romanized provinces to the south of the Danube, or from Dacia north of it.

A lot of the widows and orphaned daughters would end up married or mated to Romans and Roman subjects one way or another, too. To soldiers, or incomers without womenfolk. Their children would grow up speaking Latin . . .

The settlers would be moved to move there not least by the new silver and gold mines *discovered* by Artorius & Co., from Fuchs's twenty-first-century maps, physical and digital. Combined with better—eighteenth- and nineteenth-century style—refining techniques, those would make considerable fortunes for their backers, large new revenues for the Imperial government, and they would shed a thick dandruff of orders for food and tools and markets for services and general lavish spending all around them to grease the Romanization process.

In front of the soldiers were some of the improved *carroballistae*, field catapults, that the time travelers had designed, drawn up in neat ranks on their two-wheeled, split-trail carriages, with their ammunition limbers behind. Hundreds were coming out of the military workshops now, with the aim of giving every legion about sixty of them. Saltpeter and sulfur and charcoal were pouring into the workshops to make ammunition too.

That was a visual reminder, not least to the envoys from various Germanic tribes and the Sarmatian Iazyges and Roxolani who were also present.

They threw what the Roman soldiers called thunderballs, or Jupiter's thunderballs, or just Jupiter's Balls: sheet-bronze spheres about the size of a man's head full of black powder and lined with lead bullets held in tree resin, with a quick-match fuse through a plug on top. The catapults could throw the twenty-five-pound weight to over three hundred yards, equivalent to a longbow shot.

When they exploded, they had about the same destructive impact as a shell from a heavy mortar in the twenty-first-century American army when you took into account the extra *oomph* given by the dense formations everybody used here. They could also throw an unpleasant form of napalm-like incendiary he'd introduced that was now called *Ignis Romanus*, Roman Fire, in a pottery jug.

What a battery of six throwing *that* did to a timber-palisade fort had to be seen to be believed.

And in front of *them* were eighteen cannon cast from bronze, modeled on the twelve-pounder Napoleon gun-howitzer of the American Civil War—the only cannon in the world, right now, and the product of nearly a year of sweating-hard labor, plus plenty of fatal and maiming accidents until the locals got the concepts of *explosion* and *recoil* internalized. Lessons which had nearly killed *him* once.

Fortunately, bronze casting was something Romans were *already* good at; that had gone faster. It had been boring out the barrels that took time...and Dr. Fuchs's measuring gauges.

The Roman troops called them *tormenta*—which meant both *throwing engines* and *instruments of torture*, a sign that soldiers' humor didn't change much.

The first of the new *carroballistae* and thunderballs had been made privately, by the Americans on the Villa Lunae...and then demonstrated—

Demonstrated, he thought. *Nice neutral term.*

Demonstrated at the battle here in May of last year, when the Tenth Legion was on the brink of being destroyed by a Marcomannic host. The cannon project on the other hand had been backed by Marcus Aurelius after he'd arrived that summer, and hence by the Imperial treasury, thank God or the Gods. By then they had impressed the Roman military...and the provincial bigwigs...and then the Emperor...to the necessary level. As he'd told his four American companions, you needed a government for that sort of massive rush job. Preferably a big government with big revenues.

The twelve-pounders had helped win the final victory too, in their very first battlefield use. Not so much the casualties inflicted at the final enormous fight between the field armies of Rome and the Great Barbarian Conspiracy, though those had been considerable. The crucial thing had been their *picador* work in giving the huge barbarian host an unpalatable choice between running away and probably starving, or attacking and hoping *that* worked.

The tribes present at that fight had included allies from all across the *Barbaricum*, as far away as the North Sea. They'd chosen to attack after hours of being lethally pummeled from far beyond the range of any weapon they had, instead of their original and highly sensible plan of making the Romans come to them.

Charging *en masse* over the open mile between their start line and the Roman army... first through the flail of the cannon firing round shot and then grapeshot... then the rain of hundreds upon hundreds of thunderballs... then at sword's point with the Roman auxiliary foot soldiers who held them in place while clouds of arrows and still *more* thunderballs fell on them... then in a short, shattering battle with the fresh and eager legionary heavy infantry.

When the barbarians were already exhausted and whittled down and reeling from their losses and terrified by the supernatural-seeming long-range death.

After about a half hour of *that* they had bolted rearward in screaming panic... the rather less than half of their original vast numbers still alive by that point. Pursued by Roman cavalry, now equipped with wood-framed saddles with stirrups and raised cantles, on horses with nailed-on iron horseshoes, and holding long lances used in the medieval couched style originally invented about eight or nine hundred years after this date.

Not many had escaped, only the ones who'd run first and fastest, or had fresh horses under them, or both. Those tribal envoys sent to this ceremony from groups that hadn't been at the battle had been shown over the field of battle first, and even some of the hardened barbarian warriors had heaved and retched at the sight and smell of forty or fifty thousand corpses left to rot in the summer heat and feed the foxes and wolves, crows and vultures, maggots and worms.

It was already being avidly discussed from here to Rome and beyond, the news spread by galloping couriers. As the greatest victory Roman arms had ever won on a single day... a discussion that would be helped along by broadsheets printed in Latin or Greek on the new paper and stuck up at street corners from here to Rome and eventually from Eboracum in northern Britannia to Nisibis on the border with Parthia.

Propaganda changes when you've got paper and printing presses, not just faces on coins and statues in marketplaces and temples. And people here don't have... antibodies to it. Not yet.

Generally about a third to a half of Roman male city dwellers could read, much more than in farming country. Basically because it was just more useful there. And they were accustomed to doing it aloud for their illiterate family members and neighbors.

Few people here read silently anyway; that was considered the mark of a great scholar. Probably that was partly due to the way they ran all the words together without punctuation or spaces in ordinary everyday cursive writing. They *had* writing, but it was still more closely linked to an oral culture than it had become later.

Though all the printers they'd trained used upper- and lower-case letters with twenty-first-century Western text conventions now, and it would spread by sheer force of numbers if nothing else. Before they'd arrived, a best seller had a few hundreds of handmade copies in total, and they were *passed* from hand to hand too. Even things like Homer or Virgil only had thousands, and that meant Empire-wide in a population of around seventy million. Books had been *expensive*, costing the equivalent of a good used car in the 21st century, or an ordinary slave here.

Nearly all the books coming off the new presses outnumbered those done in the old style and they were much, much cheaper. They had the prestige of officially approved novelty, too.

Marcus Aurelius would ride the ceremonial chariot in triumph through the streets of Rome when he returned there soon, with an attendant holding the victor's crown over his head and whispering *remember you are mortal*...which he'd endure because it was customary. Rather than really enjoying the screaming adulation from the spectators.

He was an unusual man for this time and place.

And Marcus Claudius Fronto, who'd been in command under the Emperor's supervision, would get the *ornamenta triumphalia*, the *ornaments* of a triumph. Nobody but a reigning Emperor and their close relations actually celebrated a triumph through the streets of the capital these days; that had been the rule since the time of the first Augustus a century and a half ago.

The others on the platform stepped forward in their turn to be vaccinated. So did Artorius, and his four ex-students—Paula Atkins, very black and by now statuesquely full-figured rather than plump; Jeremey McCladden, who was like a slightly scaled-down version of Artorius as far as his body went and had a deceptively frank, open, snub-nosed Midwestern small-town-boy face; tall, gawky Mark Findlemann; and Filipa Chang's wiry athletic slimness.

They'd all been immunized in their home century and didn't really need the vaccine, but showing willingness now was important. Particularly since they were commonly regarded as quasi-supernatural, which was the reason Paula and Filipa were present at this military ceremony and on the dais itself. Normally nobody female except possibly an empress would be, unless they were a spectator in the distance; a fair proportion of the residents of Vindobona—of both sexes—had walked out to watch all this, and they were grouped a fair ways back of the dais.

And we all have trouble paying for a drink in Vindobonum, Artorius thought. *They know what we saved them from. Now they think they can be saved from the plague...and they can.*

Though the former Harvard graduate students were officially named Paula, Julius, Marcus and Philippa *Triarus* on their certificates of Roman citizenship, the *libellus*. With Latinized versions of their surnames tacked on the end of the *tria nomina* as a cognomen. Paula Atkins was Paula Triaria Atcintia, for starters, though women often used only the first two.

Artorius had picked Triarius as a mild joke, since it was a recognized Roman middle name—the nomen, originally a clan marker—but also meant *old soldier*.

He was literally an old soldier, himself. A graduate of West Point, and very briefly a captain in the US Army, 1st Battalion, 75th Rangers, though he'd retired after a bad wound from an IED. And done his doctorate in classical history at Harvard right afterward, starting while he was still on crutches...and receiving it not long before he ended up here.

And in a real sense, here-and-now we are *all the same clan!*

The others had been graduate students, also of varied fields of classical studies and five or six years younger than him, recruited at the request of an Austrian physicist named Hans Fuchs. Who'd claimed to have invented a mechanism for securely, precisely dating any historical artifact. That had been a bald lie to get them to Klosterneuburg, just north of Vienna, where the Institute of Science and Technology campus was located.

Fuchs had had a direct...personal...reason for wanting a range of Roman experts.

It was really a time machine, *of course,* Artorius thought. *Though I didn't believe it when he told me. Seeing was believing, though!*

Remembering the flickering stop-go sensation as Fuchs hastily triggered it when the news of World War Three starting poured in through phones and tablets, then tried to dash back and jump inside the circle of gridwork with the Americans and what they'd come to call his *baggage*.

That had been like slow motion in real life, and had given Artorius a...

Really interesting *experience and I don't want to see anything that* interesting *ever again as long as I live.*

...an *interesting* view of the flash and blast wave hitting the building the time machine was in.

Complete with watching the cracks spreading in the glass of the windows as they prepared to scatter in razor-sharp high-velocity shards through anyone standing in their path. Followed if they'd still been there by the burning building collapsing on whatever was left of your head, and then the fallout plume finishing things off if you were unlucky enough to live through all that and feel the puking, bleeding, rotting-alive sensations of radiation poisoning.

I can't really object, since Vienna and most of the cities in the world were fusion-bombed just about the same time we... left. We made it by a second or less. Though Fuchs didn't make it. Well, he made it but minus his legs from midthigh down and we buried him. And kept the very useful metric ton of baggage he'd put together for the trip!

He carefully *didn't* think of what he'd been tricked into leaving behind: a wife he'd loved since high school and married a month after graduating from the Academy, and their children, for starters. Sometimes his subconscious didn't agree with that and sent unpleasant dreams about their probable fate... if they hadn't just been erased by what he was doing here.

The dreams came less and less often, though. As far as he was concerned, Arthur Vandenberg the American had died then, killed with his family on the same day. If you repeated something to yourself often enough and hard enough you started believing it.

I'm Artorius now, and Roman. Sort of. Reformist Roman, maybe? And I've been a Stoic in philosophical terms since I found out what that was. Fate doesn't give you love, it loans it to you and can take it back at any instant. Prepare to be punched out by Fate, because that will happen, sooner or later. More than once, probably, and it all ends in death.

When everyone on the dais had gotten their cleansing wipe and scratch and bandage, Marcus Aurelius gestured Galen forward to address the assembly. Designated men in the more distant cohorts would relay his words to those too far away to hear clearly.

The Greek's Latin was fluent, but with a definite hometown Ionian accent. That wouldn't hurt, since Hellenes had high prestige in matters scientific... or philosophical, as they'd say here.

Nor did it hurt that he was physician to the Imperial family and court, and had introduced—or relayed from the Americans and gotten the credit for—the new antiseptic treatments that had kept unprecedented numbers of them alive after being wounded in action, and other measures which had cut the usual camp diseases radically. More than half of the rather light Roman casualties in the summer just past had been due to direct enemy action rather than infected wounds otherwise survivable, plus camp fevers and dysentery.

Which is unprecedented and everyone realized it.

In his own history, that probably hadn't happened for any major military campaign until World War One. And only on the Western Front, even in that one.

Galen's divinely inspired, they think: Asclepius whispers in his ear, instead of just us. Which is good. People are less likely to argue when they think it's God... or a God... talking.

"Soldiers of Rome, and foreign guests," Galen said.

Utterly terrified and bewildered foreign guests, Artorius filled in silently.

Looking at the *ambassadors* aka *hostages* huddled in clumps, surrounded by Roman "honor guards" with their hands on their swords and unpleasantly predatory expressions on their faces. The envoys snatched horrified glances at the new weapons every now and then. They'd been given luridly helpful demonstrations of what the *carroballistae* and cannon could do, with live sheep or pigs or occasionally living but shortly to be dead condemned criminals as targets. That usually hurt less than crucifixion...

Foreign guests convinced that nowadays Romans throw thunderbolts like Gods. We've introduced a lot of new stuff... starting with wheelbarrows and on to paper and printing, which took a lot longer and a lot more trial and error... but gunpowder... yeah, that gets their attention. With a bang! *People who've never seen explosions before are... impressed.*

"You will all have heard of the terrible new plague from the east," the Greek physician said. "This—"

He held up the now-empty little glass flask.

"—is an infallible preventative. Ten days after you receive this treatment, the plague will have no power to touch you. There will be a slight flush of fever, but nothing to worry you, and then you are safe from this terrible illness for the rest of your life!"

Unexpectedly, a chant of *"AVE! AVE!"* came from the troops.

Galen started a little, and you could see him stop himself from looking around for the one the accolade was directed at.

What the ampoule contained was the scabs from scratches on the shaven stomachs of calves where they'd been rubbed with matter from cows sick with cowpox. The scabs were cleaned, dissolved in distilled water and then the ampule was sealed with a careful daub of molten glass.

That was how the Victorians had done it, low-tech but effective.

They now knew definitely that the Antonine Plague—also known to historians in their native century as the Plague of Galen, from his descriptions of it—*was* smallpox. An odd, ancient variant of it, even more viciously contagious than later types, swiftly and agonizingly lethal to half or more of those infected. Diseases tended to get less virulent with time because letting their hosts live longer made reproduction easier, so evolution pushed them in that direction. They were far enough back that smallpox was *even more* dangerous than it had been in the last few centuries before it was extinguished.

In the original history the Antonine Plague had killed somewhere between a tenth and a third of the entire population of the Roman Empire, and much more than that in the concentrated masses of the cities and in the armies. That had been a fair chunk of humanity, since the Roman Empire right now held a third of the human race.

Rome had never really recovered; it had been the first painful face-plant on a long and ever-steeper downhill slope of bone-breaking impacts, with the Dark Ages at the bottom.

Though this time it won't *kill the co-Emperor.*

Imperator Caesar Lucius Aurelius Verus Augustus was an amiable nonentity, one who always looked a little guilty when his far more energetic older adopted brother was around.

He's alive because we dosed him with some of our precious stock of twenty-first-century antivirals when he got here with a fever of a hundred and five and the beginnings of pustules, Artorius thought. *The ones aimed at monkeypox... which is part of the same general family as smallpox. And we cured Marcus Aurelius' ulcers with antibiotics, too. Ulcers which are* almost *certainly what killed* him *twelve years from now in the history we studied. Live long and reign well, Emperor of Rome!*

Experiment had shown that cowpox still gave a nearly perfect rate of protection against *this* variety of smallpox, just as Jenner had found in the eighteenth century. And like its close relative smallpox, the cowpox virus was large and formed a protective sheath and could lie dormant but contagious for long periods when protected from sunlight and heat and desiccation. In the ampoules it would stay active for quite some time, if they were kept in boxes and the boxes kept in shade.

Plus, apparently cowpox was common in cows around here anyway. They'd use the vaccine to infect them if they had to— that way one dose could make thousands.

The farmers looked at us as if we were men from Mars when we asked about that, it being something everybody knows. *And in a sense we* are *like big-eyed gray aliens here.*

So far only three locals knew they were from the *future* as well as "America." There were Marcus Aurelius and Galen, who'd used their formidable intellects to jointly figure out that the Americans' cover story had gaping holes. For example, why would people from the other side of Oceanus itself know the geography of northern Europe better than the Romans who lived next door to it?

The Emperor had confronted him about it privately. *And* believed him when he told the truth and gave some demonstrations on his phone, which was linked to the military-grade laptops in the baggage. People here *knew* less, and less of their information was *accurate*; that didn't mean they were necessarily stupid.

At all. Galen and the Emperor were both scary-bright.

So was Josephus ben Matthias, the Jewish merchant who'd discovered the involuntary time travelers unconscious beside Fuchs's *baggage* and who'd given them invaluable help. But he had also mentally worried at the curiosities of their appearance like a very smart bulldog until Artorius took him into his confidence about it.

He'd even noticed that all the coins in Fuchs's chest of cash looked new-minted; they'd been fresh from an Italian firm in the twenty-first century who made replicas of Roman currency. When they *should* have had lots of wear and tear because they bore the face of Antoninus Pius, who'd adopted the current Emperors as his heirs—Marcus Aurelius was his nephew anyway—and died five years before the Americans showed up.

And he'd puzzled over the fact that he'd found the five of them... five and a half, if you counted Fuchs who hadn't *quite completely* made it into the temporal field... in a forest clearing. With absolutely no sign or track of the pack animals or carts that could have brought their metric ton of baggage to a remote spot, as if they'd dropped out of the air.

Which we did, pretty much.

Their cover story for the rest was that they were exiles from *America,* an island realm beyond Hibernia, now utterly destroyed by a terrible war fought with weapons of Godlike power. Perhaps even sunk beneath the waves, like Plato's Atlantis.

Which has the virtue of being... in a way... the truth. And it'll account for there not being any ruins when we get around to doing the sailing the ocean blue in the local equivalent of 1492. Fairly soon now. It'll be the Age of Exploration but supercharged, with an electric cable up the butt. With modern sailing ships, sextants and chronometers and accurate maps.

Galen waited until the shouts died down; the Roman soldiers were brave as you could want facing human enemies, but *everyone* in this period feared disease with excellent reason, and rumors about the plague had been spreading even faster than the virus. Their relief was palpable.

"Men I have trained—" he went on.

Paula Atkins snorted very quietly from behind Artorius. That included a fair number of *women* she'd seen to training as well, over the past eight months, for what would be scary but well-paid work... and they'd get paid just what the men would, too. It would take the rest of their working lives as well since it would be a couple of decades before *everyone* in the Empire could be vaccinated. By then enough children would have been born that they'd have to start again...

There were practical reasons for including women in the program, which she'd used to justify it: there were many places in the Roman Empire, particularly in the east or Greece, where married men would be deeply reluctant to let a male physician near their wives and daughters, and women could spread the plague as easily as anyone.

In her own mind and in English she regarded it as a strike against what she called the general *dick-worshipping-dickitude* of Roman civilization. This was not a time or place to fill a feminist with joy, to put it mildly, though there were others that would have been worse.

If we'd ended up in Assurbanipal's Assyria or Athens in Pericles' time for instance.

Galen went on: "—are even now travelling east and west, north and south, to all parts of the Empire, bearing this preventative and the means to make more of it. Escorted by some of your comrades, the brave soldiers of the Roman Empire. Together we will defeat this plague, crush it as we crushed the barbarians!"

That got him another round of cheers; not least because these were the soldiers who *had* defeated the barbarians, and they were intensely proud of their deeds. Those cheers died to disciplined silence as Marcus Aurelius stepped forward in his turn and raised his right hand high in the standard Roman rhetorical gesture for a public address, which was distinctly similar to their military salute:

"Soldiers of Rome! You will all receive this treatment today, just as I have."

"ROMA! ROMA! ROMA!"

That unified bellow was a standard response to the opening of an address by the Emperor; it didn't startle Artorius the way it had the first time. Nobody had warned him then, since it was another of those things *everybody knew* and nobody had bothered to write down ... or which hadn't made it to the twenty-first century if someone had.

Marcus Aurelius touched his bandaged left arm.

"Every soldier of the Empire shall receive it as soon as may be, and their families too. Every encampment, even the furthest, shall receive it in the next six months."

That was doable, but only with a massive effort. As for the families ... technically, soldiers in the Roman army couldn't marry while serving their twenty-five-year enlistment.

They did anyway, of course. The resulting wives and children were legitimized—and given citizenship, if necessary—when the husband mustered out or died, not least because the male children often joined the Army themselves and fitted in better than random recruits. The auxiliaries who formed the other half of the Army were recruited from *perigrinii*, noncitizen Imperial subjects, but they got citizenship at the end of their hitches and *their* mates and children did too.

Rome had always had a much more liberal attitude to extending its citizenship than most ancient civilizations... which was *one* important reason it had ended up as ruler of a third of the human race. The Imperial army was a giant Romanization machine, among other things, and a major reason so much of Europe had ended up speaking languages derived from Latin. At second hand, it was why two Latin-derived languages had stretched from the Rio Grande in south Texas to Tierra del Fuego at the southern tip of South America.

Probably even more so this time 'round, Artorius thought. *It'll likely replace Proto-Germanic in the next couple of centuries, the way it's been doing with the Celtic languages and Dacian and most of proto-Basque already. Add in a solid block from Tripoli to Morocco, too. And it'll spread explosively overseas when we bring in advanced sailing ships...*

In fact, he thought Latin might well remain a *single* language, though it would change over time as all tongues did; the written, formal form was already a bit different from what people actually spoke, though less so than English had been in his birth century. But it hadn't started to diverge *regionally* very much in Artorius' history until after the Empire broke up and that cut trade and travel to small fractions of their former volume. Hopefully in the history the Americans were making those would only increase... and literacy in standard Latin would grow too.

Less actual *regional variation right now than English in the twenty-first, in fact. Less variation between the way it's written and spoken, too.*

You knew that if you'd experienced what people *actually* spoke in, say, Jamaica or Glasgow or Freetown in Sierra Leone. All of which he had, with travel paid courtesy of Uncle Sam. Or thought about why thought was spelled with *ught* but pronounced *thot*.

The Emperor went on:

"This preventative medicine, this *vaccine*, will also be sent to the City of Rome itself and to the cities and towns along the routes to the east, from where the plague is spreading, to *stop* that spread. As a shield turns a sword! Then it will be sent to every province, every district, in the end to every village and villa and farm from Britannia to Mesopotamia. The Empire protects its citizens and subjects, with the favor of the Gods!"

A roaring chorus of:

"AVE! AVE, IMPERATOR!"

... greeted the words, shouted in unison from ten thousand throats.

Marcus Aurelius had been well-respected and fairly popular before the brief and triumphant Marcomannic War. Now the Army, at least, and as the news spread the population in general, regarded him as Julius Caesar or Augustus come again, or a new Trajan at the very least. Having the divinely inspired Galen and the mysterious and divinely favored (or possibly sorcerous or just divine) Marcus Triarius Artorius and his helpers at his back didn't hurt at all either, as rumors about *them* spread. And now he'd promised to halt a plague in its tracks.

Roman Emperors in this period—except the more megalomaniacal ones, like Caligula or Nero—usually didn't claim divine status while they were alive. The ones who did that didn't tend to live very long, either. They were deified *after* death, unless they were so violently unpopular with the Senate in retrospect that their successor didn't want to spend political capital on it.

The Emperor Vespasian, most of a century ago, had murmured: *Oh dear, I think I'm becoming a God!* as a mordant joke on his last sickbed.

That was a technicality that didn't mean much beyond the city of Rome and the upper classes. The fact that the Emperor *was* generally regarded as equivalent to a God would reduce resistance to this unfamiliar treatment. Though you had to bear in mind that the Classical-pagan concept of what a God *was* differed very strongly from that of monotheists like Jews and Christians.

Stopping cold the dreaded plague that had already slain multiple tens of thousands wouldn't hurt either once the evidence became clear to all, which would be another nice little positive-feedback cycle. The plague was bad enough to frighten everyone out of their wits, but *this* time it wouldn't actually do more than a small fraction of the original... if original meant anything here... damage.

Which means a lot *of people are going to live a* lot *longer because of us... not bad, not bad at all.*

Marcus Aurelius finished:

"*Roma aeterna victrix*! Rome forever victorious! Favored by the Gods, guarded by brave men, Rome shall have *imperium sine fine—*"

Those Latin words meant *empire without limits* or *eternal rule everywhere*, roughly. It was a quote from Virgil, though not many of *this* audience would be familiar with the poet, except some of the officers.

"—and bring all the world, all the human race, beneath the wings of our Eagles and the reach of the Pax Romana!"

Artorius nodded in grim agreement with the cheers that greeted that, unconscious of the way his face had set like something cast in raw iron.

And since this Roman Empire is favored by time travelers, Rome may actually get it. Imperium sine fine; one world, one government . . . in the very long run, a democratic one . . . and no nuclear war. Not a planet left to the rats and roaches and cringing scabby savages scuttling through ruins while they died by inches. We can do that.

He nodded again, without noticing he was doing it.

We will do that, or die trying.

⮞ CHAPTER ONE ⮜

Middle Vistula Valley
Imperium Romanum
March 10th, 170 CE

General Fronto was—inwardly—amused by how his presence made the senior centurion of this cohort a little nervous as the unit tramped north along the new road they'd built after settling in last fall.

He mentally read the man's mind:

As if the natives weren't enough, I have to look out for a muckety-muck, he mused. *Or possibly not, but I'd bet a considerable sum that's what he's thinking.*

It was a chilly spring day a few hours before noon in northern Germania, and there was a slight sogginess to the sound of the hobnails and iron-shod hooves and iron-banded wheels on the new-style bed of rolled and hammered crushed rock that covered the surface of the road. The sky was overcast, the air chill and damp though not really *cold* . . . not compared to what they'd just lived through in the winter.

And there was a smell of old wet ash and burnt wood from the roadside verges. Where the forest had been chopped back, and mostly burned to get rid of the timber and brush apart from what was hauled away to build the northernmost fort they were heading for, or to pile up for firewood to get them through the accursedly long, cold, wet, snowy winters here.

Northernmost for now. So far, he thought cheerfully. *We'll go*

another hundred miles at least this spring and summer...maybe
all the way to the German Ocean.

The men weren't even sweating much yet, despite marching
since dawn and the doubled tunics under their armor, and the
fact that many of them were wearing thick wool neck scarves
and local-style breeches and the new knitted socks and closed
hobnailed shoes rather than *caligae* sandal-boots. It was a bit of a
different smell from the one you'd get on a march by the Middle
Sea or in his home province of Asia Minor this time of year.

He'd never been a centurion himself, of course. Equestrians
could start that way, but as a man from a—fairly recently—
senatorial family he'd done his first three-year stint in the Imperial army as a *tribunus laticlavius*, a broad-stripe tribune. Which
meant a young staff officer attached to a legionary commander.

Officially with that rank you were senior to the five narrow-
stripe tribunes, and second in command of the legion...whose
commander, the *legatis legionis*, was usually a relative or patron
and one on the right side of the Emperor. Unofficially you were—

If you have any brains at all!

—there to learn the basics of the trade, the grimy details of
things that didn't get into written accounts or even very much into
old-soldier stories. That had been a bit over twenty years ago for
him, and—apart from a spell as a *quaestor* in Rome itself to make
a stab at the *cursus honorum* career path—he'd been campaigning or in garrison duty or lately governing provinces as well as
commanding troops most years since and, just last year, general
of a great field army under the Emperor's immediate supervision.

He'd *started* by commanding auxiliary cohorts, then a spell
as legate of the Ninth Claudian Legion south and east of here
at Durostorum, which had been a frontier posting back then...

You learn from the centurions, *not least. War is a trade, and*
like any other it has its mysteries.

"Don't worry," he said quietly to the senior man, the *pilus*
prior of the cohort, who was riding beside him.

The man was tough looking and stocky, brown haired and
blue-eyed and weathered, and in his late thirties. Which made
him six or seven years younger than the general, who went on:

"I've made it clear to several high-ranking men that this was
my idea and you're blameless if I get an arrow through an eye.
I need to see how the campaign is going—and it's spread out

now, not a matter of great pitched battles, so I also need to see the smaller units in operation. Cohorts at least."

The centurion eyed him out of the corner of *his* eyes, then grinned back.

"Thank you, sir," he said. "I'd heard you were a bold one, and smart."

A scar on his upper lip showed white through his black mustache and drew the lip awry a little, which blurred the Gallic accent in his fluent Latin. Then he went on cheerfully:

"But if you take an arrow I'd probably be dead too, and we could share a drink in Elysium and talk about it there!"

They both laughed, which was visibly reassuring to the troops. Who'd just spent a long, cold northern winter in log huts inside bank-and-palisade forts, and were aware that the drive northward would resume soon, aiming at the German Sea. Which meant more road-making and fort-building while your gear rusted and rotted in this damned damp climate and had to be painfully scoured every evening and the leather repaired far, far too often...and constant skirmishes at least.

They won nearly all of them, but you could get crippled just as badly or killed just as dead in a forgotten, victorious little tiff at the edge of the world as you could in a major battle.

That too is the price of Empire, he thought.

They marched in silence, keeping an eye cocked on the forest verges, until the senior centurion's head came up, and he spoke to his *optio*:

"Pass the word to be ready. Quickly, but quietly! No show!"

Then to the general:

"Our *exploratores* should have reported back by now, sir."

Fronto nodded. Scouts brought you information...or sometimes they didn't, and that was news too. Usually rather *bad* news. The centurion went on:

"This area, the local tribe is the Gutōz. The easternmost Germanii, and they're mad bastards and go blood-crazy sometimes. Some of their girls have moved in with our troops just lately, too. Not just the ones dragged in by the hair, either."

"Their women are showing surprisingly good taste, then," Fronto jested.

The centurion smiled dutifully, but then went on:

"Yes, sir, but that sets them off badly. And I have a bad

feeling ... something in the air ... it's suddenly too quiet, even for early spring there should be more noise from the birds."

Ah, good, I wanted to see how the lesser new things *do in this sort of situation,* Fronto thought as the man turned back to his business.

A lone cohort didn't rate the new *carroballistae*, much less a cannon. There were other things, though.

The men had been marching with their uncovered shields slung over their backs, bright with red and yellow and white, crossed thunderbolts and eagle wings and the sigil of their legion. Now they pulled on the straps and each shifted the scutum to their left hands in a unified ripple taking only a few seconds as their heads came up. As if that had been a signal—

Which it probably was, Fronto thought tensely.

—there was a sudden blatting, lowing, dunting chorus of oxhorns from the woods to their left, westward. On the heels of that a straggling mass of men surged out from behind the cover—you could see them before they left the trees in little bands and groups, because this stretch of road had been driven arrow straight through dense stands of huge old-growth trees, pine and oak and alder and the eerie-looking white-barked birches, with no time for underbrush to grow up since.

The *tubae* and *cornua* of the cohort sounded, the clear brassy notes of the straight and curled instruments cutting through the blatting of the enemy cow-horn trumpets and the growing chorus of their snarling, shrieking war cries. Every man in the cohort dropped his furca in unison, the carrying pole that bore his gear from its crosspiece clattering to the pavement.

The centurion slid down from his mount and moved to take his place at the fore. There was a reason the casualty rate among men of that rank was double the one ordinary soldiers suffered.

The Roman troops moved in a snapping unison, without shouts or spoken orders. They'd been marching in a hostile-country formation, a column taking up the whole thirty-foot width of the road. It was eight ranks across, with the baggage carts—four-wheeled ones with pivoted front axles and mule drawn, now, with the new collar harness—in the middle.

Now the century standards, poles with a crossbar and a wreathed open-palmed bronze hand—carried by men with tanned wolves' heads on their helmets and the fur down their backs—were moved to the western verge of the road. That was just inside the four-foot-deep ditch that ran along the straight course of the roadway, and two files of soldiers lined up along it, spaced out at three-foot intervals with the second row covering the gaps in the first.

Each hefted his pila, the long metal shanks of the heavy javelins glinting, their wielder's eyes fixed on the shaggy band shambling towards them, long hair and unkempt beards above furs and leather and often tattered wool. There were four hundred and twelve men in the cohort; the enemy were about twice that number or a bit more.

The *easternmost* file of troops turned in place to watch the woods on *that* side of the road and marched forward to the ditch. Fronto checked in that direction himself, but evidently the enemy had no more men... or it hadn't occurred to them to do anything but mass as many as they had and run forward screeching and frothing at the mouth with their blue eyes bulging.

Savages, he thought. *But* dangerous *savages. Don't underestimate an enemy—they pick up tricks fast. That was Varus' mistake and he lost three legions.*

It was the middle ranks of the legionary cohort who did something new. They set four-foot shield and six-foot pilum leaning against each other, and reached into the satchels that each had at his right side, below the usual high hitch for his sheathed gladius. Each muscular hand came out holding a *malogranatum.*

The word meant *pomegranate,* and the iron spheres did look much like them in size and shape, though each had a cord dangling from the top. The fuzz of rust gave them a mottled reddish-brown look, strengthening the resemblance.

Every third or fourth man also had a *Ronsonius.* Each of those men flicked back the brass cover with their left thumb and spun the little wheel that scraped flint on steel, while everyone held their grenade high up and away. Absolutely nobody wanted to light a fuse accidentally, once they'd seen what grenades could do. The pale blue flames welled up from the wicks that coiled down into the hollow interiors full of distilled naptha or redoubled superwine...

Fronto snapped open his telescope, blessing the makers inwardly while he did, and raised it to an eye. The savages were tall—Germanii were, on the whole, and these even more so than the southern tribes he was more familiar with. More of them had blond hair leaking out from under caps or in a few cases helmets than the folk along the Danube, too.

Even here they weren't *all* blond, though, contrary to fable down in the southlands. Where blond wigs were fashionable nowadays for women, and not only ones of ill repute—he'd sent a bale of sheared locks to his *domus* for his female kin to play with.

They deserve their share of the loot too! After all, every mother of a soldier went under the shadow of Hades to bear him.

Most of the Gutōz had round shields as the northernmost tribes preferred, simple things of planks covered in leather painted with birds of prey or bears or wolves or crude abstract patterns, probably symbols of this local God or that. In their right hands were long battle spears with heavy iron heads—contrary to fable and rumor, they didn't use flint for that, either.

Though they do sometimes when sacrificing victims to their Gods. Human sacrifices, often enough.

Here and there a helmet or mailcoat glittered gray under furs and wool, but not many and concentrated around the chief and his banner; only about half the shields had copper or bronze or iron bosses over the central handgrip, the rest contenting themselves with extra wood and leather.

Fronto grunted thoughtfully. Two to one was bad odds, though Roman gear and discipline would probably have produced a victory anyway.

"Now, though..." he murmured under his breath, sliding his shield around and drawing his long horseman's spatha. "Now, we shall see."

The new saddles made precise control of the horse easier, and gave you a firmer seat to strike, so he didn't dismount himself. Arrows began to fly toward the Roman troops from tribesmen who halted a moment to let fly...but German archery was more a dangerous nuisance than a real threat.

Nothing like Parthians. Now, their bows are deadly *dangerous.*

He batted one shaft headed for his face aside with his hexagonal cavalry shield, and it cracked across and the severed halves went *tick* off someone else's gear somewhere near. The pace of the attackers went faster and faster, and their formation grew a little more ragged—as caution, or perhaps just shorter legs,

varied their speed. It was more or less a wedge with their chief
and his standard of a bear skull on a pole at the front. What the
natives called a "swine array" after the lowered head of a wild
boar; they claimed one of their Gods—an uncouth one called
Wothenjaz—had taught it to them.

Thirty yards away, and a trumpet call familiar to any Roman
soldier rang out:

First rank, throw!

The long pila drew back, the shields went up with the left
feet, and then the heavy throwing spears flashed out in unison
as feet stamped down. Seconds later a series of hard *tock!* sounds
came back, or softer meatier *thuds*, as the points and long, narrow iron shafts pounded into bodies. Many of the Gutōz who'd
caught them on their shields were wounded too; the three feet of
narrow iron shank were designed to slide easily and fast through
the hole the elongated four-sided points made, and many of those
points gouged into faces or arms or chests.

Those that *didn't* wound also served a purpose. The iron
shanks bent, and the Gutōz discovered something Rome's earlier foes had known since the Punic Wars. You couldn't wrench
the pilum free of your shield, not in the middle of a fight you
couldn't, and the dragging weight and awkwardness made the
shield useless until you did.

The enemy line rippled as men tried to free their shields, or
tossed them aside. Then the trumpet call sounded again:

Second rank, throw!

The next volley slammed home, doing even more damage than
the first. The Gutōz were very ragged now, and a few from the
rearmost were just running away in howling panic. There was a
long flicker along the front two Roman ranks as hands slapped
down reversed on the high-slung short swords by their right
sides and the two-foot blades snapped out. The men crouched a
little, left foot forward, shields up under their eyes, each gladius
held hilt down with the blade ready to stab or—less often—chop.

And then a *new* horn-call rang out:

Light! Throw!

Fuses lit, sputtering and hissing. Arms cocked backward
and a hundred and sixty of the little bombs flew out, trailing
off-white smoke.

They could be thrown further than a pilum, being lighter. A

dozen or so burst in the front ranks of the Gutōz; more landed in the middle or slightly behind. A stuttering—

crackcrackcrackcrackcrackcrackcrackcrackcrackcrackcrackcrack—

And the same signal again, and again; each man carried four of the little bombs.

Fragments of the iron casings whined through the air, pinwheeling until they struck flesh like supernally fast saws in splashes of blood. When they landed at a man's feet he was gutted like a butchered hog, or had limbs blown mostly off.

They made nothing of armor, too. Off-white sulfur-stinking smoke blanketed the carnage for a moment, then slowly, sullenly drifted north. In the stunned silence that followed, the shrieks of the wounded were loud, but the hale warriors were too appalled to keep up their war cries.

When the front rank of the Gutōz hit the Roman line, they were many fewer than their foes, though probably they hadn't all realized that yet. Many were wounded, but they leapt down into the roadside ditch and tried to scramble up or thrust with their spears.

The Roman scuta stopped the points; short swords darted out...and then the Roman ranks were advancing, smashing the natives back with heavy shields, smash-stab-chop...

Ten minutes later the only Gutōz who weren't dead, dying or captives were a scattering running away. Fronto sniffed; the damp chill muffled even the stink of blood and cut bellies, one of the few good things about the weather here. Though not the burnt-sulfur smell of thunder powder, a new thing too.

The senior centurion came up to Fronto's stirrup iron; his blade was running blood, and he wiped it on a cloth before resheathing it, to keep it from rust or sticking in the scabbard. The scabbard was at his left hip, a mark of rank like the leather webbing over his mail-clad chest carrying his decorations. The ordinary troops wore the *lorica segmentata*, made of hoops and bands of plate on a leather backing and fastened with straps and buckles.

"Those *malogranatum* really helped, sir," he said. "Long life and health to Artorius the War-Wise and his clients! Mars Himself whispers in their ears! We'd have had four or five times the casualties without them, and killed far fewer of the barbaro-scum."

"Indeed, and may the Gods hear your words," Fronto said.

"You speak truth. Though most of them didn't stop even with the grenades."

The centurion shrugged. "Nothing wrong with their guts, sir. Brains, yes. They're so stupid they couldn't tie the laces on a sandal without a year's instruction and I'm surprised they know where to put it to make babies. But they've got iron balls, all right. They'll make useful recruits for the auxiliaries when they're tamed a bit. Like the Batavians out west—they do well in northern Britannia, I've heard from men who were stationed in Eboracum."

Fronto nodded. "Well, for now that combination of lack of wits and plenty of courage just gets more of them killed. What are *our* casualties?"

"Eighteen dead or nearly so, about twice that seriously wounded and three times more lightly hurt... with the new treatments, nearly all of those should recover."

A high shriek rose in the background as doubled superwine was poured on a wound. It prevented infection... and hurt like liquid fire. You also had to keep it under close control to keep the men from stealing sips.

"Even if it smarts! We'll put the badly hurt on the carts. We killed at least half of the Gutōz warband, or took them prisoner."

"Hmmm," Fronto said and thought, *You should never let an act of rebellion go unpunished.* "Where's the nearest village of these Gutōz?"

"About four miles that way," the man replied, pointing northwestward with a right hand that was covered in very slowly drying blood. "It's not really a village as we use the word—more of a clump of little hamlets, strung out through fields, and a chief's hall on a hill... or as close to a hill as this plains country has. I think they built up a mound under it."

"We'll drop off the wounded and the prisoners at the fort and then pay them a visit," Fronto decided. "Together with some of the cavalry stationed there."

"That'll be a cold march, sir," the centurion said warningly.

"The men can warm themselves up by putting everything to the torch. And with their women and boys when we get there!" Fronto said cheerfully. "If we wait, they'll disappear when those who ran away make it home. But they can't leave immediately, they'll have to pack food and gear or they'd just starve in the woods. We should catch them running around like headless chickens if we double-time."

"Yes, sir. Ah, these Gutōz women, they—"

"Carry concealed knives, yes, I know, Centurion." He chuckled. "You just have to strip them completely naked and thump them a little before you get to work. Forward!"

He looked at the sprays of blood and body parts where the grenades had landed, faint under the dim cloudy light, as the cohort completed its cleanup and cuffed and kicked the saleable prisoners into a clump and tied their hands and elbows together behind their backs and then linked them neck-to-neck in coffles. The wet chill damped down the flies too—in summertime in his home province, the bloody insects would already be swarming. And the dead flesh at least starting to spoil.

And we have the only thunderpowder weapons in the world, he thought. *Long may that continue!* Roma aeterna victrix!

⋟ CHAPTER TWO ⋞

Tèbié yánjiū dānwèi 32
(Special Research Unit 32)
Xi'an, China
June 25th, 2032
to
June 25th, 165 CE

Yuè Daiyu—the second, personal name meant Black Jade—
bolted upright in bed from a confused dream of fear and
flight and chaos.

It took an instant before she realized that she *was* hearing
the strobing screech of a siren, not simply dreaming it.

"*Tā mā de!*" she swore, putting the heels of her hands to her
eyes, then forced herself into action.

Starting with hitting the light switch. She'd had an hour
and a half of sleep after falling thankfully and early into bed at
the end of a long day's mental and physical work followed by a
dismal institutional dinner. At least there had been plenty of it.

Less than two hours was worse than no sleep at all, in a
way. She could feel the sand grinding in the gears of her brain.

*Another practice run! It's only been two days since the last
one! I didn't want to join the Army!*

Reaction to the siren was automatic, though, drilled in by
months of hearing that sound at unpredictable intervals day
and night. She bolted out of the sheets and threw on the clean,
sturdy field uniform that always hung ready in the little cubicle,
stamped her feet into the boots, cinched the belt with the Type

92 pistol and holster, and swung the full pack on her back and put on the billed cap.

The only thing that *wasn't* drilled in was the last-instant snatch at her mother's pendant from its place on the little bedside table.

Wàn yī, she thought: *Just in case.*

The news had been very bad the last few days—and the gaps in the news were even worse, if you kept up with things. Not even rumors on WeChat to fill the gaps, just silence.

Which means the government really, really doesn't want us to know the truth. What *a surprise!*

You learned to fill in the gaps yourself, unless you were one of the ones who just accepted the official line...which her immediate family didn't, at least not when they were strictly private.

China is not a lucky country. Especially about politics.

Her mother's necklace was old, even as a pendant; family legend said it had been handed down from mother to daughter since it was found in one of the first modern archaeological digs, over a century ago. The centerpiece was an Eastern Han bronze coin—round, with a square hole in the center—in a gold ring that enclosed the ancient metal. And it dated from the reign of Emperor Ling, 1,860 years ago...

Which is ironic, when you think about it, flitted through her mind as she dashed out the door. *I kept it secret...I wouldn't be here if I hadn't...but I* hate *the government that's gotten us into this fix...that may destroy the country! The Eastern Han were* even worse, *if that's possible. Though they didn't have nuclear weapons!*

The lights were strobing red in the corridor outside as she tucked it away beneath shirt and jacket. She turned right and trotted all the way to the operations room, just as she was supposed to; the colonel would be waiting, expressionless but watching a time readout.

She was sweating a little by the time she got there and breathing deeply, after running nearly a kilometer with twenty kilos on her back, dodging other running people at the same time. Their faces had been drawn and fixed, and many of them were sweating more than their efforts could account for.

That sweat and panting was despite being in the best condition of her life—the training here included a strong physical element, and she'd gained ten pounds on her original tall willowy frame, all of it muscle.

Her degree in Chinese historical linguistics was one of the reasons she'd been picked for this, but not the only one; youth and health were among the others. She'd also gotten mRNA vaccinations here against every infectious disease known to humankind. Including a number that were officially extinct, and survived only as samples.

The technicians sitting at their workstations or tending the hulking machinery—which she didn't pretend to understand, she was a historical linguist, not a physicist—were sweating too, under the stiff discipline.

The sweat of fear.

Like the people I passed on the way here, she thought. *Thank the ancestors for discipline, or this would be a riot of despair. But people fall back on training and habit in emergencies.*

She looked over at Liu Xiang as she took her place on the circle of gridwork, shedding her pack and lying down as the drill mandated. The building was semiunderground...because that circle was as close as they could come to the ground level of long, long ago. The roof above them was a plastered ferroconcrete dome nearly half a meter thick.

"*Shàngxiào?*" she asked quietly. "Colonel?"

He was a square-faced, stocky-fit, gimlet-eyed man just turned forty, a decade and a half older than her and about the same five-foot-seven height, which was typical of their respective generations and genders. She wasn't altogether sure what he was a colonel *in*, even after months of working together, but he'd proved disconcertingly knowledgeable about all the team's specialties.

Including her deeply obscure one.

Which most people haven't even heard of!

Here they'd all cross-trained so that they could help each other. Or perhaps replace each other if necessary. And gotten hands-on experience with other things, like field medicine and riding horses, marksmanship and martial arts and a dozen other recondite skills. Two of them had had their appendixes removed as well, and they'd all had tonsillectomies.

She was morally certain the older man had studied at some university or another at some point in his life, though. Whether he was Army or People's Armed Police or Ministry of State Security or something more obscure in the labyrinthine coils of the Chinese security state.

Which she secretly detested under a show of deep respect. The Taiwanese had...had had...democracy, which showed you it wasn't *alien to Chinese* culture as the official line went.

But you had to grant the colonel plenty of brains.

"This is not a drill," he said calmly.

I think he suspects me. But if we...get where we are supposed to go...would that matter? Not that I can see, and so would he think...I think. Our politics wouldn't even be comprehensible to the people then.

He spoke excellent standard Mandarin, but with an occasional slip that made her think he came from the northeast up near the now-theoretical Russian border. She hadn't dared to ask. Now she felt a jolt of genuine fear. That meant...

"Now keep silent," he added.

The other three members of the team trotted in instants later: Yang Biao, the mechanical engineer; Hú Bingwen, the agronomist and *civil* engineer; and Ding Àilún, their historian proper. Mostly an expert in *technological* history and its infinite details. He was indeed handsome and cheerful most of the time as his name indicated...but not very cheerful right now, and fear made his face bleak.

Do I look as scared as they do? I hope not!

They all glanced at each other out of the corners of their eyes as they took their places and lay on the gridwork inside the personalized painted outlines. Theory was one thing, reality another. None of them were married or parents, that had apparently been part of the selection process, but nearly everyone had *some* family even nowadays and they'd be thinking about them now.

That and their personal friends from university or earlier. Who would all be dead soon, quickly if they were lucky. In a hideously prolonged fashion if they weren't.

The cargo surrounded them on three sides and part of the fourth, in carefully arranged heaps lashed together with rope— hemp rope, at that. Not all that much of it was hers; some books, more data on the military-grade laptops and drives. Most of the gear was in Biao and Bingwen's care, tools and gauges and seeds and plans and working models, and they were checking it over compulsively with their eyes.

Probably as a distraction from fear of impending death...or fear of where they'd end up if they *didn't* die. All of them were older than her, but not by more than a few years—she suspected that she'd been brought in when the original choice...

Almost certainly a man, her mind added, with weary resignation and well-buried anger.

...disqualified himself somehow. The number of people with her specialty was limited, especially if you insisted on someone young and healthy and with no immediate family attachments. She carefully *didn't* think of what had probably happened to hypothetical-him then. This was an ultrasecret project and the people running it weren't taking chances...so death or a camp were the most likely destination for anyone who failed.

She hadn't *believed* what it was, not at first, though she'd carefully not said anything to that effect. If the authorities believed something, you acted as if you did, if you weren't a complete idiot or living alone on a Tibetan mountaintop...and even then there was probably a concealed camera and a drone keeping you under constant surveillance.

She still wasn't absolutely certain that it would work...though right now she strongly hoped it did.

Very strongly. Very, very strongly.

A stiffly self-controlled messenger delivered a tablet to Colonel Liu, and added as the officer flipped through the report: "The strike on Vienna will be in the first wave, sir."

"Good," Liu said, nodding. "We need no competition...no rivals...where...we're going."

Oh.

Nothing had ever been officially said, but she'd heard the rumors that this setup was a copy, and the original was in Austria, of all places. Apparently serendipity combined with good espionage had given them this chance to correct the dead-end... literally, a mass-death-dead-end...that the world seemed to be in.

May Xi suffer through the Seven Hells. He put our feet on this road! And for him...for him, I wish I believed in the Seven Hells.

Then the colonel raised his voice: "You labor to ensure China's future! You are heroes of our country!"

A different future starting far in the past, Black Jade thought; what he'd said wasn't quite a lie, exactly, but—

It won't look anything like our China by this date. Which is much better than nothing, I suppose, since there will be something besides ruins and bones.

"Commence the run!"

Fingers tapped keyboards, voices murmured low. A whining drone built; even now, men and women labored at one piece of equipment, snapping in parts and stepping back and nodding at the last instant before it went live.

Then someone's voice broke in, half a scream as they leapt to their feet: "Beijing! Beijing is gone! Multiple hits!"

Black Jade hissed involuntarily. She'd lived there for much of her life, her parents and grandparents and great-grandparents had been academics at Beijing University—had been since it was the *Imperial* University, generation after generation for more than a century. Apart from a brief exile when the Japanese occupied it, and a not-too-bad temporary rustication during the Cultural Revolution.

The thought of the blast wave leaving burning rubble in its wake...burning *people* in its wake...some nothing but shadows on concrete as had happened in Hiroshima and Nagasaki...

Biao grunted as if someone had punched him in the stomach; he was an only child, like most people their age, but she knew his parents and grandparents lived there.

Did live there. Died there right away, *if they're lucky.*

Another shout: "Missile inbound for Xi'an...breaking up... no, multiple warheads, independently steered."

Black Jade jammed a knuckle into her mouth and bit. Her parents were dead six years ago now, and her grandparents earlier than that; she had a second cousin who she'd never met. But that missile was headed for *her*. Some part of her mind scolded her for selfishness; billions would be dying soon, many millions already had...

But my *dying wouldn't help* them, *would it?*

"Initiating!" someone said.

And that means it's irreversible, her mind gibbered. She'd picked up that much from overhearing the physicists. *Nothing can stop it now, it doesn't need the equipment anymore. Whether or not it's in time.*

"Five...four...three...two..."

Flicker.

Everything seemed to freeze for an instant, and then things were back to normal...if you could call this instant of mass destruction anything resembling normal.

Flicker. Flicker.

Like a hiccup in the flow of time, freezing everything outside the circle of gridwork and slowing it down within.

"Missile warheads approaching," the same voice said, an edge to it now. "Countermissiles launching...one...two...three warheads still on course."

Flicker. Flicker. Flicker. Flicker.

The world was strobing faster and faster, like some crazed early film where things moved jerkily. Slow motion, normalcy... blurring into each other so that sound droned low...

"Missile nearing destruction radius—"

An ear-piercing whine filled the air, going up and down the scale from shrill to bass as those disconcerting moments of stasis struck. Sparks flew, and a man whose nerve had broken was caught dashing towards them in a great arcing discharge, shaking and dancing like a spastic puppet.

Colonel Liu's face was still like something carved of granite, his breathing even, but there were beads of sweat on his brow and his pupils had flared wide.

FlickerFlickerFlickerFlicker—

Everything was in slow motion now, each moment of frozen time blending into the next. She noticed his eyes glancing up... over what seemed like an eternity. Black Jade followed his gaze... and stifled a scream with difficulty. The concrete dome above them was *bulging*.

Bulging *slowly*.

It was like being paralyzed and seeing death stroll towards you at a leisurely pace, taking its time. Cracks spread, and plaster fell away from the smooth surface, drifting downward like vast snowflakes. The concrete cracked too, a huge crumbling hemisphere of it bending inward and pointed straight at *her*. As if a giant metal fist was striking it from the east.

And it is, she thought...or mentally gibbered. *A fist of red-hot air rammed forward faster than sound.*

The cracks in the thick concrete spread. She could see the steel rebar within now, snapping like thread and shooting...very slowly...sparks as it did.

Light behind that, light blinding-bright, growing, heat beating on her face.

A dull roaring noise, drawn out and slow. Screams, equally

bass and low, as the technicians under the dome saw death seconds away.

...flickflickflickflick...

Blackness.

Black Jade realized her head hurt even before her eyes opened. Hurt badly. And blood was running down her upper lip, salty and nasty in her mouth. She moaned and stirred, coughed and spat.

Then she realized she was lying on...

Dirt, she thought. *And I can smell night soil.*

That meant composted human waste used as fertilizer; one of their training trips had been to places where that was still done. Relief uncoiled within her.

We made it! We're here! We're not going to die right away!

That cut through the pain and grief. Then she heard the distinctive *shick-shank* of an automatic pistol being cocked, and shed her pack and forced herself to her feet. There was a pistol at her own belt, come to that, but she kept her hand away from the holster. She could use it, the virtual-reality training had been brutally realistic, but—

The metric ton of... stuff... they'd brought with them was intact. In the space left for an entrance Colonel Liu was standing with the weapon in his hand. In front of him were a clutch of...

Peasants, she thought. *Badly frightened peasants.* Angry *frightened peasants.*

The reason they were angry was obvious; the Chinese time travelers and their metric ton of gear had landed on a field of *nearly* ripe vegetables, bok choy and eggplant and others now thoroughly crushed and scenting the air with bruised green smells like after-hours at a market. These people probably got some of their money selling their produce in nearby Xi'an... Chang'an, this far back... and needed the money very, very badly. She was back to the times her grandparents had talked about... elliptically... when millions could starve.

Starve to death. When everyone knew that could happen, and feared it.

This... this particular time and place... wasn't friendly to the poor, either. She'd taken enough general historical courses on it to know that, very definitely.

They were frightened because the strangers and their baggage had appeared out of nowhere without pack animals or porters or wagons—though they probably hadn't *seen* the arrival, or they'd *still* be running and screaming about evil sorcery and magicians over and over again.

Be grateful for that. We didn't know if we'd have an audience!

All of the peasants were ragged, dressed in short lap-over jackets held with rope belts, with loose pants below for the men and long skirts for the women, and mostly bare feet. She could smell them from here, too, even with her nose bleeding. Old sweat sunk into coarse hemp cloth, unwashed bodies...

Colonel Liu hadn't opened fire. Black Jade didn't think that was his automatic response to any confrontation, for which she was thankful. Too many in his line of work *did* think that way.

But shoot he would if he had to, with pellucid ruthlessness. She was utterly certain of *that*. The peasants would run when they saw some struck down by magic with sounds unlike anything they'd heard before. Right now they were brandishing hoes—she noted that the heads were crude, heavy cast iron.

He called out to her.

"Your translation services would be appreciated, Doctor Yuè," he said, politely but with a snap in it. "They don't appear to understand my attempt at the language at all."

She walked—more hobbled and reeled—over to him, mopping at her lip with a tissue as she did; one of her many patch pockets was full of them.

And I'll never get any more, some distant part of her mind gibbered, under the ice-pick pain of the headache stabbing inward from her temples. *Never any more...of so many things...*

There was a trickle of blood on his neck, from his left ear. She suppressed an impulse to mop at it, and spoke to the mob of two dozen farmers...and the families behind them...with both her hands raised, palms open. Even then she blinked at little in surprise at the sheer number of half-naked children of all ages mixed in with the peasants. Knowing a total fertility rate and *seeing* it were two different things.

"Please, good people, listen to what I say," she began, in her best stab at the late stage of Old Chinese spoken toward the end of the Eastern Han period.

Or very earliest stage of Middle Chinese, she noted absently; that was still a matter of dispute. *The Shang oracle bone inscriptions are nearly fifteen hundred years before* this, *after all. Confucius has already been dead six hundred years! They wouldn't even know my name means Black Jade, here.*

China was an *old* place. Her language was one of the few that descended unbroken from an ancestor in the Bronze Age, almost alone in that it had been one country—with chaotic episodes—from that period too. Most of the time you just took that for granted and got on with your life, though her specialty made her more conscious of it than most. Here and now it was very, very apparent.

Another glance:

And they're so short! And skinny! Bent backs, missing eyes, scars, skin diseases . . . bad teeth . . . and I think they look *older than they* are. *A lot older.*

What the peasants were saying . . . or shouting . . . didn't *sound* at all like modern standard Mandarin, or even the Mandarin dialect that would be spoken here in her time. Much harsher and choppier, with glottal stops and consonant combinations that didn't exist anymore and hadn't for a long time, well over a thousand years. It was roughly like the sound reconstructions she'd spent years listening to and contributing her own mite to, but not exactly.

Sounds we hadn't used for a long time in my age. But in this one, yes, this is current, she thought, the knowledge disorienting in its strangeness.

The tone system of *Middle* Chinese was just now barely starting to develop from consonant-cluster endings in Old Chinese . . . and while the Middle Chinese system that would emerge by Tang dynasty times was ancestral to what she'd grown up speaking, it wasn't very much like it all. A little more like Min, or Cantonese, those were comparatively archaic, but not *very* like those either.

The peasants stared at her, blinking, and then some of them recognized she was female, which seemed to puzzle them.

Maybe it's the trousers. None of the women here seem to be wearing them . . . that must have happened later, it was routine for peasant women for a long, long time. Lower-class people wore trousers, upper-class dressed in robes.

The one in front brandishing a hoe—he had a few wisps of beard, mostly grey—lowered the tool and frowned. He scratched at the bandana-like covering tied around his head.

Then *he* spoke.

She caught exactly one word for certain: *djuj* with a slight "k" echo, meaning *who*.

Probably in a sentence meaning:

Who *in the name of every demon are you people and* why *have you destroyed some of our crops?*

Black Jade turned to Colonel Liu, flogging her aching head into working order by sheer willpower:

"Sir, they're speaking a, ah, a *dialect* of Eastern Han period Old Chinese. A rural, western, dialect of Old Chinese. What I know is the best reconstruction we have of the literary, court speech of Luoyang, the"—she shifted to Old Chinese herself—"the Eastern Capital—"

The old peasant caught the name of the city and spoke excitedly to his fellows. Then they all laid down their tools, dropped to their knees, and bowed their heads nearly to the ground. Some things about the strangers had probably sunk in; the quality of their clothes, their size—they were all at least four inches taller than the average here—and the sheer fact that they didn't look as if they worked too much and ate too little. They were strangers... but obviously *rich* strangers.

That made them *dangerous* strangers, to a group of peasants.

The elderly peasant...

I doubt he's more than a decade older than the colonel! Though he looks about seventy-five or eighty. Bent back, gray-white hair, not many teeth left... that makes him harder to understand too!

... spoke again; much more slowly, and she thought he was trying to mute the distinctive sounds of his local speech. He evidently knew that court language was different from his, but not enough to realize she was speaking a weird variety of it. Probably his only experience of the court language was officials in elaborate robes reading out incomprehensible decrees.

Mostly imposing heavier taxes.

She nodded, repeated what she thought he'd said back to him, and *he* nodded enthusiastically. They spent a moment more repeating the sentence to each other, slowly and carefully.

"Sir, he says he's sending his son to"—she pointed north—"Chang'an. That's, ah, *probably* what he said."

Chang'an was the ancient name of Xi'an. It had been an Imperial capital for a long time—in the Qin period after the

First Emperor unified the country, and then in the initial, earlier period of the current dynasty known as the Western Han, before the brief interregnum of Wang Mang in—

Her mind did a skip. *About a hundred and fifty years ago, as of now,* she told herself. *This now is your now... now! Forever. The machinery up... up in the... former present? It's destroyed. The world is destroyed. Was destroyed. Nothing we can do will be worse than that. Maybe these children's grandchildren will have enough to eat all their lives!*

Luoyang was a long way east of here; hence the name of the second phase of that dynasty, Eastern Han.

Her folk still called themselves *Han people* and their speech the *Han tongue* ...

Though how many of them were left after the nuclear war was doubtful.

"The boy... young man... will go fetch some sort of official. Who will probably be easier to understand, I should think."

"Excellent, Doctor," the colonel said, holstering his pistol. "You saved us considerable trouble. Possibly saved lives."

Behind her she heard groans, and when she turned her head she saw the others sitting up and wiping at dribbles of blood from noses, ears, and eyes.

"We will need transport," the commander of their party continued.

She nodded and turned back to the old-looking peasant man.

"We... will... need... carts," Black Jade said slowly, trying to make each word distinct. "Several... carts. Carts. Wagons. Things... with... wheels. Oxen. For... pull."

"Carts!" the man replied, just barely recognizable as the word to her, nodding, and pointing to the gear with a questioning expression and beaming when she nodded.

He'd caught that at least; and this close to a city, market gardeners like these probably had a few. Handcarts, if not animal drawn. Even this far back, Old Chinese had a stripped-down positional grammar, which helped.

I don't think we've invented wheelbarrows yet... not quite yet. We invented so many things... but gradually. What will come of them all happening at once?

She nodded again.

The colonel pulled replica coins from a pocket, held on a

string through their square central holes, and handed them over. The villagers' enthusiasm grew; those bronze coins were probably more than they'd expected to get from this little patch of truck.

Their baggage included precious metals and jewels, enough to make them rich by here-and-now standards.

If this official *doesn't try to have us killed and take it when he arrives,* she thought with a shiver.

There were two rifles in the baggage...but if they had to use them...

"We should keep a low profile at first," Liu said thoughtfully. "It will be some time...several years...before the Emperor Ling takes the throne, and I think it will be best if we approach him, rather than his predecessor. He will be a boy...only twelve... and probably easier to influence. First we will secure our position with the local government, then the provincial governor. Who will probably try to keep us secret, for the sake of his own advantage. Then—"

⇒ CHAPTER THREE ⇐

Municipium of Sirmium
Province of Pannonia Inferior
February 10th, 170 CE

His guest was looking curiously at the fireplace in the study office of Josephus ben Matthias, in the Pannonian city of Sirmium where he had his *domus*. Or it was the study of Lucius Maecius Josephus if you went by the *libellus* that attested his Roman citizenship, which other Jews generally didn't when they weren't dealing with the Imperial government or the Army.

If there's a difference there, Josephus thought whimsically. *Artorius says the Empire is an army that has a government, not a government with an army.*

The fire on the andirons behind a thin screen of fretted bronze cast flickering light on the scrolls on the shelves and the rows of newfangled codex books, many *printed* on *paper,* and some of which had illustrations and maps from engravings. Though that firelight was not nearly as bright as the new glass-chimney lanterns that rested in brass gimbals along the walls in front of silvered-glass mirrors.

Josephus had used pearwood for the blaze, in honor of the fact that *this* visitor was also his uncle, his dead father's elder brother, and more-or-less head of the extended family by common consent. Though *technically* that head was a scholar immured in theology back in Judea, who occasionally sent out a burst of letters explicating the details of the Law.

Though Uncle Stephanus also brought a scholar from the schools in Judea with him, Josephus thought.

That mandated a degree of caution, he thought as they chatted idly.

And he brought four *bodyguards. He was traveling in unfamiliar territory, so it's justified. But I have two...*

The scholar wasn't a priest, technically. That tradition had died in blood with the fall of the Second Temple, about a hundred years ago, confirmed by the failure of Bar Kokhba's revolt a little earlier than the time of Josephus' own birth. The man *was* of priestly descent, which enabled him to do certain things. And he'd studied in the ancient homeland; not in Jerusalem, which was a Roman colony named Aelia Capitolina now, and had been since Emperor Hadrian's time—Jews were forbidden entry to it since Bar Kokhba's rebellion.

But he'd been at the school in Yavneh founded by Yohanan ben Zakkai after the fall of the Second Temple, which was the center of Jewish scholarship in the old homeland.

And the bodyguards are Jews, too, Josephus thought. *Which is significant. Freedmen, yes, and ex-gladiators...*

Most bodyguards were veterans of the arena; it was a natural occupation for those who'd received the wooden sword of freedom.

...but three born Jewish, one may be a convert, from his looks. And my bodyguards say they keep to themselves and always have their weapons to hand. So my uncle either believes...or more charitably, fears...I am possessed by a devil, or have embraced sorcery. Not altogether surprising given the wild rumors about Artorius and his followers, but...inconvenient. I know that it is something far *stranger...but of course I cannot tell him that.*

The burning fruit wood scented the room pleasantly, as well as warming it; he noted it absently, while his mind worked through schemes to avoid a confrontation.

The truth, then, as much of it as I can tell. Truth is a weapon of great power! And I will tell it in a way that reassures him! Nor may I reveal that I know his *true purpose here. I shall treat him as if this was just family, and family business.*

There were little marble-topped tables beside their chairs on either side of the fire, with winecups and plates of small sweets made from flaky pastry, honey and hazelnuts...though the curved tripod legs of the tables *weren't* elongated fauns or nymphs, which they would have been in most Roman rooms. The mosaics in the house were abstract patterns, too, and the murals lacked human figures.

Dinner had been quietly sumptuous as well, with a roast lamb as the centerpiece, and the new potatoes and tomatoes...

And needless to say Josephus' wife Deineira had done her usual quietly competent job of ensuring none of it violated Jewish law. That wasn't easy in Pannonia, where Jews were thin on the ground and only Sirmium even had a minyan's worth of free adult males. The lamb had been slaughtered by one of their household slaves, a convert, according to the Law, for starters. There weren't any Jewish butchers in business in Sirmium, not yet, which was a major pain in the backside.

Josephus was increasingly tempted to manumit the slave, find him a suitable wife, and set him up in the butcher's trade—there was a *shmita* year coming soon, and Jewish bondsmen had to be freed then anyway. If he could prevail on some of the others of his faith here to join in, ensuring that the freedman's trade flourished, all the better. That would be a *mitzvah*, a divinely favored good deed, and a sign that the scattered Jews in the city were becoming a true community.

And that competence of my beloved... and very clever... wife is a relief when I am here at home, he thought. *What I must do sometimes when away from it... well, necessity drives us all, and at least I have avoided pork. The Most High knows my circumstances.*

"These are... among the innovations your... would *friend* be the right word? That Lucius Triarius Artorius has introduced?" his uncle said.

He moved his left hand, the one not holding his wine cup, indicating the lanterns and the fireplace, not to mention the printed books, before he went on:

"I have heard at home how such are being installed in the Imperial palaces on the Palatine, and many senators are imitating that. And these mirrors of lead glass silvered with the new acid amalgam! Amazing! Like looking at *yourself*, somehow!"

Josephus nodded.

"Yes, my uncle," he said. "The lanterns provide better light, as you see, making it comfortable to read after dark."

"Without straining your eyes," his uncle said. "Although with the way my sight has closed in... it was never keen at a distance,

but I am afraid you are a blur now. I must nearly touch my nose
to a document to read it these days, or have a secretary read it
for me. Ah, old age! It is a shipwreck!"

Josephus smiled and reached into a pocket—which itself was
another new thing.

Though most find their gaze lengthens *as they grow older. But
not all. Still, this will illustrate my point.*

He extended the pair of lenses in their wire frames to his
kinsman. They should help . . .

"Put those over your eyes, my revered uncle. Hook the curved
ends at the sides over your ears."

The older man did, and then looked around with a wondering
expression on his face that turned into a broad grin.

"Marvelous! The blurring is much less!"

Then with a frown, and reaching a hand up to unhook them:
"How is this done?"

"They are yours," Josephus said, waving a hand. "This is the
third set—the first two went to the Emperor. They alter the course
of light to the eyes, as a clear glass jug full of water does. But in
a calculated way, you see? Depending on how the glass is ground
to shape. So that it may remedy both close and long sight."

He nodded to the fireplace. "And the *ignis locus* is much less
fuel-hungry than a hypocaust. As you can feel, it makes nothing of
winter's cold, even here in Pannonia. The *chimney* carries away all
the smoke and fumes in a way no brazier can do, be the charcoal
ever so fine. I bought and freed some of the slaves that my friend
Artorius first trained to making such places of fire, and advanced
them money to start their own business, installing these innovations
here in Sirmium. That has paid handsomely and quickly—everyone
in Sirmium who has seen them wants them if they can meet the
cost, and in Vindobona and Carnuntum as well, and among the
countryside gentry of the two Pannonian provinces as far away
as Acquincum on the Danube. And the Emperor has taken it up,
which means everyone will in the end, from Britannia to Syria."

They were speaking Greek, since their family came from
Antioch in Syria a few decades ago, where that tongue was common for Jews; they still had plenty of kinfolk there. Josephus
spoke Greek and Latin and Aramaic and three other languages
well, and several more passably. He knew his uncle outdid him
there. For a merchant it was a valuable skill, even if you could

get by in Latin and Greek in most of the Empire, in the cities and larger towns at least and as far as bargaining was concerned. He went on:

"One of many *new things* Artorius has brought to us."

"Like these lenses!" his kinsman said, beaming now and turning toward the bookcase. "I can read the title there—at twice arm's length! Yes, I can see how it is the same thing as a glass jar full of water. But as you say, in a calculated way."

Well, at least he doesn't think that *is sorcery,* Josephus thought, noting the slight feeling of relief in his uncle's voice. *A good start at reassuring him!*

"And Artorius is my friend indeed, and a good and loyal one, as I strive to be to him. His new treatment saved my son Matthias' life, as Deineira told you at supper."

Stephanus nodded; he'd been pleased by that too.

"The boy seems to flourish now. A likely lad! Clever, quick-witted and well-mannered, and already well-read. Your grandfather would be proud of him. May HaShem bless you with many such fine sons, as he has me. Blessed be the Name!"

Josephus carefully *didn't* mention that the new treatment for bowel infections—rest, plentiful doses of boiled water amended with honey and sea salt, and a diet of nothing but broth and then soup and then dishes boiled to softness for several weeks—wasn't all that Artorius had provided. Though *that* treatment now saved many lives. Especially of children here in the city; youngsters were prone to stomach illness, particularly in the warm season, even more than others.

Artorius had also given him pills, made of what he called antibiotics, which had brought his Matthias back from the edge, with the shadow of Azrael's wings—the Death Angel's wings—plain on his thin pallid face.

Those pills slew the miniscule parasites that he now knew caused much disease, like unseen tiny fleas or lice in your very blood and bowels.

Now I understand *that, now that I have read the book on medicine from the new book-stamping press, and looked through the* microscope. *My household does not, apart from my wife... but they have already noticed that my commands make everyone under this roof less likely to fall ill. Everyone knows cities are unhealthy; now I know* why *they are so.*

And the pills were irreplaceable, made by means that could not be duplicated in this age, nor for generations yet to come even with the knowledge brought from the future. The Americans would be plagued beyond belief, quite possibly attacked and killed and robbed, if others knew what those medicines could do. Bodyguards and Imperial favor or no, given sufficient desperation.

It would be hard even to blame some such attackers, who only wanted to save their loved ones and families!

Absolute secrecy was the only real shield from such peril. And Artorius had trusted him with that knowledge, the instant he learned of Matthias' illness, without Josephus asking... he hadn't known about the medicine, even, at the time, though he already knew from where... from when... the strangers had really come.

And I need not... must not, for many reasons... tell my uncle of such. I will be worthy of Artorius' trust! My son's life... could any man make me a greater *gift? Could any man be a better friend, then and now? We are close as brothers, like David and Jonathan. Together we will move mountains and reshape the world itself with peace and plenty!*

He went on aloud:

"For that, I will owe him more than I could pay all my life. And speaking of paying, he has also increased my wealth in the things of this world... very considerably. Both directly and indirectly, through our partnerships, and by providing me large sums of capital on reasonable terms because he has confidence in my knowledge and my judgment."

"Reasonable?" his uncle said.

"Five parts in a hundred interest per year, or two parts in ten of the profit from a venture, usually, whichever is greater."

"That *is* reasonable! Very! Confidence in your judgment indeed! And in your honesty."

"Artorius *is* reasonable, and a good judge of men. *Baruch HaShem—*"

Which literally meant *blessed be the Name* in Hebrew, the old tongue of their people, preserved because it was sacred; the phrase was an expression of thanks to the Most High. Though most Jews now spoke Aramaic or Greek in the east, or Latin in Rome and the other northern and western provinces.

"—that He brought me to meet Artorius on the road!"

He'd actually met Artorius and his four companions and their large wagonload of baggage *off* the road, but that was confidential. He first saw them after weird lights and noises, lying unconscious beside their gear in a forest clearing... and no slightest trace of the pack beasts or wagons or porters which would have been needful to move so large a weight of baggage.

With a dying man—a corpse, within instants—a little distance away. Wounded unto death from something that severed his legs at the thigh as a flick of a razor blade might an overboiled carrot.

It had all puzzled him then, like an itch in his head that he'd only been able to scratch when Artorius told him the truth of it. No other would ever learn it from him, not even the wife of his bosom, from whom he'd kept nothing until now and who'd given him shrewd advice all their years together.

His uncle Stephanus nodded. He was a man of twice Josephus' own age of thirty-two, but still hale; hale enough to travel here from Rome, which wasn't easy even for a wealthy man in this season. And he had most of his teeth, though they were yellowed and spotted. His white beard brushed his chest, and he was dressed in a long, striped woolen robe of fine cloth, longer than Josephus' calf-length bleached tunic with the narrow purple equestrian stripes. He added a silk skullcap, being more of a stickler for the finer points of the Law than his nephew.

Apart from age they had a strong family resemblance, olive-skinned, lean and long faced and bold nosed, with eyes a very dark hazel and hair equally black before age lightened the older man's and sent it receding far back from his forehead.

"And those jewels of his you sent to be sold on commission!" his uncle said, and kissed his fingertips in delighted awe. "Ah, so wonderful! So beautiful, the way they are cut in facets! We have all made good profits from them, and so has your friend. The only problem there was remitting so *much* money to the little bankers here in this... remote province!"

Josephus nodded in his turn, accepting the *frontier backwater* that was what his uncle had really meant.

Though Pannonia Inferior and its neighbors were making rapid progress now... and it was no longer on the frontier by several hundred miles, with the entirely new province of Transdanubia now stretching far north and Dacia much enlarged to the northeast. The war with the Germanii had pumped a good deal of Imperial expenditure into trade here too.

The new northern mines were doing even more. Directly in the vast expenditures required to get them going, and indirectly because the people they employed or enriched *bought* more, and it would be years before their needs could all be locally supplied. The precious metals they produced would grease the wheels of trade as well; an Imperial mint was under construction in Carnuntum.

The little bankers have gotten bigger. And there are more societās, more joint banks. And bankers... or their sons... have started to flock here from the southland cities.

Stephanus lived in Rome, and there was no better market for gemstones in all the world. But Josephus had also sent some of the jewels by trusted courier to more distant relatives in Athens, Antioch-in-Syria, and Alexandria-in-Egypt; not even Rome could absorb all that many of the huge, flawless and cunningly faceted stones Artorius had brought with him—

Brought from his own time. Remember, no hint of that!

"The jewels have profited us all, but that has been the least of it, Uncle. There has been the *Ronsonius...*"

Which was a cunning arrangement of a brass receptacle just the right size to be gripped firmly in one hand, holding distilled naptha or the new double-refined superwine, combined with a hinged cover, a wick, and a clever little wheel mechanism for striking a spark with steel against flint. The soaked wick nearly always caught immediately, and with it you could light a lantern or a torch or a cooking fire.

They were wildly popular, being so much easier and quicker than ordinary flint and steel, and were making his whole family a goodly sum in half a dozen cities, with artisans producing them in bulk on commission. Though soon they'd be copied by others, and the price would fall.

The Imperial army had also adopted them to light the new fuses for thunderpowder weapons... and every soldier faced with field service wanted one very badly to light plain and simple *fires* when the alternative was cold food and cold sleep *in* the cold and wet. Even getting the doubled superwine or distilled naptha for them would be a profit source, in the long run.

"And those new mirrors," his uncle said, waving at the lanterns and their backing. "As good as a pool of still water, or better, and there any time you want them. *Hei-hei*, what rich ladies in Rome will pay for that! Especially in frames beautified with precious metals well worked. Jewelers of our people in Rome are making the settings now."

Josephus nodded agreement and went on:

"And much else; for instance, the new methods of accounting, which have simplified *my* business greatly. Also through Artorius I have had the Emperor's favor... not least, that the *Imperator* paid Sextus Hirrius Trogus' debts, including his debt to *me*, immediately, in full and in cash. Which made me eligible for the Equestrian Order," he added, tapping the purple stripes on his tunic. "To which he elevated me himself!"

His uncle grinned. "Rewarding two men richly but with the same money! Clever!"

Josephus acknowledged that with a smile of his own. "So I was able to repay you for your gracious loan ahead of schedule."

Which favor from his uncle was what had let him buy up Sextus' much-depreciated debt in the first place, four years ago. That had been a long-term investment, the largest he'd made to that point—he'd renegotiated it with Sextus and given him a grace period on the compounding of the interest, rather than pressing for payment and taking property from him in court. That had *started* to pay off before Artorius and his countrymen arrived, and then had given him a massive sum much more quickly than he'd anticipated, since he'd *bought* the debt for less than half its face value.

"And that money gave me the capital I needed to bid... successfully... for orders from the Imperial Army since. Nor did the Emperor's public favor hurt me in the bargaining! Bulk purchases of grain, livestock, leather and cloth. Very valuable contracts."

"Artorius is a friend indeed, in more ways than one!" Josephus' uncle said. "I would like to meet this man! Profit seems to follow in his train like flowers after rain in a desert. *Mutual* profit, the best and most lasting kind."

"You shall meet him, Uncle, if you stay with me until the spring. And you are very welcome beneath my roof for as long as you please to honor me and mine with your company."

Which was possible, because Stephanus had able grown sons to mind his business in Rome. He could afford to let them handle the daily routine, while he sniffed out opportunities... and perils. That would also spare him more cold-season travel.

"These... Americi, is that the word?"

"*Americans*, in their tongue."

Which only five people in all the world speak, he thought, with a slight shiver. *Exiles indeed!*

"These *Americans* must be very wise!"

"Artorius certainly is, and *none* of the others are slow-witted. One of the four followers who arrived with him is a Jew by ancestry, a brilliant scholar. Though fallen from the observation of the Law, alas."

"Yes, Marcus Triarius Findlemanius. He is working with the Greek doctor Galenos on the new Medical Institute. Already they have saved lives. In the Imperial family, too, by the rumors."

"Yes, those rumors are true; I get news from court now. And they will save many more. And as Marcus shows, Artorius regards our people highly. He has said to me that one good measure of a realm's success and sound governance is the number of its Jewish inhabitants and their fair treatment before its laws! And I have heard him intercede for us with the Emperor himself, more than once."

"And the Emperor listened?"

"The Emperor listened *with respect*."

"A righteous gentile, then, this Artorius!"

"Righteous indeed. And one of very keen wit, I warn you again of this in advance. One who sees through pretense as if it were a dancing-girl's dress of eastern silk. Do *not* underestimate him, or you will be sorry."

Stephanus hesitated very slightly, then spoke:

"There is wisdom, and then again there is wisdom... You know that more than one of our family's heads of household has asked me to report fully on this matter of Artorius... it is so strange. The rumors of sorcery... they are disturbing."

Of course, my uncle, Josephus thought. *Otherwise you would not be here—not at this time of year, at least! And not with a man learned in the Law, and four bodyguards! With my father gone, you are the closest of the elder generation to me, so naturally you would be the one sent to see if I have been beguiled by sorcery or bound by spells.*

Aloud he laughed and made a waving gesture with one hand, shocking his uncle.

Which is necessary, as preparation for quieting his fears.

"Oh, that! Mere superstition, the babbling of peasants and fools."

Jews were forbidden anything that smacked of spellcraft; even taking auguries, which was nearly universal among other folk. His family would cut him off if they thought that he had broken the Law so, regardless of profit and loss. They might take...more drastic measures, too.

And be quite right to do so, if Artorius were a sorcerer, he thought, and went on aloud:

"No, no, merely a better grasp on the mechanic arts and natural philosophy. Like the new bookkeeping methods I mentioned."

"Those have been very useful, and will be more so. But... these thunderballs? Throwing lightning, to kill many men with a clap of thunder indeed—is that not magical?"

"No, Uncle, I have beheld them at every stage of their construction, and no spellcraft is involved, any more than with the mirrors or the *Ronsonius*."

"Hmmmm," Stephanus mused. "You have a point there. Those are mundane enough, once you understand them."

Josephus nodded. "So are the thunderballs. A mere matter of common ingredients—saltpeter, sulfur, common charcoal—ground finely in water, combined in a new way. And thrown by physical devices, not by gestures and words of power: by catapults or the force of the thunderpowder itself for the new *tormenta*, the *cannon*."

"But they burst with a *sound* like thunder," Stephanus said, regarding him shrewdly.

"So they do. But I have also...privately, you understand..."

His uncle nodded; discretion was something Jews in the Empire learned early, whether they were rich or poor.

"...mixed and lit the thunderpowder myself, after prayer and supplication to the Lord of the Universe over it, and reciting the passages of the Law that concern sorcery. It then behaved exactly as that which Artorius makes, neither more nor less, as no evil spell could. Simply a matter of greater knowledge. As men in the time of Troy knew not the forging of iron but made their tools and weapons of bronze."

Careful! Josephus thought, as the comparison popped out. *Don't slip like that and drop clues! Stephanus is no fool. No indeed! Even travel through time might occur to him, if his mind was prompted in that direction by enough wonderments.*

"I can show you this myself, if you wish, taking you through every step," Josephus went on.

"That is a relief to me, and will be to others of our kin," his uncle said, his face clearing. "You may show me tomorrow, but I have full confidence in your judgment now."

As a shrewd man of business must, he recognized sincerity in the younger man's tone and bearing.

Then he rose. "I will return—I must visit this new jakes of yours. Ingenious, pulling on a chain to flush away the wastes! And more economical of water than one with a constant flow like a river."

He rose and left, promising to return soon. Josephus breathed out in relief. Though Stephanus could conceal intent very well...

A few minutes later, a knock came at the door, three short raps, a pause, and then another.

"Enter," he said, keeping the tension out of his voice.

It was the senior of his two bodyguards, a *Germanii* from the western provinces, tall—even taller than Artorius—but moving like a great yellow-haired cat. He inclined his head and spoke:

"Sir, your uncle came and spoke to the priest, and to his bodyguards. In no language I know or recognize." They were talking the bodyguard's birth speech, though he had some command of Latin too, and at least enough Greek to know what it was when he heard it.

Aramaic, then, probably, Josephus thought, tense but calm and clearheaded.

"Afterward, the priest put aside his scroll and sought his bed," the big man said. "And his guards, they don't look as if they expect a fight anymore."

The bodyguard wasn't particularly intelligent...except about anything to do with fighting. He wouldn't have survived six years in the arena if he didn't have a good grasp of *that*, size and reach and stallion strength or no. He went on:

"They stashed their weapons...one by one, save for the man on guard outside your uncle's rooms, making it look casual."

Josephus let out a long sigh, and relaxed truly for the first time since his uncle had arrived.

It worked, he thought. *Praise be to Him!*

"You and Hildirīks—" the merchant said.

Who was his other bodyguard. It meant "King of Battle" in the Germanic tongue; as his own meant "God Will Increase." Curiously, American names seemed to have no meaning that their bearers knew, though some of them were *descended* from Hebrew.

He had learned to speak the Germanic tongue because of its usefulness in trade here on what had been the border. It would be even more useful now—for a generation or two at least—with so much of the former *Barbaricum* now inside the Empire. There would be a total turnover in the amber trade, just for one thing, when the Imperial armies reached its source in the German Sea far to the north. Roman traders would be able to *go* to the source and buy there themselves, rather than be stuck at the end of a chain of transmission that raised the price each time the amber changed hands.

Hmmmm. There will be transport costs ... but amber is very light in relation to value. And other trades, too ... bulk timber to the Middle Sea lands, as well, with these improved ships Artorius has told me of ... opportunities!

"—can go back to your usual schedule," he went on to the bodyguard. "And you will receive a bonus of, hmmm ... fifty denarii each for the sleep you have missed."

The bodyguard grinned and ducked his head; that was most of a month's pay, but a good investment. Germanii ... warriors in general, come to that ... admired a superior who was openhanded.

They'd been in a few fights together—at the first battle with the Marcomanni in the spring three years ago, for one, when they'd brought the new thunderpowder weapons to the field. He knew he had the man's respect as a *fighter*, too, not just the deference due an employer. There had been hand-to-hand work there for both of them, as well as catapults throwing bronze balls lined with lead bullets and stuffed with the thunderpowder.

I do not like the feel of steel striking home in bone, he thought. *No indeed! But it is ... necessary, sometimes.*

He practiced with the sword with the bodyguards several times a week—wooden practice weapons, of course—and in wrestling and boxing and the all-in *pankration*. A trader on the frontier needed those skills, and he was teaching his son Matthias too.

"Thank you, sir!" the man said. "We will toast your generosity with the first cup we buy!"

Stephanus returned only a little later; Josephus thought he looked more relaxed, and he did yawn.

"I think I *will* stay until I can meet our benefactor Artorius, and many thanks for your kindly offer of hospitality. He must be a man it is well to know."

Josephus went on:

"We visit each other, and our wives and children are friendly too..."

At a raised brow: "His hospitality includes taking care with the food when we guest with him. And he has never complained of the fare here, either."

"Ah!" his uncle said, obviously impressed.

That was not common. Romans loved pork, for example, and most just didn't take any law forbidding it seriously. Josephus went on:

"But as you may imagine, he is *very* busy! Not least with this new ironworks west of here in Noricum province. And believe me, when it is producing...no later than this coming spring or early summer, probably...it will also be extraordinary. Very."

His uncle's eyebrows rose; ironworks were ubiquitous, and only modestly profitable, usually a matter for artisans rather than investors, save for the Imperial ones. And those used the same techniques; they were just bigger, with many more furnace hearths. Though steel from Noricum had a longstanding reputation as the finest in the Empire, sought-after for the best swords and razors and other edge tools.

Josephus pointed at the fireplace.

"It is to ordinary iron smelting as that is to a brazier of charcoal," he said. "Or as those lanterns are to the usual kind, or the mirrors of silvered glass are to a polished bronze disk. The Emperor has backed it, but I have also bought a portion of it, with this new arrangement for permanent shares in the *societās* that manages it. I expect that profits will accrue to all who do so within...no more than eighteen months or at most two years from the first smelting of metal...*dividends*, they are to be called. Then regularly every year, on an increasing scale."

"How so?"

"Because the works will be able to *sell* iron and steel...and gear made of them...at a *much* lower price and still make very substantial profits."

"Much lower? *How* much?"

"Less than half current prices is the plan—and higher quality than any but the very best. The production *costs* are that much lower, and some of the product...iron cast like bronze, but much cheaper, and even cast *steel*...will be entirely new. The works could sell at half or less what they plan to charge and still make a reasonable return, but it will take a good long while for prices to fall *that* much."

Stephanus looked intrigued and skeptical at the same time. Josephus went on:

"Until others catch up with the new methods, but that will take years—ten, at least, I think, given the large initial investment required and the skills needed. The Empire will have first call on those. The plan is to duplicate the new works in many different places, places where there is good ore and fuel. And not *too* far from navigable rivers ... or seacoasts ... for transport."

"With the Imperial armies having first call?"

"Yes ... but there will be a large surplus over that demand in the end. And remember that it won't just be iron; steel too, by new methods that make it much more cheaply. Good steel, cheap enough to be used for many more things; for ordinary tools, even."

His uncle hesitated and then asked:

"How much in total would you say you have made in profits that you would not have save for Artorius, if you would?"

Josephus told him, straight-faced. His uncle jerked, nearly spilling his wine.

"You jest!" he sputtered, then went on more slowly: "No, you are serious!"

The sum he'd just quoted put him very slightly ahead of his uncle in total wealth ... and Stephanus had been a very shrewd, very successful merchant in the very capital of the Empire for longer than Josephus had been alive.

"By no means do I jest, honored Uncle. That is accurate to the last denarius as of the beginning of this week; I swear it by His Name that we do not utter."

They both dipped their heads at the mention of the Most High. Stephanus whistled softly, then sipped his wine.

It was a fine white watered three to one, strong and sweet, and was from what the Romans called Syria Palaestina and Jews their ancient homeland of Judea. Specifically from the HašŠəpēlāh, the foothills between Jerusalem and the southern coastal plain of Philistia.

Philistine once, mostly Greek now, Josephus thought.

Jews were not as numerous there as they had been before the

disaster and vengeful slaughters and enslavements of Bar Kokhba's revolt a long generation ago, but some remained and their vineyards were still well regarded. Galilee was the center for their people in that region now, since it had not joined the uprising.

Rome's hand is heavy on rebels, Josephus thought. *Very heavy indeed. Praise to the Most High; let him decree we will not put ourselves in that terrible place again! It was brave, but...foolish, very foolish and destruction on a scale such as only an intelligent but wrong-headed man can manage. Bar Kokhba was able, very intelligent...and very, very greatly deluded. The voice in his head was not the Most High. Mere madness, or a spirit of wickedness, perhaps, who hated our folk.*

Stephanus stroked his beard. "You advise me to place money likewise? It seems this is to be a gold mine, as well as an ironworks!"

"If it pleases you, yes, Uncle. I would advise it. I have yet to suffer loss on any joint venture with my friend Artorius; and with the new law, you are liable for the debts of the *societās* only to the amount you invest. Safer than a gold mine, in fact—less likely to attract the roving eye of rich senators, and not an Imperial monopoly leased out."

And used as patronage went without saying.

The Roman world ran on it at the upper levels, whether it was the formal ties of patron and client or more ad hoc.

"A most clever arrangement, these permanent, freely saleable shares and the limitation of debt liability!" Stephanus said. "Clever. Clever indeed! That will free much money from being held in safe but low-paying assets, release it for more productive use... by cutting the risks, and making the shares almost as liquid as cash. And it will free money now lying captive and truly sterile in strongboxes! Though it would be wise to keep a close eye on the managers."

Far too many men thought *wealth* meant gold and silver right under your thumb, or warehouses full of goods, or land to the horizon. He and his uncle knew that real wealth was money placed shrewdly so that it was out *working* for you. Coin was just a marker, an entry in a ledger. And stores of goods *ate* money, until they were sold. You didn't make money off saleable stuff by sitting on it except in the unfortunate times of dearth.

Money...to be true wealth, money has to move constantly.

Thus it breeds, *breeds wealth for all through whose hands it passes. Unless they are too stupid, and from foolishness there is no protection save the hand of the Most High.*

"Indeed, that is the point of the new law, my uncle. I would that all our family should profit from that, as they have already with the sale of the jewels and the *Ronsonius* and the new mirrors. It is a large investment, so more capital is welcome, and it should pay an excellent return."

Josephus' slight smile stayed as he went on:

"When the thunderpowder is more widely known, it will be very useful for other things than war—mining and quarrying, for instance, or building roads in rough country. Properly applied, it can shatter the hardest rock, just as it rends men's bodies. Indeed, the new ironworks is already using it so, at a great saving in labor! Much rich ore has already been brought to readiness, stockpiled for when these giant new furnaces are complete. There is a whole *mountain* of good ore there at Colonia Ferramenta—"

Which meant "Colony of Hardware," or close enough; or possibly "Settlement of Iron Things."

"—sufficient for countless ages, and splendid forests for charcoal—also enough for ages, if carefully husbanded by pollarding and planting. Which they will be."

Stephanus stroked his beard, and his eyes were hooded in thought for a time.

"About buying shares in this ironworks—"

⇒ CHAPTER FOUR ⇐

Northern China
March 1st, 168 CE

Daiyu—Black Jade—shivered slightly.
    The six cast-iron cannon of the battery roared, belching off-white smoke that stank of burned sulfur, more powerful than the smells of horse sweat and unbathed humans and melting muddy snow that surrounded Black Jade. Two kilometers away the six-kilo round-shot struck the knot of nomad horsemen. She lowered her binoculars, face impassive but still wincing slightly internally.

The horses...and men...they spatter *when the shot strikes. I had not expected that. They splash for meters!*

She didn't have to fight down nausea anymore, though. And she'd seen what nomad raiders did in a frontier village they overran. She *had* lost the contents of her stomach at that, which had cured her of any conscious sympathy for the Xianbei. They were wild men, and barbarically cruel even by the standards of the Eastern Han dynasty.

Still, the way blood splashes so far...and the horses, they *do not choose their masters.*

Their escort of horse archers cheered. They were nomads themselves—Xiongnu, Huns, whose ancestors had come south to what she thought of as Inner Mongolia when the Xianbei drove them from the steppes further north, north of the Gobi. Rather than going west, as some had done.

They *despised* the Han as grass-eating farmers, like so many humanoid cattle or sheep. But they *hated* the Xianbei with a passion, which made them useful allies.

Now I know what barbarian *really means,* she thought.

They were also using stirrups and framed saddles, copied from the ones the five Chinese had brought from the future. The problem there was that the Xianbei would copy it too, and not too far in the future. It was one of the *immediate* inventions they were introducing, one that needed no new tools or methods to make.

Only the idea is needed there. Cannon, though ... cannon are different.

Colonel Liu nodded in satisfaction as the regular Han infantry soldiers around him cheered too. Half of them carried crossbows, which her ancestors had invented a bit later than this ... but improved models, with rifle-like stocks and sights that about doubled their effectiveness. The other half had nearly rectangular iron-faced shields graven with scowling, snarling tiger faces, and long spears.

The gun crews were already reloading after they pushed the cannon back into position, a long *hisssss* sound as the bundle of soaked cloth on one end of the ramrod met hot metal and quenched any sparks in the barrel, then a dance-like play of agility as the fresh rounds were rammed home and the touch-hole primed.

The colonel motioned her forward.

"You see what the new weapons can do," he said to the Han general sitting his horse beside him.

The man looked a little puzzled; Black Jade repeated it in better court Old Chinese, and he repeated it back to her ... with a distinct regional accent.

She turned to the colonel and dropped into Mandarin: "Sir, he *mostly* understood you ..."

"Good. I thought I'd finally gotten fluent, down in Luoyang!"

"You have, sir. You are fully comprehensible *in Luoyang.*"

Which was true. Though his accent was still vile, and prompted laughter now and then. It would not be tactful to say that, though.

And tact ... tact you need to survive around State Security. Or the nobility, here.

Her accent was still detectable but diminishing ... but then, languages had always come easily to her.

She went on:

"But his own speech is a northern dialect, and the combination of *his* learning the Luoyang speech as a grown man and *his* accent plus *your* accent made it uncertain. There is less uniformity in language here than we expected! But then, Old Chinese has been spreading in all directions for over a thousand years by now. Only to be expected that it will diverge regionally in such a long period. Even among the upper classes, since our system of writing is not alphabetic."

"Inefficient," her commander said, and shrugged. "We will introduce an alphabet, eventually...but it will be some time before a universal schooling system can be created with mass literacy in a standard speech...He seems impressed, at least."

There was a sheen of sweat on the general's face, despite the chill spring weather, and his eyes kept flicking back towards the guns. There were only three batteries of them so far, and this was their first visit to this section of the border.

The man wore a back-and-breast of black leather with red-lacquered iron scales over it, and larger scales on the shoulder pieces. His helmet looked distinctly odd to her: it was of leather padded with cloth on the inside, and had more black iron scales laced to it on the outer surface, and a hanging neck guard of the same. Pheasant feathers stood up to either side of it over his ears, which was a mark of rank; a long, single-edged straight sword hung at his waist; loose trousers were tucked into soft-surfaced knee boots beneath, both originally copied from the nomads.

His bodyguards were similarly equipped, and carried lances that often had a projecting side blade or a hook; their gear was much like his otherwise, except that it looked plainer, and his saddle and theirs were in the old style.

She and the colonel were in steel-wire chainmail with knee-length skirts split before and behind for riding, and plate-steel helmets with flared neck guards. Those were among the first from the new workshops, but more would follow later—it was just as good protection or better than the local product, and weighed about a quarter to a third less. At least the concept of mass production was something that the locals were thoroughly familiar with, in military workshops at least.

Hooves pounded; they all looked up, but it was two riders with the blazons of Imperial messengers on their chests, trotting over the rolling grassland from the south. They drew up, bowed in the saddle, and handed over a sealed scroll to her; she passed it to the colonel.

He reads *the local language well, but then, he did before we . . . arrived. Odd to say* before *of something in the distant future!*

"Ah," he said in the language they shared; that made it absolutely safe from eavesdroppers.

"Sir?"

"The Roman envoys have started talking about departing for Rome once more."

They'd been there for months when the Chinese party arrived at court. And they'd been intensely curious, and had enough contacts to follow what the newcomers were doing. Whoever had picked them had been shrewd about their abilities.

Colonel Liu smiled thinly and dropped into their birth speech, which made his remarks invincibly private:

"That would be unfortunate, since they would take news of us back to Marcus Aurelius. Not fatal—what can he do, ignorant of the devices of the future? Still, he was . . . is . . . a very intelligent man. Better he know *nothing*. But something can be . . . arranged, I think. If I can persuade Emperor Ling. That man . . . that spoiled boy . . . keeping his mind on matters of importance is like sculpting a statue from warm pig lard!"

"And if he cannot be brought to see the necessity, sir?" Black Jade said.

The colonel's smile showed teeth now.

"Something can still be arranged," he said. "With our other contacts at court. Three years is enough to develop such."

Black Jade shivered slightly again.

⋙ CHAPTER FIVE ⋘

Province of Noricum
Colonia Ferramenta
(Erzberg Mine, Styria)
May 1st, 170 CE

"This doesn't look in the least like any ironworks I've ever seen before, Tribune," said *Legatus Augusti pro praetore* Marcus Claudius Fronto on a bright spring afternoon.

In fact, if you hadn't said so I wouldn't have taken this ... place ... for an ironworks at all, he thought, turning from side to side in the saddle to take it all in.

That was difficult; it was just ... different ... from anything he'd seen before.

The weather was even mild, at least by Pannonian standards, though he wore a thick fitted wool cloak with the hood thrown back as well as his densely woven white wool tunic with the broad senatorial stripe and another plain wool tunic beneath ... as well as the new knitted-wool knee socks.

His military *balteus*-belt and spatha sword were worn over it, and tight knee-length leather riding breeks, *femoralia*, beneath. His mount was good ... though no better than that which Artorius bestrode beside him; the man was an excellent judge of horseflesh too, and was establishing a fine stud on his home estate, breeding tall chasers of fifteen hands and better. That was a very suitable diversion for a gentleman, of course, like most things to do with horses.

Still, Artorius always makes good on a promise—we've all seen that. So far, at least, so it's the way to bet.

He coughed a little as the wind bore harsh acrid smoke towards them down the slope of the valley. The road twisted to follow the upward-ranging cleft in the land and the brawling, leaping stream that ran a little distance away, occasionally sending a little spray their way. The basic scent of the smoke was burnt charcoal, familiar enough, but with an odd mealy, gritty, metallic-stony overtone not quite like anything he'd smelled before.

There wasn't as *much* smoke as he'd have expected, though. Big Imperial ironworks usually existed in a constant haze, and their workers coughed constantly... until they coughed blood and died, often enough.

Artorius and he were riding side by side a little ahead of Fronto's mounted aides and couriers, servants and baggage and the *turma* of thirty-one cavalry guards whose new-style long lances rose and fell with a steely glitter from the afternoon sunlight. Their armor came from here too, some of the first, and all made from *steel*, not just iron. Even the wire for their mail shirts was fine steel, which was unheard-of.

And won't those couched lances and the stirrups and the thunderballs and tormenta *throwing cannonballs a mile or more be a surprise next time we fight the Gods-detested Parthians in the east,* he thought happily. *And the big siege* tormenta *Artorius has mentioned, that will batter down strong city walls in a day or less... no more long sieges and camp fever killing our men...*

He grinned like a shark at the images that flitted through his mind. He'd fought the Parthians himself as a legionary legate in the bitter struggle that had greeted the new Emperors on their accession seven years ago, before the Marcomannic War. And he'd won most of those engagements, fought others to a draw... but never easily and it never really seemed to settle much.

Because you can beat *a Parthian army, if you're smart and skilled and have a little luck... and then they run off faster than you can* catch *them.*

Rome and Parthia had fought many wars in the east since the first back in the times of the Republic, when the easterners had slaughtered Crassus' army in the desert at Carrhae. That was a disaster whose memory still made Roman soldiers wince.

Though that victory hadn't let the Parthians come much further *west*, either.

Nor had the Romans gone much further east when they won

battles with the easterners. Emperor Trajan had beaten them badly, back about fifty years ago, and come maddeningly close to turning all the rich, fertile irrigated lands of Mesopotamia into new Roman provinces. Without those lowlands and the vast revenues they produced, the Parthians would be merely savages haunting the mountains and deserts and steppes at the edge of the world.

But then those promising new territories had fallen apart in chaos and rebellion as he sickened and died, and after that the new Emperor Hadrian had been too occupied with a Jewish revolt to do much.

Armenia in particular had gone back and forth between the empires like a leather ball in a boys' game of toss and catch. First one side putting its nominee on the throne there, then the other, nothing lasting. Armenia was worth having since it bred good fighting men, especially for horseback work, and its mountains had rich mines, but neither empire had been able to stake it down for long.

Nobody else on the Roman side had even come close to what Trajan had done. Ctesiphon, the Parthian capital in the west on the banks of the Tigris, had been sacked in the latest war more than five years ago now, and all Rome had really gotten out of it besides . . . probably temporarily . . . a secure hold on Armenia was a little plunder and a bad plague.

Thank the Gods that Galenos came up with a way to stop it! Apollo's son Asclepius truly whispers in his ear. Without that . . .

He shuddered at the thought.

But the reports from the east and Rome said the plague was dying down now, fewer falling ill every day, week and month as the vaccine was spread like a wall around each outbreak by the ones Galenos had trained. They were *making* more vaccine now from the east to Britannia, and soon there would be enough everywhere, and eventually they could give doses out to the remotest village or hut.

And everyone would take it, like it or not, with troops standing by.

Deaths had been very heavy in the east, maybe as much as half a million in total by now, not to mention ten thousand or a bit more in Rome itself, but he'd used his position to ensure that everyone in *his* family got the vaccine quickly. And his dependents, and then all the tenant farmers and slaves on his estates and all his clients and *their* clients, slaves and dependents.

That was merely meeting a patron's obligations to those who supported him, of course. A noble who didn't do that soon found his clients wouldn't back him when he needed it badly; a patron had to secure the loyalty of his clients by concrete favors, by being loyal to *them.*

As I support the Emperor, who is my *patron.*

What it might have been like around his home *without* the vaccine boggled the mind, a holocaust of unimaginable scale.

Everything would be very different the next time Rome fought Parthia, hopefully . . . and the reports that the plague had raged over there totally unchecked was an added gift from the War God Mars, or from Far-Shooting Apollo whose arrows carried death. Since it might well kill every third or fourth Parthian, more than any Roman army could hope to do.

After all, Rome's frontiers with the European *Barbaricum* hadn't advanced much for most of a century either . . . not since Trajan conquered Dacia . . . until the Marcomanni tried to invade Pannonia. Since then the tribes on the Danube had been swiftly crushed without much loss and a huge swath of Germania annexed.

He looked forward eagerly to teaching a similar lesson about *Roma aeterna victrix* to the easterners.

Oh, what a surprise for them it will be! Who knows? We might march as far as Alexander of Macedon did! But unlike his, our Roman conquests . . . our conquests usually last.

Right now he could spare the time to come here, to where the very latest wonders were born. Especially since the campaigning season started late in the far north, where his command was now, and his subordinates were fully capable of handling what was essentially a long mopping-up process punctuated by small battles that always ended the same way. Raids and ambushes and the odd arrow or slingstone or javelin from behind a bush were annoying, but didn't matter much in the long run unless you happened to be one of the casualties. You crucified the skulker if you caught him, burned a few villages around the spot and sold or slaughtered the inhabitants, and went on.

There had still been snow on the ground in some of the passes over the Carpathians on his journey here, after a winter in log huts. Those at least worked surprisingly well, and with an improvised *ignis locus* of sticks or rocks set in mud . . . they were warm enough you were just uncomfortable, not freezing and coming down with death in your lungs. And they were quick to run up by deeply notching the ends of the trunks and squaring off the top and bottom of the timber in that land of many tall straight trees.

Which had been another suggestion by Artorius.

Worse than Armenia *in winter up there, and I thought nothing could be!* the general reflected with a shudder. *Thank the earth-shaping* Gods *there's plenty of firewood!*

His own ancestral home was in the mild coastlands of the Aegean amid rich rolling fields of grain and pasture, and vineyards and olive groves and orchards of apricots, figs and pomegranates as well as cherries and apples.

More dampness in *the cold than Armenia, at least, up there in the north of Germania. It soaks into your bones! No wonder they keep trying to come southward!*

The crunch of shod hooves on pavement and the grinding of wheels would make their conversation private; Artorius had said that seeing the works would be better than him trying to explain them ahead of time. Before them the mountains of Noricum, outliers of the Alps, still bore winter's lingering snow. Their lower slopes were green with trees ... and now threaded with rising columns of smoke from charcoal-burners' work, turning wood into fuel for the smelters.

He pointed one hand in that direction.

"Not as much of that smoke as I'd have thought necessary, Tribune," Fronto said. "Ironworks devour charcoal, and this is to be a very large one, I believe?"

"The process we use here is more economical of fuel than those you are used to, sir," Artorius said. "You will understand that I did not make iron myself in America; my family were landowners ... mostly a grazing estate, what we called a *ranch* ... and I was a soldier, and I hope something of a scholar."

Fronto nodded. That made Artorius ... *respectable* would be the best word, he decided. Respectable by Roman standards.

The *novus homo* went on:

"But I'm familiar with the principles our American artificers used—if nothing else, weapons are mostly iron and it behooves a soldier to know where they come from."

The general inclined his head in acknowledgment; that was why *he'd* made a point of visiting the local Imperial ironworks whenever he was moved to a new province on the frontiers.

You got less in the way of embarrassing surprises about supplies if you did that.

"With some trial and error over the past couple of years,
we've duplicated the essentials," Artorius said.

He added a short phrase in the mysterious tongue that the
ex-Americans used among themselves. It was the oddest-sounding
language Fronto had ever heard, even more than Aramaic or
Armenian, a hard rasping-nasal staccato that grated on the ear.

In this case, what the other man murmured under his breath
sounded like:

The essentials as of about eighteen-thirty-five.

Whatever in Hades' name *that* meant.

Fronto smiled and gestured friendly agreement. Artorius had
a reputation for being brusque and acerbically direct. And he
lived up to it in his no-nonsense way, like Cato the Elder come
again with all the ancient blunt Republican virtues that some
now considered vices.

But his *voice* was carefully respectful of Fronto's rank, and
bore less of the odd accent he'd noticed when they first met, back
when the Roman armies crossed the Danube. Now it could almost
be that of any scholarly Pannonian *eques*, though in appearance
he might have been Gallic or German...save that his blue eyes
had a bit of a slant and were narrower than you might expect.

*Like his client, that woman Philippa who knows so much
of horses...and even more strangely, of mathematics...but not
nearly so much so,* he thought. *Just a hint of what she has in
full. Though the tint of her skin and hair would be quite normal
around my home estates.*

Romans were a mixed lot too these days, of course, and more
so all the time; they could *look* like anything from Egyptians...
or even Nubians...to Germanii.

But then, we started *that way, you might say. Romulus and
Remus recruited shepherds and land pirates, escaped criminals
and runaway slaves, and they* stole *their brides from the Sabines
by force. They violated a* sacred truce *to do it! Banditry, really,
by a bunch of peasant bullies and thugs living in thatched mud
huts on the Palatine Hill behind a log palisade...but on a grand
enough scale, with the favor of the Gods, banditry becomes an
Empire. With Empire comes law and prosperity.*

Fronto was always conscious of accents. His own family spoke

Greek at home in western Asia Minor, but he'd been expensively tutored as a child to make sure his Latin was that of Rome's elite, and was doing the same with his own children so that they'd be equally at home in both tongues, both spoken and written.

Even my daughters! You never know what matches may be made.

Many men born of the upper classes throughout the Empire, equestrian or senatorial, spoke Greek as well as Latin...

Still, Latin is the language of state, of command. And of the Army... mostly. Even auxiliaries usually learn it. And it is the tongue for addressing the Senate.

The further west and north you went in the Empire the less Greek you heard, too, except in the bigger cities like Rome and Carthage, or ancient Hellenic colonies like Neapolis or Massalia or Emporeon.

Artorius pointed ahead; growing larger as they rode up the valley toward the spanking-new dam of stone and earth that ponded back the river were four great circular towers, separated by several hundred yards each. Forty Roman feet high at least, constructed of roughly shaped stone set in concrete... and they tapered a bit from base to summit, and were broad enough to look a bit squat.

Like fortress towers but a little larger than most.

Flames burst from their summits occasionally, with a high-pitched shrieking sound that made him soothe his horse reflexively as it shied at what sounded like a whistle blown by the lungs and lips of Jupiter the Best and Greatest.

"What *are* those, Tribune?" Fronto asked, pointing to the towers. "Surely not..."

Now he could see that an endless bucket-chain-like arrangement ran up a sloping framework to the top of each, bearing loads of charcoal, broken iron ore and some other crushed rock. Brought there by wagons from up the valley that ran on wooden rails strapped with iron on top; it looked like they coasted down and were hauled back up—empty, or nearly so—by mules.

"Yes, those are the furnaces, excellent general. The heart of Colonia Ferramenta," Artorius said.

Fronto nearly jerked his reins in surprise, and his horse snorted questioningly. He'd seen iron-smelting furnaces more times than he could count; they were simple clay columns not much taller than a tall man—than Artorius, say. And no bigger around than two men could span with linked hands.

In an Imperial working, dedicated to supplying the constant iron hunger of armies and fleets, there might be dozens or even hundreds of them pockmarking the ground. With several slaves squatting near each all day to work the bellows and more bent double hauling baskets of ore and charcoal on their backs.

Though he supposed some were using *unarotas* by now. *Wheelbarrows* was the term in the American language.

"*Furnaces*?" the Roman general said incredulously, blinking. "Furnaces big enough for the smithy of Vulcan!"

Lame Vulcan was the God in charge of artificers and craftsmen. Or He was dubbed Héphaistos, if you were speaking Greek, as Jupiter was also Zeus Pater. Some said these days it was a sign that Latin and Greek had a common origin, an ancient mother tongue from which both descended. The Emperor was writing a book on that, when he had some spare time.

"Not quite *that* big, sir," Artorius said with a chuckle. "The fourth is just finished and started producing this week. The concrete needs time to set and it's slower in cold weather, we had to keep carefully banked low fires on the hearths for weeks. Then they're thickly lined inside with a special brick in a careful shape. That brick has to be renewed now and then, but not often."

These giant things... Fronto thought, and went on aloud:

"How is that possible? No bellows could supply enough wind! Not with a thousand slaves for each, all *working* at the bellows!"

"Ah, we use...there, sir!"

Artorius pointed. They'd come level with the first of the towers...

Furnaces like fortresses, Fronto thought, shaking his head in wonder. *Artorius is Vulcan's favorite son indeed!*

...and a long shed with a roof but no walls yet ran beside it. A waterwheel turned at one end of it; that was familiar enough from gristmills, though this one was bigger than most, had iron bracing, and the blades seemed to be curved instead of straight boards...and the millrace delivered water from the top but a little back from the summit, so that...

"The wheel will turn in the same direction as the water flows in the lower race!" he said.

That meant less back pressure and more work for the same flow. He added:

"Ingenious!"

Like all of his new things, Fronto thought silently. *His native homeland is destroyed utterly, apparently, as utterly as Atlantis in the philosopher's fable, but Rome... Rome benefits. Who knows how long the war with the Marcomanni would have lasted without the thunderballs and* tormenta *and new roads and the other* new things? *Perhaps with other barbarians... the Sarmatians, for example... aiding them too, beyond the Great Barbarian Conspiracy that we nipped in the bud. Truly, the Goddess Fortuna's wheel turns to favor Rome!*

The shaft from the waterwheel ran for some distance, with short squat stone pillars cut into U-shapes with greased iron liners on top to support it, and iron collars on the shaft at each resting point. But the timber of the shaft was not straight; instead it bent back and forth at morticed, metal-braced joints like the key design often painted on walls below the ceiling. The outer faces of the extensions had heavy poles on lateral pivots moving back and forth as well as up and down as the shaft turned.

Those in turn connected via more pivots with other poles that were pulled back and forth horizontally...

"To convert the circular motion of the waterwheel to back-and-forth!" he said.

"It is called a crankshaft, sir," Artorius said. "Because it is cranked—bent back and forth."

"Also ingenious! But what are those things like great straight-sided barrels? I see no bellows."

"Those *are* the bellows, in a way. See how the moving rod pulls the iron-rimmed circular plate inside each tube of wood backward and forward resting on greased iron strips? The row of hinged insets in each opens with the backstroke, letting the air through... then they snap shut as the plate... the piston... is pushed forward. That provides the draught, more powerful than any bellows worked by men or animals. With six pistons working at different stages of the cycle, as there are here, the amount of air is continuous."

Artorius' finger went to four large brick structures between the...

Air-pumps, I suppose, Fronto thought. *Odd to think of pumping air as if it were water! Though I suppose that is what an ordinary bellows does too... Air can push things itself—hence the sails of ships, and the new windmills, so it must have... would* weight *be the right word? Very* odd, *so* odd *to think of air* having weight! *Yet... it must, the logic is irrefutable.*

...and the impossibly huge furnaces, each flanked by a tall, narrow brick tube, easily twice the height of the furnace. Three of those were pouring out smoke to add to the tang of the air.

"And see how the hot air from the top of the furnace is moved to those block structures by pipes? They are called *preheaters*. The gas from the furnace *burns* in the preheater, too, making it hotter still."

Fronto peered. "Are those pipes *iron*?" he said with astonishment; they were huge, big enough that a man could crawl through them, or at least a toddling child. "Lead pipes for water I have seen, of course, and even bronze sometimes for public fountains and the like, but *iron*?"

"Yes, from the first liquid iron of the first furnace. There are four preheaters for each furnace...blast furnaces, they are called. Inside each preheater is a checkerboard of the special brick I mentioned; it is called *firebrick*. The hot burning air from the furnace heats the bricks until they glow. Then the outrush is put to the *other* preheaters, and the air from these piston bellows is put through the hot brick before it enters the furnace at the base. That heats it—which *again* reduces the amount of charcoal needed still more, and increases the heat in the furnace, melting more iron from the same weight of ore."

"Hmmm," Fronto thought, trying to visualize it.

Then it was as if something went *snap* in his head and he said:

"Yes! I see! Instead of being vented to the air and carrying *away* the heat from the burning charcoal, the hot fumes of the burning... or the charcoal itself, in a way...is used *twice*! Most ingenious!"

He was subtly flattered by the look of approval Artorius gave him. Fronto supposed some broad-stripe men—the common phrase for those of senatorial rank—might be *offended* by approval from a man born a foreigner. One only granted Roman citizenship a few years ago and even more recently raised to the Equestrian Order, the lower end of the noble class...

But then, his own family had only been entitled to the broad stripe since his grandfather's time, at the end of the reign of Trajan, not long before his own birth. And they had been granted Roman citizenship by Vespasian during the First Jewish War two generations before that, for services rendered to the State, which together with their wealth had made them equestrians.

We had to work *at being Roman. We climbed the ladder by our own strength! And I...I have added to the fame of my line, become the conqueror of the Germanii...under the Emperor, of course...and eased the way for my children.*

Artorius nodded and went on: "These furnaces don't produce blooms which must be hammered to expel slag. The iron is fully liquid, and the slag—helped by the limestone which is tipped in with the ore and charcoal as a flux—all runs off...carrying far, far less iron with it than the old way."

"It's a *nova res*, a *new thing*," Fronto said, impressed.

New thing was the general term that had grown up for the innovations the Americans had introduced, with *Pannonian gear* as the alternative words for things like stirrups and horse collars, huge, improved freight wagons and nailed-on iron horseshoes.

"Some of the liquid iron is cast into things like cannonballs, as you have seen recently in the north, sir, and the cost is much, much less than bronze shot was. Some to stoves or cookpots or other uses, like the fire plates at the back of an *ignis locus*. The *cast iron* is very hard, harder than steel. So hard that it is brittle."

Fronto chuckled. "An iron *stove*? What a luxury! Perhaps for the Imperial palaces, eh!"

Artorius shook his head. "The cost is less than one-tenth of the iron that you are used to, sir. At least that much less, perhaps more. And casting is easier and cheaper than smithwork. So it may be used for many things...cast-iron plowshares, for instance."

Fronto felt his ears perk up at that. He'd seen the two-furrow riding plows the Americans had introduced on the Villa Lunae, which now belonged to Artorius. They did a better job than the usual wooden walking plows, did it much faster and with less labor and fewer draught animals. So did the disk harrows, and the seed drills needed much less seed than hand sowing the same acres, and you could weed the fields with animal-drawn cultivators since the grain was sown in straight rows, thus raising yields still more.

He intended to have it all introduced on his own estates just as soon as he could; he'd already made a start. Along with a raft of other improvements and the new crops from America, brought here as seeds when Artorius and his clients fled the terrible war there—maize and potatoes, sunflowers and tomatoes and those *very* tasty peppers and such.

The *vilicus*, the manager, on the Villa Lunae had told him that all together the *new things* there had cut costs by four parts in ten, and increased yields and profits by even more. But the plowshares on those riding plows he'd seen were thin sheets of soft wrought iron hammered over carved beechwood. If they could be *cast* from iron, iron that was very hard, they'd last much longer...and if the iron was so *cheap*...

Visions of greater revenues from his estates danced in his head, *almost* as satisfying as the vision of Parthian armored cataphracts lying dead in windrows, or screaming and flailing at themselves as gobbets of burning *Ignis Romanus* ran under their hauberks.

Though not as amusing *as that,* he thought, smiling at the pictures his mind painted.

Or those damned elusive Parthian horse archers flogging their mounts as they fled from cannon fire in howling bulge-eyed terror and shat their saddles.

Artorius went on: "Some of the cast iron is turned into ordinary bar iron in the finery furnaces you see there..."

He couldn't see the details of that, but a hammering noise carried to them, louder than any he'd heard before, a heavy CLANG...CLANG...CLANG.

"And bringing the cast ingots in still glowing red hot in those closed wagons on rails saves fuel too, so it's cheap to do. Just for one example, all horse owners will be able to afford horseshoes eventually."

Fronto grunted thoughtful approval. Horseshoes made a *big* difference in how often hooves chipped and cracked, and the Roman cavalry throughout the Empire from Britannia to Armenia would all have them by the end of this year, along with framed saddles, raised cantles, stirrups and instruction in the couched lance. The stirrups gave mounted archers a big advantage too, increasing the weight of bow they could draw by a full third and making it easier to control the horse by leg signals.

If horseshoes could be made cheap enough for civilians who could barely afford a horse...horses were much faster than oxen, and now they and mules could pull just as hard with the new collar harness...

Time is money, he thought, a saying popular in Pannonia these days.

"Some is made into steel—by pouring the molten iron into crucibles with saltpeter, which does it rapidly and cheaply," Artorius said and went on over his shoulder:

"Dablosa!"

One of his ex-gladiator bodyguards came forward; the man looked prosperous, from the fine armor he wore and the gold and silver ornaments on his harness and the hilts of his weapons, and the tall chestnut horse he rode, almost as good as his employer's.

"Sir? You wish?" he said with respectful courtesy.

In fluent Latin but with a strong Dacian accent the Roman general recognized from auxiliary cohorts recruited there.

"Show the lord Fronto your new sword," Artorius said.

"Lord," the man said and drew his blade with an arena-style flourish.

He presented it hilt forward across his left forearm … which had a guard on it, not of boiled and varnished leather but of smooth steel.

The weapon was a horseman's spatha, with a fairly broad double-edged blade of about thirty-four inches tapering to a wicked point. That made it a little narrower and a foot longer than an infantry *gladius*. Though those had been getting a bit more substantial lately in a swing of military fashion, after getting shorter for the *previous* three generations. Soon they'd be back to the twenty-four inches they'd been in the divine Julius Caesar's time.

He took the sword and sent it whickering in a figure-eight through the air with an experienced flick of the wrist—it was nicely balanced by the solid-steel pommel, as nicely as any blade he'd ever held. And it had an odd guard, like a steel letter *S* squashed down into a near circle, that looked like it would give very good protection for the hand. He knew from experience that on horseback you couldn't completely rely on your shield for protection; you had to be able to parry and block with the sword as well.

The blade rang sweetly with a sound he recognized when he tapped it with the hilt of his dagger, too, so it was both hard and resilient. The edge was good as well, knife sharp but not honed so fine that it would turn on bone.

"Excellent Noric steel," he said approvingly.

Wise men didn't stint their bodyguards, and steel weapons from Noricum were among the best, as good as any fine forging from Syria.

"As good as any I've ever seen!" he went on. "Expensive, but worth it if you can … wait, though you said …"

Artorius grinned as he replied, an infectious expression.

"Yes, sir. With this saltpeter process...where I was raised it was called Heaton steel, after the inventor...fine steel like this will *also* cost only a tenth or less of its present price. Perhaps a twentieth part or less. Low enough to equip *all* Roman soldiers with blades as good...and at a lower cost than for the, umm, less-good ones they use now."

"Vah! *Deodamnatus!*" Fronto swore, his eyes slitted for a moment in calculation.

Soldiers in the Roman army technically owned their own personal weapons, armor and gear: the cost was deducted from their pay, and then they usually sold most of it back when their enlistment was over, to add to the lump sum of twelve years of pay that made up their pension. When they weren't given land grants for farms instead, which would become commoner again with the fresh conquests adding to the *ager publicus*, the land that was at the disposal of the Empire.

Conquest paid well, especially with the *new things* helping. And veteran colonies were nearly as good as garrisons and cost a lot less, since the land was booty in the first place.

If the troops could all be *sold* fine blades like this...and at a lower cost, but the deductions stayed the same or didn't diminish as much...and the armor could be upgraded too...

More effective troops and *at a lower cost!*

"The accountants of the *fiscus* will weep for joy, Tribune," he said sincerely.

Over three-quarters of all Imperial revenue went to the military, every year...even when there *wasn't* a major war on. Or to the closely related tasks of building and maintaining roads and forts. His home province of Asia Minor had been webbed with Roman highways during the reigns of Trajan and Hadrian, which made defense—or attack—much easier.

He handed the sword back to the guard with a nod and smile—intelligent men were polite to bodyguards, too, and you were polite to the bodyguards of men whose opinion you valued. Then he ventured a jest:

"And the *a rationibus*—"

Which was the title of the equestrian official who managed the Imperial *fiscus*, the treasury.

"—will sacrifice oxen...or possibly his children...to the Gods in your name."

They both chuckled at the mildly scandalous remark—Romans considered human sacrifice a mark of barbarism, and had since the Punic Wars at least—and Artorius went on:

"Not to mention that scythe blades and axes and saws and sledgehammers and other tools can be made from the steel too."

"That would be useful," Fronto said. "Very!"

Too expensive to be practical now, but possibly not in the future he'd just glimpsed. Steel tools were stronger and springier and kept an edge *much* better than ordinary iron. For many uses they were just impossibly expensive... or had been. He went on:

"Especially steel axes and saws in the north! You would not believe the forests there once you're north of the Marcomannic lands. Endless! The cleared ground is just patches and the only big areas without trees are the bottomless bogs where the rivers spill in floods, or naked rock in the mountains. You have to fell timber to move anything but the *exploratores*, the scouts, even a pace ahead. And the forests swarm with savages as a poor man's hair does with lice."

He glanced down at the road they were riding on, recognizing the type.

The roadbed and its ditches had been shaped from cleared dirt by a simple horse-drawn earthmover called a *Fresno scraper* by Artorius. Then the beveled soil had been rolled with column drums to firm it up and covered in a surface of broken rock, the bottom eight inches of three-inch broken rock, then another four of two-inch that was a little thicker in the center, to produce a low curve that shed water.

Then *that* was rolled and pounded until the broken bits of stone locked together, a method the more cunning since most of the hooves and wheels and boots of ordinary traffic also worked to keep it consolidated. Just here it looked like dark-gray furnace slag, though limestone was commonest elsewhere.

Traditional Roman paved roads were five *feet* deep, with shaped rock in layers often set in concrete even before the paving surface was added.

This was just as good for animal-drawn carts or hobnail-booted feet, shed water about as well, resisted hard frosts in cold areas more strongly, and was fifteen to twenty times faster to build and required a lot less skilled labor. Plus it was easier on the hooves and legs of horses than solid stone blocks.

It did need a bit more maintenance, but that was easy enough. You just dug up the surface around a pothole or rut or wet spot with picks, added some more crushed rock—piles of it were kept spaced along the new roads—and pounded it down with wooden blocks on poles until everything was smooth once more. And every few years you added a little across the whole surface and rolled or pounded it in.

Fronto went on aloud:

"These new roads . . . by the *Gods* they're quick to make! That's been a great help in the north, Tribune. If it isn't rocks up there, it's bogs; and if it isn't bogs, it's forests of giant trees, and the winter is cursed long and cursed cold even compared to Pannonia or the Caucasus. And with more snow than either. The natives strap long boards with upturned tips to their feet and *glide* over the snow! Thunderpowder helps with cutting through rock for roads in the high country, too. *And* breaking it up for the pavement."

"I am glad to hear it, excellent Legate," Artorius said. "Do you think you'll reach the German Sea this year?"

Fronto shrugged. The German Sea was about 640 Roman miles as the crow flew from the Danube between Vindobona and Carnuntum, the capital of the province of Pannonia Superior.

That knowledge also came from the *new things*, the uncannily accurate maps drawn to scale on the *paper* . . . stamped onto it, actually, like stamping a seal on your ring into wax. That made the relevant ones cheap enough to issue to every commander of a cohort or cavalry *ala*, even in the Auxiliaries. You could measure off distances with a ruled stick, or your thumb at a pinch, and along with the *very* new north-pointing needles called *compasses* they simplified travel greatly. Now you could tell which way was north, even in a winding valley in the fog.

And the maps made strategy easier to think out.

And . . . not least . . . they greatly reduced your chances of getting lost when you were campaigning away from known country.

And you need not rely so much on possibly treacherous local guides, either.

Before, everyone had assumed the northern sea was much, much closer. Currently the vanguards of the Roman armies were a bit over three-quarters of the distance, say 440 miles from the old border.

Say also twenty or thirty days march on good roads . . . now that there are *good roads where there were only muddy deer tracks before.*

And they were pushing ahead as the snows melted and the mud became slightly less bottomless and roadbuilding became practical again.

"We'll reach it in this campaigning season, if Fortuna spins her *rota* in our favor," the Roman general said, invoking the Goddess of Luck and Her sacred wheel. "We'd be there already if we hadn't had to march against tribes well west of the Ouistoula river, and raid east of it."

"As the divine Julius did over the Rhine when he conquered Gaul," Artorius said...which was a flattering comparison.

"Exactly. We're more than halfway down the Ouistoula, now that the ice is more or less gone...it was never solid, but there was too much for riverboats."

"Yes, the Vistula," Artorius said, as if making a mental note.

That sounded a little odd. *Ouistoula* was the Greek name for the river; the Latin spelling was *Vistla*.

Fronto continued: "And we've put some light galleys on it, with your new *carroballistae* throwing thunderballs and Roman Fire. And a few with twelve-pounders in the bows. We have a good road over the mountains to the navigable part now, and with the new wagons and harness our supply train is able to get us what we need, when we put it together with what we've plundered from the natives. That lets us use enough troops that we can overwhelm resistance quickly, and empty bellies for the natives drives the lesson of *Roma semper victrix* home."

Rome forever victorious, Fronto thought again to himself with satisfaction, and went on:

"When we *do* reach the German Sea we'll have the unsubdued Germanii tribes between there and the Rhine, the *Agri Decumates* and the Alps boxed in on three sides. We have outposts on the eastern side of the Elbe now, and bridgeheads over it. Four sides, when we get ships on the water up there. Ships with cannon, and *carroballistae* to throw Jove's Balls."

"And the new provinces reduce the Barbaricum between the Rhine and the Vistla by a quarter...or perhaps a third... already," Artorius noted.

"Just so! When the Rhine legions and their auxiliaries are re-equipped—"

At Artorius' raised eyebrows he specified:

"—that'll be finished soon—we can subdue everything in the pocket that's left in no more than a few years. *Possibly* as little as one campaigning season!"

"If Fortuna keeps smiling at us," Artorius added.

Fronto laughed agreement and went on: "Varus...and better still, the fine army the accursed fool lost...will be well and truly avenged."

Romans, particularly military men, remembered the disaster that had cost Rome three full legions in the Teutoburger Wald forest. *And* the prospect of bringing Germania into the Empire, even though it had happened a hundred and fifty years ago. It had been one of the few real and serious defeats in the reign of the first Augustus.

Publius Quinctilius Varus' name was not recalled fondly.

At all, Fronto mused. *As the first Emperor said...repeatedly... Quinctilius Varus, give me back my legions!*

If prayers and sacrifices affected Hades' choices, the man would be enduring an eternal fate that made Sisyphus' look like soft rest in Elysium. Avenging his *defeat*, though, that was a different matter.

Many slaver and drool at the thought, now that it looks to be practical, Fronto thought happily. *And I, I have the* glory *of it! After the Emperor, of course. But he deserves his greater share, it was his policy that set the stage...not least, that he quickly saw what Artorius and his clients could give us after that first victory with Jove's Balls saved the Tenth Legion and Vindobona. He bound them to his person by favor and largess, and they to him by acceptance. And hence Artorius and his clients are solidly loyal to him. Remember that! Marcus Aurelius is not a man* anyone *can safely underestimate, for all that he's not really a soldier himself.*

Being a successful general was all very well...but it could carry risks of its own, if an Emperor became suspicious that you had secret thoughts of wearing the purple yourself. Marcus Aurelius was no Domitian or Nero or Caligula, no mad monster seeing plots under every leaf and lashing out unpredictably, but he wasn't a trusting fool either.

Fronto went on:

"Not all that much fighting so far this spring. Once the native tribes up there get a taste of the thunderballs and cannonballs and *malogranatum* which I can testify personally shred a charge nicely—they wail and weep and puke and run. Or lick dirt at our feet. And the news of our great victory over the Marcomanni and Quadi spreads and sows a good and wholesome terror. Late last year and early in this we've had some brushes with that folk you called Goths when you warned us of them. The native name is something like Gutōz, but I call them filthy blond swine myself. Mad bastards and savage ones, but primitive compared to the tribes along the old border and we hammered them badly last year and again this spring. *And* they don't like Jove's Balls or Roman Fire or cannonballs—now that we have more cannon. Not the old bronze shot nor the new iron stuff from here! Or case shot and grapeshot."

He felt cheerful. The prospects ahead filled his stomach with delight, even better than a fine feast with good wine and naked dancing girls wiggling their backsides.

"So it shouldn't take more than two or three more years at the very most to bring *all* the Germanii *under the wings*. Many have surrendered without a fight and more will. The length of our European frontier will be nearly cut in half once Germania is pacified! Especially since the Sarmatian tribes east and west of Dacia have submitted now, and the Bastanarae too. Dacia isn't a thumb rammed up into the *Barbaricum*'s arsehole anymore and surrounded on three sides by stinking, dangerous barbaro-dung. It stretches from the Danube at Aquincum to the Black Sea and the Tyras river."

That parlous position of Dacia's had become more obvious with the new maps. It had set his teeth on edge every time he looked at one that showed political boundaries, and others had the same reaction.

The new eastern frontier of the Empire would be much more...

More tidy, that would sum it up. Tidy, running from northwest to southeast, and shorter by more than a third, and needing a smaller garrison. Say four or five legions and an equal number of auxiliaries to hold the Germanii down for the first generation, less once they're reconciled to living under the wings. Also it will put the remaining legions needed on the new frontier much, much further from Rome. Another month's marching distance, which all Emperors will appreciate! No foreigner has ever overthrown a Roman Emperor. But the Roman legions have, and more than

*once, though not in the past few generations. And the ones on
the Danube and Rhine were uncomfortably close to the City and
to Italy. Soon the garrison camps will all be much further away.*

"I hadn't heard about the Sarmatians yet, sir," Artorius said
thoughtfully. "Just that they were talking with our envoys. I've
been—"

He waved at the ironworks.

"—busy."

"That's just this month. I saw to the last of it on the way
here, and the reports will be reaching Rome about now. After a
few demonstrations of what the thunderballs and bronze *tormenta*
can do to distant formations of horsemen they crumbled like...
like snow in the spring, up here! One ball took off the head of
a rearing horse *and* the chief riding it at three times long bowshot! And another sight of the battlefield where we broke the
Marcomanni and Quadi and their allies. The bones and tatters
of hair cover nearly a square mile there, with weeds and saplings
growing up through the ribs and eyeholes of skulls. A third or
better of the Iazyges and Roxolani left for the Pontic steppe when
they saw they couldn't persuade enough of their countrymen to
fight us. Plenty of room for *colonia* of veterans, and plenty of
land to sell cheaply to new settlers."

"The Pontic steppe is where those tribes came from originally,"
Artorius said. "I don't think the ones there now will welcome
them with open arms, or joyfully offer them half their grazing.
Whether or not they're relatives."

Fronto nodded. "And the others went on their knees and
brought tribute to lay before us, horses, cattle, gold... *And* we
conscripted many of their young warriors for the auxiliaries,
they'll be useful in the east."

"And won't make trouble north of the Danube," Artorius
observed. "By the time they muster out, the ones still living will
be Romans themselves for all practical purposes, wherever they
settle. Probably in the east, in fact."

"Just so! The new frontier will run up the Tyras river—"

Which was on the western edge of the Pontic steppe itself.
Artorius nodded and murmured something like:

"Dniester."

And then at Fronto's curious look:

"The Dān-Ister, as the Sarmatians call it."

Fronto nodded agreement: "—then northwest through the higher country and down the Vistla—"

He used the Latin rendering of the river this time, since it was apparently the one Artorius was used to.

"—to the German Sea. That's what I've recommended to the Emperor, at least, and I am confident he will agree. A glance at the new maps shows that that is the most convenient stopping point, and it won't take long to do. By the end of this year possibly, or by the middle of the next at most."

"That will do nicely, sir."

Artorius grinned, and added in a pawky accent that imitated the old-fashioned crisp speech of someone reared in the upper-crust mansions of the Empire's capital:

"It will do as a stopping point…For now, perhaps. For now…"

They shared a laugh, and Fronto went on:

"Yes, *imperium sine fine*, as the poet put it! That will be a shorter length and easier to hold securely than the Rhine and Danube, with cheap river transport along most of it, and access to the Black Sea for nearly half, and to the German Sea for most of the northern portion. The tribes east of it aren't much except for the Sarmatians… *they* can be formidable… and the ones to the west…"

He smiled, or at least bared his teeth.

"…well… *they'll* all be dead or on their knees soon."

They passed the last of the furnaces, and a wilderness of trampled mud, piles of beams and bricks and logs and new roadways where humans and horses, oxen and carts, labored to run up other buildings. More quarters for the workers, and workshops to make finished products, amid those already functioning.

Fronto cocked an eye at the gangs laboring amid the ring of hammers on nails and the snarl of saws in wood, while wheelbarrows and wagons full of brick and stone and mortar went by.

"Working fast!" he said, and chuckled. "Your overseers must wield a wicked whip!"

There was an echoing silence. Fronto looked over, a bit surprised, but Artorius' face was carefully blank. It was odd, since all he'd done was pay him a complement.

The man cleared his throat and spoke:

"In fact, sir, I am using a bonus program here—rewards for good work, ranging from more food and better quarters through permission to marry, to cash. So that if a man works sufficiently hard and well, and saves what he earns, he will accumulate a *peculium* sufficient to purchase his freedom in, oh, five or six years. I find it reduces supervisory costs very considerably. And we have few runaways."

"But if the men are freed on such a scale, who will do the ordinary laborers' work?"

"The same men, sir, mostly. For pay. Since we need far fewer men than the old ironworks, we can afford to pay good wages."

"But they'll save them to buy land, or at least the smarter ones will," Fronto said, interested.

"We can afford to pay better than an ordinary peasant farmer can make. That too will lower costs, I believe, sir. Then they can rent houses with gardens... buy them from the ironworks *societās* eventually... raise chickens... and buy their own bread and potatoes at the bakeries and commissary shops we'll rent out to men who take up the franchises. And the laborers will buy pork and mutton and beef now and then too. Pannonia and Noricum are producing more crops and stock these days, what with the new seeds and better methods, and will grow more and more as they spread. Potatoes do well in wet upland areas like this part of Noricum, for instance, where grain won't yield very much, and an acre... or less... of them will feed a man for a year as far as basic... bread-like stuff... is concerned. Two or three thousand acres of potatoes would feed this whole *colonia*, at least for basic... bread-like-stuff."

"*Carbs*," he added in his own English speech.

Fronto frowned. Cash and the prospect of manumission was often used to get highly skilled slaves like doctors or accountants working harder. But not on this scale, that he was aware of, and not for common laborers. It was...

A bit disturbing. Though I couldn't say why, exactly.

Artorius went on:

"This works will produce around eight or nine thousand tons of iron and steel a year when it's fully built, with around four to five thousand workers, sir. Including the charcoal burners, and clerks and so forth."

Fronto dismissed his momentary unease. It was buried under astonished delight, reinforced by Artorius' reputation for never boasting beyond what he could really do. As a former provincial governor and present commander of armies, he knew that the entire *Roman Empire's* production of iron as of last year was not much more than ten times that.

Give or take, nobody knows precisely. But as a rough estimate, that's about right, he thought.

Which probably required at least three hundred thousand workers, half a million if you included those who labored at it part time in out-of-the-way places. Iron was usually made locally, wherever there was ore and fuel.

Here...

"How?" Fronto said.

"Many different things, sir, each reinforcing the other."

"Ah, that word you told the Emperor when the three of us spoke just before the last big fight with the Marcomanni... *synergy*, if I remember it correctly? Caesar Augustus was quite taken with it."

"That's it, sir. The big furnaces smelt much more of the iron in each unit of ore because they are so very hot, and they need much less fuel to make each unit of iron, and both those mean less labor, as does the thunderpowder to help quarry the ore and flux, water-powered machinery for crushing it, for blowing the draught and lifting heavy forging hammers and so on. And powering machines, too... lathes that can cut iron, for example, and drills that can bore into it. We've a few of those now and more and better ones will follow. And the cheaper steel makes the tool bits for those..."

Fronto whistled; turning iron like a wooden leg for a table was also a *new thing*. He could see how it would assist many operations.

He mused aloud:

"Then ten plants like this could double the whole Empire's iron supply, with one-tenth of the labor. At one-tenth the maintenance cost in food and housing and clothes as well. Or wages, for the free workers. And twenty... they would give us twice last year's production at a small share of the cost! It would take many, many such works to match what we *spend* on producing iron now. And *that* many would have iron as cheap as rocks!"

"We're planning... the Emperor has endorsed the plan... on twenty to start with, yes. All about this size. One every two years for the first few, then one every year, with men who've learned the skills here teaching others, sir," Artorius said. "And those workers not making iron anymore by the old methods can do *other* things; grow more food, make shoes and cloth or wagons... In the long run it'll also be good to have many works bidding against each other for contracts."

"Twice our current production at a small fraction of the cost," the general mused.

Then he thought for a moment, and went on:

"But can the Empire *use* that much iron?"

"Oh, yes, sir. Since it's so much cheaper, iron and steel will be used for much more, things that wooden tools are used for now or which aren't done at all. Cheap cast-iron *rollers* for the new style of road, for just one instance, pulled by working stock. That will make roadbuilding even faster because we'll need fewer men hand pounding the broken stone."

Artorius gestured and went on, some enthusiasm showing through the measured speech:

"It'll be the same for all the crafts, more tools and cheaper and better. And it will cut the cost of equipment for the legions to the same degree. For instance, iron horseshoes will become cheap enough for *everyone* to use them... and that will mean more work from and longer lives for the horses... more work done *with* the horses..."

They pulled up in front of the Praetorium of the *colonia*, a colonnaded courtyard-centered building a bit like the *pars urbana* of any Roman villa on a gentleman's estate... except that there were chimney stacks through the red-tile roofs. That meant fireplaces...

I must see to that back home on my domus *and villas,* Fronto thought. *It's warmer there than here, thank the earth-shaping Gods, but winter can still be damp and chilly. Especially when you get old, which I hope to do someday. And firewood for hypocausts is a bit scarce these days back home. If we could limit it to the bathhouse... that would be convenient.*

"And you have these *cast-iron* stoves for your kitchen staff, I suppose?" Fronto said genially.

"Yes, sir, among the very first. Here and back home... that is to say, on the Villa Lunae. You'll be eating the results tonight!"

"I am a man of *war* and hence a man of *iron*, so why not?" Fronto said with a laugh. "It's bound to be an improvement on trail rations and what we eat in the north among the savages—it's no wonder they lust to kill with the diet they have, bland isn't the word. Or what they serve at a *mansio*, where they just *think* they have good cooks for the travelers. Though at least those have baths."

He saw Artorius' wife on the portico of the building, and checked his horse a little so that they could greet each other first. Stewards and their staff bustled about to see to his followers and gear—the low-ranking ones who wouldn't be bidden to the formal dinner, though they'd eat better and sleep softer than usual. His four young tribunes, who were of course all *equites* themselves, dismounted and waited for introductions. A groom came to hold his horse.

The lady Julia was a woman past her midtwenties now, and he'd wondered a little at why Artorius had wed her—especially since he'd done it *after* he'd received the Emperor's favor, along with elevation to the Equestrian Order and broad estates. One of which he'd swapped with the *eques* Sextus Hirrius Trogus for the Villa Lunae, at the same time as the wedding that made them brothers-in-law.

All of that Imperial favor meant he could have made a *much* better match. With a new bride rather than a widow, a virgin in her teens, from a more prominent family, and with more than a token dowry. After the great victory over the Marcomanni a bit later... that would have been not just possible, but easy.

For example a better match with my family. My eldest daughter Flora is just sixteen now, and highly suitable. I'd propose it at once if he weren't already wed! He's going to be a broad-stripe man if he lives another decade, or I'm a Barbary ape. Old senatorial families die out... well, many of them live in Rome, it's hard on children there... And new ones arise. As my kin did!

Granted that Julia's family, the Trogi, were of the Equestrian Order themselves and had been since Julius Caesar had been a young man, elevated to that status by Pompey the Great.

Great as compared to what? Fronto thought with a smile; people had been making that joke since the man was alive.

That made hers a *very* respectable lineage. Her elder brother, Sextus Hirrius Trogus, was rich... by provincial Pannonian standards, at least... and a major landowner around Sirmium southeast of here. Though he'd been burdened by debts until Marcus

Aurelius rewarded him for helping Artorius by paying them off and giving him a lifetime's tax exemption to boot.

Most of those debts had come to him indirectly, via the Lady Julia's wastrel first husband. Her father had picked a man of good birth, but hadn't investigated his character as thoroughly as he should.

So she'd been a widow rather than a virgin, and she'd been twenty-six when they wed, quite old for marriage to a man in his thirties. And with only one surviving child, a daughter who Artorius had adopted and given his name as part of the marriage contract.

Though she'd born Artorius a son since; the boy was several years old now, in the care of a nursemaid standing behind Julia, and from his looks flourishing. But you should be careful about becoming too attached to a young child, since so many died in their first few years.

Hmmm. He's not swaddled... is that some local Pannonian custom?

Women usually couldn't help that love for a newborn, of course, and so got more grief. It was one more reason to thank the Gods who'd made you a man.

He looked at Julia with dispassionate appraisal. Yes, a comely face, full of character and life as well, with light russet-brown hair and greenish eyes showing the Gallic strain in her family's bloodline. Even white teeth showed as she laughed as well, an unusually fine set for someone her age, as pretty as...

Well, Flora has good teeth too! he thought a little defensively.

Yes, and he'd seen and heard with his own ears that she was witty and for a woman very learned, which would appeal to a scholar like Artorius. And she blossomed as she saw her husband and took his hands as he stepped quickly up to the portico. Their smiles at each other were like a private letter that only they could read.

Not a splendid figure to match the face and good teeth, though, he decided judiciously.

She was broad enough in the hips, but a bit too big in the bust to be quite fashionable, and rather tall for a woman.

And wearing that new garment... the bra, it's called.

He shrugged mentally; doubtless Artorius had his reasons, and she was pleasant socially. She and Artorius greeted each other decorously, but there was obviously true affection there, and from the lingering handclasp passion too. Her daughter, Claudia, was eleven—only a few years from the marriage market herself, bound to be courted eagerly given her formal, legal adoption by an Imperial favorite. And she threw herself *at* Artorius with *filial* eagerness, if not overmuch decorum; obviously she thought of him as her true father now.

He laughed and swung her effortlessly up and around and put her back down, smiling; the man was strong, too. Then he grinned as his young son regarded him dubiously and jammed a little fist in his mouth, and the fond father tickled the boy's nose with a finger, laughing outright at the grimace and grin that produced.

Fronto swung down from his horse—stirrups made that *so* much easier, and no need for a slave on hands and knees to provide a way to get up *into* the saddle in a dignified fashion either. He made his bows in the moment between politely allowing family to come first and overlong, impolite hesitation. He was of higher rank and birth, but there were other factors at work. Artorius might be a *novus homo*, a new man . . . but he was one with *extremely* good prospects, as well as a friend and fellow soldier.

Fronto took a bundle from the new-style saddlebags of his mount, and after the first greetings presented it to Lady Julia with a flourish. She unwrapped the cloth and twine around it and then stood frowning in puzzlement with the *libra*—one Roman pound—weight across her palm.

"Well, thank you very much, excellent Legate Fronto," she said politely, looking up at him with a question in her eyes.

You could read it: *A silver ingot?*

Gifts from guest to host were common, but a lump of precious metal would seem . . . crude, from a man born a gentleman and reared as one. Usually guest gifts were more symbolic, or picked because they were unusual or humorous, or special produce from the guest's own lands. Fronto himself often gave amphorae of ripe figs preserved in spicy wild honey, a specialty of his home estates.

Now he grinned and inclined his head.

"The very first yield from the new mine at Cowl Mountain, in the former Marcomannic territories, *Domina* Julia."

Which were now in the center-west of the brand-new Province of Transdanubia, and a swarming construction site that made this ironworks look small. The ingot had been from a test run to prove the ore, using the new smelting methods.

"Ah!" she said, and beamed at Artorius. "My lord husband's discovery!"

Fronto nodded:

"Just so, lady," he said and turned to Artorius:

"And it is as rich as I hear you promised, in that staff meeting with the Emperor in Carnuntum—the one nearly three years ago, right after the Quadi night attack that you alerted everyone to just before they struck."

Which illustrated why everyone with two denarii to rub together hastened to invest in anything Artorius did if they could manage it. Fronto did himself, nowadays. There were quiet but intense scrimmages to be *allowed* to invest where the Tribune did.

He went on aloud:

"The *fiscus* accountants are delirious with joy at how many talents of silver it will produce, and at the way your new refining methods...what are they called?"

"*Sartagine amalgamation*," Artorius said absently; he was obviously distracted by a thought. "Pan amalgamation."

"—your *pan amalgamation* yields so much more silver from the same ore; they have just now sent men who've learned it to Hispania to apply it to the Imperial mines there as well. And to try using it on the old mine waste, possibly that will pay too! Five more of the mines in the new territories will be producing silver by the end of this year, and that one further east is already yielding gold. Enough taken together to pay all the costs of the Marcomannic War quite soon, and this year's campaigning further north as well!"

Artorius reached out and touched the cold shining metal, shaped like two blunt triangles joined point-to-point and bearing an Imperial stamp. He seemed pleased, though commendably not showing it much. He had a tenth share in the new-style permanent limited-liability *societās* that managed the mines on lease from the Imperium in the recently added provinces. That had been assigned him on the Emperor's orders, because he'd given the location of the precious metals in the first place and the improved refining methods; and he'd given each of his four American clients a tenth of that share for their own.

It would pay abundantly.

Fronto...and nearly all the prominent men who'd been at the meeting, which he hadn't, but a friend had sent him the news... had put money into it too. The Senate would be very pleased as well, when they realized that it would enable the special war taxes to be scaled back very soon. The Emperor didn't *have* to take the Senate's opinions into account. But wise Emperors, of which Marcus Aurelius was emphatically one, did. Because taken as a whole, the senatorial families had too much wealth and too many clients to ignore. And after all, army commanders and provincial governors were drawn from their ranks. Save for a few special cases like Egypt.

The wearer of the purple could afford to anger *some* of the upper crust, as long as the Army supported him, but not all. Marcus Aurelius was firm, with a hard hand when it was absolutely essential, but popular. With most of the upper classes now more than ever.

And with the masses, too, for what little that latter was worth.

Fronto smiled at the future, his own and the Empire's.

Roma aeterna victrix! he thought. *Imperium sine fine! Next... Parthia. After that...who knows?*

⮞ CHAPTER SIX ⮜

Rome
Palatine Hill
July 15th, 170 CE

Fronto didn't wear a toga as often as many men of senatorial family did. He wore military gear—including the elaborate fancy form generals donned for ceremony—much more often. But when you were appearing before the Senate itself in the capital of the Empire it was obligatory, and he flattered himself that he'd carried it off with aplomb.

He smiled. The Senate session that had ended a few minutes ago had just voted him the *ornamenta triumphalia* for a third time, an almost unprecedented honor... and it wouldn't make the Emperor apprehensive because he was the one who'd introduced the motion, sitting on his throne chair between the two consuls.

The glittering gold wreath wrought like laurel leaves was around his brow, with its dangling gold ribbons; his tunic was embroidered with palm leaves, and his toga was entirely purple with an edge embroidered in gold. An ivory baton was in his hand... Though he intended to change as soon as he was in the house he'd rented. It wouldn't do to go about clad like an Emperor!

Particularly since the current Emperor hated ostentation and only wore the costume when he had to for ceremony's sake. He supposed Marcus Aurelius knew that not all men shared his taste for plain clothing... but, no, it wouldn't do.

Though there will be a bronze statue of me in the Forum of

Augustus; the artist will be doing his sketches in the next few days. And I can commission a statue of myself in this garb, and put it in the hall of my domus *back home ... and my descendants can display it too! True and lasting glory!*

The senators had also voted Marcus Aurelius a new name—*Germanicus*, for his deeds north of the Danube, with a round of quite genuine cheers.

And unlike previous recipients of that honor, Marcus Aurelius hadn't just scored a victory or two over the savages. He'd *conquered* Germania, and already annexed most of it—as provinces, not via the more dubious and generally temporary means of client kingdoms. And it looked to be settled for good and all with the recent cascade of surrenders.

Even wild Germanii savages can act sensibly, if you kick their balls up around their ears hard enough and often enough.

The speech Marcus Aurelius had given had also mentioned the new northeastern frontier of the Empire, and it was the one Fronto had recommended and discussed with Artorius that spring. Some of the senators had been surprised—the ones who knew things were going well, but not *how* well.

The Emperor had departed, and the session of the Senate was over. Hundreds of the Senators in their broad-stripe togas were pouring out of the Curia Julia, discussing the blizzard of good news as they went through the great bronze doors and into the hot sunshine—

And haunting stink, Fronto thought.

Like most men who spent much of their time in the countryside, he found cities appalling until the nose wearied of noticing it.

—of the Forum. To greet their entourages of clients, or to clamber into their litters and be born off to their mansions with their clients trailing along behind in order of importance. He'd be using a litter himself this time, though he usually preferred a horse—the costume he was wearing and the regulations on daytime street traffic in Rome made it inescapable.

The original *forum of Rome ... ornamented by Emperors, but not founded by them. Smaller and less glorious than Trajan's forum, but much older,* he thought, looking out from shade into the bright Italian summer sunlight.

Fronto lingered in one of the doorways to the portico for

a moment, looking around; this building had been begun by the Divine Julius himself, and completed by the first Augustus decades later.

It was an oddly austere sight—even with the additions Domitian had added a very long lifetime ago, more than eighty years past. Things from the first Emperor's reign often were rather bleak by today's standards.

The council hall of Julia—which was what "Curia Julia" meant—was about eighty feet long and sixty wide, with three broad steps at the rear, which could hold five rows of chairs each, and a high painted ceiling. The walls were veneered in Carrara marble for two thirds of the way up; that had been a new thing in the time of the Divine Julius and only really common in that of the first Augustus.

At the far end was the Altar of Victory, with a lovingly painted statue of Victoria—the personification of triumph—standing on a globe and extending the conqueror's wreath in one hand. The floor was the most luxurious aspect, *opus sectile* work in which colored marble was inlaid into stylized rosettes in squares alternating with opposed pairs of entwined cornucopias in rectangles, all worked in green and red porphyry on backgrounds of Numidian yellow and Phrygian purple.

His smile grew broader. His grandfather had come back from his first Senate session in late middle age and ordered a smaller duplicate of the floor in a new dining hall in one wing of the family *domus*.

Then he sighed and headed toward the exit. There was a string of would-be clients waiting out there, ready to try and get personal notice...

The price of success and glory! he thought dryly. *And that's just the* rich *and* powerful *would-be clients!*

A senator and his narrow-stripe client fell silent as he passed, glaring at him with barely hidden hostility. He briefly inclined his head in a polite response—the senator was of a very old family, which made that advisable. Old family was a mark of distinction... and a rather rare one. Turnover in the Senate was high, as families died out, or lost interest in a distinction that kept them in Rome a good deal and stayed at home. You could be a Big Man locally instead if you didn't want to plod through the *cursus honorum* or spend a lot of time on battlefields.

Unless you want to be a general with the ornaments of a triumph awarded to you. Three times, by the Gods! he thought smugly.

Senator Lucius Funisulanus Firmus knew he shouldn't be scowling at the hero of the hour as he strode by. He did it anyway, and it was all the more provoking when he got a polite nod in reply.

"Damned Greekling," he muttered under his breath. "And *dressed* like an ancient king of Rome!"

He spoke once the erect, soldierly, darkly handsome figure was safely out the entrance and into the milling...and rather loud...crowd beyond. That gave more than adequate cover, if you weren't too close to anyone else. You were never entirely sure if an agent of the Praetorian Prefect, one of the *Frumentarii* spies, was listening if you were elbow to elbow with others.

His client Marcus Bruttius Rusticus nodded; he was a slim man in contrast to the senator's stocky figure, with a...

Lean and hungry look, the senator thought; Marcus was a well-to-do *eques* with estates in Campania, and a *domus* here in Rome, but also an ambitious one. *Which makes him very useful.*

"His Latin is good," Marcus said. "But you can tell it was learned from tutors."

"Greeks are well enough as teachers of rhetoric and actors and doctors, and for those who'd fritter away their time on hair-splitting philosophy," Lucius said bitterly. "Though I prefer common sense. But in the *Senate*? Bad enough it's overrun with Gauls and Spaniards and Africans these days, now they're adding Greeklings! Hadrian started it—he was a Philhellene."

"Fronto wouldn't have been getting the ornaments again if it weren't for this Artorius," Marcus said. "At least *he* hasn't been promoted to senatorial rank!"

"Not yet," Lucius said sourly. "What's one more accented foreigner? Oh, excuse me, Roman citizen...for all of five years! And an *eques* for just under three! My ancestors..."

He fell silent for a moment as someone he didn't know well came into earshot, and then they strolled towards the great bronze doorway.

"And a violator of the *mos maiorum*," he added, naming the *customs of the ancestors*—sacred in the eyes of upper-crust Romans.

"Indeed. All these innovations, these *new things*!" Marcus replied.

Lucius nodded vigorously. "I said as much to the Emperor," he said sourly.

"And, sir?"

"He replied that the most ancient Roman custom of all was to seize any opportunity that presented itself to win victory or make Rome greater. But Rome grew great by the *sword*," he said, his voice growing earnest. "By courage and discipline and strong right arms, not by cowardly...perhaps sorcerous...innovations. But Artorius is cursed lucky. *Deodamnatus*! The Emperor is in his belt pouch. Or his *pocket*. Another new thing!"

Marcus smiled. "Yet he has made many enemies," he said softly. "Sir, something might be done with that."

Lucius stopped and gave him a sidelong look. His own voice dropped.

"Not many in Rome itself," he said. "Too many are taken in by the victories. The Emperor first and foremost! And the other *new things*. Merely useful for money-grubbing, most of them. A senator should dismiss money and concentrate all his virtue and action upon public affairs—"

"Ah, but that wasn't quite what I was thinking of, sir," Marcus replied with a slight smile. "Artorius is dung. And for that, you use a pitchfork. Ideally one with a long handle and sharp tines on the business end. There are Germanii who—"

He went on. Before long the senator was smiling and nodding.

Luoyang, China
July 20th, 168 CE

"Antikles, son of Onetas, of Alexandria-in-Egypt, do not assume you have any secrets from us," the woman...her name meant Black Jade, of all strange things...said.

Antikles started violently at the accented but fluent Greek; the chains around his wrists and ankles rattled. His head still hurt from the blow—with a cloth cylinder filled with damp sand—behind the ear that had knocked him out when they finally tracked him down where he'd been hiding.

But he felt his mind frantically trying to remember what he...and the others, presumably all dead, now...had said to each other.

Assuming that nobody at this court spoke Greek! he thought bitterly.

From his own smell and itches, he'd spent most of the time he'd been unconscious in a dungeon, and one just as filthy here as they were in Alexandria.

This room was one of the ones the strangers had taken over in the palace. Most people here squatted or knelt or sat cross-legged on the floor. On mats of wicker for nobles, or on carpets: the Emperor and the very highest had low platforms that raised them above others . . . and they still sat cross-legged or knelt. Emperor Lin himself sometimes used a folding stool of northern nomad origin when he hunted or traveled, but mainly as a stepping-stone to horseback.

These people were different, he saw. They had four-legged chairs with backs and arms, and high tables—evidently they ate sitting rather than reclining. The five of them *were* all sitting, while he knelt before them—and two guards with clubs and long knives stood behind him.

"I kneel before you, Mistress Black Jade," he said—in Greek.

Which is true literally and *metaphorically,* he thought.

"Not before me alone," she replied, face blank. "Also before Colonel—"

She used "cohortarch" as the military title, cohort-commander, a Hellenic adaption of a Latin term.

"—Liu. He is in command here. If you do not fear me, fear him."

She shifted back to whatever language it was these people spoke among themselves. Antikles was frightened, but he deliberately allowed it to leak out and show itself in his face and body—as if he was trying to conceal his terror and failing. It never hurt to have an enemy despise you, the more so if you were in their power.

As he cowered, he listened carefully. Whatever these strangers spoke, it certainly wasn't the Han tongue, or anything closely related to it as far as he could tell. He'd learned the local tongue quickly, and he spoke both the Empire's major languages himself, and had a smattering of Egyptian and Aramaic and was fluent in two Indian languages. He'd hired locals from there to teach him, accompanying him back and forth on voyages out of Berenike on the Red Sea coast, to use the long voyage time usefully.

Interpreters were expensive, a general pain in the arse and might be dishonest or after a concealed agenda of their own.

Close attention when they spoke it had shown none of the similarities of vocabulary that you noticed if you grew up speaking Greek and learned Latin later. Terms like mother and father, which were *mater* and *pater* in Latin and *mitéra* and *patéras* in Greek. In his times in India, he'd noticed that there were similarities there, too—mother and father words similar to both Latin and Greek, and fire was *ignis* in Latin and *agni* there.

Nothing like that had hit his ear with the strangers. And at times it was as if they were *singing* when they spoke with each other.

Black Jade turned to him. "We will question you about Rome and your mission here. You would be well advised to tell the truth!"

"I will tell you everything," he said, letting his teeth chatter.

That wasn't hard. Just remembering how this Cohortarch Liu had dealt with the eunuch official was enough for that—extending his hand with the little black metallic thing in it. Then the sharp crack of the noise, unlike anything he'd heard before, and the man's head erupting and shattering as if it had been hit by a lead sling-bullet. One from the hand of a God.

Many of the Han courtiers had screamed in terror. He nearly had himself.

And I will let them become overconfident, he thought. *Something may be done with that. Even if they are powerful sorcerers.*

➣ CHAPTER SEVEN ⇐

Western Dacia
Roman Empire
May 20th, 170 CE

"Looks good," Jeremey McCladden said, standing in the stirrups and shading his blue eyes with a hand.

Or Julius Triarius Claddenius does it, he thought sardonically.

That was the name on the *libellus* that had granted him Roman citizenship; he was just a citizen so far, though he already had more than enough to meet the property qualifications for membership in the Equestrian Order. All of the Americans did, but only the Prof had bothered to become a narrow-stripe man, as the locals put it. Since the Emperor had invested him with fairly high military rank, which automatically both needed and carried the status of an *eques* with it. You couldn't be much above middling-centurion level unless you were that at the very least.

Romans had no equivalent of his name, Jeremey, either. Understandably, since it was Hebrew in origin. For that matter, ninety percent of men used the same twenty or so popular *praenomena*, the first names. The *cognomena*, the last names that were rough equivalents of an American surname had started out as peasant nicknames too, and still showed it.

So Spurius means bastard, *and Crassus means* fatso, *and Arvina means* lard-ass, *and Flaccus means* floppy-eared, he thought. *And Cicero means* wart-face. *The upper crust... what Senator Fatso said in reply to the noble address of Senator Lard-Ass, with crucial commentary by Wart-Face. Nobody laughs at it, either. Unless they're drunk.*

They'd both gotten here, to what he thought of as central Hungary just east of the Danube, very newly annexed to the Empire, by a long day's travel starting at noon. Him, Filipa, and their respective entourages, the military escort...

And it doesn't bother me being nearly alone...just one other American...and traveling around, he thought. *Not anymore. All five of us are getting* used *to being here. It's been months since I got one of those weird feelings of* this can't really be happening *that make you feel like you'll wake up and it'll all be a dream. Baptism by total immersion!*

They were east of Acquincum—what he thought of as Budapest, on the good macadamized road that had been pushed through after the annexation.

Got to stop that, he mused. *Get used to the local terminology, too! It's been going on five years now and this is where you're going to stay. We're sixteen Roman miles east of Acquincum and it's never going to be Budapest—the Magyars are hunting or herding reindeer somewhere in Siberia right now and they'll probably stay there. Until the Romans arrive!*

The city of Acquincum had been a border town until recently; now it was well *behind* the border, thanks to the Americans and the rapid end of the Marcomannic War. It would still provide a good market for fresh produce, and the Danube was a major transport corridor. In fact, the city would grow fast with the flow of trade and settlers now that the river Danube was all *inside* the Empire on both banks from its source to the Black Sea.

With big-ass mines up north, now, too. It's a pretty river, he thought. *Mostly. As well as useful. I'll get a house in Aquincum too...but the country is a lot healthier for kids, here. Your priorities change when you're a parent. Plenty of game for hunting here, as well.*

It was good-looking land; the mounted members of the party had halted on the crest of a gentle swale. To the north in the distance was a set of forested hills carpeted in big ash and oak and beech and maple. There were more trees stretching out into the grassland along several smallish rivers, what an American would call big creeks. Southward and eastward was a very gently rolling plain of loess soil—airborne fine dust, originally, back a long time ago during the last glacial period—under what he thought of as tall-grass prairie rippling in the warm green-scented breeze from the south.

It reminded him of what he'd seen of little scraps of native vegetation in southwestern Wisconsin, fragments of the great grasslands that had covered the eastern and central Midwest before the white settlers arrived to put them under the plow. They'd stopped now and then to sample the soil and it was black as coal and rich as cake. Most of the *species* were different, but the overall *gestalt* was very much the same as the prairie parts of his home state.

Birds swarmed, including high V's of ducks and geese and whatnot with their cries drifting down. You noticed that here; birds were fantastically abundant, and ground-based wildlife only a bit less so. The Roman members of the party... and Sarmatian and Germanic and Celtic, all Romanized to various degrees... looked up at the birds with obvious hunt-and-feast thoughts.

And so do I! he thought. *Face it, dude, you were* destined *for the second century CE. You're more comfortable here than you ever were in the twenty-first. Especially at Harvard. That was... talk about acting a role!*

He smiled to himself and recited under his breath:

> *"Lay on, MacDuff*
> *Lay on with the soup and haggis and stuff*
> *For though 'tis said you are my foe*
> *What side my bread's buttered on you bet I know!"*

Flowers starred the thigh-high grass, long spikes of blue bugleweed, round white adder's meat, the yellow buds of archangel and many more, nodding in the wind that bent it in waves and rustled in an endless soughing amid an intensely flowery smell leavened by horse sweat. The grass was vivid green where it wasn't the odd straw-colored leftovers from last year, and the leaves on the trees had that sharp-cut early summer look. There weren't any herds of cattle and sheep and horses around here right now, since the bulk of the Sarmatian nomads who'd lived here—which was the Roman name for tribes who were sort of Early Northern Iranian types—had left after the still-new annexation.

They'd be fighting for their lives well north and east of here, back on the steppes north of the Black Sea, where their ancestors had come from long ago. Needless to say, their distant relatives to the northeast weren't inclined to share the grazing.

His five bodyguards were all mounted too, all ex-gladiators, Germanii except for a Sarmatian, all freedmen and all tough as nails. They liked working for him too; he wasn't dimwitted enough to neglect the men he depended on to guard his life. First-rate pay and perks, and they respected his dogged approach to learning the local fighting skills.

There was a coach stopped over a dozen yards away on the tail end of the macadamized road, another concept they'd introduced to the Roman army. Ditches and then rows of stakes with twists of cloth tied to their tops stretched away eastward, showing where the extra mileage *would* go when the legions got around to linking up this stretch with the older province of Dacia further east. They'd be putting in another twenty miles or so this year...

Dacia had been shaped like a thumb stretching up from the Danube with the tip pointing northwest. Now it was two and a half times larger, and a quasi-rectangular block.

The vehicle stopped behind them was modelled on a Western stagecoach but on new steel springs; his two girlfriends—

Concubines, dammit, he reminded himself.

That was the Roman word, and it implied a quasi-contractual relationship. Not to mention that he was their *patron*, since he'd bought and freed them when he got them knocked up that first year on the Villa Lunae.

His *concubines* Livia and Valeria were in that, with the kids, all four faces peering out with the personal maids and nannies in the background; he had a son and a daughter going on three now, formally adopted and hence legitimized, and there would be more in the future. Both the girls were also somewhere around nineteen going on twenty to his thirty-quite-soon, which was A-OK by Roman standards. They were also *very* good friends with each other, which upped the entertainment quota as far as he was concerned.

And it's all OK by my standards, he thought sardonically. *Some of the others get a bit tight-lipped about it sometimes. But Liv and Val are plenty happy about it. They're freedwomen now, and their kids are full citizens—since I freed them before the births—and they're a rich man's kids and heirs and have good prospects... including looking after their mothers eventually.*

Fil and *her* girlfriend, Sarukê, were there too, also on horse-back, armed like him with sword and dagger—they had cased bows, he had one of the new crossbows slung from his saddle. Though they didn't bother with bodyguards yet. Sarukê had been a bodyguard herself since she'd gotten out of the arena years ago, courtesy of Josephus ben Matthias. She still thought of herself as chief bodyguard to the Prof...

Artorius, he thought. *Get it straight, dude!*

...though that was more and more theoretical. She also thought of the Prof as her pledged war chief. Sarmatians had that mind-set, and she was fanatically loyal and very probably would be for life.

Both his party and hers had big baggage wagons along, late nineteenth-century types drawn by six horses each. Those held their tents and gear and supplies, and one of them had two red deer carcasses gutted and headless hanging by their heels from the rear hoop of the canvas covering. Yearling males, and plump with the good grazing set free here when most of the nomads left. Sarukê had shot one from the saddle yesterday with her bow, displaying casual ease after a brief whooping pursuit, and he'd gotten the other with his crossbow as it ran past. They'd all be eating venison tonight.

There were a round dozen of servants, wagon drivers and roustabouts along too, more than half of them his. And most of a *turma*—squadron—of cavalry in the official party from the provincial governor's HQ.

Marcus Abronius Metellus pointed to one of the creeks. He was a centurion with the sideways crest on the helmet slung at his saddlebow, one risen from the ranks like around half of those indispensable military professionals, and self-educated. He was also on the staff of the governor of the enlarged province of Dacia and an equestrian by social rank, promoted into that too. A lot of the practical side of Roman administration was in the hands of army men like that.

He rode well, in a stolid, no-nonsense fashion, and had an air of hard common sense. Shown not least by the new-style saddle with stirrups he used, and his ease with it. The squadron behind him used them too; from their looks and accents they were mostly from far-off Britannia. Auxiliary cohorts and *ala*—cavalry regiments—got moved around a lot.

Like most Roman soldiers... those who *stayed* in the Army after the initial brutal training and constant marching and drilling... the centurion also looked strong in the way that someone who ate well and worked very, very hard did.

And tough enough to chew rocks and shit gravel, as the Prof puts it in that down-home Texan way.

He was in his thirties and looked older to American eyes the way most people here did, between weathered tan and scars. Otherwise he was a generic south-central European, brownish hair and gray eyes and blunt features, except that he was only five-seven... which was tallish for this period and place. And two inches over the Roman army's minimum height requirement.

The five ex-Americans were all towering-tall by local standards; the two women among them were as tall as the average Roman man or a bit more, and the three men were all skyscrapers by local standards. He was five-eleven-and-a-bit himself, the shortest of the American males, and had gotten used to looking at the tops of peoples' heads. That did no harm—they were quasi-supernatural to most locals, and Gods, demigods and incarnate spirits were *supposed* to be tall. Most of the locals weren't surprised to meet such, since their stories were full of things like that.

For that matter, Sarukê was five-nine. Her people had a high-protein diet, mostly meat and dairy products with bread a minor element since they traded for their grain or got it in tribute rather than growing it themselves, and she'd been the daughter of a minor chief who ate well all her childhood. The roving life of nomads exposed them to less disease, too.

"There, sir."

The centurion pointed.

"That little river is the division between your land and the... ladies'... fields."

He accompanied *ladies*—which was *dominarum* in Latin—with a sideways glance at Fil and Sarukê. Like many Romans he found them distinctly *odd*, but the Americans' quasi-supernatural prestige kept him polite; so did their connections to the top in the form of Marcus Aurelius' patronage. And Fil's Korean looks helped with that, vastly exotic here, like an elf maiden out of a Romano-Celtic tale. Romans often didn't take women very seriously... except when high social rank or great wealth or supernatural mojo or a combination of the three adjusted their attitude.

Then they transitioned seamlessly to deference: he'd noticed inconsistency didn't usually bother them.

Jeremey nodded. "Fil?" he said.

"Well, it's excellent grazing and hay land," she said...in Latin. "Good land for horses, and we can begin our breeding program right away. Good for crops, too, of course."

They generally used Latin unless something had to stay *strictly* private these days. English sounded very, very strange to the locals; not just an unknown language, but a weird one. There weren't any with its stripped-down positional grammar in this part of the world either yet, and its sounds were eccentric too.

Sarukê nodded vigorously, her long reddish-blond braid bobbing.

"Good for cut hay, raise fodder," she said. "They say, winters milder here than...where my tribe Aorsi come from."

That was her tribe's name for themselves; their homeland was in what he thought of as central Ukraine, around and southeast of the site of Kiev in his home century.

Winters there aren't Siberian, but it's not for want of trying, he thought. *Brrr! Wisconsin was bad enough! Living there in tents and felt huts on wheels...brrrr! No wonder they're tough and brave—the fires of hell would be a welcome relief.*

The Roman centurion came from what Jeremey thought of as Switzerland, the portion that was the province of Raetia here; it had been part of the Empire for over a hundred years, since early in the reign of Octavian, the first Augustus. Many of its people had Roman citizenship. His legion was stationed in Pannonia Inferior—which meant Downstream Pannonia, in Latin—and he was on detached duty with the Britannian cavalry *ala*, regiment.

The legion would probably be moved several hundred miles north and east in the not-to-distant future, since that wasn't on the frontier anymore.

"Milder winters than where *I* came from, *Domina*," he said—the title meant roughly *respectable lady*, which Sarukê rated because she was the...

Recognized mate, he thought. *Sort of like Antinoüs with Hadrian, only innies instead of outies and they're the same age, pretty much, which Romans find very odd. Takes a little getting used to, you keep running into really, really different concepts of what human beings are here.*

...of someone with Imperial court connections.

Romans didn't have any concept of "being gay." Not beyond the most basic *likes boys* or *likes girls* level. Their concept of sexuality focused instead on who was pitching and who was catching. All penetration was masculine, all passive roles were feminine regardless of your sex, it was all tightly linked to social standing, and most Romans...Roman *men*, at least...assumed that when women had sex together it was all dildoes.

Dick worshipers, he thought, mentally quoting Paula Atkins. *Jesus in the foothills, and people thought I was a knuckle-dragger on feminism before we landed here. I'm a bleeding-edge leftie by... no, not by a second-century viewpoint, they don't have that concept here. Well, maybe some esoteric Greek philosophers centuries ago...*

"It's mountains there in Raetia," the centurion went on. "Snow and ice in sight of the valley where I was born, even in summer."

Sarukê nodded to him, cordial enough. "Ah, have heard mountains make things colder."

The centurion grinned. "And poorer, lady. It's a good place to come from...once you've left."

Sarukê looked at him for an instant, then chuckled as the mild joke penetrated her rather eccentric command of Latin. Centurions were quite well paid. Then she turned to Jeremey.

"Where you build villa, think you, Jem?"

Her Latin was accented much worse than his, with the choppy sibilants of her original East-Iranian native language. Which was not quite like anything he'd heard in his native century—it was as close to Proto-Indo-Iranian as it was to anything spoken back up in the twenty-first, and a third of the way back to Proto-Indo-European. Just for starters it had a fiendishly complex inflectional syntax, which included joys like three separate grammatical genders.

She'd been born far northeast of here, and captured by Roman troops—auxiliary cavalry, to be precise—when the raiding warband she'd been in was smashed on what had then been the northeastern frontier of Dacia. Then she'd been sold as a slave, ended up a *gladiatrix*—a female gladiator, which was uncommon and considered mildly scandalous but not unknown among the kinkier sort of arena afficionado—until she was bought and emancipated as a bodyguard by Josephus ben Matthias.

Who'd now and then taken full advantage of the way Romans didn't associate *female garb* with *warrior*. Not until their faces were rubbed in it, or their ribs slotted by a dagger.

She'd been there with him when the Americans woke up alongside Professor Fuchs's body, in full Amazonian Sarmatian fig...and ended up working for the Prof. Saved his life more than once, in fact, and probably...

Our whole shebang, he thought. *God...or the Gods...know what we'd have done without her, that first year or two. Hell, I know—we'd have done badly, or very badly, or very, very badly, as in* get killed *badly.*

Jeremey thought the Sarmatian amazon was one smokin'-hot lady in a big, strapping blond country-girl athletic way, if you didn't mind some tattoos and scars...and scary, as well.

Fil lucked out, he thought. *She's happy. But spare me from luck like that! Scary as* hell*, you betcha.*

"Well, I'm not certain yet," he said.

The land he'd purchased—at a nominal price; it really paid to have connections here, and they all did, with a vengeance—was about twenty Roman square miles. Or, as they'd put it, around twenty-four thousand *iūgerum*, which was a unit about two-thirds the size of an American acre. That was huge by Roman standards. Even great landlords here usually owned multiple smaller units of a few thousand acres at most scattered across whole provinces and beyond.

To avoid bad weather in one spot...

And because there weren't all that many economies of scale in agriculture. Some, but lots of bottlenecks too...Until we arrived!

His gifts from the Emperor included several thousand acres of land from the *res privata*, the vast imperial estates, all rented to tenants of various sizes. Imperial properties were all leased out, since they were just too large—over twelve percent of all the farmland in the Empire—to be managed directly, even in part.

But with the modern agritech they'd introduced, currently at about 1870–1880 standards, a unit this size was fully doable. And without renting chunks of it out, which landlords here had done because of the need for massive amounts of harvest labor... Which had been much reduced by cradle scythes, and when they got the McCormick reapers to go with the riding plows and disk harrows and multirow cultivators and seed drills they were already using...and a second sugar-beet refinery...this was prime beet land and Romans hadn't had any sweeteners but honey until they arrived...

His father had run a seed-and-feed business in a small Wisconsin town, and Roman agriculture had been his study focus, so he'd been the closest to an agricultural expert the five Americans had. Except for the Prof, and his family had been ranchers in West Texas, which wasn't like anyplace around here. He went on aloud:

"But offhand, I'd say I'll put the HQ... the villa... there"—he pointed northeast with his riding crop—"in the lee of those hills, see where the slope breaks from steep to gentle? That'll break the storm winds in winter, it's protected from the north and east. Well drained, close to timber and firewood and building stone, and it'll have a good view southward over the bulk of the open country, what'll be the fields. The village for the farmhands a bit further east. Easy to build small dams and bring running water in, too. Which means it'll be easy to set up a slow sand-filter system."

That meant an arrangement of sand in a stone or concrete box with a drain at the bottom. Only a few Romans understood *why* it worked so far, but most Romans were absolute pragmatists about anything technical once it had been demonstrated that it *did* work. They weren't terribly inventive themselves, but they'd take anything useful and run with it and tinker with it and do it on a bigger scale than anyone else.

Slow sand filters purified water by biological action, the film of algae that grew in the first inch or so, and if you had a natural flow of water it didn't need powered pumps or any chemicals.

Just an occasional shutdown and raking and some fresh sand. De nada!

The neighbors of the Villa Lunae had taken it up, once experience had shown it cut disease massively—and given the prevalence of slavery here, big landowners had a direct interest in doing that besides saving their own intestines and their families'. A dead slave was a dead loss, and even an ordinary laborer's cost was usually equivalent to the price of a good new car back up in the twenty-first. Though the campaigning and prisoner-taking of the successful incorporation of the Barbaricum had knocked prices down by about a third for a while.

A few cities in Pannonia Superior had started using the system too once the urban bigwigs had grasped what it meant for *their* health. The Emperor was deep in plans to put Rome's water supply through it likewise... which would cut the mortality rate in the great city a good deal, possibly down to replacement level so that it didn't need to suck in tens of thousands of countryfolk every year just to stay even.

Fil and Sarukê leaned their heads together and spoke...in Sarmatian, which Fil had been learning as fast as she could. They'd all known Latin when they arrived here, though that had required weeks of work to be comprehensible beyond commonplaces through their weird accents, which were now a lot less obtrusive but still noticeable. All of them except Paula had known Greek, too, and she'd learned it since.

They were all good at languages—the Austrian physicist Fuchs had specified classicists who *did* know the old tongues, which had made them a minority in 2032's academia, though a substantial one.

And when he was in the Rangers, the Prof always took a copy of Xenophon's The March Up Country *and* The Meditations of Marcus Aurelius *with him in his pack—both in the original Greek.*

Fil pointed north and a little west. "Good idea, Jem. We'll do something similar over there—not more than a mile or two, depending on which valley looks best. Sheltered from the north wind in winter, like you said. And plenty of good sites for water-mills, too!"

He nodded. "Ah, that's a thought. Flour's more profitable than wheat, if you're close enough to ship it without it spoiling. Ditto sugar."

They were...and with the Danube close, close enough to other markets up and down the river in terms of transport costs and reach. When the canal around the Iron Gates downstream of here was done—it was in the planning stages now, with surveyors swarming over the rocky site—they could ship it to the Black Sea and from there into the Mediterranean. Miter-gate canal locks were another thing the Roman engineers had taken up and run with. Fairly soon they'd have the Rhine and Danube connected, too.

There were plenty of cities down in the south there, and they all wanted flour and salt meat...and now potatoes and cornmeal, too. Ultimately the new northern territories would want wine and brandy; and with grain and the new-crop basic foodstuffs cheaper, markets for meat would expand as the common folk had more money in their...

Pockets, not belt pouches, soon enough! Of course with the Emperor's gifts and our shares in the new mines, we're rich anyway... but I sort of fancy myself as a squire and I surely don't want to live in a Roman city. Even with our antibiotics, they're deathtraps. Just visiting them is dangerous enough. No wonder they always put wine in their water if they can afford it. Literally *a lifesaver!*

The two women were deep in a conversation in Sarmatian and bits and pieces of Latin and Greek, leaning together and smiling.

And Fil and Sarukê both love horses... in sort of different ways... I like riding myself... and breeding better ones will help with modernization, now that we've got stirrups and horseshoes and collar harness going across most of the Empire. And it'll be fun to have them in visiting distance—I even miss Mark and Paula, now that they're down near Rome getting the Galen Medical Institute started. Guess I'm more sociable than I thought. Or homesick, now and then; the five of us are as close to home as we're ever going to get. Home is ruins and fallout now, for a deeply weird value of now. This place is rough and tough, but it's inside heaven's gate compared to that.

"Good for us to be fairly close," he said, and then cocked an eye at the sky.

He dropped into English for a sentence: "Not as if you can hop a plane to somewhere warm in the winter, either; no spring break in Florida."

Fil nodded and rolled her eyes; a few years ago she'd observed that thirty miles was ten or twenty minutes where they were born, and an endless aching whole day in the saddle here. That had been after a day-long ride in cold fog-drizzle-rain. They'd both been horse enthusiasts in their teens back home, and the Prof had been in the saddle from the age of six on his family's ranch, but even so...

Romans did a fair amount of traveling, and by second-century standards it was easier in the Empire than anywhere else, with Roman roads and organization. But to the Americans it was brutal here even though they could stop at a *mansio*, the official guesthouses strung out along the Roman highways. Even riding a horse or sitting in a horse-drawn carriage was physical work, and it felt so *slow* if you were in a hurry.

You *could* do a hundred miles a day with relays of horses...

but that wrung you out like a damp cloth. Only specialists like Imperial couriers did that often.

"Looks like it's going to be a nice night, but we should camp soon. It rains half the time here," he added, falling back into Latin.

"Oh, the dry season's starting...still, you're right," Fil replied.

"Tomorrow we can pick exact spots, drive stakes along the boundaries, things like that."

Sarukê nodded, then grinned, showing white, even teeth.

Her folk had better smiles than Romans, usually, since they ate less bread and other carbohydrate-rich foods and hence had less plaque. Plus she'd have caught the improved, gene-modified version of *Streptococcus mutans* from Fil, which chased all the *bad* bacteria out of your mouth. That and regular brushing solved a *lot* of problems. Which was fortunate since Roman ideas of dentistry usually involved metal tongs and a long, strong pull...

The Sarmatian spoke:

"Takes time, with Romans, make camp. We Aorsi, good weather like now, we just stop wagons, light cook fire. Sleep *under* wagon."

Filipa Chang lay back and felt her breathing slow. She and Sarukê lay sweaty and entangled on what amounted to a broad wool-stuffed futon encased in linen sheets—all of it innovations. So was the big dome tent with interior partitions and jointed supports, though the legions were copying it, especially for officers.

The Sarmatian grinned at her and stretched and lay back with one hand behind her head, and Fil's head on her shoulder.

"Why do you *yell* like that?" Fil asked.

It had been sort of an ululating screech at a critical moment...

I'm used to it by now, but...God, did it startle me the first time!

"Why not?" Sarukê replied. "Makes things feel better. Why you *not* yell? At first, I think...thought? *Thought* I'm not doing things right for you."

"It's...not the custom, where I was raised," Fil said.

And I don't like giving Jem entertainment, she thought. *Although he and his girlfriends were making enough noise earlier! He's in bro-hog-heaven, with a threesome anytime he wants it. Men! Though I've got to admit, compared to Roman men American ones look like models of enlightenment. Even Jem.*

Romans also had less...much less...sense of body privacy

than Americans in the twenty-first. The lower classes because they were crowded together on top of one another in one- or two-room peasant huts or city apartments or slave quarters, and the upper because they had servants swarming around *all the time*, sex and defecation included, which still struck her as sort of gross.

Not to mention what their public bathrooms look like . . . that's the baths and the privies. Everything out in the open, like it's a coffee shop, and conversations accompanying their bowel movements. That's much more stressful than gossiping in the caldarium, the hot room.

What body-privacy qualms Romans *did* have were deeply alien, mostly upper-class women being modest . . . though they thought nothing of using a chamber pot in front of female friends or servants of either gender. And Roman attitudes towards sex were deeply, deeply strange. Nothing like her home milieu, nothing like what she'd covered in undergrad survey courses of early-modern or medieval Western Civ, and *certainly* nothing like modern or ancient Korea.

Sarmatians were even less concerned with privacy—they might be nomads roving over the vast Eurasian plains, but they *lived* fairly densely packed with entire extended families in a tent, or a small hut on wheels. You could ride out on the steppe for privacy . . . but that risked anything from hungry wolves to another clan's warriors out to carry on a blood feud. Their attitude to human and animal wastes was unpleasantly casual too, even by Roman standards, since they moved on from by-products every couple of days instead of trying to make them go away. They wore more clothes than Romans because their native climate was colder, and that was about it.

And Sarukê's spell in the arena didn't help. Like being imprisoned in a cross between a football locker room and a concentration camp run by professional sadists. She doesn't talk much about it . . . and I don't blame her. Twitches and moans in her sleep sometimes. I'm glad she started taking baths before we met, though!

≫ CHAPTER EIGHT ≪

Rome
Palatine Hill
June 1st, 170 CE

"So your son Verus continues to heal well, sir," Galen said as they walked toward the room some steward had selected for the upcoming audience. "The process is nearly complete, even though last year's operation was... well, radical."

Marcus Aurelius let a sigh of relief escape him. He'd been frightened when Artorius... via his Jewish client Marcus, who'd come south with Galen to start the new medical institute, and his wife Paula, the one of Nubian appearance... had said in confidence that originally his son Verus had died young from an infection after an operation to remove a growth from his ear.

Though he flattered himself he hadn't shown it. Besides a father's natural anxiety, not the least of his fright was a growing conviction that Verus' elder brother Commodus wouldn't make...

The best possible Emperor, shall we say. Artorius hasn't said anything about him, and I... I have been afraid to ask outright. But that silence is an indication in itself. Of course, his information dates from nearly two thousand years beyond this day! It might be... wrong, or exaggerated. Yet I cannot shed my worry... he must have read some equivalent of Tacitus about the events of my life and my family's...

Verus, now, Verus was quite young, only six, but commendably intelligent, and already showing flashes of a sense of duty. The Emperor had been planning to have them both named

Caesars—heirs—as soon as possible, so that the succession would be settled firmly before he died himself. He would have done it years ago, if he hadn't been in Pannonia and then across the Danube organizing the basic fabric of the new provinces.

Almost anything was better than a disputed succession and civil war.

Almost, almost! But there is always something worse. A bad enough Emperor invites assassination, and that produces civil war too, more often than not. Rome was very lucky with Domitian's killing; he was followed peacefully by Nerva, and he by Trajan in short order, and after that Hadrian succeeded him and adopted my adoptive father Antoninus Pius. Two twenty-year reigns, more or less, and then my father's twenty-three. A long lifetime of good Emperors, longer even than the reign of Augustus.

He smoothed a frown from his face with an effort of will. If he let a son of his who couldn't be a good Emperor succeed to the purple . . . or who at least could be a *well-meaning, intelligent, passable* one, like his immediate predecessor Antoninus Pius . . . he wasn't doing the boy any favor. He was inviting his own son's death beneath a knife, as well as disaster for the Empire as a whole.

Which would be a violation of duty both familial and public.

Now . . . now I shall wait a little. Festina lente, *as the saying goes—hasten slowly. That served the first Augustus well, and I should remember it. And I may well live longer than another eleven years, since Galen and Artorius between them have cured my stomach pains. Though one cannot count on such things—a flowerpot might fall on my head tomorrow, or I might slip on wet marble and break my neck getting out of the baths. Still, if I do live longer, it will give me time to see my sons' worth as grown men even if they are still young, and make a good choice on which one shall be my primary heir. Or there are Verus' children. They are my grandchildren . . . he is my adoptive brother and married to my daughter, after all, which is why I gave one of my sons his name.*

The other current Emperor was a nonentity as a ruler and a bit slothful and too fond of his own pleasures, but Marcus Aurelius had been raised with him, and regarded him fondly despite his weaknesses. There was no reason his sons should be exact copies of him, either. Sons and fathers, by birth and by adoption, were often very different.

"The operation went smoothly, with the new opium compound *injected* to banish pain, sir," Galenos said. "And we had a healthy slave of the appropriate blood type standing by, but that was not necessary, since the loss of blood was minimal. There are few large blood vessels very near the bone behind the ear."

Injection was another of the *new things*; that and transfusions of blood. He had followed the tests necessary for transfusion with fascinated interest. They involved adding the red cells from one man's blood to those of another under the *microscope* and seeing if they clumped and burst. If they did not, especially if they did not from *multiple* others, some blood from that one might be transferred to another, making up for that lost by wounding or cutting.

They were speaking Greek, so Galen used *kyrios* as a respectful but not servile form of address. The physician went on:

"The tumor Marcus mentioned was there, yes, but still quite small last year. All of it was removed. And there has been no infection. As is usual with the new methods, though not in every instance."

That it was an infection that had killed Verus in the history Artorius and the others had studied went unmentioned. But that was another major reason why major surgical interventions were... or had been... avoided until absolutely, unavoidably essential with quick death the only alternative. That and the hideous pain, which could inflict lasting damage on a patient in itself. Now both those things were different here in the palace, and soon elsewhere too.

So odd, to think of a world where most *live into old age, to seventy years or even more! Yet that* is *possible, I now know.*

"I will visit him this evening, and his mother is with him now, and the nurse that you trained," the Emperor said with relief. "The *Augusta* Faustina and I shall make a public sacrifice of thanksgiving soon. Good work, Galenos. Good work indeed!"

He smiled, looking forward to his next duty as a pleasure.

"And now we shall see the results of my embassy to the furthermost east! From what our friend Artorius has said... the realm there, China he called it... is second only to Rome! Together, we are two-thirds of the whole human race. Strange to think of Parthia... and even India... as mere way stations, lowlands between two high mountains."

"Rome is more than that as of these last few years," Galen

observed. "The remaining independent Germanii surrender more often than not, now, as soon as our troops arrive and throw a few thunderballs. And Rome bids fair to grow still more. As Rome grows, so grows the shadow of its laws and its peace."

"Rome grows more prosperous within its boundaries, as well as in size," the Emperor noted. "Already the increase in Imperial revenues is very notable."

The embassy Marcus Aurelius had sent eastward in his first year of rule had consisted of a half dozen carefully chosen men, besides escorts and servants and rich gifts. The first stage of their trip had been a voyage from the great Red Sea port of Berenike, east to Taprobane, the large island just south of India.

That was a regular trade route, but beyond it little was known...or little had been known, before Artorius and his clients brought accurate maps of the world's lands and oceans. That was four years after the embassy left, of course.

Only a single ambassador had returned, with a scar on his face that had *nearly* taken his left eye, and he now had a limp and much more gray in his hair than the years he'd been gone could account for.

He *had* made it as far as the Land of Silk and returned; that was literally the other side of the world.

A great accomplishment. And he worked as a deckhand to get back from Taprobane to Berenike! Obviously, disastrous bad luck at some point.

Though when Artorius found time to commission some of the better sailing ships he'd mentioned...the first was nearly complete, and a crew selected and in training...then it would be a matter of only three months or so either way. Less time than it took to get from Eboracum in northern Britannia to Nisibis in the Empire's southeast by overland travel, even on Roman roads.

When the scar-faced ambassador was ushered into the great room, he scarcely bothered to look around. Instead, when seemly greetings had been made, he spoke urgently and quietly from his position in front of the Emperor's chair. Marcus Aurelius had had the servants bring him a stool, but he looked too agitated to use it.

"Sir," he said—in Greek, using *kyrios*, which could also mean *lord*.

He was an Alexandrian who'd made voyages to India before

being chosen for his mission, a merchant and a clever one, dark
and quick moving as the Emperor remembered him. There were
few who knew Latin east of the Imperial border and few who
spoke Greek much beyond India, so his knowledge of several
Indian languages had been an asset. Those were spoken most of
the way to China. All the ambassadors had spoken several, and
all had been men who learned a new speech easily.

"What I have to say should be for your ears alone, Caesar
Augustus, until you decide what can be bruited abroad."

The Emperor's brows went up, but he made a sign and the
clerks left the room. Another, and the two Praetorian guardsmen
banged their pila on the bosses of their scorpion-blazoned shields
and left too, though you could see that they did so reluctantly.

*Which shows commendable dedication to duty . . . or perhaps
curiosity instead.*

And they . . . very probably . . . spoke no Greek, but best to take
no chances. The men came from the Italian countryside, mainly
that from Rome northwards, but they lived in Rome . . . where
nearly every tongue known to man was spoken by *someone* in
its million-strong population. Greek quite commonly, and it was
even odds a guardsman picked up at least a little of it.

That left him and Galenos, and the man glanced at the doctor.

"Galenos has my absolute confidence," Marcus Aurelius said.

In fluent and accentless Hellenic speech, the sort a scholar
or gentleman used. As he'd learned in boyhood from his tutors
in his grandfather's house, and polished on his own in Athens
as a youth.

"Speak, Amyntas."

The man paused a moment more, passing his hand across
his face and collecting his thoughts. Marcus Aurelius waited
patiently. It had obviously been a horrific journey and the man
had suffered greatly, and he'd been penniless when he arrived in
Berenike and only a belated recognition by a kinsman had saved
him from begging in the streets.

It was necessary for the good of the Empire, but that did not
reduce the loss and pain.

*This is the same room in which I heard the first reports from
Pannonia,* the Emperor thought suddenly, glancing around while
he waited for the man to collect his wits. *The first reports of
Artorius and his thunderballs.*

The opus sectile marble floor with its patterns and the view out the pillared garden-plot terrace reminded him.

And the murals of Actium on the walls, the sea battle that settled it would be Augustus who'd rule the Roman world. Octavian, as he was then. I remember thinking how showing Cleopatra as an Egyptian sorceress was nonsense. That was the first news from Pannonia, apart from Galenos' letters from Artorius. News of the Tenth's victory over the barbarians three, no, four years ago. Courtesy of Artorius and his thunderballs, their first use in this time. So much came from that! And from my decision to go to Pannonia myself!

Even the smell was familiar from that time, now that the weather was warmer, the incense and garden flowers warring against the city-stink of Rome's huge population and their beasts of burden rising even to the Imperial palaces despite all the sewers and aqueducts could do.

And now I know it causes disease and death, as well as a bad smell! Hence now my Empress and my children spend the summers mostly beyond the City, under the care of a physician trained by Galenos or the man himself, and all that they touch or eat is carefully checked.

Amyntas took a deep breath and began:

"We arrived in the southern part of the Han empire after twenty months of travel, sir ... they call themselves after their dynasty, which has ruled for nearly four hundred years. Their name for themselves means *Han People* ... we arrived, after no more than the usual hardships on our way from Taprobane, the island to the south of India. Storms and sickness and the odd fight with pirates and bandits and such, nothing out of the ordinary. And the increasing difficulty of making ourselves understood—past Taprobane few speak Greek, and sometimes we had whole chains of interpreters. So many languages! But for half the distance the priests at least spoke some Indian tongues and could interpret for us."

Marcus Aurelius nodded. He better appreciated how *far* that was now, with Artorius' maps of the world. Especially the one on the surface of a sphere that could be rotated, which was endlessly fascinating and required less thought than those laid out flat on the new paper, which distorted sizes somewhat.

Would I have sent them, if I had known truly how far it is?

He thought for a moment, then nodded inwardly.

Yes. Trade does use that route, though few make the whole voyage themselves, instead handing goods over four or five times. When we have time to build more ships such as Artorius knows of...

"Only one of the four of us died on the way, that was Aindrea, poor fellow, of some fever. We arrived nearly two years after we set out from Berenike at a city on a great river, named Nanyue."

"Their capital?" the Emperor asked, interested.

"No, sir. A southern outpost, though a large one, in lands very hot and damp and more recently acquired. Their capital is far to the north, inland, on a great plain laced with rivers and dug canals of amazing length."

The Emperor pursed his lips. If someone from Egypt said a canal was of amazing length, it had to be long indeed. Though Artorius had plans for such, and the Army engineers were enthusiastic.

The man went on: "It is called Luoyang, or a name that translates as *Eastern Capital*, and the climate is much like...oh, what I've heard tell of Macedon or Epiros. A strange city, with an eerie beauty that owes nothing to Greece, but almost as large as Rome, I think—larger than Alexandria, certainly."

"Ah, remarkable!" Marcus Aurelius said, wondering why the man looked so haunted.

Alexandria was the second-largest city in the Empire, and in every ordinary way second only to Rome, though the men of Antioch-in-Syria or Carthage might dispute that. Egypt was the richest and most populous single province after Italy, and then there was the very valuable trade with India carried on from its Red Sea coast, which usually provided between a tenth and two-tenths of the Imperial tax revenues. Often more than all the Gallic provinces together, or about half that of Hispania Baetica with its great silver mines.

Amyntas went on:

"We were bidden to the Emperor's court in the north within a few months. Their ruler—"

He used *autokrator,* the usual Greek translation for *Imperator.*

"—had just newly come to the throne. He was...is...quite young, only twelve then, and was very curious about the outside world, though he is not a...ah, a shall we say, a very *serious* young man."

Meaning he plays at being Emperor, like my adoptive brother Lucius Verus, Marcus Aurelius thought with regret. *And relies on others to do the actual work.*

His emissary went on:

"Much of the routine business of administration is done by eunuchs there, oddly enough, not merely guarding the Emperor's women as is done in Parthia or India. Many of them are very corrupt. They and the other party of officials...who are students of an ancient sage...Chonxeus, his name would be in Latin... are often at deep odds."

Very corrupt? Which from an Alexandrian *means very corrupt indeed,* the Emperor thought; the men of the city had that reputation, and it was often deserved.

"We were entertained hospitably and given tutors to learn the language, forms of courtesy, and something of the script. Which reminds me of the old one the Egyptians used...much of it does not represent *sounds* at all."

"They have heard of Rome, then?" the Emperor asked.

"Yes, sir, but only by garbled reports passed hand to hand. As soon as we achieved some fluency, the Emperor...his crown name is Ling...bade us to come and entertain his banquets with descriptions of Rome. All went well..."

The man stopped and shuddered, and put both hands to his head, fingers gripping until the flesh under his fingernails showed white. Marcus Aurelius waited patiently, and Galenos caught up with the notes he was making on a diptych with several sheets of paper in it, bound at the hinge with a copper coil.

A deep breath, and Amyntas continued:

"But then the summer of that very year, five strangers—four men and a woman—arrived from a great city to the west, a former capital of the Han empire, it is called Chang'an. Bearing curious weapons and tools, some of sorcerous appearance, and in strange clothing. Officials reported...if I translate the calendar accurately...that they had first shown themselves in late June... the twenty-fifth day of June...some years previously..."

"How many years?" the Emperor asked sharply.

"Ah...it would be CMXVIII ab urbe condita, sir. On the twenty-fifth of June. Near Chang'an..."

Marcus Aurelius stiffened, and he noticed Galenos doing the same. That was when *Artorius* and *his* four companions had appeared in Pannonia. To the very day.

And they also wore very odd clothes, from what the merchant Josephus said, and carried astonishing things!

Amyntas continued...he'd probably heard nothing yet of

Artorius beyond a few garbled rumors. He'd been understandably obsessed with getting to the palaces, at that. Probably to the
exclusion of all else, a fixation of the will that had carried him
halfway around the world.

"They looked much like the local people. Much the same
complexion as we around the Middle Sea have, hair an ordinary
black but always very straight by nature. Yet flat of face and with
small noses and tilted eyes, so—"

He put his fingers to the corners of his eyes and pushed
them up; the Emperor was reminded forcibly of one of Artorius'
fellow exiles from the future. The woman named Philippa; her
original cognomen was something like *Chang*, now rendered as
Chania. Artorius had a little of that appearance himself, though
otherwise he looked Gallic or Germanic.

Ah. But she said her parents came from another realm there...
Korea, it was called... which was a rival to China and ally of
Artorius' America. Artorius' great-grandfather fought in a war there,
and returned with a bride already pregnant with his grandfather,
so he is one-eighth of that blood too.

"But they were dressed differently from the locals... in trousers and jackets, almost like Germanii or Sarmatians... only the
poor wear that there, nobles dress in long robes, but *these* clothes
were of very fine cloth, finer than any I have seen and not wool
or linen... or cotton or silk, either. And even I could tell they
spoke the language with a strong accent. They—"

A few minutes later, he stumbled to a stop at Galenos' profane
exclamation—a rarity for him—and Marcus Aurelius' angry scowl.

"No, lord, I *swear* what I said is true. They actually did smite
the eunuch who denounced them with something that made a
loud noise, gripped in one hand. And his head split apart as if
struck by a slingstone—as if it were a *melon* so struck—"

"I believe you, Amyntas," the Emperor said. "I believe you
wholly and without reservations, for reasons you do not know
as yet. You are not the cause of Galenos' distress or my anger,
and it shall not fall on you. Continue."

He did, finishing: "And Eudoxos was hacked down. Antikles, I
do not know his fate, he was elsewhere and like me he had made
friends among the locals, merchants as well as nobles. I ran..."

Amyntas put a hand to his scar. "I ran bleeding... escaped...
hid with friends I had made..."

An hour later the man left, exhausted but considerably more cheerful at the promised reward for his perils and exertions... which Marcus Aurelius had decided would be the combined reward that he *and* his comrades had been promised.

"His journey back to Rome would be worthy of a poet. Even Homer!" Galenos said. "For perils and trials, it rivals the trials of Odysseus."

The Emperor nodded: "Hence my reward to him. He deserves it."

It would buy him a comfortable gentleman's standing for the rest of his life, a good marriage and an inheritance for his children, without making more voyages... which he probably wouldn't want to do ever again. Come to that, he probably wouldn't leave the vicinity of his native city, once he got back there, except to visit his new country properties. He'd probably traveled as far as any man had in all the years of humankind.

And his news is cheap at the price, Rome's ruler thought, feeling his mind churning with what he'd just heard.

The Emperor looked at his court doctor... and confidant, and increasingly his right-hand man for certain matters. Their shared knowledge made that inevitable, and the Greek physician and philosopher's keen wits made him the more valuable.

"Artorius must be informed of this. Immediately! That was identical to his descriptions of one of the weapons of his own time! A *pistul*, he called it, like a sling that throws a lead bullet too fast to see. As his *cannon* do their balls of iron or bronze, but much smaller."

Galenos nodded. "I will travel to Pannonia myself, Caesar Augustus, if you think that advisable."

He obviously *did* think that himself. Marcus Aurelius considered for a moment, and then nodded agreement:

"Yes. Nothing must be committed to writing... to *paper*... as yet! The... particular secret involved must be kept if humanly possible. We must have time to make preparations, if there are other travelers from the future, and we must do so untroubled by general panic. And to make those preparations, we must have Artorius and his clients here to furnish the information we will need."

Galenos looked around, and after reading his notes one more time lit them from a lamp and dropped the flaming pages into a painted pot used for waste.

The Imperial chancellery was switching over from papyrus to the new paper as fast as it could; it was better and now that the local workshop was in operation and expanding quickly, run by the young nephew of Josephus...

Simonides, his name is.

...it was much cheaper too. Mostly here in Rome it was made from linen rags, which could be bought abundantly in this great city. Everyone wanted it now, including the legions with their constant intricate recordkeeping, and there would be other workshops soon. Here, and in other large cities... perhaps even in Alexandria too, in a few years.

"We will question Amyntas further tomorrow for details; then you will leave the day following, or the day after that—preparations may take that long. Bring Artorius and as many of his American followers as possible here *immediately*."

"Yes, lord. Marcus and Paula can manage the Institute well enough while I am gone; I shall inform them of this news this evening, counseling them to keep it strictly secret?"

The Emperor nodded. The Galen Medical Institute was now in full swing, heavily subsidized by grants from the *res privata* and constructed around an Imperial villa a suitable distance from Rome... and upstream from it too, with a water system using the slow sand filters as an example to the students.

It taught the new medical methods Galen had put together from the future's books and the Americans' suggestions, and would spread them across the Empire. As yet it was in its early stages and many of its students would become teachers themselves, but it was already turning out scores of physicians. Eventually, hundreds and thousands; and they would take copies of the books with them.

Galenos' prestige... already great before Artorius arrived and massively increased since... would ensure that students were plentiful, and from all districts of the Empire. So would the results, when they returned home to employ the new techniques. Young military doctors were being told that only those who studied there could expect advancement, too. There was even a houseful of female students, watched over by Paula.

Marcus Aurelius went on firmly:

"I will dictate an order that you are to be given every facility at each and every fort, military station and *mansio—*

Which was what official staging posts, with quarters and fresh horses and supplies were called; they were spaced out regularly along all the Empire's main roads for the use of messengers and officials and military men. Though others could use them, for a stiff fee—that helped defray the expense. Artorius thought they could be used as the core of a *postal service*, an intriguing concept.

"—and that you may commandeer any other assistance you need from the authorities military or civil. And an escort from my horse guards will accompany you. Don't grind yourself into illness with haste, I cannot spare you. But don't dawdle either."

The Emperor smiled—slightly, as he usually did.

"If nothing else, with whom could I discuss this...secret... save with you?"

Galen frowned in thought. "With Artorius and his fellows, sir...I find him...and some of them, Marcus and Paula not least...very interesting."

"Yes, I agree. But they are also profoundly strange, especially when discussing their own...time and place. With you, I can speak as to a peer, a man of my *own* time and place."

Galen blinked. "I had not thought of it in those terms, sir... but you are quite right."

"Go then; and take all due care."

When the Greek had left, Marcus Aurelius rose and went to the edge of the court outside, looking downhill and across the splendors of the forums built by his predecessors and out to the huge expanse of tiled rooftops, marble columned temples and twisting streets that was Rome.

Artorius told me that his future world was divided among hostile powers, with weapons that are to thunderpowder as that is to a little boy's toy wooden sword, he thought. *Weapons that could destroy even so great a city as Rome with one blow. China was the greatest of them next to his America. Ultimately a war between them and their coteries of allies destroyed his...his world and his...time. A horror indeed! But now that is of more than academic interest, because it* might *happen here. Not in this generation, if I understand him correctly, but...eventually. May the Gods spare us!*

Near Luoyang, China
July 2nd, 169 CE

"So," the Han general said.

He was tapping one gloved fist into the palm of the opposite hand as the second row of soldiers lowered their smoking flintlock muskets, and his eyes were narrowed in thought. Then he went on:

"This weapon has a longer effective range than a crossbow, but not *greatly* longer. It takes about the same time to reload as the new model of crossbow—though the ammunition is not reusable."

They are smoothbores, Colonel Liu had told her a few days before. *Rifles eventually ... but since nobody else has firearms at all, why magnify the difficulties of manufacture?*

The general went on: "And these muskets are considerably more expensive. What makes it more desirable? I see why the *cannon* are; they hit far beyond the range of our crossbows, or the bows of nomad horse archers for that matter. *That* is crucial. They cannot attack us in masses—and if they disperse, their fire is much less effective."

Colonel Liu nodded. "Respected sir, muskets strike harder than a crossbow. They will pierce any armor a man can wear. It requires much less strength to use; anyone who can load and raise the weapon will hit with the same force. With the bayonet attached, it can be used as a spear and quarterstaff at close quarters, which a crossbow cannot be. A line of the bayonets will stop cavalry, while the rows behind that shoot them down. And it is easier to learn to use for peasant conscripts."

His accent was still strong, but Black Jade's sensitive ear no longer thought it a barrier to understanding. She hoped she could cease to accompany him to these *demonstrations* soon.

Helping spread the new seeds ... and new spinning and weaving methods ... and paper and printing and better medicine and much else ... was more ...

Much less *likely to give me nightmares,* she thought. *And* these *things make the nightmares about home worse. Death and mutilation are death and mutilation, whether done with swords or muskets or fusion bombs. This China needs weapons to subdue the barbarians to the north; they will raid and rape, burn and plunder and kill and carry folk off as slaves otherwise. But I do not like to see...or smell...their consequences.*

The targets—clumps of condemned criminals lashed to posts—stretched out for about two hundred meters from the firing line.

Liu's voice dropped as they walked forward. Black Jade swallowed in distaste; she didn't like coming close to the results of volley firing. Especially since the troops were using buck and ball—a combination of one full-sized musket ball and three smaller shot, rather like a big shotgun. Some of the targets were still writhing or whimpering, though a man with a spear was silencing those.

We think of ourselves as Chinese, and these people as Chinese... but they don't speak the same language as we do. Not literally, and not metaphorically either. I thought our government was cruel—and it was. But impersonally so. These people...they often revel in cruelty and laugh at screams. Often enough. And those that do not, it just does not disturb them.

"And sir..." Liu said quietly to the general. "These weapons are useless without ammunition...which the Imperial government has a monopoly of, one which cannot be broken at any time in the near future. Not for many years, hopefully."

"Ah," the general said again, drawing the word out and nodding.

Which means they cannot be used by peasant rebels, either by deserters or if stolen, Black Jade thought.

The great rural uprising of the late Eastern Han—the Yellow Turban revolt that shattered Chinese unity and ushered in an era of warlordism and then the endless strife of the Three Kingdoms—wasn't due to start for another fifteen years. Since the time exiles knew exactly who would organize and start it...it had been Zhang Jue, an Imperial general and Taoist faith healer, and his two brothers, Zhang Bao and Zhang Liang.

It never will. I think those men are already dead. No doubt wondering why *they were killed to the last instant. And the eunuch faction has been overthrown—their oppression was a major reason it started. And we are improving life, at least a bit.*

Smaller, less organized, spontaneous uprisings against savage taxation, extortion and forced labor were already breaking out like measles, though. The Eastern Han dynasty had been tumbling downhill toward its doom when they arrived, and shoving it back up the slope was...

Very difficult, she thought ironically. *Cannon and muskets...* *they are expensive, so expensive that a government is necessary to* *employ them in any numbers. A large government, at that. You* *cannot face an army that has them unless you have them too.* *That will enforce unity while we reform the abuses... but that is* *easier to say than to do.*

They came to the first row of bodies. Black Jade kept her face expressionless, though her nose wrinkled slightly at the smell of blood and feces—the last from fear, or punctured bowels, you couldn't tell the difference. Flies buzzed, bright noon sun picked everything out in unforgiving detail, including the heavy lamellar armor of laced iron plates... and how both varieties of lead shot had punched through it and into the bodies beneath.

The general's eyebrows rose.

"Impressive!" he said. "Armor stops many crossbow bolts and arrows."

"But not bullets," Colonel Liu said.

"Yes, I see." The general nodded thoughtfully. "Little could live within two hundred paces of a line of men with these... and with cannon as well for greater distances... and the ease with which they can be learned... hmmm..."

⇒ CHAPTER NINE ⇐

Galen Medical Institute
Near Rome
June 2nd, 170 CE

The core of the Institute had been an Imperial villa, just far enough from Rome—and upstream of it—that the city-stink didn't come here often, not up into these rolling, well-drained hills. Instead the scents through the open windows—which looked down on the main courtyard—were of wax and clean stone, water and flowers and pine trees and cypress with someone cooking lunch off in the background.

Buildings were going up throughout the gardens and fields, eventually enough for a thousand students...and with central heating, not the Roman hypocaust type but based on late-nineteenth-century American models, and running water put through sand filters, and flush toilets.

Right now there were about a hundred students, a fifth of them women...

And us and Galenos and a few more instructors, Mark Findlemann—Marcus Triarius Findlemanius—thought. *Doing well by doing good...until this bastard of a thing hit us. Drop back into the Roman Empire, and it eventually turns out fine... until someone else does it too.*

He slumped his long, lanky form into a chair—a compromise, with a back and armrests but without the X-form frame that Romans would associate with a *curile* chair, a status marker.

His wife Paula—Paula Atkins, originally—came into the room,

tall and statuesque and very black. Mark's mouth quirked slightly. They'd never have gotten together if being back *here* hadn't shown how much they had in common.

I think we're both on the spectrum too. Me more than her, but her too. Common as dirt in academia, which accounts for a lot of things.

"She's asleep," Paula said, and rolled her eyes very slightly.

Boy, but children are work. Even with a nanny-wetnurse and maids and cooks, children are a lot of work.

His mouth quirked a little more broadly. If he said that aloud, he knew exactly what she'd say:

Ya think, dude? And more work for the mother, *at that. And here...there's a lot more reason to be afraid for them here. Thank God for those antibiotics and antivirals! And the info on how to use them.*

"So...Chinese time travelers," he said instead.

She sat in the chair across the—ebony, inlaid—table on the mosaic floor.

"Worse than that," she said aloud.

His brows rose, and she went on: "Chinese time travelers, sent by the Chinese *government*. If they were just..."

"Random Chinese scholars, like us?" he supplied. "Tricked into a time machine just as the world blew itself up?"

"Right. We could compromise with 'em. But..."

"Yeah, that's not likely," he said. "From what that Greek merchant told Marcus Aurelius they're armed and want to take over."

Her lips tightened. "Right. Bet you anything their honcho is secret police or something like that. Maybe all of them are."

They looked at each other and sighed.

"Well, there's one good thing," he said, and at her raised brows: "We'll probably see the others sooner than we thought we would and we don't have to ride to Pannonia to do it...no! Don't throw that book! Not the pillow either!"

She grinned, dropped it and came over and sat in his lap.

"How shall I punish you instead, then?" she said, or purred.

And there are good things about marriage. Oh, yes!

∋ CHAPTER TEN ∈

On the way to the Villa Lunae
Pannonia Inferior
(Downstream Pannonia)
July 2nd, 170 CE

That crowd in Carnuntum was dicey, Artorius thought.
He'd been on horseback then, too—which hadn't helped,
since it was a serious status marker and they weren't feeling
benevolent towards their superiors. The core of it had been charcoal burners and ironmakers from out of town, frightened out of
their wits by news of the great new ironworks west of here, at
Colonia Ferramenta in what his age had called Styria and this
one knew as Noricum.

It would produce at prices they simply couldn't match and
not starve.

They filled the rather narrow, paved but untidy street from
edge to edge; the shopkeepers and artisans had slammed and
bolted their doors and shutters, and were probably waiting tensely
inside, their families behind them and clubs or knives or a veteran's sword in their hands.

But there were unemployed wool-fullers and others in the
crowd too, thrown out of work by fuller's earth used instead of
urine and wooden hammers moved by water mills or windmills
replacing human feet—one mill like that could do what eight or
a dozen fuller's shops had done before.

Others who'd lost income when the local legion was moved
further north...The odor of a crowd in this age, sweat soaked

into unwashed wool but fresh sweat too, seasoned with anger. Faces contorted in rage and fear and fists were shaken.

Not unjustified. If they can't get work, they can't feed their families.

Unfortunately, the Roman government had neither the inclination *nor* the means to do anything about it out here in the boonies. People in Rome got what amounted to income support in the form of subsidized bread, but that was as much to prevent riots near the center of power as for any real benevolence.

And they're looking over their shoulders because there are still troops... auxiliaries... in the fort east of town and they'll slaughter townsmen without a qualm if the authorities tell them to. So would my own bodyguards, if my life's threatened.

He could hear a hand clap to a sword hilt behind him as a lump of horse dung flew by. Then he stood in the stirrups and shouted:

"Good people! Citizens of glorious Carnuntum!"

Fortunately his accent was faint enough now that it didn't grate on the ear; it could have been just the way someone from a few dozen miles away spoke. This was a trading town, among other things, and they were used to odd turns of speech. It did sound like an educated man's Latin, though.

The growing growl of the mob died down a little. He went on:

"My friends, my countrymen—I understand your anger. But there is no need for fear, for yourselves or your families. I will guarantee, on my word as an *eques*, that those of you who wish it will receive land grants in the new province north of the Danube. Grants of fifty *iūgerae*, which is to be the new standard."

That knocked the brabble down by an order of magnitude; thirty acres was a considerable area by second-century standards, what a prosperous yeoman would command, enough to feed a family well and have a surplus to sell. Maybe enough to buy a slave girl to help out in the house and with the children, or a field hand.

Land grants in *colonia* hadn't been common for some time—but then, neither had new provinces been conquered in some time. Even those of them who were townsmen came from peasant families not too far back, had relatives who still farmed, and knew the basics of the trade. Men looked at each other and you could see the thoughts running through their heads...

Calculating the risks. But people have a different way of think-ing about *risk in this century. Just* living *is risky, here and now.*

"And there will be help in stocking and buying tools for the farms," he added.

A fresh brabble arose, but not as angry this time. He made a downward gesture with both palms.

"In two weeks I will return, and there will be clerks in the town basilica to take names and issue land warrants. The State will help organize the move," he said.

Men were looking at each other, and a few were covertly dropping items they'd snatched up.

"And for those who don't wish to farm, there will be employ-ment making charcoal at Colonia Ferramenta, east of here," he said. "At good prices, too—"

He quoted a figure per pound of charcoal which produced muffled swearing and hasty counting on fingers.

The crowd began to break up. He was still getting scowls and dirty looks from a fair number, men who'd been satisfied with their trades and life in Carnuntum as it had been and wanted no change. But they'd sensed the turning in the mood of the crowd as a whole, and nobody wanted to attract the attention of the town council . . . or of the five ex-gladiators who were riding behind him, and the stevedores and wagon drivers behind *them*. They didn't have swords and armor . . . but they did have whips and clubs, belt knives and tools like axes. And they were *his* men. If you were a good employer you got loyalty in a fight, here and now.

He blew out a breath and wiped a hand across his brow. His chief bodyguard Dablosa the Dacian leaned forward in the saddle and spoke:

"Nicely handled, sir," he said. "I wouldn't have wanted to try and fight our way through a crowd like that, there must have been a hundred of them, and there might have been women throwing roof tiles down on us."

"Hundred and thirty-five," Artorius said, and grinned. "And a roof tile was how King Pyros of Epirus got it, a long time ago."

Dablosa nodded. "Heard of that, I think. And even with the wagoners added in . . . we don't have more than twenty. Even Hercules can't fight two."

The Dacian frowned. "I wonder why there weren't many weavers?" he added. "Your *new things* have hit their trade hard."

The gathering had thinned enough that they could make their way again, slowly. Artorius chuckled.

"Because the weavers can sell all they make, and now they can make enough more that even at lower prices they're better off," he said.

"Ah!" the Dacian said, nodding offhand. "Yes, everyone wants a spare tunic and more blankets if they can get them."

Artorius nodded. Nineteenth-century-style spinning wheels and flying-shuttle, kick-pedal looms and the other innovations increased productivity of the various stages of making and finishing cloth by five to fifteen times.

But there was a lot of pent-up demand for more cloth here. The average family's ideal was to have three sets of clothes for each individual—one to wash and hang to dry, one to wear, and a better set kept for festivals, weddings, funerals, feast days and attending a sacrifice at a temple. Which was a modest enough goal, but only a largish minority had been able to get that much until just recently. Now hoarded coins were being spent.

"And fulling is cheaper, too," he added.

Then he stretched in the saddle, glanced up at the sun and said:

"Let's get going. I want to make the Villa Lunae by sundown."

Dablosa laughed. "Now that I'm a married man...so do I, sir! It will be good to see my son, too."

He jerked his thumb over his shoulder, to where a girl in her early teens sat on one of the wagons with a bundle beside her.

"And Aelia is going to be *very* grateful for some household help!"

"Sir!" Dablosa said, five hours later.

Artorius motioned with his head, and the bodyguard moved his horse forward until they were riding side by side. And he was glad that the gurgling in his gut had died down without needing to use the ever-diminishing store of antibiotics.

My intestines and immune system must be knowledgeable *about the local bacteria...finally,* he thought. *If that wasn't just anxiety about the mob. Only took four years and a bit! We'd all have died in pools of our own crap if we hadn't had the drugs!*

They were south of the big quarry that supplied Carnuntum with building stone, too. Ahead the Roman road stretched arrow straight. This part was two generations old, built to connect the frontier forts with the cities further back, with stone-block pavement starting to show the depressions of ruts worn into the hard limestone by metal-shod wheels as the westering sun cast shadows. The turnoff to the Villa Lunae...which he now considered home—wasn't far ahead.

Which is another demonstration of why macadamized roads are better, he thought, glancing down at the pavement. *And home... home is where the heart is. Julia, and little Lucius.*

It was in the afternoon, but still bright with that central European summer light; the *climate* was more like areas much further south in North America as far as warmth and cold and growing seasons went, but the changing hours reminded you that...

You're not in Texas anymore. Great God...or Gods...above... but the Gulf Stream makes a big difference.

"What is it, Dablosa?" he asked.

He'd learned to take the man's judgments very seriously indeed when it came to anything involving his bodyguarding job. You didn't survive eight years in the arenas, even provincial ones, without developing an almost supernatural ability to sense danger. And he'd been a hunter in Dacia before that, and since then around here.

"Sir, there's something...that patch of woods ahead. It's making the hair on my spine bristle!"

The other four bodyguards looked at each other, but Dablosa made a gesture and they rode along as if unconcerned.

Artorius nodded, concealing the sudden pounding of his heart and that heightening of every sense he'd come to know... and dislike.

Right, he thought, after a moment's careful attention. *Not enough bird noise.*

That was something even he, who'd been a hunter at home before and after and during his spell in the Rangers when he had time, had had trouble with here at first. There were so *many* birds, and anytime not in the dead of winter they were noisy. Unless something frightened them...which human beings stopping in their territories did, unless you were very, very still and quiet.

What Dablosa had done with the signal to the others was good craft too. If someone caught you by surprise, they had a massive advantage. If they *thought* they were going to catch you by surprise but you'd sussed them out, the advantage swung over to you.

"Good call," he said to Dablosa.

Then raising his voice very slightly, smiling as if unconcerned:

"There may be trouble when we reach the woods ahead. Bandits, or assassins. Don't give them warning; be ready to fight."

The woods would put whoever it was...if it was someone, and not just the birds having a hissy fit...on their right sides. That meant something here, because it meant your shield arm was on the other side. All the bodyguards had their shields hanging off their shoulders by the strap, with the grip near their left hands. They also had knee-length hauberks of the new steel wire, and helmets on their heads.

But I'm not wearing armor, and my shield's hanging from the saddle. Oh, well...

Dablosa was between him and the wood as they came near; the man took his job seriously. The wind grew a little cooler as it came from under the trees—big trees mostly, with brush on the verge; what he thought of as English oaks, hornbeams, tall, straight ash trees with their smooth gray bark, beeches...

Forests of any size hereabouts also had lots of deer, boar, wolves and brown bears and occasionally even aurochs, and this one covered at least five or six square miles.

A flock of bustards suddenly burst out of the shrubby growth along the edge—big males, the largest birds in the world that actually flew. Gray and black and brown above, white or whitish below...rare and endangered in his day, common as dirt now... flogging themselves into the air...

That brought a thought, and one he acted on instantly.

"Shoot those birds!" he cried, making his voice light and cheery. "They're your dinner if you can get them!"

Dablosa had his bow out and an arrow on the string in seconds. So did two of the others...

"Wothenjaz! *Haaa, Wothenjaz! Slahadu, slahadu!*"

Eight men burst out of the brush, screaming: invoking the God who guided warrior souls to the afterlife...and then just shrieking:

"*Kill! Kill!*"

The one in the lead had a sword—a Germanic style of blade, a long single-edged slashing weapon. The rest had swords by their sides and were carrying shields and long, heavy battle spears, and several of them had armor, mail shirts or leather covered in iron scale.

That would have been bad odds...except that three of the
bodyguards already had arrows on the strings of their bows, and
had turned their horses with their knees as if to launch casual shafts
at the flight of bustards...who were now winging it well behind
them and rising fast. It had taken the birds a fair bit of time, of
course...each of them weighed thirty to forty pounds all up.

Dablosa drew to the angle of his jaw and shot. The flat snap
of the others' bowstrings followed in less than a second. One
plowed into a shield boss...and the hand on the grip behind it.
The spearman's snarl turned into a howl as he tried to shake the
shield loose, leaping up and down in the same spot and waving
the arm and arrow-transfixed hand.

Another slammed into a man's thigh just *below* his shield.
The broad, barbed head ran through without nicking the bone
and came out the other side in a gout of red blood; the man
lost all interest in the fight and tried to hobble away before he
fell on his face, twitched and died—there were a lot of big veins
and arteries in a human thigh, quite capable of dropping your
blood pressure to unconsciousness in a few seconds.

Dablosa's shaft went *over* the leader's shield and into one eye,
just below the flared rim of the helmet with a sheet-bronze boar
atop its crest. With a hard *thock* of steel penetrating bone. That
was very impressive marksmanship...but Sarukê had known
what she was doing when she recruited his bodyguard squad for
him three years ago.

The leader of the war band dropped back in an arching spasm,
sword flying in one direction and shield in the other.

The rest of the attackers checked, aware that the odds were
suddenly even and they hadn't surprised their targets. Artorius
snatched up his shield by the grip in his left hand, and whipped
out the long spatha cut-and-thrust sword at his hip with his right.

"Get them!" he shout-snarled and put his heels to the tall horse.

A little to his surprise, the wagoners behind him snatched
up axes and clubs and ran towards the action too...

Ten minutes later he looked up from bandaging a man's shoulder and saw Dablosa walking down the row of dead enemies, a
puzzled frown on his face.

"Don't worry, Marcus," he said gently to the pain-drawn face
of the man lying back on the leaf-scattered grass. "If you can't

use the arm full strength when you've healed, you'll still have a place, and full pay for the rest of your life. You were wounded in my service, and protecting me."

"Thank you, sir," the man said.

He saw the glance the others gave him and then each other. That made him an exceptional employer by Roman standards... though in the half-civilized places most of them came from it was what a chief would do. He pretended he hadn't seen it, and went over to Dablosa instead.

The senior bodyguard had pulled the helmets off all the seven dead men who still had faces, and there was a frown of puzzlement as he walked from one to the other. Artorius finished wiping off his spatha—there was a nick in the blade he'd have to see to, he always took care of his gear himself—and asked:

"What is it, Dablosa?"

The Dacian nodded to the corpses. "Sir, they look skinny."

Artorius nodded; plenty of people in this time and place often did, and it was currently even more common north of the old Roman border, where he was fairly confident they came from.

"And?" he said.

"But sir, they're all *tall*. They have the height of nobles. And fighting-man scars, the most of them, though they're all pretty young. Some look like they're from last year."

Upper-class people were taller nearly everywhere here, with the exception of those who suffered through multiple fits of sickness as children.

He'd once read that as late as 1914 sons of English members of the House of Lords were a full five inches taller at eighteen than people from the bottom of the social pyramid... though they'd attributed it to genetics back in Edwardian England, rather than nutrition. The dead Germanii looked as if they'd average a bit over five-eight or -nine, above average for their people and well above the Roman norm. Dablosa himself was about that height, though built like a scarred, trigger-quick muscular brick.

"There's a lot of nobles fallen on hard times up there," Artorius said, jerking a thumb toward the distant Danube and the new territories over it. "Since the big battle, and Rome taking over."

"Yes, sir, there are. But look at their *gear*. It's good, first rate. And they had plenty of money. It doesn't... it's not..."

The accent in his Latin had been getting stronger.

"...if they had good fighting gear and lots of money, why weren't they *eating* well? And if they weren't eating well, if they were too poor, where did they get the gear and money?"

Artorius opened his mouth, shut it with a snap, and thought. He nodded soberly, acknowledging the sharp judgment. There were times when he still felt like an alien here, and this was one of them.

Then he spoke to the rest:

"All of you. Show me the contents of these men's belt pouches. I may need it for my...my own purposes. You'll get the same weight of cash if I do."

Weapons and whatever the dead man had on him were recognized perks of winning here, but the bodyguards all trusted him, and the rest of the staff followed their lead. A saddle blanket went down and the contents of the Germanii warriors' pouches were poured out on it.

He whistled as he bent over the brown, high-smelling wool, though that scent was mostly lost under the fecal smell of violent death. Dying men often shat and pissed themselves, though not always, and ripping open bellies had the same smell-impact.

Silver denarii, more than twenty each, he noted.

A denarius was a Roman silver coin worth about thirty to fifty dollars at 2032 prices; one was equivalent to about twice a blacksmith's daily wage. Though translating values was tricky; that was taking the price of bread as the basis for comparison, and everything was relatively expensive here except labor. That was a product of the low productivity of the economy.

But that's equivalent to ten thousand bucks or so, he mused. *Someone with ten thousand in his belt pouch isn't going to live on day-old porridge.*

All of the coins were recent, too, bearing the face of Marcus Aurelius or his co-Emperor, Verus.

The leader had had four golden coins. An aureus was worth many times what a denarius was, twenty-five or thirty times as much, though it was about the same size. But much heavier... and much purer gold than a denarius was silver, ninety-eight percent as opposed to eighty-five.

He looked more closely and then cursed softly. One of the gold coins had a milled edge. That was *very* new; the mint in Rome had just started doing that, using a steel multiple-coin press and stamp made up at Colonia Ferramenta to hammer the round gold blanks. That would make shaving or clipping the coins much easier to detect, which was a perennial problem. It would be a long while before they circulated much beyond central Italy, though.

He picked up the coin. *Virtually no wear,* he thought.

Then he tucked it into his pouch and threw down two older ones to replace it.

The unwounded guards...ones who didn't have wounds that restricted their movements, at least...had gathered around him.

"I think that these men had a grudge against me, for helping defeat their tribes," he said.

Everyone nodded; you did the dirty to enemies whenever you got the opportunity. It was part of a warrior's honor.

"But they had help from someone with a lot of money. Take the extra and have a drink on me: You all did very well here. Get Marcus into the wagons on some blankets and we'll head for the villa."

He touched his own belt pouch, where the coin rested wrapped in a piece of cloth—a handkerchief, though Romans didn't have exactly that concept and would have thought of it as a rag.

And the praetorian prefect should hear of this, and the Emperor, he thought grimly. *I'm going to be sending them a parcel.*

Early the next morning, in the master's bedroom of the Villa Lunae...

Mary's face was smiling, that infinitely familiar, slightly crooked smile he'd first really seen when he was sixteen. It had struck like a thunderbolt then, and every glance was a repeat. He never tired of it.

They were in Amarillo together, them and their three children. He was happy that they were, though the offer of Professor Fuchs to examine his artifact-dating machine had been *very* tempting. Still...

Artorius...still Arthur Vandenberg in the dream...smiled back, though he kept his eyes mostly on the road. Traffic was sparse, with most people staying at home listening compulsively to the news.

All of which was *bad* news. Very bad indeed.

"I'm glad you're with us, Art," Mary said; she was cradling

their youngest in her lap. "Things ... aren't good at all. Maybe we should go out to the ranch—"

Light. Light from the city ahead of them, brighter than the sun, blinding. Arthur threw up his hands. Mary screamed and twisted in her seat, putting her body between the fire and her child. The other two screamed from the back seat as well.

Arthur felt his flesh burning, long after he should have been dead...

And woke, with a shout that was half a scream itself. Julia's hands were on him, shaking firmly.

"Wake, husband, wake," she said softly.

He clutched at her, weeping unashamed. Her hands soothed him, until he was conscious of the world once more.

"It gets less frequent, but no easier," he said eventually.

Julia smiled at him—for a moment he was conscious of how like Mary's expression it was, then he dismissed the thought.

"You are a man of deep feelings," she said. "But a brave one."

He picked up a cloth from the bedside and scrubbed his face, smiling back at her.

"Well, it's dawn," he said. "And the last day of harvest. Much to do!"

"Here also, husband," she said, reaching for him.

꞊ CHAPTER ELEVEN ꞊

Villa Lunae
Pannonia Superior
July 18th, 170 CE

"Welp, it works!" Artorius said that afternoon, in English and with a sense of profound satisfaction. "They've all worked this year, and downtime for repairs hasn't been very much at all. Yee-and-I-mean-it-haw!"

You only had two weeks to get the wheat harvest done here in eastern Pannonia Superior, and for that matter in most of the Empire. The method you used *had* to be reliable; the best invention in the world was worse than useless if it broke down in the middle of the harvest and left you no alternative.

And if the harvest fails, people starve. Starve to death, he thought. *We had the cradle scythes to fall back on, though. This time at least.*

He nodded again and went on:

"Improved to the point of being good enough to use, I'd say. This harvest proves it."

"At last!" Jeremey McCladden replied, sitting his horse next to the older man's and pounding his fist on the pommel.

His voice was halfway between thankful prayer and heartfelt curse as he went on:

"After three goddamned *years* of effort! First it worked for three steps . . . then it broke. And then a dozen steps . . . and it broke again . . . then a hundred yards last year and it goddamned *broke* . . ."

"Iterative development," Artorius said. "It fails...until it doesn't."

That was how Cyrus McCormick had done it in the Shenandoah Valley in the 1830s, too. You couldn't anticipate everything, so you did your best, pushed it to failure, fixed what failed and went on.

"And this was a Type B, at least partially—they needed new techniques, as well as the idea," Artorius added. "New materials, at least."

They had the additional advantage over the original inventor that they knew it *could* be done, and be done with hand tools in a rural setting. But you needed things Americans in the 1830s had been able to buy, but Romans didn't have...or had, but only for expensive, specialist uses. Like decent steel, or gears.

Until just recently, he thought. *Amazing what you can do with a ninety percent drop in costs.*

He turned in the saddle and looked back along the big square field, the wheat stubble pale yellow-gold under the hot summer sun and the heads of the grain a brighter color. Green showed beneath the cut stalks, the clover undersown into this fall-planted crop in the following spring. Men and women were stooping over the last long row of neatly cut wheat, gathering it until they had a bundle as big as they could reach around, then using a twist of straw to bind it into a sheaf.

That was traditional. Others followed along behind, putting them into carefully built stacks of a dozen sheaves each, which was an innovation.

That meant the grain heads were all off the ground—less likely to be eaten by vermin, and drying much faster because they were out of the nightly dewfall.

If the rain holds off, he thought, cocking an eye at the fleecy white clouds that dotted the faded blue Central European sky. *But propping them up that way makes them shed water better too.*

Then he grinned to himself. His father and grandfather had used the same distrustful skyward glance on the family ranch, a country dweller's inherent suspicion about the weather. Though they'd *wanted* rain much more often. *This* place had about three times the rainfall of the Vandenberg ranch in the caprock country. *That* place had been just on the westernmost edge of country where wheat was possible.

His grandfather had often added: *and if the damn crick don't rise,* with a laugh, running a hand through his silver-shot raven-black hair, his strong Texan accent at odds with his half-Korean face...

Though creeks were thin on the ground in the aridity of West Texas. That saying probably came from the family's time in Tennessee, as they followed the frontier on the long, long generational march south and west. From the time the first Vandenberg stepped ashore in Philadelphia, more than two and a half centuries before he'd...

Ended up here, he thought.

The workers stopped and raised a cheer when they heard the man driving the reaper cry *whoa!* as the last of the grain fell under the creel and cutting bar, and the moving canvas behind that ejected it neatly to the side.

He hauled on the reins to halt the two-mule team pulling the replica early McCormick harvester. Half a dozen young men sprinted forward, seized him and bore him on their shoulders in a circuit around the machine while the rest cheered and pelted the group with wheat stalks and the mules rolled their eyes.

The grain was reaped...and in a couple of days, they would all get a massive blowout party, the harvest festival sacred to the Gods—in this case, the *Cerealis,* the grain-harvest celebration sacred to the Goddess Ceres. Down in southern Italy that was held in late April; later here further north, of course.

And they know there'll be food *enough for the next year,* Artorius thought. *People have a* direct *interest in the harvest here, not just a financial one.*

The estate workers—

A lot of them still slaves, alas, he thought.

With a wry twist of the mouth. That was one ancestral custom he'd never wanted to see reborn.

Though here and now...it's not reborn. It's been the rule since time immemorial. But more and more freedmen every year. I can't go faster because I can't risk too much hostility from the neighbors. And I need less labor for this estate, which means I can free the surplus ones and get them farms north of the river in the new territories, or loan them enough to set up as craftsmen on their own if they have the skills.

The laborers of the Villa Lunae all thoroughly approved of his innovations, whatever their status. They cut the workload considerably. And everyone was eating better, too, with fewer mouths to feed plus heavier yields from the new crops and the old.

Meat three times a week! he thought ironically. *Still, it's a start.*

There were half a dozen guests sitting their horses nearby, neighboring landowning gentry and some of the bigger freehold farmers who didn't quite make it to that status, and they were gaping at the machine. Even his brother-in-law Sextus Hirrius Trogus was, and he'd been among the first to copy the new methods and crops. This had been one of *his* estates, until Artorius had swapped some of the Emperor's gifts further south for it, at the same time he married Julia, Sextus' widowed younger sister.

Who would be the head of the Trogus family, in a just world, which this isn't, any more than the time I was born into. She's a hell of a lot smarter, not that he's stupid. Damn, but I was lucky to meet her! And lucky she liked me, despite all our differences.

He smiled. Paula had said—a bit acerbically—that was probably because even a retro-fossil like him from the twenty-first-century backwoods was a good bargain for a woman by the standards of *this* era.

Josephus ben Matthias was there too; he'd brought his uncle... and his wife and children... for a long visit, which had been interesting, and stayed after the older man left and escorted his wife and son and daughter back to Sirmium; she was expecting again, though only just. Stephanus was a canny old bird, and they'd agreed to correspond after he got back to Rome.

And so's Julia expecting. I think I shocked her when I said I hoped it was a daughter this time!

The thirtysomething Jewish merchant was nodding sagely. Though he didn't own farmland himself, he traded in its products... and had a sound practical knowledge of how things were done and what the economics were. He was also beaming at the thought of what the new reapers would do. Roman crop yields were surprisingly good—when the Americans had arrived they'd found them equivalent to late eighteenth-century levels in Holland or England, around here—but Roman farming was extremely labor intensive. There just wasn't any alternative.

Increasing labor productivity *and* raising yields *and* introducing new, heavy-yielding crops like maize and potatoes really, really increased the amount of marketable surplus over the subsistence needs of the workers who grew them. Which blew the upper limit off the percentage of people who could do *other* things besides raising their own food.

About eighty-five percent of the Roman Empire's population were peasants and farmworkers, but now they didn't have to be, not anymore. With the Emperor's backing, the innovations were spreading fast...

And all of the neighbors are using the new saddles with stir-rups, Artorius thought, amused. *Having the Emperor and the Army take 'em up convinced even the most stick-in-the-mud.*

There had been two saddles in the baggage the late unlamented Fuchs had put together, rather old-fashioned handmade Spanish ones from a small company named Zaldi who specialized in that sort of thing, and a disassembled model to make them easier to copy. Bought with what Fil had called the scientist's oh-naughty-so-bad use of pilfered R&D money. From an Andalusian firm, which was as far away as you could get in Europe, to attract less attention before his planned temporal bugout.

How time flies! Josephus brought us here that first summer because we needed somewhere secluded and Sextus owed him favors. I agreed because it was closest to Vindobona of the choices he offered. Just chance...and how chance matters!

"*Finally* we have it going," he said to Jeremey, and raised a hand. "No criticism implied! I'm just glad we...*you*, in fact... finally cracked it."

"Well, you did get the metalworking lathes and boring machines going too, at the new ironworks," the younger man said. "That was a big help. Screws and bolts and homogenous metal bars. And being able to use actual *steel* instead of the hand-hammered crap they call wrought iron here. That's so soft I could carve my initials in it with my fingernails, and you have to hammer-weld it to get a decent-sized piece and the welds are lousy too unless you pay in diamonds."

Sorta crude *new metalworking,* Artorius thought, grinning back. *Very crude. And courtesy of those measuring gauges Fuchs sent along, too, as much as anything, when we finally got time. And the little working models. But each iteration of the lathes and stuff is better, not least because we know the trajectory and don't make false starts. We'll be able to make more gauges ourselves this month, and send them out all over. And we don't have to hand-cut all our screws with files anymore, hurrah!*

One of the guests swore again, luridly, and gazed at the reaper with naked lust.

"And I thought your cradle scythes were marvelous!" he said.

Those were ordinary scythes with a frame of wooden fingers above the blade and parallel to it; they knew about scythes here and used them for hay, but hadn't for wheat or barley because you'd lose too much grain if the stalks were scattered and had to be raked up.

The cradle scythe's wooden fingers caught the cut stalks, and a tip every swing or two deposited them in neatly aligned rows ready for the binders.

With a sickle, one harvest worker could cut a quarter of an acre a day, or a third if the crop was light. With a cradle scythe you could do between two and three complete acres a day, an increase of eight or ten times. That had massively cut the cost of the grain harvest, and sped it up; more and more big operators were dispensing with the expensive hired harvest gangs that had been necessary before, and had written enthusiastically to their relatives and friends further distant about it.

And they'd be writing to *their* relatives and friends, and so on. Rome didn't have a postal service yet—the nearest thing were Imperial messengers for government correspondence—but private individuals could correspond over vast distances, from one end of the Empire to the other. *If* they weren't in a tearing hurry and had some money. That was why the closest thing they had to *public opinion* beyond the very local type started at the top of the social scale and trickled down.

Big landowners couldn't keep enough slaves for the grain harvest if sickles were the best tools to be had, since the extra hands would be near idle most of the year and eat every day regardless. One of the drawbacks of slavery...from the owner's point of view...was that slaves *had* to eat. You couldn't turn them off and park them in a shed if they weren't needed, and in farming country everyone's labor needs moved in synch so you couldn't hire them out either.

So they hired free men at high wages, from their tenant farmers, or towns, or distant, congested hill-country districts, or small freehold farms nearby with too little land to employ and feed all the working members of the peasant families. With the cradle scythes they could cut back on that substantially.

But with this reaper, one man and two mules could cut *fifteen*

acres a day; it was a self-raking model, so only the driver was
needed. That was another productivity jump of seven or eight
times over the cradles.

Fifteen acres a day for a single worker was about sixty *times*
what sickles had done...and were still doing, across most of the
Empire and absolutely everywhere outside it.

"Fifteen acres a *day*? With one man and a pair of mules?"
the neighbor said, when Artorius mentioned it. "You can do your
whole harvest on this *latifundium* in a day or two!"

"Not quite, Lucius, my neighbor," Artorius chuckled—in Latin
that was a natural way to phrase it. "I have five of these now,
all working well. That's seventy-five acres a day with five men
and ten horses or mules if the machinery doesn't break down..."

Jeremey rapped his knuckles on his head and made a local
gesture with thumb and two fingers to avert bad luck. The *vilicus*, a freedman who did the routine management of the Villa
Lunae spat into the bosom of his tunic, for the same reason but
more emphatically.

"—so about two weeks for it all. Or a little less. No quicker
than before."

"Binding and stooking will be faster, with the men you don't
need cutting working at it."

"Yes, even so," Artorius said.

He actually used a double affirmative: *sic, ita*, in Latin.

"And definitely less time than that when I get a few more.
I'm planning on having...oh, ten of them. Maybe twelve, to have
spares on hand for when there are breakdowns."

The half of this estate run as a single large farm from the villa
itself had around a thousand acres put to fall-planted wheat and
barley, with a little less on the outlying tenant farms that occupied
the other half of the acreage. The villa sold more than half the yield
of its own grainfields—much more this year, with corn and potatoes yielding well and feeding the workforce abundantly—but the
tenants ate most of theirs, and often paid a share of it as rent. That
would change as they grew more corn for polenta and cornbread,
and more spuds. Not to mention canola and sunflowers and the rest.

With ten or twelve mechanical reapers, the small grains *could*
all be cut in about a week to at the most ten days...and with only
one man—

Or woman, he reminded himself. *You sit and hold the reins.*

Ain't easy nohow, as granddad said, but it's not like swinging a cradle scythe all day from can to can't, either. That takes heavy muscle; some women have it, but not as many as the men.

—doing the cutting per machine.

Before the Americans arrived, Sextus' *vilicus* here had usually hired over a hundred extra laborers at grain harvest, or a hundred and fifty if the crop looked very good. At one or two denarii a day each for at least two weeks; three to six thousand denarii, the biggest single cash outlay of the farming year, and the workers had to be abundantly fed and expected to carry some of the harvest home for their families.

That was twice or more times a skilled artisan worker's usual daily wage, not counting the perks and payments in kind. At harvesttime the honchos were over a barrel and everyone knew it.

Binding and stooking and carting and threshing would take longer, but back in their first year here Jeremey had managed to get an early, primitive, nearly all-wood threshing machine invented in Scotland in the 1780s working, after a lot of frustration and cursing and kicks. That had been one of the many functioning scale models that Fuchs's baggage had included; sizing them upward wasn't exactly *easy*, but having them certainly helped.

The estate had four of them now, slightly tweaked; before that, about a quarter of the labor force's total annual hours had been spent beating the sheaves with flails and then tossing the wheat in a breeze with paddles to separate the wheat and chaff. With a constant risk of rain damage to the thatched ricks, the grain was kept in until it could be threshed. Big nineteenth-century-style wagons drawn by mules with horse-collar harnesses hauled the wheat in faster than oxcarts, too.

In a month *this* year's wheat and barley would all be safely in the new granaries, or off on the roads to Vindobonum and Carnuntum and Sirmium. And the straw and chaff would be composting with manure to be spread in the fall when the winter wheat was planted, or on the maize and other spring crops later.

They'd charged for the first copies of the threshers, but all the bigger operators in the neighborhood had them now. Full-sized models had also gone out to tour a lot of the Imperial estates, the *res privata* that encompassed about twelve percent of all the farmland in the Roman Empire. Models of the thresher, and the rest of the new equipment too.

Soon a lot of people aren't going to be working themselves into early graves stooping with sickles. Or spending the winter beating on sheaves. Because of us! Artorius thought, pleased and proud. *And since the* res privatas *are scattered from Britannia to Syria, everyone will be exposed to the new stuff and new crops. That's something to be proud of too. And corn... potatoes... all that means people won't necessarily starve to death if something hits the wheat that year. Plant breeding we can bring in gradually.... Romans already do that a fair bit by rule of thumb, and it'll get better when they know the why of it.*

The guests—except Sextus, who as a kinsman was staying at the villa too—parted with polite good-byes scarcely concealing naked envy.

One lingered. "*Quid, Domine Artorio*'?" he said bluntly, jerking a thumb behind him. Which meant: How much, Mr. Artorius?

"Two hundred fifty denarii," Artorius said. "From the workshop at Colonia Ferramenta. Plus wagon fees and paying one of their craftsmen to show it to your workers."

The man was a substantial freehold farmer and owned twenty slaves including his cook and housemaid, which made him solidly middle class by Roman standards. So he'd need one, or two with a spare... though the spare could be used too, which would cut his harvesttime and weather risk.

The man winced. That was about half the price of a field-hand slave each. Before the Americans arrived, no single piece of farm gear cost anything like that, except a wine press or water-powered gristmill. Most of the equipment had traditionally been made locally and on site, out of wood or leather with metal only where unavoidable.

On the other hand, the reaper was able to do the work of *sixty* field hands, or the even more expensive free migrant workers.

That many freemen would cost *seven* hundred a week, in fact. He'd probably only hired about ten, but even so he'd make the investment back in a couple of years, besides the reduced danger of disastrous loss to bad weather.

"You must spend money to make money," Artorius said.

Josephus nodded vigorously, but the farmer stared at both of them blankly, shook his head and said:

"You said they'll be available next year? I'll start saving, then ... all the Gods damn it, you have to run fast these days just to stay in the same place!"

Sextus chuckled as the farmer rode off still shaking his head; he was a cheerful man in his forties with thinning reddish-brown hair and graying beard, a little heavyset by Roman standards, which made him quite fit by American-civilian ones in 2032 ... though by then the new drugs had finally gotten cheap enough that more and more people were thin, reversing a trend generations old.

Before fusion bombs made it all moot, Artorius thought.

While stopping his mind wandering back uptime with an effort of will. That got a little, little bit easier every time. The nightmares had gone from once a week to once every couple of months, too.

"And I will be first to get these reapers, after you!" Sextus said, almost gloating, and clapping his hands together.

First crack at the new tools and seeds was part of the agreement they'd reached in the land swap that had accompanied Artorius' marriage to Julia. Getting the grain in fast was *important*; bad weather at harvesttime could cut the yield drastically, and unlike the lands around the Middle Sea, it could rain here at any time of year.

Prestige was involved, as well as money. He'd be cock of the walk among the landowners of the Sirmium area, and their envy would mean higher status.

Plus deluging Colonia Ferramenta with orders. Probably a few of the workers from there would move out and set up workshops closer to the grain-producing areas of the region, manufacturing reapers on their own ... then graduating to small factories ...

"Just so, my brother-in-law," Artorius said.

They rode back toward the villa along roads of graded dirt, some of them graveled, and Sextus looked at a field and frowned.

"Is that *whole field* in turnips? Surely you don't need them to feed your workers, now?"

"No, I don't, but I'm raising them as fodder for the cattle and sheep and pigs."

Sextus nodded. "Well, with that lifting-plow thing you showed me for the potatoes, harvesting them wouldn't be too hard."

"And once they're on the surface, you can feed the livestock on them in the field—and they'll be dunging it at the same time, which will increase yields and save labor. With grain cheaper, more people will be buying more meat and wool and leather."

Norfolk Four-Course Rotation, he thought to himself. *Courtesy of Turnip Townsend, eighteenth-century reformer; the Romans use grass leys with clover in the mix and they store hay, but that's about it as far as fodder is concerned. Though with an extra year of clover here, and with the New World crops thrown in... So call it the Pannonian Seven-Course Rotation.*

He looked up at the sun; all the Americans had acquired the skill of telling time by the position. Mechanical clocks would be possible... someday. When they had the time.

All of us got better at that except Mark, he thought with a smile.

Mark Findlemann... or Marcus Triarius Findlemanius... was one of the most intelligent *and* one of the least practical men Artorius had ever met, either here or in their native century. *He* couldn't do it within two hours without a sundial, unless he stopped to do the math in his head. *Then* he was more accurate than any of them.

He and the nearly equally intelligent and much more practical Paula were in Rome now... just outside it, rather, at the building site of the new Galen Medical Institute. And raising their first child; she was about a year old now. Which was one more reason they weren't *in* the great city except for visits, during which they virtually held their breath and after which they scrubbed down with the new surgical soap and thought deep antibacterial thoughts. The letters they'd sent about the health situation there were hair-raising.

About two deaths for every birth, Artorius thought with an inward shudder.

Preindustrial cities of any size were all demographic sinkholes requiring lots of migrants from the countryside just to maintain their population, but reading about something and seeing it yourself were different things. Moving from the country to a town here was a reckless gamble, a gamble with your life...

And your kid's lives.

... and the bigger the town the more reckless it was. That was a major reason none of the Americans had lit out for the big city; they had Fuchs's store of antibiotics and antivirals, but those wouldn't last forever.

Rome today is better than, say, Shakespeare's London... it was five burials to one baptism there if I recall it rightly... but that's because of the Roman aqueducts and sewers, and I suppose even bathing with all and possibly infectious sundry is better than not bathing at all which is what the English did then more often than not. Marcus Aurelius and Empress Faustina had about twelve kids, and only four of them lived to grow up...four are dead already. We'll change that, too. Not immediately for anyone but the Emperor, but give us and Galen some time...can we get people careful about not letting flies land on their food soon? Hmmm...well, Marcus Aurelius is doing that with his palace staff now, so it'll probably be imitated...starting at the top and spreading down...

Which might have interesting consequences—fewer senatorial families dying out each generation, for instance.

They turned for home; Josephus and Sextus and Jeremey and he rode first, with Dablosa the Dacian and Balþawiniz the Chamavian riding behind them, the bodyguards' usual position. They were both ex-gladiators, both freedmen and both had been with him since the winter of the first year, recruited by Sarukê from among her arena acquaintances. The other three were back at the villa guarding his wife, young son, his adopted daughter Claudia and their home.

The bodyguards had saved his life more than once; he'd thrown them all lavish wedding parties with local girls and they looked to be lifelong employees now, with apprentices they were training up. To *their* way of thinking they were well-treated retainers of a respect-worthy warrior chief who'd see they had a home in their old age...

If they live that long, he thought.

...and grandchildren to make sacrifices at their graves.

"Remember the first time we rode to the Villa Lunae?" Artorius said to Josephus. "From Vindobonum?"

"Yes, that was at harvest time too, four years ago now. And you quoted Homer to me—the scene where Héphaistos is working a harvest scene into the Shield of Achilles," Josephus said.

Artorius nodded, and recited the lines again, with a distinctly better accent he'd learned from Julia:

> "He placed it on the estate of a great man
> Where the hired men
> With sharp sickles in their hands
> Were cutting the crop..."

"And I said *some things never change*," the merchant said, and looked around.

The fields were all cut now; in some of them workers were using long-handled, two-tined pitchforks to toss the sheaves onto big mule-drawn four-wheel wagons with pivoted front axles... also an innovation, at least for farmwork. It had been two-wheel oxcarts on that day. These carried five or six times as much with only one driver, and much faster.

"Little did I know!" the merchant added.

And I thought how odd it was to see a countryside so full of people, Artorius thought. *Not exactly John Deere combine-harvester empty now, and it won't be for a long, long time if ever. Certainly not in my lifetime, but not as crowded by a long shot! Which gave me an opportunity to free a lot of the labor force, and some of them are working for wages.*

"I'd just finished planting the new seeds that day," Jeremey said. "And I rode out to meet you."

He jerked his thumb to a field of rustling green maize planted in late April and now starting to tassel out, the stalks half again the height of a man. They'd planted a little over three hundred acres this spring, and it would yield more bushels than the whole wheat and barley crop.

"And there it is!"

Jeremey had been sent on ahead to the Villa Lunae with the seeds, since that was very time constrained. His field of study had been Roman agriculture, and he was a small-town boy by origin. The son of a man who owned a seed-and-feed business in rural Wisconsin, where his family had had a huge truck garden because his mother was an organic enthusiast raised on a farm, and he'd helped his father—and visited a good many farms—in the course of his teens. Plus learning to ride horses from his older sisters.

He'd managed to get everything possible into the ground in time to be harvested before first frost, though it had been close. With the seeds intended for this climate, at least. The next year yields had been much higher... It had been geometric progression since then; a few acres the first year, hundreds the second, enough to actually *use* the third. Now they and their neighbors were all cashing in on the clamoring demand for seed of the new crops from people a bit further away, too.

Spreading like ripples in a pond, Artorius thought. *And the Emperor has been helping...*

"Oh, which reminds me, I got a letter this morning from the procurator of the *res privata* in Egypt, Prof," the younger man said. "Sent along to his Pannonian equivalent with a copy to me, then referred up here when my *vilicus* said I was visiting here. On papyrus, not our paper, but what the hell, give them time."

"Ah!" Artorius said. "And?"

Jeremey let silence stretch for a few seconds; he had a rather nasty sense of humor sometimes, and his eventual grin was sly after he'd used a doom-and-gloom expression just long enough to put Artorius' teeth seriously on edge.

"The cotton and indigo and the rest all came in fine, and there's a lot more of it than last year," he said. "There'll be enough seed next year to plant much bigger areas. And the sweet oranges and limes and eucalyptus and bananas and mangoes and so on are still growing well—though we'll have to wait years for those. Like the hickories and whatnot here. And the rubber plants and cinchona for quinine and that sort of stuff are growing...not that that will do us any good for a while, they need a wet tropical climate to really yield."

Hmmm. Maybe we could acquire Sri Lanka, for a start? Artorius mused. *Start something like the East India Company? Romans... well, Egyptians and Egyptian Greeks...already trade there...*

Jeremey went on: "But they'll supply *seed* when we need it. The cottonseed'll be handed out to all the *res privata* estates there next spring, at least the ones that can do some summer irrigation, and they'll have orders to share with the local farmers and landowners as soon as they can. It's good long-staple stuff, gene tailored to be disease resistant and it repels bugs all on its own. The windmill pumps are working out too, the Nile Valley has a consistent wind from the north."

Artorius let out a breath. Cotton cloth was a luxury import from India here and now, very nearly as expensive as silk from China. Egypt and some of the other eastern provinces could produce plenty of it, though, and had in his own time. In a few years, Rome wouldn't be sending tons of precious metals east to buy it anymore. Ordinary people would be able to wear it, too, eventually—they'd introduce cotton jennies when there was enough to use. Which would be a major benefit in hot weather, and for—

"Cotton underwear, hot damn and hallelujah!" Jeremey continued. "Drawers, at least—we won't be able to do elastic waistbands for a long time. Not Fruit of the Loom, but three-quarters of the way there."

He said it in English. None of the ex-Americans particularly liked the Roman linen loincloth, the *subligaculum*, though Paula and Filipa liked the *strophium*—the breast band that was the Roman answer to a bra—even less. They'd had bras done up by seamstresses since, and the Empress Faustina had taken it up when she saw Paula and asked *how is that possible*, and *that* meant it was spreading like wildfire in aristo female circles.... Paula thought that if cotton got cheap enough she could introduce disposable tampons, too.

Artorius himself wasn't conscious of the loincloth anymore unless he thought about it for some reason, except when he put it on or took it off.

Josephus gave Jeremey an odd look, and then shook his head. Hallelujah in English was recognizable to his keen multilingual ear as the Hebrew *hallĕlūyāh*, which meant *Praise Ye the Lord*.

For that matter, he'd recognized the source of Jeremey's name the first time he'd heard it: also Hebrew, *Yirmeyah*, from *May Jehovah Exalt*.

He'd been a bit bemused at the knowledge that Christianity had become the faith of the Western world, and at how that had carried bits and pieces and sometimes chunks of his people's faith into a broader sphere. He hadn't been all that happy about it either, and he sincerely hoped it wouldn't turn out that way this time around. Jews and Christians were much closer and more similar here and now than they'd become later, and Jews were much more numerous than the upstart heretics who thought the Messiah had *already* arrived.

More numerous so far.

About like conventional Christians and Mormons back uptime, Artorius thought. *Complete with the newcomers with an extra book doing a lot of missionary work.*

That didn't mean they *liked* each other.

Cousins often didn't. Artorius had been on nonspeaking terms with several of his, in the Texas Panhandle. Over everything from politics to his decision to take his doctorate at Harvard and live in Boston and leave the ranch to his younger sister and her husband to run, with himself and his wife and kids as a sleeping partner and frequent visitor.

Christianity won't necessarily *happen the same way now,* Artorius thought. *Though we'll never know, not for sure—none of us will live that long. But Christianity in the Roman Empire really took off in the crisis of the third century and after. This world looked bleak enough that focusing on the next was...more encouraging. If we succeed, by the middle of the next century they'll be well into their Industrial Revolution...building steam engines and railroads and settling Argentina and Australia.*

In the history he'd studied, the Roman Empire had come within a fraction of an inch of total collapse in those desperate times a few generations up the line—plague, economic collapse and a galloping hyperinflation that wiped out the banking system that had surprised the Americans with its sophistication.

About as good as eighteenth-century France's...for a while. Now we're making it better, with joint-stock banks and share issues for brokerage. Next...checkbooks! Josephus likes that idea.

And after the disastrous reign of Marcus Aurelius' son Commodus...endless civil wars and usurpations for generation after generation, secessions of whole provinces *also* lasting several generations, barbarian invasions and mass piracy...

Diocletian and Constantine had hauled things back together for a while, but big chunks of the central and western parts of the Empire were spiraling downward even before the final collapse. The east did much better...until the ruinous wars with Sassanid Persia that set the stage for the Arab conquests of the seventh century.

But we've already made a lot of changes. No Plague of Galen, not really, deaths maybe a twentieth or thirtieth of what they were the first time 'round and smallpox is now a solved problem...for residents of the Empire. And even for things we can't vaccinate against, quarantine and better sanitation and knowing that germs exist and what to do about them will work wonders. And it looks like the Empire will take in the whole of central and a lot of eastern Europe now, just for starters, as far as Scandinavia and Poland and Moldova and western Ukraine. More territory later. The economy's gotten a major prod up the ass from the tech we've introduced with more to come, there's paper and printing, a lot of intangibles like germ theory and algebra and modern astronomy and limited-liability corporations... and not least, Marcus Aurelius may live into his eighties now after we cured his ulcers. If there's no crisis in the next century... who knows what'll happen?

The exchange with Josephus and Jeremey had brought back memories of his first visit here. They passed a creaking Dutch-style windmill—also an innovation—amid a thumping of wooden hammers fulling cloth, and turned north as they approached the big lake. That was an improvement too, if you didn't like the thought of fulling cloth by trampling in human urine with bare feet.

There had been changes that he smiled to see when they reached the villa itself, the *pars urbana* that was the landowner's dwelling. The mansion was a two-story structure of stone ashlars covered in cream-colored stucco, built around two colonnaded courtyards gracious with pools and fountains and flower beds. It ran east-west, with a four-story square tower at the left rear corner and a platform overlooking the lake with a big swimming pool.

It still looked imposing, and still roughly resembled the reconstructed Villa Borg he'd seen in the Saarland... but there were chimneys through the red Roman tile roof now, some of them smoking. And now the baths and the swimming pool on the rear terrace had bottom drains.

And showers, hot damn, he thought.

The *pars rustica*—two further courtyards, single story and much plainer—no longer housed the workforce in little *cellae*, small single rooms for each family.

Instead there was a modest village now, off a bit eastward toward the red-fringed shore of the big lake that stretched out of sight north and south, and nearly so to the east. It was composed of plastered and whitewashed rammed-earth cottages on stone foundations and cellars, whitewashed and topped with tile roofs, even the smallest big enough for a kitchen and several bedrooms. Each had a chimney too, giving all the families their own hearth, and small cast-iron stoves were being imported from Colonia Ferramenta.

The cottages were grouped around a square; he'd taken the design from central Savannah's colonial period, and each cottage had a thirty-by-ninety plot for a kitchen garden and a chicken coop. There were public buildings there too at each end, bigger versions of the cottages and likewise tile roofed—a school which all the children now attended half the year from age six to twelve to learn reading and writing and the new arithmetic, a bathhouse...also with showers and individual tubs...a bakery, a laundry and a tavern. The free tenants would be able to use those too.

And a big fountain in the center of the square where they could all draw water, water that now went through slow sand filters upslope and was actually fairly safe to drink.

He'd instituted strict sanitary regulations, installed an artificial-swamp treatment patch for the wastes, and had a nurse-midwife trained in the new methods on watch from a little clinic. The infant mortality rate had dropped by eight-tenths already. There was a modest shop too, so the workers could get used to handling money and buying things for themselves against the eventual day of emancipation. The bonus program let nearly everyone earn a bit of cash at least. And the women were using modern—nineteenth century—spinning wheels and treadle looms in the *pars rustica*, vastly more productive than the equipment they'd grown up with, and selling what they didn't need themselves.

They got cash from that too, all their own.

It'll look even better when the trees grow, he thought critically.

"Well, well!" Jeremy murmured in English. "The game is afoot, Batman!"

"That's 'The game is afoot, *Watson*,'" Artorius said automatically; he'd been a Conan Doyle fan in his youth.

As he spoke he looked up sharply. The young man had exceptional eyesight, and he'd made out what took a few minutes to become clear to the others: a tented encampment in the tree-studded pasture north of the *pars urbana*. Closer still, and he frowned when he made it out as a detachment of the *Equites Singulares Augusti*—the Imperial Horse Guards, an elite cavalry unit, with their horses grazing the meadow.

The subdued manner of the grooms who came to take the horses at the villa's gatehouse made him frown. Something had definitely upset the usual routine. When Galenos came out of the gate and waved, Artorius eyebrows went *up* in surprise instead.

As far as he knew, Galen had been back in Rome for good, getting the new Medical Institute started, along with Mark and Paula. Those two had had their Roman-style wedding here the year before last, but left with the Imperial party.

He'd been planning on a brief visit to the capital himself, in the winter season when it was less dangerous.

Now that I'm not needed for the directly military stuff, he thought. *I can concentrate on modernization . . . and pitch a centrally run post office complete with stamps to Marcus Aurelius . . . And it would be good to see Mark and Paula again.*

"*Salve,* Galenos my friend," he said after they'd shaken hands.

He stepped aside with the wiry Greek; nobody would mind, though they'd be intensely curious. He and Galenos were both known to be close to the Emperor, and it was just presumed that much of what they said was in strict confidence and composed of State secrets.

"I bear news from Caesar Augustus," Galenos said quietly . . . in Koine Greek, which would be an additional bit of insurance since it wasn't much spoken around here. "It concerns your . . . arrival. Your original arrival in Pannonia."

Artorius thought, intensely enough that sight and sound and even the smell of roses faded for a moment. Marcus Aurelius knew *how* he'd arrived. Or at least as much as Artorius did himself since he had no idea how Dr. Fuchs's time machine had actually worked, which meant this was important.

Very important. Very, very important.

"Best we discuss it with everyone who . . . knows," he said. "After dinner. That'll save repetition."

⇒ CHAPTER TWELVE ⇐

Luoyang/Eastern Capital
Palace District
August 19th, 169 CE

Colonel Liu had called them together for dinner. Somewhat to her relief, Black Jade had found that the historical estimates were right—chopsticks had come into general use in early Han times and they were standard by now. You could get rice in Luoyang, too, if you were prepared to pay enough; most people in this area ate millet porridge with spoons, though a pita-like flatbread of wheat or barley was also common.

And they eat dog and magpie and owl now, she thought with a shudder. *The beer and yellow wine aren't bad, though. And their tea tastes...very strange.*

They'd taught their own cooks to make modern Chinese dishes...

And everyone expected me to do it, she thought with weary resentment.

...which were mostly what was being served—some of the dishes had become popular here at court as well, especially the ones with hot peppers. There were enough peppers now for the spicy dishes *she* liked—those had been among the things that Hú Bingwen had planted near Xian their first year here.

Everyone was laughing at a joke he'd told about his time south of here; he'd just returned from a spell in the Yangtse valley.

"More seriously, the double-cropping rice and the transplanting frames are both doing well, and so are the wheat varieties we brought with us, both those for around here and the southern types. And the cassava and sweet potatoes and sugarcane and rubber are established on the southern frontier. They will spread on their own, now."

Servants came in and carried away the dishes and set out beer...now made with hops...and rice wine and the...

Highly idiosyncratic, she thought.

...local idea of tea.

"And the new coal-fired blast furnaces have—" Biao began.

Colonel Liu cleared his throat. Biao fell silent, and so did the others. Black Jade felt a pang; gatherings like this had become rarer. Except for the colonel, all the male members of the party had high-born local wives now—some more than one wife—and growing families of children.

Her mouth twisted. She was *not* interested in local men; their ideas of what a wife should be were horrifying.

Or local women, she thought, and stifled a sigh.

A few experiments in university had convinced her that wasn't an option for her. Despite the general shoddiness of the three or four young men who'd been trying to court her at any given time back then. Some women enjoyed the surplus of males that selective abortion had unfortunately produced; she didn't.

It just made the men more pushy and desperate.

A goodly number of court ladies had made erroneous assumptions based on her clothes and demeanor and issued invitations ranging from the subtle to the blatant.

Natural enough, from their viewpoint, she thought with exasperation, with a slight roll of the eyes. *The way I dress and act... seen through local eyes...*

"Yes, Colonel?" she said.

He looked around the table; it was circular.

"You are aware of the thinking behind our...expedition," he said. "That we could build China up to the point where it would become the world, and the world would be China as it expanded and supplanted all others. One world, one state, one language and culture, one *people.* It would be almost automatic, so there was no hurry. We would lay the foundations with technical progress and political...reform...and all else would follow naturally, just as China's expansion under the Qin and Han did but vastly more so."

"And no nuclear war," Àilún said, his eyes distant for a moment.

"Yes, of course," Liu said. "No Three Kingdoms mutual slaughter either, provided we could introduce a few reforms... getting rid of the eunuch faction, for starters, which we've done. And the new farming and manufacturing methods would increase government revenue without grinding down the peasants and producing the Yellow Turban revolt. Steady expansion, by land. And by sea, when we introduced better ships."

He drew a deep breath. "But I have received alarming news. You know that the Marcomannic Wars, and the Plague of Galen, should be occupying the Roman Empire right now. That is the only other state comparable at all to China in this period."

She nodded. They'd all read synopses of events further westward. In the abstract, it was horrifying; a great civilization stumbling into ruin, and along with it the ruin of millions of lives. That was no reason China shouldn't take advantage of the events, of course, since they'd happen anyway—the time travelers were too far away and too busy to prevent it even if they wanted to.

"Well, I have received news from merchants based in Nanyue who trade to India."

Another deep breath. "The Marcomannic Wars... are over."

Everyone sat up and took notice at that, and glanced at the others. That struggle was supposed to last for *fourteen* years of mutual ruin.

Liu continued: "The tribes north of the Roman frontier on the Danube have been broken by new weapons—thunderballs, they are called. Cast by catapults, they explode and scatter lead shot with deadly effect. And the story tells of other weapons—bronze tubes which throw shot so fast it is invisible and strikes down foes a mile distant."

This time the silence echoed. Colonel Liu pulled something from the pocket of his jacket and passed it to Black Jade. She unfolded it, wondering at the feel—paper had been invented here in China about two generations ago, but this was smoother and *neater*, somehow. They hadn't gotten around to improving it yet. When she'd opened it, she almost dropped it in shock.

There was *printing* on the inside. In the Latin alphabet and the Latin language, which she knew, but with twenty-first-century Western text conventions—upper and lower case, and punctuation...

Biao and Bingwen and Àilún passed it from hand to hand,

with muffled exclamations...and swearing. They were all familiar with the Western alphabet, of course, and could speak—or at least read—some English.

Liu folded it again. "Without doubt, this means that the strike...our strike...on Vienna just as we...left...failed. And the merchants said the Roman traders they met—Greeks, in fact, mostly from Egypt, but Roman subjects...boasted that a new treatment by the court physician Galen—"

They all nodded to show they remembered who he was.

"—renders them immune to the plague that began years ago after the Roman sack of the Parthian capital, Ctesiphon. They say this new treatment...they even call it a *vaccine*...is being spread rapidly, and they had small scars on their left arms produced by it."

Several of the men around the table grunted. Black Jade felt as if she'd been punched in the stomach herself. They'd started on their own immunization program years ago—the Plague of Galen hadn't reached China until the 170s CE, as far as historians in their own age could see, but why take chances?

"Gunpowder weapons, and vaccines, and paper and printing," Àilún said; technological history was his specialty. "For Europe...from a thousand years to seventeen hundred years too soon. Many centuries even here. And who knows what else that they did not mention?"

The colonel's face set like stone. "This...changes everything," he said. "We can no longer take our time, and merely plant seeds that may come to fruition later. Here is what we shall do—"

Black Jade listened numbly.

Liu wants to start a cold war *with these...these time travelers to Rome. But that means a division of the world! Nuclear war, again—the world destroyed, a few centuries down the road to the future!*

She'd gone along with Liu's plans: there was no alternative... or there had been no alternative. Now...

He will lead the world to destruction!

⇒ CHAPTER THIRTEEN ⇐

Villa Lunae
Pannonia Superior
July 18th, 170 CE

Galenos looked around the dinner table, a little bemused despite the familiar murals of garden scenes on the walls with nymphs and fauns cavorting. And the floor mosaic's portrayal of empty oyster shells (highly theoretical this far from the sea unless you paid their weight in gold) and scattered nutshells, olive pits, fruit rinds, and grape stems.

He wasn't unduly shocked that Artorius' wife and not-quite-marriageable-age adoptive daughter were present...

Though the new knowledge indicates that marriage should be at least four or five years after first menses, he thought automatically.

...and several other women who were respectable...or at least somewhat respectable and not *hetairai*, paid companions. He suspected his *ancestors* would have been from his readings in the classics, but two centuries of Roman influence had left its mark in the Hellenic lands, particularly in the uppermost of the upper classes.

And he'd spent much time in Rome itself. Much of it at the Imperial court, at that, which was very much a world on its own, with its own mores and customs.

To Romans, women of the family dining and taking part in the conversation at a meal with guests—even at some types of public banquets—was accepted as routine. So were guests bringing along *their* womenfolk. And nobody doubted that the women of

173

the Imperial family had political weight of their own, far more than most senators. An *Augusta*, an Empress, could often expect posthumous deification like her husband, and her image—and those of her daughters—would be broadcast in temples and monuments from Britannia to Syria.

Nowadays, the Imperial court also used forks as they did here. Marcus Aurelius had been very taken with the way they made eating tidier at Artorius' wedding feast here in this very house, and ordered sets made up for the Imperial household. Galen had been impressed himself.

Of course what the Emperor did...if he was popular at all... instantly became fashionable in Rome. And Marcus Aurelius was now very popular indeed, after the triumph of the Marcomannic War and the massive extension of the Imperial boundaries.

What Julius Caesar was to Gaul, our Caesar Augustus is to Germania, was the latest saying in the capital. *Except that the Divine Julius took eight years to conquer Gaul, and our Augustus took two to annex Germania.*

Imitating everything from his haircut to his determinedly modest clothes was all the rage, as were titillatingly risqué blond wigs shorn from Marcomannic captives for the elite's womenfolk.

That imitation currently included rich men flaunting *gold* and *silver* forks. And keeping an elaborate, costly knife-and-fork set on their belts, or accidentally-on-purpose obvious in a pouch, so that they could produce and flourish it at dinners with those who hadn't caught up with the newest trend. That sent the little eating implement cascading down the social scale like a slow avalanche in the Alps.

And I approve wholeheartedly, now that I know diseases can be spread with a touch of hands or even a single finger. Or a breath! No, what's really *strange is that it's a rich man's house and a dinner with guests and we're all sitting upright on chairs. And all* the chairs have backs, not just the one the *paterfamilias* uses.*

Romans and Greeks shared the habit of reclining on cushioned benches at any but ordinary casual family meals, or at least the gentry and wellborn did, like his family in Pergamum. Artorius had done that at his wedding feast, sharing a couch with his bride, as was customary with Romans. Evidently his land...distant in time as well as space...found that habit unpleasant or difficult to acquire, and he'd imposed his own customs under his own roof save for the most august, formal occasions.

Sextus Hirrius Trogus apparently wasn't distressed, and also wielded knife and fork with aplomb. Artorius had taken Josephus aside for a moment and whispered in his ear; the Jew had grinned and slapped him on the shoulder.

Probably Artorius told him the food is ritually clean for his ethnoi *despite his family having left,* the Greek thought. *Except for those marked dishes, which he has* not *sampled. Artorius has a reputation for brusque directness, yet he also shows great tact at times. It is no wonder that his clients are devoted to him! He is like a kindly father to them.*

Lady Julia murmured a phrase and burned a small crust in a lantern flame, the usual Roman sacrifice before a meal. Made to the Penates, the household spirits that had originally presided over the pantry and storehouses.

Josephus looked aside at that, and murmured something under his breath, then sat down and spread a napkin over his lap like the others.

The sequence of courses was also a little different from aristocratic Roman custom. There had been trays of little savory nibblements first, carried around by servants; that was the *gustatio*, as was standard with wealthy Romans. Josephus had gotten a special small tray of his own, without the bits of ham.

Poor Romans counted themselves lucky if they could get a loaf and some oil for dipping rather than what was left of yesterday's stale pea-and-barley porridge, of course, as the poor did everywhere.

But that was followed with soup by itself—an excellent one rich with tasty wild duck from the great lake just eastward, and vegetables that included the new ones—and then a salad also reigning alone, mostly of lettuce.

I approve. It is an aid to digestion and promotes regular movements of the bowels.

Among other things the salad included the novelty of prepitted olives so you didn't have to spit the kernels out on the floor, and the bright-red *tomatoes* and sweet peppers the Americans had brought. Those had just started to show up on the Imperial table in Rome as a rare treat. The fiery ones were ingredients in what Artorius called *BBQ Sauce*, a spicy concoction that Romans near-universally adored and he rather liked himself. It added a welcome complexity to grilled or roasted meat.

And the salad was dressed with a touch of vinegar as well as olive oil, which added a certain piquancy.

I admit that eating a dressed salad with a fork is...much neater.

The main course was a roast lamb, glazed with honey infused with garlic and the new peppers. It had been roasted with peeled, quartered potatoes around it besides various vegetable side dishes. Galen found potatoes nourishing but rather bland most of the time. *These* were excellent and had soaked up both the lamb's taste and that of the glaze.

He tore off a bit of a white wheat roll with his left hand—on a special side plate, which was an excellent idea too—and touched it to the shallow dish that held the dipping oil.

"Hmmmm," he said, and tried more.

He'd assumed it was olive oil. It wasn't, though it had a similar feel in the mouth, but it was nutty, earthy, smooth, with just a pleasant hint of bitterness.

"Whatever this oil is, it's excellent!" he said. "Even if it isn't olive."

"From the *helianthus*, the sunflowers," Artorius said at his enquiring look. "When cold-pressed it's quite tasty, I find. I was surprised, since we didn't do it that way where I came from, and where I was raised it was blander than this."

"Indeed! A pleasant change. And here far from the lands where olives grow, it will be well received!"

Sextus smiled at his brother-in-law.

"*I* remember how surprised you looked the first time you tasted it," he said. "You didn't expect it to sell as well as you promised me it would when you first sowed the sunflowers, did you?"

Artorius glanced upward. "Perhaps not for food," he said, and his wife Julia chuckled and winked at her brother. "That was a pleasant surprise, yes. But for scraping off at the baths, and for cooking, I did expect it to do well. And it has! And for making the new, mild soap that is pleasant to use."

"Well, it's also much *cheaper* than olive oil, this far from the Middle Sea," Julia put in. "Or at least it *will* be, as more grow it and press the oil. Soon we will all have abundant oil at no great expense—as they do among the olive groves of the Middle Sea. I admit I like the new *sapo* too; it is gentle on the skin, it makes you very clean, and the lavender gives it a lovely scent that lingers."

"And you can feed stock on the cake once the oil has been pressed out," Jeremey said cheerfully.

"And the flowers are so pretty; a whole field of them...that is as if the sun has rained drops of brightness on the earth," Julia answered. "Even brighter than wheat or barley at harvesttime."

Dessert was fresh fruit, peaches and apricots, and dried figs and dates, and a cake of unusual appearance. The outer surface was covered in a smooth substance that looked like white soft cheese, but tasted very sweet without the characteristic smoky tang of honey.

"Thank Jeremey for that," Artorius said, when the Greek mentioned it.

The younger man nodded; he was sitting between two pretty, well-dressed young women who were a little subdued in Galenos' presence...

Ah, his concubines, the Greek remembered. *They were slaves here. He bought and emancipated them when they became pregnant by him and adopted their children...a son and a daughter, which legitimizes them by Roman law, and they're* already *full Roman citizens since their mothers were freed before they were born.*

They were also both pregnant again; about five months, he judged. Artorius' wife very probably was too, but not nearly so far along. From the pair's adoring looks at Jeremey...sincere ones, as far as he could tell...they still appreciated how lucky that all made them. They'd gone from slave housemaids in their teens to the free and affluent mothers of children who'd probably go far. Even if Jeremey married into a respectable line later, their future and that of their children would be secure.

That was another difference between Greeks and Romans; Greek cities in their independent days had guarded their citizenship far more jealously. The freed slave of a Roman citizen *was* a Roman citizen, with only a few restrictions on office holding or enlisting in the legions without special permission. Though also still in that patron-client relationship with their former owners that Romans set such store by.

The freed slave's *children* born after emancipation were citizens in full, equal to any other. Their grandsons could be senators, broad-stripe men.

In their glory days most of the free Greek *poleis*—city-states— had required that both parents be citizens and granted exemptions very, very sparingly. Galenos remembered reading how even the great statesman Pericles—who'd been voted high office in Athens repeatedly and played the citizen's Assembly like a flute in that city's days of great power as ruler of the Delian League—had had severe problems getting his son by his mistress Aspasia enrolled among Athenian citizens.

Which may well be one reason Rome *rules the world, not* Athens, he thought. *Those two are not wives, but respectable enough. Their children will probably be in the Equestrian Order, easily. And their grandchildren... possibly even senators! There are plenty in the Senate who have freedmen or freedwomen in their bloodlines. At the very least their children will be rich and influential, certainly: Julius... Jer... em... ey, in the American language... is very knowledgeable in the management of estates. That book of his,* Rerum Rusticarum, *looks as if it will replace* Columella's De re rustica. *Marcus Aurelius has sent copies to the provincial procurators of the* res privata, *and that means most big landowners and their bailiffs are clamoring to buy it too.*

"It's *sugar* that makes it sweet," Jeremey said, at Galenos' inquiring look when he'd tasted the icy-looking coating. "*Saccharo*, in Latin."

Galenos frowned as he searched his memory, then nodded:

"Ah, Pliny mentions it, and its sweetness! But he says it is derived from India? And used only as a medicine?"

"The Indian variety is from the pressed juice of a... call it a tall reed. That is then boiled and filtered. It needs hot weather and much water; it would grow well in Egypt... especially southern Egypt... under irrigation, but not many other places in the Empire. This tastes the same, but it's from a special type of beet instead that grows well here in Pannonia and would in many parts of the northern provinces, and parts of Italy and Hispania too. We had the seeds of them along, and I've built a refinery for them on the property the Emperor granted me and another here on the Villa Lunae, and one's under construction on my new land in western Dacia," Jeremey said. "Ought to be a big market for it, honey's expensive by comparison. And what's left over from pressing the beet pulp makes good stock feed."

Galen chuckled dryly. "Between that and the pulp from the sunflowers, your livestock will be pampered!"

Jeremey smiled. "As stuff for bread and porridge gets cheaper, people will buy more meat. And fruit, and vegetables and cheese and wine. More livestock means more manure, too, and that means higher yields. A . . . in Latin it would be *moving loop of virtue*."

The interior of the cake was dark, moist, rich, and studded with raisins and nuts. The tastes were very distinct, sweet without the familiar tang of honey disguising them, as well as slivers of carrot that complemented the other flavors well.

The nuts in the cake included some he'd never tasted before.

"Peanuts, they're called," Artorius said, when he asked. "It's *just* warm enough around here by the lake for them to yield a little, but they ought to do very well closer to the Middle Sea, I've sent some there. To estates of the *res privata* on Cyprus and in Syria, for starters. They hold a lot of oil, too. It can be used for cooking, and to grease the works of machines, and to make a better variety of soap . . . *saponam*."

"And the crushed and pressed pulp . . ." Jeremey began.

". . . is good feed for livestock," Philippa finished dryly.

"Speaking of what does well, how's your new land going?" Artorius said, raising his brows.

"Quite well. Got a fair amount of field broken to the plow for winter wheat, the sugar refinery will be done next year, and the gristmill. I've got the villa planned, too, and an architect from Acquincum working on it . . . young guy, he got the concept of scale drawings like—"

He snapped his fingers and went on:

"—and he's very taken with that. Interested in the fireplaces and the new-style plumbing and flush toilets too."

Philippa nodded and spoke with casual boldness:

"And we've started breeding horses on ours, next door to Jem," she said, and touched the woman beside her on the arm.

Philippa was the most exotic of the Americans in her looks. Her skin was very slightly darker than Galenos', about the same as, say, Legate Fronto's, but her face was distinctly high cheeked and flattish, with a small straight nose, and her eyes seemed slanted. Her hair was a conventional enough raven black, though very straight and tonight worn in braids around her head held with jeweled silver pins.

Her eyes look *that way because of the fold at the corners*, Galenos reminded himself; it was medically interesting, but not important as far as he could see. *Common in the furthest east, I am given to understand.*

She was sitting next to Sarukê, the Sarmatian amazon. The Sarmatian woman was even taller than the American—about five foot nine, hers were a very tall folk, perhaps because they were nomads who lived from the meat and milk of their flocks—with pale almost colorless gray eyes, reddish-blond hair and a face that was comely in a bold-boned, hawk-featured way. The two were lovers, and had been since before Galenos arrived in the north with the Emperor; they neither flaunted nor hid it. It wasn't exactly the normal, conventional love of man and youth...for one thing they were the same age, both around thirty, and obviously intended to make a life together for the rest of their span. But it wasn't exactly totally different either.

Though some men resented such liaisons bitterly as a trespass on the Gods-granted prerogatives of the male.

Galenos shrugged mentally. He didn't think so himself. For that matter, most men were also deplorably ignorant of the basics of female anatomy and thought that a penis or something like it was absolutely necessary for pleasure in sexual congress.

Philippa was in Roman male garb, more or less—a calf-length tunic of fine embroidered wool, basically, worn unbelted indoors but often bloused up through a belt to knee-height when doing something active out of doors.

Though she tells me that would be very much a woman's garment in America! Old-fashioned *woman's clothing, at that. So by American standards, Roman and Greek men all wear women's clothing!*

He hid his smile at the thought.

Sarukê was in the garb her tribe wore on the steppes north of the Black Sea. That was loose trousers tucked into soft strapped boots, and over them a long-sleeved shirt-tunic. But she didn't stink, the fine cloth was clean, and she had shed the rude ronyish manners her folk were said to have and used knife and fork like her companion.

Josephus' freedwoman and bodyguard when the Americans arrived, Galenos remembered. *And a gladiatrix for a while before that, captured on a raid against Dacia.*

He thought the ancient myths of Amazons might originally have come from those steppe folk. Fighting women weren't exactly common on the plains north of the Black Sea, but not all that rare, either. Their title there was a Sarmatian word which translated as *man-killer.*

Captured from a raiding warband and enslaved and sold as a gladiatrix, his mind prompted—it took notes constantly, and read them at need. *Josephus bought her from the arena in Carnuntum and freed her to be his bodyguard. Head of Artorius' bodyguards later, and she helped spread the new horse lore after learning it from Philippa.*

"We get more too over Danube east here... *of* here," the Sarmatian said in her rough but fluent Latin. "New west part of Dacia province, like Jem say—next to his land."

Galenos nodded; that northern extension of the Empire originally conquered by Trajan was now much bigger to both east and west. Currently it ran from Pannonia Inferior and newly declared Transdanubia to the Black Sea in an irregular rectangular block if you looked at the maps, with the Danube to the south and west, extending north to the crest of the Carpathians and east to the Tyras river, what Sarmatians called the Dān-Ister. It would be divided later, as Pannonia had, if that proved of unwieldy size.

Roman settlers... anyone from the older provinces, in fact... were being encouraged to move in, not least by land along the new roads, sold at nominal prices. The previous natives on both sides had been mostly wandering herdsmen, distant relatives of Sarukê's people, and more than half of them had left ahead of the annexation. Most of the land there was *ager publicus* now, the "public fields," and apart from the one part in ten or so set aside for Imperial estates it would be used for new settlers. Whatever their birth tongues, their children... or grandchildren, in some cases... would speak Latin.

Land prices there were particularly nominal if you had what the Americans called *pull* with the authorities, which of course they did. In abundance. Army veterans got their smaller plots for free, but those had been increased in size too on Artorius' advice. The amount of land one ordinary rural family could handle was going to grow a good deal in the next generation.

"Yeah... I mean, *sic, ita,*" Jeremey said. "Not far east of the Danube around Acquincum... it runs north-south around there... so there's cheap water transport right on the doorstep and a market. *East of Budapest,*" he added, a phrase in the mysterious English language, then returned to Latin:

"Got a nice big chunk, about twenty-four thousand *iūgera,* Fil and Sarukê got the same right next door. Good black dirt, reasonable weather, and just a little drainage needed on some spots."

"Unless you're set on duck hunting," Fil said with a grin. "Swamps attract ducks. And geese."

"Well, there is that too, now that we've got shotguns... even if they're muzzle-loaders. Nothing better than roast wild duck!"

"Except venison stew," Artorius said.

"Well, yeah, if you don't spoil it Texan style with those damned hot peppers that leave you feeling like you've swallowed red-hot embers..."

They both grinned at that, and Julius went on:

"Excellent ranching country for livestock, good for wheat, good for sugar beet, good for corn, *really* good for sunflowers and canola, passable in spots for vineyards and potatoes... and it's mostly grassland, so with the new plows we're breaking it in quick... plant alfalfa, then start a regular rotation... plant woodlots..."

"I thought you didn't *like* farming," Artorius said with a smile.

"It's a lot more fun from horseback, pointing with your riding whip and telling other people what to do," Julius/Jeremey replied with a sly grin.

"And fine land for horse, too," Sarukê said. "We two breed, Fil and me. *Big* horse. For cavalry, and for pull cannon, and even bigger, heavier for pull new big wagons, farm gear."

Philippa nodded enthusiastically.

"With selective breeding," she said. "We've gotten a small herd of those Gallic ones, from the Ardennes, for base stock, and we'll cross back with hotbloods, maybe Arabians. Four or five horse generations and we'll have the equivalent of *hunters* and *Percherons*."

Those two words were in English, but he caught their meaning from the context. Her name meant *Lover of Horses* in Greek, and she did and had taught her partner how to use the *Pannonian gear*, as it was called. They'd both done the initial teaching of Roman cavalry troopers—aided by the humiliating ease with which Sarukê beat their best in practice matches with lances in the couched style when she had a wood-framed saddle with stirrups and raised cantle and they didn't. Usually knocking them out of their old-style saddles, often into a full head-over-heels circle involving broken noses and teeth.

Philippa had also taught the new arithmetic—where a number's values were positional—and new systems of bookkeeping that many merchants and the Imperial fiscus were adopting wholesale, and was writing a book on what she called *algebra*.

Which from a few hints unlike the strictly practical aspects promised to set the cat among the philosophical pigeons well and truly. Galenos grinned at the thought. He had philosophical inclinations himself, but a lot of the theoreticians had sneered at philosophy from an actual practicing *physician* with his hands in blood and muck.

As if they *don't squat to pass stool and walk on air instead of dirt!* he thought. *Less arrogance from them* now, *though. Considerably!*

Algebra promised to sow more chaos than even the new heliocentric astronomy, which had prompted fistfights in the schools in Athens and Alexandria, with near riots in the streets as well as mere passionate debate...particularly when accompanied by the new telescopes. There weren't many of those yet and the military had first call on them, but a few Imperially owned ones had been lent out where it would do the most good.

And the stars being suns like ours, just more distant—oh, the outrage!

Marcus Aurelius had laughed aloud when Galen proposed that loan of the farseeing instruments...he loved Athens and had been an enthusiastic student of the Stoic school of philosophy there, but found some parts of its customs as practiced among the learned classes exasperating.

Hundreds of copies of her exposition of algebra would go all over the Empire, when it had gone through the book-stamping process, what the Americans called *printing*. Though there were even more copies of the books on the new medicine, ones that bore *his* name. His text on antiseptic wound treatments and surgery and childbirth had two *thousand* copies in its Latin version, and nearly a thousand in Greek.

More than any other book written down, except Homer! he thought with pride.

And more would be needed soon.

Though I know people who lock themselves away when they come to understand the concepts of bacteria *and* viruses, *or flee to mountain cottages, glaring at anyone who approaches them,* he thought. *It's almost like being surrounded by evil spirits! Only with a microscope, you can* see *them. And the new soap and double-refined spirits can slay or banish them.*

Artorius cleared his throat when most of those present had finished dessert.

"Honored guests...my dearest Julia...the excellent Galenos has brought news from Caesar Augustus."

Which was a respectful way of referring to the Emperor.

"I must ask that we have privacy to consider and consult about it; Caesar Augustus has so ordered."

Sextus rose at once, with a slight smile; he was deeply proud of being an Imperial favorite's brother-in-law. Pride even beyond the practical benefits, which had included payment of his debts and a lifetime's tax exemption. He'd been prominent in his home city of Sirmium before Artorius arrived, but he might as well have been an uncrowned king there now, and far wealthier too from being among the first to use the *new things*.

"Julia, my sister, shall we retire? I would like to see my nephew and niece, play with them and give them my departure presents since I'll be leaving early tomorrow."

He and his sister, Artorius' adopted daughter and Jeremey's two companions rose, nodded and smiled, and left. So did Sarukê, though she whispered something in Sarmatian in Philippa's ear first, which made her laugh and feed the other woman a last piece of the cake on the end of her fork. The servants had been warned away, too.

"So," Artorius said, when the Americans and Josephus were alone with the physician.

That left out only Paula, Marcus, and the Emperor not present— of people in the present year who knew where the five had really come from.

Or when *they really came from, rather. That story about the western land called America and how it was utterly destroyed was...in a sense...true. How what is technically the truth can mislead! Clever of Artorius, to conceal the truth with...truth.*

"What's up, Galenos? What's up that couldn't be written down, at least?" Artorius said.

He was notorious for being blunt.

"I agreed to wait because I did not want to spoil your admirable dinner," Galenos said briskly. "A delay of weeks would matter, but a few hours did not. The situation is thus: Caesar Augustus sent an embassy to the furthest east, in the first year of his reign."

"I know," Artorius said.

He had even less tolerance for blather than Galenos did himself.

For which I admire him, Galenos thought. *He's... blunter about it with those of high rank, too. As if it does not occur to him that he might offend, or he does not care if he does. Marcus Aurelius finds that a relief, after oceans of flattery. When Artorius makes a compliment, you know he sincerely means it.*

The Greek went on: "They left nearly four years before your arrival, just after the death of the previous Emperor. Two months ago... now... one of the ambassadors returned, alone, badly scarred, penniless, the sole survivor. He told us—I was present—"

Artorius slammed his fist down on the table when Galenos finished, hard enough to make the plates and cutlery jump, his lips moving in silent curses.

He ignored the pain.

In fact, it's welcome, the ex-American thought. *God damn! I can feel the winds of fate blowing on the back of my neck, and it's nasty as hell!*

"Shit," Jeremey said with equal disgust; Galenos would know what *that* English word meant, at least. "Crap and crapitude."

Then he swore in Latin, ending with a sigh and:

"*Stercus accidit.*"

Which meant *shit happens.*

Josephus was open in his alarm; he'd proved himself as a brave man more than once, but unlike most Romans born into the Equestrian Order, he didn't make a fetish of stern, controlled *gravitas* unless it was necessary for an audience.

"They... they are also from your time?" he said.

"With an *automatic pistol*? That's what the weapon the ambassador described is called. Yes," Artorius said, his voice flat. "*Hades,* yes. *Deodamnatus.*"

Philippa sighed wordlessly and put her face in her hands for a long moment.

Artorius saw Galenos' shrewd glance taking in their reactions; probably Marcus Aurelius had asked him to check if the Americans were surprised. The Emperor trusted Artorius as much as he did any man... but a Roman Emperor couldn't trust *anyone* absolutely. Not if he wanted to live long, rule until he died of natural causes and be followed by his chosen successor.

"And here I was hoping I wouldn't have to do anything

more than work on long-distance canals and sailing ships...
that first one's a-building... slowly... down in Trieste... Tergeste
in Histria... and they're starting another at Ostia. And getting
the machine tools improved now that we're making reasonable
measuring gauges ourselves," Artorius said, weary disgust in his
voice. "Now, I'll have to... bring some other projects forward."

He glanced out the window that gave onto the gardens, colorful
flowers, wall murals, bright mosaics and splashing fountains. It was
still light, the long, lingering evening of summer in central Europe.

So much for contentment and a quiet family life, he thought.
*Hell, so much for looking forward to cotton underwear again! It'll
probably be used for bandages first, packaged sterile field dressings.*

"I have something to show you," he said to Galenos and went
on to the others: "You guys need to see it too. I was hoping it
wouldn't be necessary, or at least not soon, but... oh, well. Crap
and crapitude, as Jem says."

They rose and walked in a group out into the inner courtyard's peristyle.

"Wait a minute," Artorius said.

When he returned with a four-foot cloth-wrapped bundle in
his hands they followed him toward a door that gave onto the
shallow slope that led down to the lake eastward. Fieldstone steps
marked it at intervals.

Jeremey was talking to Fil behind Artorius:

"I always wondered why Vienna got hit in the first round of
strikes," he said. "That's Vindobonum now," he added to Galenos
in Latin. "Destroyed just as we... left."

Fil made an enquiring noise, and he went on, in Latin: "It didn't
make sense to waste a first strike on an unimportant neutral city
like Vienna... Vindobonum. Mopping up, yeah. But right away? The
Chinese must have known about Fuchs's time machine, somehow."

"Yes, the *mi-chin-nom ssi-bal*—" Fil said, and went on from there.

They hadn't talked about it much; the subject was too painful. But Artorius knew she *really* didn't like the Chinese government. He didn't speak more than a little Korean himself, though
his grandfather's mother had been a war bride from there, who'd
arrived in the US pregnant in 1953.

Which had created a tremendous hullabaloo back then—at
the time there just wasn't anyone of East Asian descent in the
neighborhood—but nobody had been nervy enough to do much

when the man who'd brought her in was a combat veteran. Especially one who'd won the Distinguished Service Cross, just one step down from the Medal of Honor, and whose father was a prominent local rancher.

Which hullabaloo granddad used to talk about with a shit-eating grin, Artorius thought. *I recognize some of what she's saying, though. Great-grandmother could cuss a blue streak when she wanted to. She spoke good Texan by the time I remember her, but she didn't find it satisfactory for swearing.*

She'd died when he was about ten and she was around eighty; she'd been in her late teens when she arrived in the early fifties. But he remembered her vividly, white-haired and bent but still crackling with vitality and keen witted.

Fil had just spat out *byeontae saekki,* which meant something like *fornicating perverts.*

She was describing the Chinese rulers...in highly unflattering ways involving incest, bestiality and an intense desire that they be boiled to death in human shit. Though they were, in a sense, already dead...if *already* had any meaning in a time-travel context.

I'm one-eighth Korean and it didn't matter much of a damn, he thought. *Real important to her, not surprising given her background.*

"—were behind that Kim bastard who nuked Seoul," she finished.

Her mother and father had been born in the South Korean capital, and come to the US as children with their emigrant parents. She'd had family links there she kept up, spoke the language and had visited now and then. They'd all avoided thinking about things like that as much as they could. It would have been pointless self-torture...but now there was no alternative.

Then she went on in Latin to Galenos:

"They destroyed the place my ancestors...my grandparents... called home, with a bomb that uses the...the same fire that heats the sun. One such weapon will slay a great city, kill everyone in it...millions upon millions...and poison the lands about it with a wasting death. Thousands of those were used."

Artorius could see Galen flinch. That wasn't surprising... since he was very smart and had an excellent imagination. And nowadays he knew how big the sun was and how far away and had *some* idea of how it worked.

"They will not have such?" Galenos asked.

Dawning terror marked his face at the thought of Rome...or Athens or Pergamum...laid waste in a flash of sun-fire.

"No," Artorius said. "Definitely not."

Galenos blew out a breath of relief; so did Josephus. Artorius went on:

"Far too bulky, if they wanted to bring anything else, and they would. They didn't expect to have anyone else from our time here. And it would be impossible to *make* such weapons here. Not for a century...more likely two or three at least. You would need that much time to build the tools...and many more regressions beyond that."

Jeremey went on thoughtfully: "Yeah, but Seoul, that *was* a strategic target, capital of an important country and one close to China at that. Vienna?"

He dropped into English for a sentence: "Just a bunch of dwindling, aging Krauts...well, call 'em Krauts in three-quarter time. Not even in NATO."

"Let's keep it in Latin," Artorius said...though he doubted there was a way to say *Kraut in three-quarter time* in that language. Speakers of Proto-Germanic were not noted for their classical music here...to put it mildly.

And Fil's eyes were bright with unshed tears. Latin might make it less visceral, a tiny bit easier to handle than the same words in their birth tongue. Jeremey wasn't the most considerate of human beings—that probably wouldn't even occur to him.

"Galenos, the Chinese empire was our nation of America's great rival and greatest enemy," Artorius said.

"And the greatest enemy of my ancestral country, Korea, where my parents were born," Fil put in. "Koreans were close allies of America."

Artorius added: "The rulers of China started the war that destroyed our world."

I think, Artorius mused. *I'm morally certain...nearly.*

They'd never know for sure, and everyone had been on a hair trigger for months before that. You couldn't say for sure who'd fired the first shots in the naval clashes around Taiwan either—it might even have been some Japanese skipper's itchy trigger finger. Things had snowballed from there, slowly at first, then getting worse and worse while the five of them were in the air from America to Vienna. The big one had hit just as Fuchs brought them into his lab and showed them the time machine.

Artorius... Arthur, then... had been convinced the Austrian physicist was either crazy or that it was some sort of scam. Until the time machine actually *worked*.

"They must have had spies in the... in the place of study..." he went on.

There really wasn't a classical Latin equivalent of *laboratory*.

He'd noticed men and women who looked East and South Asian there at the time, but that was standard anywhere on a scientific team in the West in 2032. And the spy working for the Chinese might have been blond and pink, for that matter.

Probably would have been, in fact.

"...of the man who invented the device for traveling through time. From what you said, it seems they duplicated it... and used it just as our world destroyed itself, as we did. Or rather as Fuchs did, without our knowing."

Which was another argument that they started it; how would they have known the precise time otherwise? Though they *could* have had everything kept ready on general principles, including several teams on alternating watches, and the one on duty bugged out when the bombs started flying...

Or for all I know, they might have gotten it working just in time, the way Fuchs did. Or both.

"Five Chinese... and probably about the same amount of baggage Fuchs put together and we brought here. Mark was convinced that was some sort of limitation in the machine, or Fuchs would have sent ten tons of gear or more. And it looks as if the machine could only go to *this* time. Otherwise, why not go earlier? Or to the immediate past? So there's probably the same limit on... on distance in time as there is with weight," Artorius mused.

Galenos nodded. "Marcus said as much to me, when I explained this to him and Paula. He called it a nonfalsifiable hypothesis, though... what an interesting concept! But we know of these other travelers in time, and they do not know of you. Surely that is an advantage?"

Artorius laughed bitterly, and continued at Galen's questioning look:

"Not as much of one as I'd wish. They don't know about us *right now*... maybe. But as soon as they hear the Roman Empire has thunderpowder weapons...and that news will be traveling quickly, it'll be the talk of every caravanserai from Nisibis in Syria to Bactria before long, not to mention merchants trading with India...they will most assuredly know exactly what occurred. We haven't been trying to keep our presence secret in the sense that *other time travelers* would realize what we were...no reason to and many drawbacks if we tried. Until now."

"And they probably bombed Vienna to prevent us...or someone like us...from coming back here," Jeremey said. "We only made it out alive by one *second*..."

That was in English, necessarily.

"Call it one heartbeat...or less than that," he added in Latin.

"Yes, I think that's likely," Artorius said. "And when they hear about the thunderpowder, they'll know they failed."

He turned to Galen: "*We* want to give the world one government to keep the peace. A Rome that truly has *imperium sine fine*."

"*Pax Romana*," Galen said, and sighed. "I will admit we Hellenes never came close to that, whatever our other accomplishments. The Romans fight each other occasionally...and not a hundred years now, since the Year of the Four Emperors! We did it *continually* until we were brought into the Empire, and Greek cities still quarrel in the courts and by intriguing with governors. Alexander's generals and their descendants were the worst of all! If Alexander had lived longer...but he was a reckless man. One who undermined his own health with drink and who courted danger constantly. No surprise he died; he was lucky that he lived past thirty, and he must have had a very strong constitution."

"Yes," Artorius said. "I think these other...travelers in time... have the same idea...but a different idea of where to start. If they succeed, *China* will be the world, not Rome! *Their* version of China, which I assure you would be a very nasty one. Probably with nobody but Chinese in it. Rome welcomes those who take up Roman ways, makes them Romans. Not swiftly but very surely. They would not."

Goddammit! he swore mentally. *We survived the first bit, got our feet under us, we rescued the Tenth Legion when Prince Ballomar brought the Marcomanni across the Danube; that got the Emperor here; we called the Quadi attack on Carnuntum, and Marcus Aurelius believed me when I told him where we really came from. Then the Romans won the Marcomannic War fast and cheap. Everything was set! With what we were going to give the Romans, unifying the world would have been automatic. And not too drastically bloody because... to coin a phrase... resistance would be increasingly... obviously... totally futile. Hell, there wouldn't even have been a global warming problem once industrialization got going! Not if they knew about it in advance, and the world population would probably never have hit eight billion. Now it's all in the chamber pot again. The only good thing is that nuclear war's out of the question for now... and that only applies if we get this settled. Before science and technology get that far. It would take generations, centuries, but if the world's divided into hostile blocs... we know where that ends up.*

He smiled again, also an unpleasant expression—it felt unpleasant from the inside and probably looked that way.

"We had a saying about that, where I came from: Ask the Uyghurs about it, but do it fast if you want an answer."

Galenos frowned. "Uy-gh-urs?"

"A people who lived in the western part of the territory China ruled. They... some of them... didn't look like the Han, and had a different language, religion and so forth."

"Ah," the physician said. "And they were persecuted. But why be quick about it?"

"Because there weren't many of them left, and fewer every year, month, week and day. I think... yes, right now their ancestors... some of their ancestors... would be there. Tocharians, our historians called them, speaking a language related to Latin."

As they spoke they'd been walking down stairs and then along a sloping graveled trail from the terrace that kept the *pars urbana* level. When they were near the edge of the reedbeds on the lakeshore, they could see that half a dozen stakes had been planted in the soft soil, each four inches thick and six feet high.

That had been done at Artorius' direction last week, out to a distance of six hundred yards; there hadn't been any urgency then.

Servants were decking them out when they arrived, then left in a hurried clump as soon as they'd finished. Most of them still thought thunderpowder was supernatural, despite it having been first made here from commonplace ingredients.

Don't want to be around when the spells fly, Artorius thought. *I'm a good magician to them... but still dangerous.*

A legionary shield, twenty pounds of laminated wood and leather and metal rim shaped like a section of the skin of a column, was on a smaller stake in front of each post. The poles themselves bore Roman helmets and *lorica segmentata*, the armor of plate hoops and bands that legionary soldiers and some auxiliaries wore, directly behind each shield as if there were living Roman soldiers there. It was realistically *battered* armor, too, bought secondhand and in need of repair if it had been intended for use again.

Artorius unwrapped the bundle. Galenos looked with interest.

"Ah, like the *stock* you made for the new crossbows. That curved place for the hand, a straight one running from it to brace against the shoulder, and the trigger inside the metal guard."

"They are both copies of something I was familiar with," Artorius said.

The stock from my favorite Kimber Open Range deer rifle, in fact, he thought. *Back in a closet in Boston, which means probably finely divided particulate matter now for a truly weird value of now, but I recall it fondly. And Mary's venison stew with peppers and mushrooms and collard greens, that was* fine *and no mistake.*

That time healed was a cliché, but usually true. He could remember his wife ... his high-school sweetheart who he'd married a month after graduating from West Point—with only a gentle sadness now, not the stab of piercing grief.

Well, there are *the nightmares. But they're getting less frequent. She'd wish me happiness from heaven.*

"Like the cannon!" Galenos exclaimed, peering at the barrel. "Only much smaller!"

Artorius nodded. "This hammer on the side sets it off," he said. "When you pull it back—"

There was a metallic *click* sound as he did, and the once-familiar feel of a spring-loaded mechanism pulled to engage a catch.

Which was oddly nostalgic.

"—it also advances the narrow strip of pewter from this coil below the hammer."

He tapped it with his right index finger.

"There are dimples in it, and little pieces of a compound that burns with a hot flame when it is struck hard and quickly. Forty of them, then you replace the roll; this slanted edge on the underside of the hammer is sharpened and cuts off the last piece of the pewter strip as it strikes. The fire travels down this small tube here and ignites the thunderpowder in the barrel. Which is thirty inches long and about half an inch wide. We're going to use the same system on the cannon soon too, replacing the fuse that has to be lit by hand with a flame. And on the new *siege cannon* and their shells and the business end of the *rockets*."

Galen nodded. "Flame from the Ronsonius won't be necessary anymore," he said, naming the lighter that Artorius had...

Invented, people think. Copied and adapted, really, he thought. *Hence the name!*

"Not for lighting fuses on cannon," Artorius agreed.

But they were a massive improvement on striking sparks with flint and steel, or carrying a clay pot of embers around.

"Soldiers will still want them. A cold, wet bivouac goes much better with a fire! And hunters, and housewives."

He dropped the butt of the weapon to the ground, and ducked his head through a loop that supported a rectangular leather pouch. When he opened it there were three rows of loops, each holding twelve cylinders of paper, and each cylinder fastened in three places with thread.

"These contain the thunderpowder, and the bullet—the projectile, in this paper *cartridge*. The bullet is shaped like a cylinder, with a blunt point on one end and the other hollow so that the gasses from the thunderpowder expand it. These grooves around it hold oil as a lubricant. The hollow base makes it grip spirals cut into the barrel on the inside."

"Why?" the Greek asked.

He was curiosity incarnate, about many matters.

"That makes it much more accurate, like the feathers on an arrow."

Galenos repeated the word *cartridge* several times to himself to memorize it.

"The feathers on arrows are sometimes curved to make it twirl in flight," he said thoughtfully. "The same principle?"

Artorius nodded and bit off the end of the paper and spat it to one side, amid a taste of salt and sulfur.

God bless the docs, he thought, sensing the reassuring strength of his molars.

He and the others had been dosed with the new gene-tailored *Streptococcus mutans* before they left Boston for Vienna; it had just been released for general use. In its natural state that mouth bacteria caused plaque and cavities, in fact most of the problems humans had with their teeth that weren't caused by clubs or brass knucks or ingrown wisdom teeth.

The altered form didn't do any of that... and would supplant the unaltered form virtually every time. He'd had oral swabs applied to the Imperial court, and to everyone on this estate, and a good few others. Galen was doing the same in Rome. And it would spread every time someone who had it kissed anybody... kissed them on the lips, at least. Eventually everyone on earth would get it, and dental problems would do a deep nose dive though they wouldn't go away altogether.

Then he poured the powder down the barrel, reversed the cartridge, shoved it into the muzzle with his thumb and drew an iron rod that normally rested in a tube in the forestock. That had a ball on one end and a slightly flared piece on the other; he used that to tamp the bullet down with two firm strokes. The crumpled paper acted as a wad to hold everything in position.

Then he replaced the ramrod, brought the weapon's butt to his shoulder, looked through the aperture sights, and pulled the trigger. The hammer snapped down...

Crack!

Galenos jumped a little as the rifle spurted smoke, and Artorius let the once-familiar recoil move the muzzle up—that happened after the bullet left the muzzle.

Harder thump than an M7, or even a hunting rifle. Not too bad, though, he thought. *Helps that it's fairly heavy, just under ten pounds.*

He'd used this before, but he'd ridden alone out into the woods to do it.

Three-quarters of a million men had died in the US Civil War in the 1860s, and most of the battle casualties had been inflicted with weapons not quite as good as this one.

Needs must, he thought.

The first of the shields and *loricae* quivered as the shot rang out. Artorius repeated the process five more times, pausing twice to adjust the sights. The whole process took just under two minutes. Then the whole party walked out to the target posts, through the drifting puffs of smoke that the mild breeze bore slowly away.

Galenos' eyebrows went up. There was a neat round hole in the first shield; on the inside was a collar of splinters. And a puncture mark in the lorica as well... front *and* back.

"It strikes hard!" he said.

"This will penetrate any armor a man can carry and move in," Artorius said, patting the weapon he carried in the crook of his left arm. "Any made of metal, or any other substance available in this age. And kill or badly injure the man inside."

Which was why metal armor went out of fashion about the time flintlocks came in, the ex-American thought. *We'll jump straight to the percussion lock here, with this tape primer... which makes it a lot more reliable than a flintlock. One misfire in five hundred or maybe a thousand, as opposed to one in twenty-five.*

With the last post, the helmet lay thrown back on the ground, another of the neat holes in the metal over the brow, right above where the soldier's left eye would have been.

"And it'll penetrate a cataphract's armor too," Artorius added, referring to heavy cavalry in head-to-toe scale and mail and lamellar protection.

"Six hundred yards," the Greek said, looking back. "Thrice the effective range of a bow, and it hits harder."

Well-armored men shed most arrows, even from powerful laminated bowstaves, until the range was well under two hundred yards... at which point the armored attackers weren't more than thirty seconds from skewering your liver with sword or spear. Archery was much more effective against men in cloth or bare skin... but those weren't the ones you had to worry about, usually.

"But slower to shoot... six shots, you made," the Greek said. "A bowman could shoot a dozen shafts in the same time."

Artorius nodded. "It can shoot faster if it's loaded from the breech, about as fast as a bow, but that will take another... year, perhaps two or three. Of this model, Colonia Ferramenta can turn out a hundred or so a week to start with... and will, as soon as my messenger gets there."

Once other, useful things are put aside for now, Gods damn it! Artorius thought. *Useful for something besides killing people!*

"A couple of thousand by this time next year, and increasing numbers after that," he went on aloud. "Plus plenty of ammunition, shaping lead is easy and saltpeter production is adequate now."

After rerouting some major sewers into leaching beds, he thought. *The ones in Rome should come online in the next six months. On the upside, what's left afterward is good fertilizer.*

"And the campaigning season is different in the east," Galenos said. "The winter is best there, in the lowlands of Mesopotamia, at least. There the summer heat can kill you and the rivers flood early in the hot season too. Better in winter for travel from Syria to there, too—that is when it rains, and when fodder grows to pasture work beasts. Outside the absolute deserts of sand and rock, that is."

Artorius nodded; he'd campaigned there himself, up in his home century.

"But there are two more things you should know about this," he said and tapped the weapon again.

At Galenos' raised brows he went on:

"Six hundred yards is about as far as you can aim at an individual man-sized target and hope to hit it unless you're very good and a bit lucky. At massed formations, though, it's effective at up to twice that range. Twelve hundred yards. It will still pierce armor and kill."

The Greek nodded thoughtfully. Nearly all formations armies used here in a pitched battle *were* massed. They had to be, given the weapons used…or that *had* been true until very recently.

Very, very recently.

"And a man can learn to handle it well in…oh, no more than a month, if he's shooting at targets every day. More practice is good, but by then the average soldier will be more than skilled enough to use the weapon well, and keep it clean, which needs hard work. Particularly if someone tells him the range."

He'd designed an aperture sight, placed well back, behind the hammer. That made it much easier to shoot well than the nineteenth-century originals.

"Ah!" Galenos said, visibly startled. "But to be a good *archer* takes many years of practice. You must almost be born at it."

Filipa nodded. "I've been practicing with the bow for years now, and I'm nowhere near as good as Sarukê," she said. "I'm *pretty* good with a sword."

She patted the spatha she'd belted on when they left the house; her tunic was bloused up through the belt in the usual fashion, with the calf-length hem now falling to her knees. Usual for men, at least: women's tunics were long enough to brush the foot for the upper classes, and at least lower-calf to ankle-length for the plebs. That was the main difference between male and female tunics.

"But the bow…no. Not compared to her. *She* started on that when she was about five or six, about the same age as when she started riding a horse."

"What's the cost?" Josephus asked, frowning in thought.

He had a good grasp on logistics, including the limits on what even the Imperial government could afford.

"It will come down as they're produced in numbers. To start with . . . about the price of a legionary's panoply. Armor, helmet, shield and weapons. Eventually a quarter or a tenth of that, about the same as a sword."

"The *previous* cost of a sword?" Josephus asked, and Artorius nodded.

"The ammunition?"

"About three times the cost of an arrow."

"Hmmm . . ."

Colonia Ferramenta was turning swords out at much lower prices now, and the quality had gone up. Artorius went on:

"Much of the skill necessary to make these is built into the machinery, and we've finally built full-scale metalworking lathes and drill presses and milling machines from the models we brought in the baggage. Only a few so far, and very crude by our standards . . . but machines beget machines, and each generation is better than the last."

The merchant nodded in turn, paused for a moment tapping his thumb on his chin while he thought, then spoke:

"That's practical, then. Especially with the new mining revenues. And even with the active campaigning in the north, the total under arms there will be less than the old Rhine and Danube garrisons put together. That will free legions for other tasks without increasing costs too much."

Artorius smiled bleakly at him and clapped him on the shoulder:

"We had a saying: Amateurs talk tactics, dilletantes talk strategy, and real soldiers discuss logistics."

Josephus shrugged. "I've been in fights, but I'm not a soldier. Costs, though . . . costs . . . those I understand well."

"And costs set the limits of the possible, my friend, in war as well as ordinary life," Artorius said, and turned to Jeremey. "Jem, if you were these Chinese time travelers, what would you do over there among the Eastern Han?"

"Get a hold on the Eastern Han emperor," he said promptly.

"That probably won't be hard, he was . . . is . . . a weakling by all the historical accounts," Artorius observed. "Not interested in much but sex and partying—he left government to the eunuchs.

198

S.M. Stirling

They ran it into the ground, selling offices and screwing more taxes out of the commoners. Then there was a mass peasant uprising—the Yellow Turbans. It was all downhill for China after that."

"The peasants won?" Fil asked, interested.

"No, they lost. They always do, pretty much. But the *warlords* the Imperial army there produced won..."

"The way they always do," Jem said, with a grin.

Artorius frowned: "...true enough...and then they promoted themselves to kings."

Jeremey shrugged. "Wouldn't be too hard to get a grip on someone like that. They'll wow him with novelties...new drinks and ways to get high...and medical stuff to help with the consequences. Stomp the stuffing out of some enemies with new weapons, impress the military, then *take work off his hands.* Should have him under their thumbs fairly quick."

Artorius nodded. "Sounds plausible. They'll probably back the Confucian faction, too."

"And then double-cross them?" Jeremey asked.

"Not necessarily. Sort of...undermine would be my guess. Promote interpretations of the analects that they favor."

Jeremey went on: "And then they'll start ramping up industry there...farming, too, probably they brought seeds the way we did, but I suspect they'll have concentrated on making stuff and planted the seeds the next year, except for the fall-sown stuff—that would work if they were packed right. Weren't the Eastern Han about to slag down around now? One of those warring-states phases the Chinese had? The warlords you mentioned?"

"Yes, around the same time as the Roman Empire hit the really, really bad phase of the third-century crisis. Fifty years from now or a few more, the last real Han emperor falls in 220 and they were starting to get warlordism before that. They call what followed the Three Kingdoms. A *lot* of mutual throat slitting plus nomad invasions."

Galenos winced a little. Artorius knew the Americans' descriptions of what the next century brought to the Roman Empire had astonished and horrified him...and Marcus Aurelius even more.

But that *history will not happen now. The problem is that we don't know what will happen...and now less than ever. We have plans...but the enemy, those dirty dogs, will have plans of their own.*

"Yup, but after that? When you learned about us?" Artorius went on aloud.

"Ship arms to the Parthians," the young man from small-town Wisconsin said, again promptly; he'd obviously been anticipating that question.

"Why?" Artorius asked.

Because I'm interested in your reasoning, he added to himself.

Jeremey went on: "They'll be making weapons anyway, same reason we did—to deal with barbarians north of them, like the Huns... I think the Huns are active there now?"

Artorius shook his head. "The Xiongnu *may* have been ancestral to the Huns, but they got overthrown in Mongolia proper about...oh, seventy years ago. Some moved west, pushing other nomads ahead of them in one of those billiard-ball cascades, some settled in Inner Mongolia. Mongolia's run by the..."

He consulted his phone, a once-automatic activity now preceded by a glance around to make sure that nobody local was looking.

"...Xianbei, they're called. Sort of proto-Mongols. Fighting the Han right now and giving them hard trouble...in our original history."

"Well, anyway, the Chinese will give the Emperor stuff to wallop them. And any rebels he gets. And then backing Parthia would tie us...tie Rome...up there while they brew some other devilment."

"Thunderpowder weapons to Parthia?" Galenos said, visibly alarmed.

"Yes," Artorius said. "Quite likely, if we give them the time."

And Galenos' hometown is in Asia Minor. Not really close to the Parthian border...but not all that far away, either. Ditto with General Fronto's family estates, apart from the stuff they have to own in Italy.

There was a regulation about that, requiring senators to invest a percentage of their worth in Italian land. It was intended to keep the price of land there up, among other things.

Aloud he went on:

"That would be logical...if we wait long enough for it to happen. Hmmm. But wouldn't that be risky for them too, Jem, in the long run? Up the cost of expansion, at least."

"Not much, if they don't show them how to *make* the weapons," Jeremey said. "Just give them...or sell them...the end product and ammunition. The early versions, at that, if they're switching to better stuff the way we are. Parthia's not nearly as big or advanced as Rome and they don't have their own set of time travelers, thank Je . . . thank the Gods for that, so they'd probably have the devil's own time—"

In Latin that was *the demons* rather than *the devil*.

"—duplicating things even with examples in their hands."

"Without help from our Chinese fellow exiles," he added with an ironic lift of one light eyebrow, vivid against the outdoors-tan of his face.

Looks more grown-up now than he did when we arrived and a bit less of a wise-ass, Artorius thought. *Well, we each get a day older every day. He's got kids now, too, that changes people—alters their time perspective, if they're smart enough to think in those terms, which he undoubtably was.*

"Which help they wouldn't get," the younger American said.

"You do sneaky good," Artorius said, and Jeremey visibly preened a little. "Yes, that's what they'll likely do as soon as they realize there are time travelers here too . . . plus sending spies and assassins."

"But those would stand out," Filipa said thoughtfully. "I mean, I get odd looks anytime I go to a new place. East Asians are scarce as hen's teeth here and now, not *completely* unknown but near as no matter. It would take them time to find people who could . . . blend in here. Ones they could trust, at least."

Artorius nodded in turn. "We'll have to try and get to Parthia before *they* do."

Fil held up a finger, frowning in thought: "Speaking of Tocharians, China rules the Tarim basin now . . . and didn't the Tocharians look like Europeans?"

"Yes. Central Europeans at that, but they wouldn't speak . . . no, I lie, their city-states had long-distance trade connections, early Silk Road stuff, *some* of them would speak Greek at least. And Indian languages—Buddhism's just getting started in the Tarim now but it's well established in a lot of India and Central Asia. It died out there later, but not for, oh, five . . . maybe eight . . . centuries from now, after the Islamic expansion. Which won't happen now."

The Americans all nodded. The probability of the same someone being born four or five centuries from now was vanishingly small, one of the quantum-chaos butterfly-flapping effects monkeying with history would inevitably have. You were who you were not just because of your parents but because a specific sperm met a specific egg at a specific time and exchanged specific genes. As the ripple effect of alterations spread out, it became vanishingly unlikely that anyone would get that precise genetic cocktail ... which meant that you wouldn't get the same people to *be* parents anyway.

It might take some time to affect, say, New Guinea, but it would eventually and a lot sooner than centuries from now. The Middle East had already been shaken up and probably nobody from the history we learned was being born there right now.

Jeremey frowned. "And if we do get to Parthia first ... maybe they'll try to arm that empire east of the Parthians ... what's it called ... the Kushans, I think, right?"

Galenos nodded. "The nomads who destroyed the Bactrian Greek kingdom," he said ... and sighed again.

The last truly independent state ruled by Greeks, Artorius thought. *The furthest and last of Alexander the Great's offspring.*

Julius/Jeremey pulled out the little black oblong of his phone, after checking that nobody not in on the secret was close enough to see anything. They weren't as useful here as they'd been uptime in the twenty-first, but the milspec portables Fuchs had included in the baggage set up a local network, their AI breaking the phone's codes with contemptuous ease.

Galenos took a deep breath and visibly steeled himself again: like Marcus Aurelius he'd accepted that they weren't magic in the sense he used the term ... but that was a distinction without much of a difference from a second-century point of view. He *had* accepted that they were the equivalent of a messenger system fast as light, a counting board, a well-organized huge library with knowledgeable research assistants moving too fast to see, and numerous other useful things as well.

Paula and Marcus had theirs at the Institute—or rather, she had his *and* hers, because he couldn't remember that they had to be used in secrecy when he was in a brown study. And they had one of the ruggedized military-style laptops and external drives, and a solar-charging unit. They both spent a lot of their time there translating the petabytes of medical knowledge stored in digital form to Latin and Greek and putting it onto paper as a step toward printing it. That had the added advantage of increasing *their* store of medical knowledge as well.

Artorius and Jeremey and Fil did that too, on other technical subjects as well, tedious and irritating as it was—Latin and Greek just didn't have the technical vocabulary and it had to be invented and explained. Part of the correspondence they all exchanged was to make sure that was uniform.

Jeremey's thumb danced over the phone's surface to supplement his verbal commands in English, and then he said in Latin:

"*Sic, ita*—the Kushans—their emperor right now is named Huvishka, and the records say he's a peaceful sort who reigned over a Kushan golden age without major wars. Rules Bactria and Sogdiana and a big, big chunk of northwestern India...including what we called Pakistan. Bet you our Chinese counterparts arrange a tragic accident for him."

Galen looked at him oddly, then chuckled with a sour expression as implication of the phrasing came clear. All the ex-Americans had acquired reputations as wits...entirely unintentionally, simply by repeating translated stock phrases that hadn't been invented yet.

"Another war," Filipa sighed. "Buddha and Jesus singing the same chorus, but I hate wars."

"Yes, and amen to that," Artorius said.

She'd seen combat in the Marcomannic War, not least because Sarukê wouldn't let Artorius go into danger alone, and she wouldn't let her lover do so either. She'd done quite well, saving her partner's life at the risk of her own on one notable occasion. And unlike Sarukê to whom it was just a trade, and one she was good at, she'd detested every minute of it, too.

Jeremey nodded absently; Artorius thought that the only thing *he* disliked about combat was the danger...and he could ignore that when he had to.

And Fil was looking forward to a quiet country life, writing books...translating them, at least...and breeding horses with Sarukê. I think they were thinking about kids, too. Hell, I was looking forward to spending my time mostly with Julia and the kids and doing constructive *projects like the ironworks and canals and better farming gear and machine tools.*

"At least one more war, and probably...I foresee...hard times," Artorius said aloud.

And to himself:

How many times do I have to retire from the Army before it finally sticks, *God dammit?*

⇜ CHAPTER FOURTEEN ⇝

Near Rome
August 25th, 171 CE

The pigs were squealing a thousand yards away, each of the two hundred beasts held upright against the post behind it by a loop of rope under their forelegs, two rows of them. They thrashed and screamed too, and dust rose up under their sharp rear hooves from the wheat stubble. That was short and uniformly cut this year, with medic clover pushing up between the rows of white-blond straw.

This was an Imperial estate, and it had been harvested with cradle scythes months ago, which reached lower than sickles had done. The seed-drill rows and the medic were new as well.

Artorius could smell the pigs too; not absolutely unlike a similar number of humans, but stronger and ranker and more fecal—the hogs were showing what they thought of the whole situation in unmistakable digestive-system terms. They didn't absolutely know they were about to die unpleasantly, but he suspected that *they* suspected it.

That sharp wit...by quadruped standards...was the reason he'd never wanted to raise pigs personally. Despite a childhood fondness for their BBQ'd ribs and one he'd picked up in the service for spiced ground-pork kebabs, Bulgarian style, what they called *kebapche*. He'd introduced both of those here, of course.

He was convinced that pigs were smart enough to usually realize *why* human beings kept them around and fed them. Unlike

203

most edible domestic stock, to whom it was—very briefly—a terrible surprise at the end of what they thought was an enviable life being pampered by friendly if bossy aliens.

That was why swine were dangerous, particularly en masse, too, whether wild or domestic. They mostly did *not* love humanity in general or any individual human in particular, not unless they were raised like pets. And being omnivores they were perfectly prepared to reverse the who-eats-who if they got the chance to sample bipedal monkey meat.

"Proceed, Centurion!" he called, raising his arm.

The commander of the Praetorian Guard cohort raised his, too—the high-ranking spectators were about a hundred yards behind his unit.

His voice was too distant to make out the order he gave, but the *tubae*'s blare carried well as it transmitted the command—which was why the Romans used them and saved verbal commands and sometimes whistles for small-unit management.

The first two ranks of the guardsmen went to one knee, their big curved rectangular scorpion-blazoned shields up and the long metal shanks of their pila bristling in a row of more than two hundred staggered points, with the butts grounded in the dirt beneath the stubble. That would present an impenetrable shield against charging cavalry at hand-to-hand range. Horses would take risks if they were well trained, but they usually wouldn't impale themselves unless blind with panic.

Men will. Sometimes, Artorius thought.

But in the open lowland spaces of the Middle East, Parthian horse archers could lethally harass from quite some distance, about a hundred to two hundred yards in an attritional hit-and-run. Another short, sharp series of notes rang out from the *tubae*, the long straight trumpets, and the *cornu*, the curled ones.

"Load; load in nine times," Artorius murmured to himself in English, sitting his horse beside the Emperor's mount.

That had been the Civil War order for training men with muzzle-loaders, and these weapons were pretty much like a Springfield rifle-musket.

With a few tweaks.

A select half-dozen bigwigs were present too, including Legate Fronto and the newly appointed governor of Transdanubia, Marcus Iallius Bassus. Both were in muscled breastplate, crimson waist sash and pseudo-Attic-style helmets with fore-and-aft crests of crimson-dyed horsehair, the Roman equivalent of dress uniform.

The Emperor's younger son, Verus, was there too. The boy was seven, and *not* in the sort of miniaturized military outfit that had given Gaius Caesar Augustus Germanicus his childhood nickname that had stuck into disastrous adulthood—Caligula, meaning *little boots*.

Verus was in a well-made tunic bloused up through a belt to knee-length, tight leather knee britches, a small cloak, and boots...but the openwork *cothurnus* type usually used by riders around the Middle Sea, not hobnailed military ones.

It was a miniature version of adult dress—of what his father was wearing now, in fact, minus the Imperial diadem. He did look like a smaller version of his father, too, minus forty-odd years; there was also a neat scar behind his left ear.

Which shows we saved his life, Artorius thought.

That scaled-down adult dress was standard for children here most of the time, once past toddlerhood and toilet trained—but apart from the size, it was simply what a gentleman would wear out riding or hunting in the countryside. And there was the *bulla*, a round gold protective amulet worn on a thong around the neck, standard for freeborn male Roman children before puberty and the ceremonial first donning of the *toga virilis*.

Girls wore one shaped like a crescent moon.

The third and fourth ranks of the Guards carried the new rifle-muskets. They also had two ammunition pouches on their *balteus*, one to either side of the buckle, and a twelve-inch socket bayonet on the left opposite their swords. And over the bayonet's scabbard was a buckler secured with a snap-on hitch, round but otherwise more or less like the central boss of a legionary shield with a similar internal handle.

Sort of like a steel soup dish.

They couldn't carry a scutum *and* a rifle-musket, but the buckler was much better than nothing.

Now each right hand went to a pouch, while the rifle went down with the butt between their feet...feet that *were* in *caligae*, though in northern climates closed shoes with hobnails were becoming more popular. The cartridges came to their mouths, and they bit off the end, poured in the powder and then reversed the bullet and rammed it down on the propellant, wadding the

paper above it. Then the rifles came to port arms, held across
their chests, and their right thumbs went to the hammers.

Another set of calls from the trumpets.

The order rang out, and the men obeyed: the muskets pointed
at the sky, and the multiple *clickclickclickclick* sounded as their
thumbs pulled the hammer back and the mechanism advanced
the pewter tape with its evenly spaced dabs of mercury fulminate.

The next command was: "*Iaculamur!*"

The tubae echoed it, in a *new* call that would be spreading
through the Imperial army about now. Two hundred plus rifle-
muskets came level, as eyes peered through the round circle of
the backsight, pushed up on the stepped ramp that supported it.

"First rank... *surculus!*"

More tubae calls, and then a huge:

BAAAANG!

Even at many yards distance the sound of over two hundred
of the rifle-muskets going off in less than a second was loud,
though it wasn't as sharp a crack as the weapons he'd been
raised with. Young Verus had his hands pressed to his ears, and
a delighted smile was on his face as the burnt-sulfur smell came
to them and the wind carried the smoke past them at a tangent.

"Second rank... *surculus!*"

BAAAANG!

The two rows were staggered, and each had the usual Roman
three-foot, standard-order interval between its men. That had
originally been to allow them room for sword-and-shield work
and for rotating the men in the first rank, but it worked well for
this too. The front rank ignored the shots going off a foot and
a half from their ears... which wouldn't do their hearing any
long-term good, but...

*War has casualties. As the way my leg bones ache in cold
weather bears witness, and I don't hear as well as I did, either.*

They had the muskets butt-down again, and were going
through the loading drill as regular as machines.

Artorius lowered his binoculars; the heavy lead slugs were
kicking up dust all around the pigs, blasting sprays of splinters
out of the stakes and plowing into their bodies too. The Emperor
and some of the others had brass-and-leather telescopes to their
eyes, what the Americans had been able to cobble together from
local materials and the invaluable little lens-grinding machine

in Fuchs's baggage. Which they were trying to duplicate, with increasing success now that they had nice clear lead-glass and crown-glass production going. They'd probably get the new ones— they had half a dozen under construction—working about the time something in the original irretrievably broke.

Or I hope *so. Very much hope so.*

They weren't as good as his field glasses . . . but they were a lot better than the Eyeball Mark One, and the second iteration had less blurring and distortion than the first draft of a dozen or so. *Those* had gone down the chain of command when the better models arrived; the artillery had first call on them, followed by the scouts, in Latin the *exploratores*, and then the officers of the line units.

The 'scope was particularly useful for Marcus Aurelius, who was short-sighted. They'd made up some eyeglasses for him too, reading ones and distance models, and he'd been touchingly grateful. Apparently they let the Emperor see better than he had since he was a small child, though they were crude by twenty-first-century standards and heavy to boot.

Still, they're a hell of a lot better than nothing at all, which is what the ruler of a third of the human race had access to before we arrived. We'll make better eventually, too.

The reloading and firing went on until both ranks had fired three times—about six hundred and eighty bullets sent downrange toward the targets.

The Emperor motioned his party forward as the riflemen stood easy, with their weapons by their sides, and the front two ranks came to their feet again. Some of the horses shied a bit as they approached the hogs, who were mostly dead now, or bleeding and convulsing, or making pitiable sounds as they shivered and twitched and drained out.

Marcus Aurelius frowned, and said something to the head of his mounted bodyguards. The troopers rode closer and finished off the beasts with economical lance thrusts in the neck. The Imperial party followed more sedately.

There were muffled cheers from the Praetorians, quickly snapped to silence by their officers, backed up with whacks from the brass balls on the end of staffs of an *optio* or *tesserarius*, or the centurions' vine sticks. The cheers were because the Praetorian cohort would be eating the pigs at a roast-up with plenty of the wildly popular BBQ sauce, since he'd brought several kegs of it south with him.

And Romans mostly love French fries too.

Pork was always popular with Romans—it was the only four-footed beast that they raised specifically for food, unlike sheep and goats and cattle who provided wool and milk for cheese and power for pulling plows and carts. Then meat, but only when they were past other work; lamb and veal and kid goat were luxuries for the rich.

Romans loved ultrastrong tastes and sweet-sour contrasts, so the sauce was a valued extra. Anything with hot peppers, in fact, and they adored tomatoes, and sugar was a revelation to them. He'd yet to meet more than a very few Romans who didn't enjoy Texan-style pit barbeque after they hopped and swore at their first acquaintance with jalapenos.

Homemade versions were already spreading along with the new vegetables, including mind-boggling combinations like French fries with garum on top, the sauce of fermented fish guts that Romans also adored. Large crates of seeds and some experienced gardeners had been sent down for the Imperial estates just outside the City last spring. That had been the fruit of the Villa Lunae's gardens, where they'd planted the up-time sacks Fuchs had bought with his pilfered R&D money. And from others who'd adopted them early when he had enough to distribute to neighbors and friends and his brother-in-law.

If you used most of the output for new seed, growth was by geometric progression, and by now Pannonia was pumping out enough for thousands of acres, with its neighbor provinces catching up fast.

American-style pizza with tomato sauce, onions, cheese and a local sausage equivalent to pepperoni and the new sweet peppers and well-established mushrooms too was just about as popular. There were *tabernas* and street vendors selling it in towns and cities in Pannonia Superior and Inferior now, and in Colonia Ferramenta in Noricum, and he'd heard at least one had started up in Rome too. Besides their inherent tastiness, the new crops and foods had the prestige of Imperial favor.

A decade or two for the new crops to spread, and there would be pizza and BBQ sauce and French fries, hamburgers and polenta and cornbread, from one end of the Middle Sea to the other. Possibly in *vicus* towns just behind the Antonine Wall in Britannia, for that matter, and serving the new forts in freshly conquered Germania.

Potatoes would be even more important in the cold northern lands where untimely rain and rust spores sometimes wiped out the wheat crop.

Spaghetti and marinara sauce here in the south, too, soon enough. People eating better...

When they got close enough for detail work, the deep, narrow stab marks of the lances didn't obscure what had happened to the pigs beforehand. The half-inch puncture marks of the bullets were unmistakable, and so were the exit wounds the size of a child's fist left by the massive soft-lead slugs. Those were speckled with bone shards and strings of fat and connective tissue just visible beneath the welling blood. The minié rounds had less shock on impact than the smaller, high-velocity bullets he'd been used to, but they made up for it by being about five times as heavy.

The wounds are different... but just as brutal.

Some of the swine had been hit in the head; those were the fortunate ones who'd died quickly, as their brains spattered downrange.

Legate Fronto was counting. "I make it... about seven in ten struck," he said. "Half of those killed, half wounded to one degree or another. And armor wouldn't have helped them, of course. It would only slow them down... so strange to think of *armor* being a useless encumbrance!"

He rapped his knuckles on his muscled bronze breastplate as he spoke. It was a marker of rank as well as protection, of course.

"Only if the people you are fighting have these weapons too, sir," Artorius said.

Marcus Iallius Bassus nodded, but added:

"True, Tribune, and so far we are fortunate that our enemies do *not* have them, so that our armor is useful and our opponents' is worthless—we have the best of both worlds. But that will not last forever. Your thunderpowder is not hard to make."

"The *rifles* are difficult to make, though," Artorius said. "We're making them in quantity, but it takes machinery that is hard to make... unless you have our models for the tools to make the tools, and can produce the right qualities of iron and steel cheaply."

Bassus nodded and made a hand gesture, then turned his gaze to Fronto.

"And yes, Marcus, that is the share of hits—"

Roman conversations could be a bit confusing, since there were only about twenty personal names in common use. If you put your head in a tavern door and shouted *Marcus*, every fourth or fifth man would look up.

"—but the troops were calmer than they would be in actual battle. And they knew the range precisely, and the targets weren't moving."

Fronto nodded in turn.

The two men were technically of the same rank—*Legatus Augusti pro praetore*, which meant they could administer provinces where more than one legion was stationed, or command a force of more than one legion themselves. Wise Emperors picked such men very carefully . . . and then worried about it. Fronto was *functionally* higher ranked, though he was polite when dealing with his peers. Roman ranking was less articulated and precise than the system Artorius had experienced in the twenty-first century anyway.

He suspected that was at least partly to keep higher-ranking types competing for the Emperor's favor, but it *was* inconvenient.

"Indeed, Marcus," Fronto said.

The men were friendly rivals, and on first-name terms . . . and both had the praenomen of *Marcus*. He went on:

"But the enemy would be in bigger masses on a real battle-field, and many more ranks deep . . . and they would all be on horseback if it was Parthians in the open field. Horses are bigger than men, and will not face danger as well as brave men with good training and discipline do."

"Depending on how well the *horses* are trained," Bassus noted.

"Yes, but there are limits to that. And what use is a horse archer or cataphract without their steed? Whether it is dead, or wounded, or simply frightened into bolting?"

"*Ita*," Bassus said, agreeing but slightly reluctantly. "These weapons would be useful anywhere, but more so in open country like the eastern frontier with Parthia. Or the steppes north of the Black Sea, of course, but we're not campaigning there. Not yet. Not for . . . oh, ten years or so, at best."

"Just so," Fronto replied. "By the time we *are* campaigning there, we won't be short of them. But for now . . . even many of the mountains and uplands there in Parthia and the border country are open and bare."

Artorius grinned to himself behind a grave front; that was

a grudging admission by Bassus that giving the forces in the east priority for the rifles was a good idea. Bassus was governor of Transdanubia now, promoted from Pannonia Superior to the greater challenges and rewards of a bigger, newly conquered province where everything had to be built from scratch.

His family originally came from what the Americans thought of as western Switzerland, whereas Fronto's was from Asia Minor, and both had most but not all their land in those locations—since senators were legally required to own at least some land in Italy. Since they were both of senatorial rank, such origins mattered little to most Romans; the upper aristocracy was a world of its own, unlike *equites* who were often deeply rooted in a particular place.

That Transdanubian governorship was *particularly* rewarding since it contained massive new mines of precious metals. A little discreet skimming wasn't really considered *corruption* by Roman standards. Particularly not when you just used insider knowledge to make investments.

Calling that actual *dishonesty* would produce nothing but odd looks at the lunatic, or an assumption of bitter envy.

He was also in line to succeed Fronto as commander in the north, in charge of subduing the little that was left of independent Germania. He'd have more than enough troops given the widespread demoralization among the natives there at Rome's newfound supernatural-seeming weapons. And the legions and auxiliaries under his command would have plenty of *carroballistae* throwing Jove's Balls, and quite a few twelve-pounder cannon, and lots and lots of grenades... but not the rifle-muskets, not yet.

There would be glory and reward for extinguishing the last remnants of the independent Barbaricum... but probably not as much as the war in the east. Fighting savages wasn't as rewarding as conquering civilized lands with great cities.

So for now the rifles would be reserved for the expeditionary force sent against Parthia. The Emperor would be in overall charge of it and the campaign, with Fronto as his second, which meant he'd be its commander under Marcus Aurelius' overall supervision. Marcus Aurelius' co-Emperor and adoptive brother, Verus, was a nonentity, but would be moderately useful here in Rome, presiding over ceremonies... and reminding people that Marcus Aurelius was Emperor and very, very popular... and well liked and respected by the Army, to start with.

Fronto should *be trustworthy, and he's smart; he knows how popular the Emperor is with the Army too... and the Senate and the Equestrian Order... and the common people, for that matter. He's not as smart as the Emperor, but right up there. Marcus Aurelius thinks so, at least, and he's a good judge... and he also thinks that Fronto doesn't* want *to be Emperor himself, he prefers being a general. Which pays well here... if you win. Lots of booty, land, and slaves. And there hasn't been a civil war in the Empire for a long, long time—not since Vespasian and the Year of the Four Emperors, really; his second son Domitian went bad and was assassinated, but Nerva followed him peacefully. Three generations of peace... long may it last!*

Paranoia was a standard byproduct of Roman court politics at this level, but Marcus Aurelius had told him you had to keep in mind that *suspecting* everybody was just as self-destructive as *trusting* everybody. If you did that, you ended up with nobody at all actually *being* trustworthy, if only in self-defense against your mad suspicions.

That was a death spiral that had only one probable end, under an assassin's knife, or being strangled in your bath, or other ends even more unpleasant. As several previous imperial reigns bore witness, though not recently—the Antonine dynasty had been lucky that way. Mainly because they'd lacked sons until now, and had adopted near or distant relatives instead.

The new *Legio IV Italica* would be coming with them; it hadn't taken the field yet, but it was ready to. The Praetorians had gotten the first shipments of the rifles. *IV Italica* would come next, with Praetorians on detached duty teaching their on-staff instructors.

The newly reequipped legion would train others further east in turn as the supply of the rifles grew. Also accompanying them would be the Ninth Claudian legion, formerly stationed at Durostorum on the lower Danube, which had been part of the Army that had beaten the Marcomanni and Quadi and their allies in the Great Barbarian Conspiracy. Durostorum was well behind the frontier now, and no longer needed troops beyond some auxiliary cavalry to remind the locals in the newly acquired territories who'd won and to patrol against bandits.

After their trip to Parthia, the Ninth Claudian would probably be moving to... and building themselves... a new base a few hundred miles north and east on the west bank of the Tyras river, what he thought of as the Dniester. Complete with its massive train of camp followers, tavern keepers, artisans and their families, and the unofficial wives and children of the legionnaires. That train of hangers-on and veterans made legionary bases spreading centers of *Romanitas* and civilization in general...

And compared to sword work or even how to throw a pilum well, rifles are simple *to learn. A month or two and you're nearly as good as you're usually going to get, at least for standing or kneeling in ranks and doing volley fire... and they already know how to do unit maneuvers, mastering a few new ones won't bother them.*

They'd have four thousand stand or better of the rifles by the time they left for the east, enough to equip half the men in two legions, with a couple of hundred more following along every week by then. Romans knew about mass production and already used it for things like ceramics, and they'd taken to interchangeable parts like ducks to water once they had a supply of accurate measuring gauges.

Roman pragmatism, he thought. *They're just good at being practical, and they mostly don't give a damn where an idea comes from if it works in battle or makes them money or makes life easier.*

Cross-training would have the men ready when the weapons arrived, and the same would apply as other legions were reequipped. The eastern legions weren't usually regarded as a match for the northern and western ones... but they'd had years of hard campaigning in the *last* Parthian War to sharpen their edge and polish them up just recently. Roman soldiers served twenty-five year enlistments, which was a big help in sustaining institutional memory. Centurions were mostly lifers, too, and all the camp prefects—in charge of training, among other things—were senior centurions themselves.

"These are *wonderful*, Tribune Artorius!" young Verus said, turning to him with his face glowing. "These rifles are like... like each man can throw little thunderbolts!"

And I was so *tempted to name them "boomsticks,"* Artorius thought, smiling at the thought of an old movie watched on a laptop during a deployment.

"Why do you think they are wonderful, young Caesar?" he said aloud; that was the boy's formal rank now.

Meaning, heir apparent, he thought. *Commodus is too, unfortunately, but give Marcus Aurelius an extra twenty years and his elder son may very well party himself to death first. Or get drowned in his bath by a frustrated boyfriend, or poisoned by a courtesan.*

"Why...why, they can reach much further than a bow."

"Yes, they can, young Caesar," he said, nodding.

"And didn't you say, Tribune Artorius, that they are easier to learn to use than a bow?"

"Much easier," Artorius agreed. "You can become useful with one in only a month, given good instructors, and a good shot in two or three. And master how to care for the weapon as well."

The Roman name for instructors was *doctores*, and they had plenty of them; military ones were *campidoctores*, "instructors of the camp." Putting *them* through the rifle training first had been a major force multiplier. Plus Roman career military men were usually brutally straightforward about using anything that demonstrably worked. Much of their equipment had been copied from one enemy or another anyway, and they knew it...which was why their short sword was called the *Spanish* short sword, and their standard helmet the *Gallic* variety...and before the Americans arrived, their four-horn saddle had been of Celtic origin too.

Not great at inventing things themselves, but at using them... then tweaking them...then making them in masses...yeah, first-rate.

Verus frowned, obviously thinking hard. "And...and the Parthians are very good archers, everyone says," he said. "But that won't matter as much when our men have these? Especially as they can pierce any armor from beyond the longest bowshot!"

"Yes," Artorius said. "They are slower to load...for now... but the greater range makes up for that, and they can pierce armor at five or six times the maximum range of a bow. You see clearly, young sir."

Verus waved a fist in the air.

"So we will *crush* them!" he said enthusiastically.

"Perhaps," Artorius said, grinning at the boy's enthusiasm. "We can prepare, but the Goddess Fortuna's wheel also plays a role in all war. Now, young Caesar, why would it be good that we crush them?"

"Well...well, the glory!" Verus frowned. "And, and Rome should rule everywhere! My father is a *good* Emperor!"

Marcus Aurelius spoke, with a slight smile, more a matter of eyes than lips, and a quick friendly glance at Artorius. He was taking extra care with Verus these days, and was often happy with the results.

"Yes, my son, Rome should rule every land and all the human race, should have *imperium sine fine*, that is true. But *why* must Rome rule? Not every Emperor is good, remember..."

Despotism tempered by assassination, Artorius thought. *That's a long-term Roman problem. You get a pass if you're a good Emperor...but not everyone has the capacity.*

"...though we have been lucky the last four reigns before myself and your namesake my brother and co-Emperor."

The boy gave him an astonished glance; he'd obviously never questioned that Rome should have *imperium sine fine*, which meant rule without limits in time or space. At least since he'd been old enough to realize that Rome didn't *already* rule the whole world. From a child's view on the Palatine Hill, it probably looked as if it already did for quite some time after toddlerhood.

"But Father..."

Then he visibly frowned and concentrated. "To spread the *Pax Romana* everywhere, Father."

"Yes, my son, that *is* why," the Emperor said. "And it is good...*very* good...that you see this clearly."

Verus glowed. Marcus Aurelius was sparing with praise, and it meant something when he bestowed it. The Emperor went on:

"In Rome's domains, peace rules, the Roman peace, and Roman law. Men prosper and live without fear of their neighbors beyond ordinary crime. Outside Rome's empire, there is only war and the law of the sword. We wage war to bring peace, and to make all men brothers. Brothers in *Romanitas*."

"There isn't always peace with brothers, my father," Verus said.

With the hint of a frown and a pouting lower lip; he and Commodus didn't get on very well, and that was getting worse as he got older and wasn't just an annoying brat anymore. To Roman eyes, provisional adulthood started considerably earlier than in Artorius' home century; you put on the *toga virilis* at puberty, pretty much. Verus would be there in less than a decade. You weren't *fully* adult until you married, and for upper-class men that wasn't until you turned thirty or so, as opposed to the late teens for women.

The past is another country; they do things differently here. And Verus didn't get older, in the original history. In this one he'll live longer...already has, a bit. Let's see what we can make of that, Artorius mused. *He seems a smart enough kid, and basically good-hearted. That's not something you can make happen, though you can scupper it—there's a random element. Bad you can produce, good requires some luck.*

Marcus Aurelius laughed at his child's words.

"Yes! That is truth! Well, my son, that is where the *law* comes in..."

Marcus Aurelius settled into his chair with a sigh, and signaled the others to sit as well; Artorius, the Praetorian Prefect, Sextus Cornelius Repentinus, and the *Princeps peregrinorum*, the head of the *Frumentarii*, the Imperial secret service. This was a smaller room, looking out from the second story on a colonnade and the gardens and fountains in the courtyard below. The guardsmen were outside the door, though that had taken a direct command from the Emperor.

The spymaster was a nondescript man, fit but not someone you'd notice if you passed him on the street, and he'd started as one of the *Frumentarii* agents himself. He also preferred that nobody addressed him by his name...

Now he produced an aureus and dropped it on the marble of the tabletop with a clink. Marcus Aurelius looked at it with a sigh.

"There is no question but that someone *in Rome* paid the Germans who attacked Tribune Artorius?" he said.

"Yes, sir," the head of the secret service said. "There are plenty of Germanii who'd like to kill the Tribune—"

His voice was clinically detached, and he glanced at Artorius. The ex-American nodded soberly back at him. You had to decouple your emotions...even when someone was trying to kill you... or you couldn't think clearly. The other man's brows rose a little, and there was respect in his voice as he went on:

"But the new milled-edge coins are currently produced only by the Imperial mint here in Rome, and few of them are yet seen outside the City. That will change when the mint in Carnuntum starts producing from the yield of the new mines in the recently annexed provinces, but it is true for now."

If you just said *the City* everyone knew you meant Rome itself.

"None are in circulation in Pannonia, to date," the spymaster went on. "Someone must have taken a bag of money northward to hire the assassins—to equip them, pay them, transport them to the site of the ambush Tribune Artorius reported in his letter. And probably to give to their families, so that they wouldn't worry about them."

"Careless," Artorius said. "If they hadn't included that coin, we would have no one to suspect. Or rather, far too many to suspect any one person."

"They probably expected the ambush to succeed," the spymaster said.

"Yes, but you should always take possible failure into account," Artorius said. "Particularly when it comes to keeping secrets. A tactical failure can become a strategic disaster if you don't."

"Very true, Tribune," the spymaster said. He turned to the Emperor:

"There is no doubt that someone in Rome...someone wealthy, probably an *eques* or even a senator...is behind this, sir."

Marcus Aurelius frowned. "But why? Tribune Artorius is a great benefactor of Rome! The Senate is overjoyed at our victories!"

Repentinus spoke, after exchanging a glance with his subordinate:

"A *large majority* are overjoyed, sir," he said. "That is not the same thing as the Senate as a whole. The victories and the accession of territory...and the *new things*...have upset long-standing balances of power and wealth. There will be those who are injured, or feel that they *will* be injured, or who are just affronted that they must consider the *new things*..."

The Emperor shook his head and sighed. "I would be surprised, if only I had not had experience with the..."

His brows slanted downward in a frown, and he held up a hand for half a minute; everyone else in the room fell silent.

"As a matter of fact, several senators have complained to me in very much those terms," he said thoughtfully.

And Marcus Aurelius is an Emperor it's safe to complain to, Artorius thought. *He may not do anything if he disagrees with you after considering the matter, but he won't have you killed because you did.*

The spymaster reached into a pocket—an innovation—and pulled out a pad of paper, thin board covers joined at the top with a coil of bronze wire that pierced the wood and the pages within... another innovation. He produced a third, a wooden pencil.

"Could you give me their names, sir?" he asked.

Marcus Aurelius did, but then held up his hand again before he spoke:

"This must be investigated, but with discretion. No arrests without my specific authorization, and for that we must have significant evidence."

Repentinus sighed, and so did the head of the *Frumentarii*. "Sir," he said. "A few arrests...some, ah, strict questioning..."

"No."

Marcus Aurelius voice was flat.

"That is final, understood?"

The spymaster sighed. "Understood, sir. I will set agents to tracing the movements...conversations...and whether any clients of the men you named have suddenly departed for Pannonia this year. Or sent agents of theirs."

"It would have to be a very *trusted* client," Artorius said thoughtfully.

"Not to turn informer? Most certainly!" the spymaster said, nodding to him.

"And therefore not a slave or freedman, probably," Repentinus went on. "And therefore more conspicuous in his movements. Hopefully."

"I will leave the investigation in your capable hands," the Emperor said. "Be swift, but careful. Inform me as soon as you have definite evidence, a full report. Discretion...will be necessary then, too."

The dark-faced head of the Praetorians exchanged another look with his subordinate. The *Frumentarii* occasionally arranged accidents...

"In the meantime, the war with Parthia will occupy me. Proceed with speed, but with care. Is that understood?"

Artorius smiled thinly. "I think it will take time...and effort...for whoever is behind—"

He pointed to the coin.

"To...ah, arrange any more attacks. Particularly in the east."

"Yes, Tribune," Repentinus said, and his subordinate nodded too. "But keep your bodyguards about you here in Rome. And on our way eastward!"

Marcus Aurelius nodded. "In fact, you should proceed to Ostia immediately," he said. "You can say it is to oversee the *Renewal*, the new ship. Ostia is smaller than Rome and more regular—fewer dens of iniquity where knives may be hired."

"Well, it also has more sailors in need of money," the spymaster said. "But fewer in total than Rome's desperados, yes, sir."

Artorius nodded. "I'll go at once, sir," he said...

Stoically, he thought ironically, and knew there was sympathy in the ruler's brown eyes.

The philosophy he and the Emperor shared didn't make that sort of sacrifice feel any better, just equipped you to deal with the emotions...if you worked at it.

Damn! More time away from home and Julia and the kids!

The head of the *Frumentarii* lifted the doorknocker on the portal of the mansion and rapped sharply twice.

Very prosperous, for a merchant, he thought.

It was fairly plain...but then, many wealthy men preferred not to flaunt their riches on the exterior of their houses, especially if they came from outside the magic circle of established families. Yet property this close to the Esquiline Hill was never cheap—for one thing, it was within easy walking or litter-bearer distance of the Gardens of Maecenas, and the Baths of Trajan. It smelled better than most districts in the central city, too, because big mansions were usually connected to the sewers, officially or unofficially.

"Wait here," he said to the two men accompanying him.

It was an hour past midnight, and the noise of the City had sunk to a background clatter—wheeled traffic wasn't allowed in most of the daytime, so heavy deliveries were made at night. That was safe enough, but you didn't go out after dark in Rome alone and on foot and without an escort, not if you looked like you were worth robbing.

It *might* have been safe hereabouts, because the *vigiles* patrolled much more in affluent neighborhoods...but possibly not, and it would, oddly enough, be more conspicuous than traveling with a group. His escorts weren't carrying swords—that was illegal for ordinary civilians, and still very conspicuous if you had an exemption. They did have long knives and walking sticks that could double as clubs. He wasn't wearing his toga, either: that was an announcement you were affluent and on your way to or from a party at this hour.

The two men wrapped their dark hooded cloaks closer about themselves and leaned against the stucco on either side of the polished oak and iron of the entrance. That...and their trained stillness...made them much harder to notice and very, very difficult to actually identify. Anyone who *did* notice them would also notice their height, muscles and the smooth way they moved, and avoid them unless very drunk. With a perfectly accurate impression that there were long daggers and coshes filled with wet sand under their clothes.

A little slot in the door opened, and then the light of a lantern—one of the new style with a glass chimney—shone out.

"This way, sir, please," the young man carrying it said as he opened the door.

The spymaster noted absently that he had a slightly eastern look—he might have been a Syrian or Greek, and both were numerous in Rome. Or just someone from Neapolis or the other southern Italian cities. He also noticed that the usual cubicle for the household night watchman was empty.

The young man led the way through the darkened house, through a garden courtyard with a fountain, and to a room where he knocked three times.

"Enter," a man's voice said.

It was an *older* man's voice, though he also sounded as if he still had most of his teeth, and with a slight sibilant accent. Someone who'd spoken Greek as a first language, he judged, and probably Syrian Greek at that. Which accorded with the information he'd gathered when the merchant first sent him a message. The man was a Jew, but nevertheless very well connected.

The young guide closed the door, standing inside it for a moment while he put the lantern on a ledge. Then he bowed and conducted the spymaster to a chair before a desk; the man behind it rose and bowed as well. He also took off a pair of *spectacula*, as the new...very new and so far very expensive...corrective lenses in a frame were called.

The spymaster returned the bow with a polite inclination of his head, and seated himself on the chair that stood alone on an eastern carpet, over a mosaic of abstract patterns. The light from behind him brought out the rugged features of the man behind the table with its neat stacks of documents and its counting board and new-style ruled paper book for accounts.

"Domine Stephanus," he said politely as he seated himself.

"Lord," the Jewish merchant said in return, sitting in his turn. "Will you take wine with me?"

"That would be most welcome," the head of the *Frumentarii* said.

The young man slid forward noiselessly to pour for them both, and then stood beside the table.

Not a slave or servant, though, the spymaster thought. *A relative, then... which is good. This Stephanus has some idea of how to keep a secret.*

The wine was an excellent white, though not Falernian, and watered around three to one. The Roman intelligence officer glanced his way as he took a sweet pastry and nibbled at it; food and drink made him a guest. Most Jews took that very seriously indeed... though not all, of course. In his experience they tended to be a clever lot, with fewer actual dullards than most, but with the same variation in morals as any other tribe in a somewhat different pattern.

And when they make mistakes, their cleverness can trip them up, he thought.

"This is my grand-nephew Simonides," Stephanus said. "He is very trustworthy... and has played a part in acquiring the knowledge you seek."

"Ah. You have the thanks of the Praetorians... and the *Frumentarii*... and I think the Emperor, when he is informed... for that."

The older Jew inclined his head in turn; he looked to be in his early sixties, but in sound health and with a tan that spoke of his recent travels.

Now he opened a box, and brought out a coin—a gold aureus that the Roman recognized as one from the new stamping machinery at the mint.

"Very similar to the one Artorius discovered in the pouch of the Germans who were hired to kill him in Pannonia."

"*Baruch HaShem* that he was spared," the older man said. "He is... very important. And we had heard of the coin from him."

"Indeed," the spymaster said. "He is important. Besides the Emperor, in some ways the most important man in the Empire."

The younger man spoke: "This coin was *probably*—"

Stephanus glanced his way, and the Roman nodded acknowledgment of the uncertainty.

"—probably, I say, identical to those I made as part of a payment...down payment, you understand? Earnest money?"

The Roman nodded. Even large dealings usually involved *some* cash.

"On a large consignment of linen rags."

Stephanus put in: "Which my grand-nephew purchased for his papermaking plant."

"Ahhhh," the head of the *Frumentarii* said. "And since he sells much of the output to the Imperial government, the new stamped coins from the mint would be part of *his* payments."

"Yes, indeed," Stephanus said respectfully, giving him a considering look. "Simonides, explain further."

"The linen rags are delivered in bundles," the younger man said. "And usually in small lots, brought into the gate of the factory by ragpickers. But this spring, an *eques* delivered a much, much larger shipment...nearly a ton...from Neapolis. We have begun to attract the material from that far away and since it's relatively light, it will bear the cost of road transport."

The spymaster nodded silently; the cost of shipping was something he met often in his trade.

The young Jew went on: "He requested a substantial down payment in coin, and I obliged him—the price was reasonable, considering the bulk and the quality, and I'm trying to build up a reserve and having some difficulty doing so—demand outruns supply for paper, so far. I had just received some of the new coin, my first, and thus I paid him in it."

The Roman leaned forward. "An *eques*?" he said.

"One with estates in Campania, some near to Neapolis," the young man said, his voice carefully neutral. "By the name of Marcus Bruttius Rusticus; that was the name he gave, and I checked with correspondents in the area and it was the truth. He made the deal in person, not through a freedman acting as his agent, which I thought odd."

The spymaster nodded. It was. Not as odd as, say, a senator doing so, but unusual. The Jew went on:

"I remarked that a letter of credit would be more convenient for both of us, and he laughed and said that he would be dealing with ignorant, illiterate barbarians, who wouldn't have any use for such except to wipe their arse with it. I thought that odd...

a landowner in Campania dealing with savages? Of whom I have experience, through staying with relatives in Pannonia."

"Josephus ben Matthias," the spymaster said...and attracted startled glances from both men. "You were his...would *apprentice* be the word? For some years."

Their well-concealed surprise was not least because he used the style they'd have done among themselves for the name. Rather than the Roman-style *tria nomina* on his certificate of citizenship.

Simonides nodded: "That is so—I was resident in Pannonia for some time, as you say staying with my uncle Josephus ben Matthias. So I was involved in dealing with the *new things* from the beginning."

"Marcus Bruttius Rusticus," the Roman said. "Yes, I am familiar with his name."

A client of Senator Lucius Funisulanus Firmus, he thought; it went through him with a jolt. *Who complains often of the* new things, *denouncing them as innovations contrary to the ways of the ancestors...my, how some men let their tongues wag! A rope about their own necks, sometimes.*

"You will understand," Stephanus said. "There is an element of conjecture in this."

The intelligence officer nodded. "There always is. But investigation will show whether that is a coincidence...or not. My thanks and my gratitude to you, *Domine* Stephanus. And to you, excellent Simonides. This simplifies my work considerably, and I owe you a favor."

"I am a Roman citizen, as is my grand-nephew," the merchant said. "That carries duties as well as privileges."

"You are to be commended, and you show that your grant of citizenship was well deserved; that is an example of antique virtue," the spymaster said politely.

The Roman rose, and left after a further exchange of courtesies...

Once outside in the darkness he bared his teeth in something between a smile and a snarl. He could *feel* that this thread was connected to his target. The Praetorian Prefect didn't like Artorius much...but he respected his wits, and recognized his importance to the Empire.

The spymaster shared both sentiments.

❧ CHAPTER FIFTEEN ❧

Leaving Ostia
Port of Rome
Aboard Imperial Roman Navy ship Renovatio
October 1st, 171 CE

"Impressive!" Mark Findlemann said.

The imperial flotilla was leaving from what the Romans called the Portus Urbis Romae in the bright light of early morning, with a cool wind blowing from the northeast.

His wife Paula Atkins... or Paula Triaria Atcintia if you wanted to get technical and Roman... snorted quietly beside him.

Portus was a huge collection of engineering works just north of the mouth of the Tiber river and the old river-port city of Ostia, aimed at providing safe anchorage for the immense fleet of merchantmen that served the needs of what Romans often simply called the City.

Massive even by our standards, Mark thought.

Rome was sixteen miles to the east as the crow flew... much longer by river barge... and the grain for every loaf its million-strong population ate came through these harbor works. So did most of the olive oil they dipped it in; there was an entire hill in Rome, hundreds of feet high, made up of smashed oil amphorae from southern Hispania.

And the warehouses here were also stuffed with *pickled* olives from all over the Middle Sea, jugs of garum—fermented fish sauce—jugs and barrels of wine from a similarly broad range of origins, of salt fish, salt pork, dried sausages in oil, cloth ranging from ordinary wool and linen to extraordinarily expensive silk and cotton, jugs of honey, cakes of dyestuffs, figs preserved *in* jugs of honey, dried fruit of a dozen kinds, ton after ton of raisins, sawn planks and raw timber, bar iron, brass slabs, exotic hardwood timbers, decorated pottery, ornamental Egyptian porphyry and marble... And on and on, down to colorful Middle Eastern rugs, which here and now had more figures in them than in his native era.

Right now it was buzzing like an overset beehive, as the Imperial flotilla—carrying the Emperor, hangers-on, civil servants...

If there's a difference, he thought.

...cohorts of Praetorian guardsmen, legionnaires, auxiliaries and supplies prepared to depart in everything from lean Liburnian patrol galleys with two banks of oars to ordinary tubby Roman merchantmen... and this ship and her sister the *Imperium Romanum*, built in Tergeste in Istria at the head of the Adriatic.

And when we're gone the regular port bureaucrats will weep for joy and sacrifice to the Gods, Mark thought.

Cranes creaked as they swung netfuls to and fro; files of laborers trotted up and down gangplanks with loads on their backs in sacks or amphorae or crates... or now, occasionally pushed heaped wheelbarrows. Harried centurions and bureaucrats and clerks waved—paper, now, the city of Rome was actually exporting paper—documents in the air and screamed commands, insults and combinations of the two and kicked lower-ranking people up the backside or hit them with sticks...

Gulls in vast flocks flew overhead... marking everything beneath with their acidic white dung, along with flocks of pigeons doing likewise. Both occasionally breaking into panicked, squawking flight in all directions from their usual perches on eaves or docks or brightly painted marble statues or bronze ones with eerie inset glass eyes as an eagle or hawk cruised by and eyed them. The ship sheds—sloping ramps roofed over by arched brick for war galleys—were all vacant, having launched their vessels as part of the escort flotilla.

So was the brand-new mitre-gated drydock where the *Renovatio* had been built, launched and fitted out three months ago.

"Impressive," Mark said again; in English this time.

"Smelly," his wife Paula commented.

Deliberately *un*impressed and shifting their three-year-old daughter—also named Paula—to her other hip. She was dressed in what Romans would regard as respectable lower-upper class garb; a long-sleeved yellow tunic that came down to her instep, a *stola* over it—fine white wool, secured over the shoulders by straps—and a wrapped, embroidered cloak. Her feet bore tooled-leather sandals.

"Well, yeah," Mark said.

Absently patting the child on the head and getting a gap-toothed beaming smile and...

"*Tata!*" which was Latin for daddy.

...in return, before she returned to her fascinated observation of the crowds and buildings and ships.

The air was full of port smells, starting with pine pitch and tar and cut wood. And from there on to everything from spilled and spoiled wine to the contents of chamber pots, though the city sewers emptied elsewhere, to unidentified general decay and the dung of horses, mules and oxen that hauled carts through the streets and barges along the in-city canals.

Not to mention bleating herds of sheep and goats, also being shepherded up gangplanks to deck corrals where they'd await their unpleasant fate on the trip to Syria. They were physically expressing what they thought of the whole process. Squawking chickens were carried on likewise, head down with their feet trussed on either side of a pole, or in baskets.

"But impressive! And less smelly than it was when all Rome's sewage went straight into the Tiber."

He deliberately didn't look out westward at the distant lines of waves breaking against the broad breakwaters of the outer port.

Fortunately the spray was mostly hidden by the long rows of arcaded buildings *on* the breakwater. His stomach twinged in dreadful anticipation every time he *did* glance that way.

"Think of the underwater concrete!" Mark said. "We didn't figure out how that worked until the late twentieth. And look—"

He waved an arm. The seventy-odd acres of the octagonal inner harbor Trajan had built were ringed by massive four-story warehouses of mass concrete and stone rubble faced with brick. Each of the eight sides was about a thousand feet long. The warehouses reminded him of the Boston Public Library...which had been modelled on them.

Interspersed among them were offices and temples resplendent with colored marble, gilt Corinthian capitals on the tops of the shining white columns, red (or colored) roof tile and brightly painted stucco—there was something that was officially an Imperial palace, too, at the northwestern corner, with its bright colors and long colonnade. It was stuffed with administrators, mostly, though Emperors did sleep there when they were in Ostia.

More of that showed over the roofs, the huge city colosseum, the bathhouses—you could see only a few of the biggest of the forty-odd that served the population of a hundred thousand or so—and *insulae*, apartment blocks... mostly rather better than their equivalents upriver.

Though you *couldn't* see the lively street life of dock wallopers and off-duty sailors and craftsmen, street-food vendors and the corner *taberna*-restaurant-bars with their cheerfully obscene graffiti and the farmers' markets selling veggies and fruits and the shipping firm offices with *Hello, profit, walk right in!* in mosaic at their front doors, and...

Outside was the Claudian harbor, a bit older and enormous—more than eight hundred acres enclosed by two great breakwaters to north and south, also topped with buildings... and at the western entrance the giant stepped lighthouse tower, the *pharos*, on an artificial island in the middle.

A pillar of smoke rose from it now; at night, there would be the lights of fires. The project to replace the open wood fires with banks of kerosene lanterns and the new silvered-glass mirrors was underway.

More than six hundred ships were at anchor in rows out there, mostly to get them out of the way of the hundred-odd ships bearing the flotilla. Although fifty or sixty were yet more supply ships, waiting to leave.

"Think of the engineering!" he said.

"Think of the slaves who did the work," she replied dryly as she tossed back the golden silk bandana she wore around her close-cropped wiry hair; it fell to her shoulders in a vaguely Egyptian-looking way. Fine-tooth-combing the way the rest of them did against intrusive insect life wasn't practical for her, since he estimated that she was about ninety percent West African by ancestry and her hair was tightly curled.

"And what they got for it," she added.

"Not much, agreed," he said. "Still, without it Rome would starve."

"A city of imperialist parasites," she grumbled.

"*What has Rome ever done for us?*" he replied, grinning. "*All right, but apart from the sanitation, the medicine, education, wine, public order, irrigation, roads, a fresh water system, and public health, what have the Romans ever done for us?*"

There was an almost audible pause as she caught the reference and groaned quietly.

A rising cheer came from the crowds landward. Massed trumpets sounded, high and shrill in unison with an eerie wailing, and the stamp of hobnailed sandal-boots on paving stones beneath it. He peered gratefully in that direction.

Marcus Aurelius was—of course—on horseback, with a number of mounted men around him. His Imperial Horse Guards, of course: and a number of bigwigs...including Tribune Artorius.

He suppressed an impulse to wave; *gravitas* forbade.

Also around him were several centuries of Praetorians, this cohort now uniformly equipped with rifles, which attracted awed glances from the bystanders. Their bayonets gleamed and moved in a uniform ripple, behind the flapping standard of crimson silk hanging from a crossbar and topped by a golden spread-winged eagle with its claws on the silver thunderbolts of *Jupiter Optimus Maximus*.

On their armor and the cheekpieces of their helmets was the rather sinister-looking Scorpion blazon of the Imperial Guard.

There was a golden wreath embroidered on the silk of the banner, with the letters SPQR inside it, for *Senatus Populusque Romanus*, the Senate and People of Rome.

"I still think the Prof should have named the rifles *boomsticks*," he murmured. "He told me he was really tempted."

"Oh, God, not *more* ancient movies!" she muttered back at him. "At least he had the excuse of filling time while he waited to be deployed when he was in the Army."

"Well, he read books too...In the original languages, even then."

"There are limits to the number of times you can read the *Meditations* or *Anabasis*."

"No limits on how often you can rupture yourself watching *Life Of Brian*, though."

"A joke isn't as funny the second time," Paula observed.

"It *isn't?*" Mark said, and they stared at each other in momentary incomprehension.

The *Renovatio* and the *Imperium Romanum* were moored with their port flanks against the pier bumpers. Their near-identical and deeply alien appearance was attracting odd looks from every mariner, and strutting pride from their officers and crews.

Both were nine hundred tons displacement, toy tiny by twenty-first-century commercial standards, much bigger than average but not outlandishly *huge* by those of Antonine Rome. There were ships a bit bigger hauling grain from Alexandria-in-Egypt and oil from southern Hispania and wine from North Africa.

Professor Fuchs's capacious baggage had included plans and models of various types of sailing craft. The *ultimate* model for these two had been a tea clipper, the *Cutty Sark*, but with less extreme lines and simplified rigging.

And Germania will be exporting lots of oak and beech and whatever, now that it's in the Empire and with transport costs dropping. People will build sawmills along the rivers there. Hmmm. Big pines for ships' masts as well, I suppose. Maybe hemp for ropes, too? Flax and hemp and linen grow well up there, if I remember rightly.

Everyone bowed as the Emperor halted before a dockside altar and the ceremony began. Paula handed little Paula off to Demetria, their ex-wetnurse and now just nurse, to make the gesture. The teenaged Pannonian freedwoman—a freckled redhead of vaguely Celtic background—took her with cheerful competence. Little Paula was thoroughly used to her, of course.

An hour and a half later the *Renovatio* cast off from its tug in the outer harbor, and set the sails on its three masts and between them. The outer—Claudian—harbor was calm as far as waves were concerned, but much windier.

There was a gasp from the spectators . . . now mostly the sailors and human cargo of the fleet on better than a hundred ships . . . as the sails cascaded down from the tops of the three masts to the bottom and bellied out, three each for the foremast and mainmast and two fore-and-aft gaff sails on the rear. Along with the triangular staysails between the masts and between the foremast and the bowsprit over the sharp cutwater of the bow.

The two ships heeled slightly and gathered speed, already faster than the best a Roman sailing ship could do by the time they breasted the southern gap between the breakwater and the island that bore the *pharos*. Outside the harbor the sea was intensely blue, and topped with whitecaps on the long rollers.

Mark Findlemann gulped, as he felt sweat break out on his brow. He turned and dashed for the leeward rail, hanging over it and giving his breakfast back to the waters.

Oh, God! he thought, before coherent thought vanished.

Ten days later he was empty, not hungry, but not quite so nauseous, as the fleet threaded its way through the Straits of Messina between the toe of the mainland Italian boot to the east and the heights of Sicily to the west. The water was calm and blue, the breeze mild and notably warmer than it had been at Ostia and bearing only the scent of sea, and the shores on either side were green with the winter rains and crops and orchards and vineyards.

The strait was shaped like a southeast facing funnel here, gradually widening from about two miles at the entrance to ten a bit further along.

Paula was beside him, holding their daughter; Demetria and her younger sister—also bought and emancipated—were having their belated breakfast. He'd been here before... or nearly two thousand years from now... when he'd attended a conference on his area of study, which had been Roman libraries, publishing and book diffusion.

"Pretty," Paula said.

"Pwetty!" her daughter chimed in... in Latin, of course: what she actually said was *bew'us*, her best try at *bellus*.

Should we teach her English sometime? he wondered vaguely. *Yeah, probably.*

"And blessedly *calm*, oh joy, oh rapture... wait a minute," Mark said, with a vague feeling of alarm.

He levelled his binoculars; the leather case jarred a bit with his tunic-cloak-and-sandals outfit. It was still easier than adjusting to wearing a knife, but that was just a universal tool here, not a declaration of ill intent.

He'd had his vision surgically corrected in his late teens, like most people nowadays...

Or up then, he thought absently.

...but he still had a ground-in tendency to peer and squint and occasionally to shove nonexistent glasses back up his nose with a thumb. Now his thumb moved the focusing screw.

Liburnians, he thought. *Painted blue-green.*

That was the standard warship of the Roman Mediterranean

fleets, which in this area and period mainly patrolled—usually quite successfully—against pirates. There just weren't any rival nations or navies around the Med. These three had their masts down and absent...which meant they were stripped for action. The two banks of oars flashed on either side, and they could make seven knots that way...which was quite fast, for this era.

The problem was that the fleet escorts for this convoy *didn't* have their masts down. And these had come straight out from behind the hill blocking the view of a little cove—they drew less than a yard and could handle shallow water well. And they were driving straight for the two sailing ships...

"Paula," he said quietly. "I think you'd better take the kid to our cabin. Shutter the windows."

She followed his gaze, nodded tightly, and called to the two nursemaids and disappeared down the walkway. Demetria grabbed her own son, Lucius—he was four—by the ear as she passed.

Mark turned on his heel and trotted up the other stairway, one of two at either rail that led to the aft quarterdeck. The Emperor was there, talking to the ship's captain, and the Prof... Artorius...was there too, watching the operation of the ship's sails with a slight smile of aesthetic appreciation.

They are pretty.

"Prof," he said. "Those Liburnians?"

His head swiveled, and he frowned. "Yes?"

"They've got their masts down...not just down, they're not on the decks in the frames either...and they came out from behind that rock, the little cove. I just happened to be looking that way. They must have left the masts on shore."

Artorius' face went still as a mask for a second; then he nodded tightly and walked over to the ship's commander.

"Captain, those Liburnians. I think it's an attack on the Emperor. Probably Parthian agents."

The man's head whipped around in shock; he was young, under thirty. The Prof had deliberately picked men with their names yet to make to command both new ships, those without a long emotional commitment to established ways of doing. His lean Mediterranean face went white beneath the olive complexion and the sailor's tan and the cropped black beard.

The Emperor looked, frowned and spoke: "I will go below for a moment," he said calmly. "You don't need to be distracted."

He left, and the captain exploded in a volley of orders. Men dashed up the ratlines—the rope ladders—to the rigging, and jerked free the reef-knots that let the sails drop to their full extent and billow free in taut curves.

Normally they were kept reefed, so as not to leave the rest of the fleet behind...except when the *Renovatio* and her sister were putting on demonstrations of speed and control, literally sailing circles around the fleet.

The ship heeled as the sailors at the wheel spun it: the *Roman Empire* followed suit as it read the *attackers to port* signal that ran up to break out from the top of the rear mast.

Marcus Aurelius came up the steep stairway from the deck— the door to the quarterdeck cabins gave out onto the main deck—and trotted upward, with a half-century of Praetorians in tow, and stood to one side, observing calmly and occasionally raising his telescope...the Mark II...to one eye. Besides their rifles, some of them had old-style scutum shields to protect their charge against arrows.

Mark could see that set the teeth of the captain and the Prof on edge...

But nobody's saying *anything, and the Emperor looks as...as if he were watching a chariot race,* Mark thought. *Man, he's the real deal with that Stoic stuff!*

Paula came back up from stashing little Paula. That set *Mark's* teeth on edge...but really, either the rams cleaving the water at the galley bows would strike, or they wouldn't. The *Renovatio* and her sister were picking up speed, but as far as he could see the galleys were still going faster. You couldn't call up a wind when you needed it the way a steamship could shovel on more coal.

It's a comfort we have cannon and they don't, he thought.

Iron round shot smashing timbers and sending waves of blurring-fast splinters a couple of feet long in every direction...that could spoil your whole day. He'd had a lot more experience witnessing death and mutilation since he got here. In the second century, dying wasn't something that happened doped-up in a hospital.

The courses of the two big sailing ships and the three galleys were curving lines drawn on the calm surface of the water... constrained by the shoals nearer the shores.

But we draw more water than they do, Mark thought; as long as he kept it abstract, he could stay calm and think. *And why not keep it abstract? I can't do shit to alter what happens, I've already done my bit. Deeper keels. They've got more freedom of maneuver this close to shore.*

The whole Roman fleet was going point to point and hugging the shore, because the escorting galleys had huge crews and needed to take on water and supplies at short intervals. Roman merchantmen of this era usually took open-sea courses when they could.

More crewmen were dashing to the guns; both the new ships had ten cast-steel eighteen-pounders to each side, and four more as bow and stern chasers.

Like a Master and Commander *rerun!* he thought, smiling slightly.

"What's so funny?" Paula asked with a tight expression.

Mark opened his mouth, then closed it and shook his head.

"Absolutely nothing," he said sincerely. "Just having a bit of difficulty believing this is real, you know. That's all."

"Tell me," she said. "But it's *bloody* ... I use the word advisedly ... real."

It was: deck planking and timbers drummed and squealed as the sailors cast off the ropes that kept the guns bowsed up to the bulwarks, and pulleys squealed again as they adjusted their aim by heaving on yet more cables to the signals of the gun-crew *tesserarius* as he bent over the breech and stared down the barrel.

The black low-slung weapons on their four-wheeled carriages suddenly looked a *lot* less like exhibits in a living-history exhibit.

He gulped, noting carefully the dark curved lines drawn on the deck to mark the extent of their recoil when ... if ... they were fired.

If nothing goes wrong or breaks. If that happens they could smash into you anywhere.

Remembering the bloody scenes in the doctor's station in that movie with the actor playing Maturin sawing away on shredded limbs suddenly made his stomach feel much less contented.

"They're still gaining," the Prof said flatly.

The captain of the *Renovatio* ... who was a Greek from Neapolis and had a name Mark couldn't remember at the moment and spoke Latin with an accent ... nodded tightly.

"Not much wind," he said, looking upward at the pennants streaming from the mast.

Then he spoke to his signaler, and more flags went up. Suddenly the *Roman Empire* fell off from its course and turned, moving with a majestic show of inertia that was much, much faster than it appeared.

The foremost Liburnian drove for it. It was less than fifty yards from smashing its ram into the ship's side at the rear when the ten broadside guns fired.

The lightly built galley *exploded* as the cannonballs hit. Spouts of water and spray... and body parts and ship parts... erupted skyward. When the spray cleared and the wind bore the bank of smoke southeastward they could see the long slim galley's hull, but it looked as if giant sharks had taken bites out of it at irregular intervals from bow to stern, and it had wallowed to a stop. Blood tinged the water around it to a light pink, and as he watched men staggered to the rails and threw themselves overboard, catching floating chunks and paddling for shore pushing the floats ahead of them... or just flailing and sinking.

That left the ship that had fired its cannon behind the two surviving galleys. It came about and resumed its previous course... but was falling very slightly further behind.

Some of the sailors of the *Renovatio* froze for a moment, before barked commands and blows from rope's ends got them moving again. Mark heard low whistles and amazed swearing in three or four languages—including one he'd come to recognize as Egyptian since they left Ostia. Egypt was where a lot of the Roman navy's sailors came from in this area. And the swearers were taking the name of a round dozen deities in vain.

Starting with Isis and moving on all the way to Mithras, he thought, swallowing heavily.

Blowing up floating targets evidently wasn't the same as seeing the results for real. He carefully didn't turn the binoculars on the wreckage. Marcus Aurelius did look through his telescope—for a moment, and then lowered it.

"The *new things* don't kill people anymore finally than sword, spear and arrow," he observed to the Prof... or to Tribune Artorius, as he'd think of it. "Death is death, after all. They do act more... quickly, though."

"Yes, sir," he replied. "Let's hope they act quickly *enough*. I think this must be the Parthians."

"Well, we have sent them an ultimatum demanding complete

surrender," the Emperor of Rome said. "I think this constitutes their reply."

Artorius nodded grimly. "And that—"

He inclined his head towards the wreckage.

"—is *our* reply."

The two remaining Liburnians spread out behind the *Renovatio*—just far enough apart that the stern chasers couldn't be brought to bear on them. The *Roman Empire* was falling gradually further and further behind; its bow chasers boomed, but the balls didn't strike, though some of them came close.

Mark found himself glancing up at the sails, and unconsciously straining his back muscles and making puffing motions. He stopped...when Paula's ironic sideways glance made him suddenly conscious of what he was doing. Just then Artorius spoke briefly to the Emperor, and then longer to the captain; Mark couldn't catch what was said, but both the stern chasers fired...and recoiled violently until the thick ropes stopped them, coming twanging taut.

Neither ball struck, though one came close as it skipped over the ocean like a thrown stone on a huge scale, striking four times before it sank. The crews sprang into their reloading ballet, amid the strong burnt-sulfur stink of black-powder smoke. He noticed that they didn't reload with round balls; instead a stiff leather cylinder went down the muzzle after the long shussssshhh of the wet sponges on the hot steel, and the linen cylinder of gunpowder and wooden sabot.

"What's that?" Paula asked curiously.

"Grapeshot," he said grimly. "Lots and lots of iron balls about the size of a big marble. Like a shotgun shell."

"Oh," she said.

She wasn't usually much interested in weapons.

"Oh," she added after a moment's thought, looking queasy.

Nothing wrong with her brains, he thought. *Or her imagination. Imagination can be a drawback, sometimes. Galleys are packed with people. Nothing on them will stop one of those iron balls, either.*

Mark stepped over to the Prof's side. "Going to do something?" he said quietly.

The Prof looked at him, and Mark felt a flush of pride at the nod of sober approval...and that it was directed at Paula too.

"Yup," he said quietly—in English. "Have to. If there was just a *little* more wind..."

He looked up at the sails and shrugged. "Galleys can't keep that speed up forever. The rowers would collapse. But they'll catch us in a few minutes, they know it and we know it, unless the wind Gods relent. They don't seem to care about getting away afterward. So..."

He shrugged again, and Mark stepped back. Just then four of the Praetorians came up on deck and handed out canvas satchels to their comrades. The guardsmen slung their rifles over their backs and put the satchels on, hanging by shoulder straps so that they rested at waist height to the right. Then they lined the port rail and went to one knee.

Which makes them less visible, Mark thought. *And the enemy—*

Anyone who was threatening his daughter and Paula *was* the enemy, sure enough, and he was surprised by the vehemence of the wave of hatred that left an acid taste at the back of his mouth.

Another volley of orders went from the captain to the mast officers and then up to the sailors on the rigging.

"I could swear we just got a little slower," Paula observed.

Mark nodded. "Yeah. The Prof and the captain have something in mind. Get ready to hit the deck."

He glanced sternward, something he'd been avoiding. That let him see a half-dozen archers bending their bows in the bows of both galleys.

"Now!" he said, and dropped to the planks.

Paula joined him instantly. That let him peer at the four hands at the twin wheels...and watch half a dozen of the Praetorians grouped around them, holding up shields, the way another set was around the Emperor. Several arrows went *thunk* into the curved canvas-covered plywood. One went quivering into the deck not far from his eyes, giving him a nerve-wracking view of the barbed iron arrowhead that had struck hard enough to half bury itself. Somewhere close a man shrieked in pain.

The captain barked a command, and the men at the helm spun the wheel. The *Renovatio* heeled sharply, twitching its stern to starboard—to the right, if you were facing the bows. Suddenly he could see the galley there, and it was unpleasantly close, close enough to see the faces of the men drawing their bows...

And see them realize what the fact that both the stern chasers were now pointing directly at them meant.

BOOMBOOM!

The double explosion sounded, shatteringly loud, and the thick ropes twanged as the four-wheeled carriages slammed back. Unfortunately he was still looking at the bow of the galley; and the men there *splashed* under the invisible onslaught.

He glanced quickly aside. That let him see the Praetorians coming quickly to their feet as a wrenching *thump* shivered through the ship, some of them staggering a little. The other galley's ram had struck there, well to the left of the rudder... but not very fast, since the galley was only going about a knot faster than the ship it pursued.

And every one of the Praetorians had a *malogranatum* in hand, with the fuse sputtering. They all threw, nearly in unison, and twenty of the little bombs arched out.

"*Suck on this, Gods-detested pirate whoreboys!*" one of them screamed amid the chorus of grunts, in Latin with a strong rural north-Italian accent.

Crackcrackcrackcrack—

The quarterdeck gun crews were throwing themselves on their steel-and-wood charges with frantic strength, reloading with another double charge of grapeshot.

Mark could see the Liburnian falling away, its foredeck and forward rowers' benches a ghastly chaos with blood running out the scuppers.

BOOMBOOM! and the heavy guns shot backward. He closed his eyes before the smoke cleared, and said to Paula—a little loudly, after the stunning impact:

"I think we should go below; Paula will be stressed out."

"So am I," his wife said, hoisting herself erect. "So am I, honey."

The *Renovatio* was slowing as sails were struck, and two longboats were filled with sailors and guardsmen, ready to row back toward the wrecks.

He didn't envy any prisoners they took.

On the other hand, I don't sympathize in the least either.

⇒ CHAPTER SIXTEEN ⇐

Harbor of Laodicea-in-Syria
November 1st, 171 CE

"Notice the looks of raw envy and covetousness the other skippers are giving the new ships?" Mark said to Paula. "Especially since that little...ah...tiff off Sicily?"

Oh, thank God the part on ship is over! ran through his mind as the *Renovatio*'s crew tossed its mooring ropes to the quayside; he suppressed the impulse to dance a jig of joy.

Gravitas, boy, gravitas! *You're marooned among stoics... literal Stoics, a lot of them. So you're not seasick anymore...but get a whiff of the city, that stink's memorable. Grave, calm, self-possessed...and suppress the impulse to kiss the pavement when you get ashore. Unsanitary, anyway.*

The Emperor was aboard, which imposed a certain restraint. He was standing on the poop deck resplendent in muscled, inlaid bronze breastplate and crested, relief-worked helmet and purple cloak and carefully—ceremonially—knotted purple sash, with Tribune Artorius and several other bigwigs in attendance and Praetorian guardsmen at the ready...with their new rifles by their sides.

Or their boomsticks! he thought with a smile. *And that getup's something I know Marcus Aurelius only does because it would shock people if he didn't. The Romans lucked out with him! So did we, for that matter—he was smart enough to see through our cover story, and smart enough to believe the truth. With him solidly behind us...things got a hell of a lot easier. Our Chinese counterparts have a party-hearty adolescent dimwit instead.*

The hills behind the town...medium-sized city by local standards...and the fields around it were green here too, where they weren't new-plowed brown misted with just-visible winter wheat, which meant the winter rains were underway here too. Though a lot of the land just outside the city wall was in truck gardens, or orchards.

Winter rain made this the season to move armies dependent on horses and oxen, especially if you had good solid Roman roads to march on, out of the mud. It didn't get really *cold* here this time of year—the climate reminded him of San Diego, where he'd visited relatives. In the summertime it would be sweating-hot and everything around here would be burnt brown; that was when the locals drove the sheep and other livestock up into the highlands and hills.

"Sort of *lustful* envy combined with sheer sweating hatred because they don't have what this ship has?" Paula went on. "Yeah, I noticed."

"As we sailed circles around the fleet," Mark chuckled.

He generally thought of his name as Marcus now, when he was speaking Latin and thinking in it. Usually pronounced *Marku'*.

Paula Atkins...Paula Triaria Atcintia, officially, herself...nodded again. She had the usual long golden-silk bandana around her close-cropped head.

Thank God or the Gods I found an article on that flower that grows in Dalmatia in one of the books I was translating! Mark thought. *A natural insecticide, and all you have to do is grind up the flowers and seeds and then keep them in the dark. Long live pyrethrum!*

Orders had gone out late last year that the estates of the *res privata* in the relevant part of Illyricum were to cultivate the flowers and send the powder on in tightly sealed amphorae... at very attractive prices as a cash crop for the tenant farmers.

Not many Romans knew—or if they'd been told, really deep-down believed yet—that the various bugs carried *diseases*. Though Galen was spreading that knowledge as fast as possible, with empirical demonstrations at the Institute.

Just about everyone *hated* the too-familiar insect life anyway, though, in a resigned what-can-you-do fashion. Anyone who *could* pay *would* pay to have something that got rid of them without incredibly laborious work, and rich people would buy it for their multitudinous servants as well because bugs were no respecters of rank. That would snowball down the social scale as prices dropped.

"Well, we were *literally* sailing circles around them," Paula added, tapping the deck with her sandaled foot and wrenching his mind back from its digression. "And upwind, too. These ships are prettier, too, in my opinion. Most of the Roman ones look...tubby. Except the galleys, and they stink to high heaven. Literally."

"I think they look better too, but I also think they just look very *strange* to the Romans."

Colonia Ferramenta—which literally meant Colony of Hardware—had supplied the cannon and iron fixings and chains. And there was Colonia Chalybe—which meant Colony of Steel— under construction in northeastern Gaul even now, in what he thought of as Lorraine in eastern France; they'd stepped up the expansion program after the...

Bad news from China, he thought uneasily.

Once *that* Colonia was going, others would follow at an accelerating rate, two a year and then three until the Empire was swimming in cheap iron and even cheaper steel by second-century standards.

Grinning, he added aloud in English...of a sort:

"Arrrr! Avast! Scunder the upperforetops'ls, wi' a wanion! We'ums be a-sailin' now! Arrr!"

The new three-masted ships were still much longer and slimmer than Roman merchantmen, which did tend to be tubby and only about three times longer than they were wide. Also the new vessels were sharp bowed, and built frame first rather than as a shell of planks with the reinforcing structure added afterward, and caulked with tarred hemp and sheathed below the waterline in rolled sheet copper.

All that made them much stronger and more seaworthy and less prone to shipworms.

Nearly all of that was what the Prof had called Type A innovations; things the locals could do with the tools and techniques they had, once they'd been given the idea...and you'd convinced them it was worth the trouble.

That got easier and easier: partly the Emperor's backing, and partly the Americans' record of success to date aweing people into submission. Or activating their greed, which was *even more* effective.

Pray we don't screw the pooch on something big! he thought.

Marcus Aurelius walked down the gangplank. An altar had been erected, with doves and a bleating lamb ready for sacrifice. He stepped forward and raised his hands...

Paula winced. "I bet you've been *waiting* to do that Long John Silver shit," she murmured *sotto voce*. "God damn Walt Disney, anyway, he was a prime son of a bitch. Come to think of it, that's unfair to bitches, even the canine variety, much less brilliant, forceful cast-iron *metaphorical* bitches like me."

"And..." she added with a bright sadistic smile, "...now you know what morning sickness is like. Children are wonderful in the abstract, aren't they?"

They were planning on three...at intervals.

"There are...well, were...you know what I mean...worse hobbies than old movies," he said, in an exaggerated aggrieved tone. "And I sympathized right through the morning sickness, didn't I?"

"Sympathy shmimpathy," she retorted, grinning too. "You did hold the bucket, I admit that."

"Well, you held mine on the trip here. We're well matched!"

"And I'm your main link to the human race," she replied dryly.

Which I suppose is true enough. I spend a lot less time involuntarily alone since we got together. Of course, she had to come right out and say "let's go to bed together" before I realized what she'd been hinting at. Funny, I get things like that in books, *but not so much in real life...*

A permanent galley with cast-iron stoves and a table in the Emperor's or captain's dining quarters were innovations too. Dinner invitations had left the guests very thoughtful.

Two more ships like these were under construction, in Ostia and over where the first one had been built at Tergeste at the head of the Adriatic. That would go much faster, now that the workforce in both places had some experience.

He cleared his throat, and returned to more impersonal matters:

"The merchant skippers have been taking notes too," he said.

She rolled her eyes. "Yeah, you can hear them thinking: *My Gods! My greed!*"

The Roman Empire had a massive set of long-distance trades

in bulk commodities, by sea or river wherever possible—they even shipped ornamental building-stone blocks from Asia Minor to Britannia sometimes. As well as everything else going from everywhere to anywhere.

Not to mention imports from the East like silk and spices.

Ships like this would increase profits drastically, and hence the volume of trade. They were three or four times faster just for starters, with an equivalent saving in the merchant's capital tied up in transit, *and* more reliable, *and* had more cargo capacity per ton of displacement *and* needed far fewer hands per ton.

Word would spread quickly after this as the chartered vessels scattered back to their usual runs, and spectators, speculators, traders and shipbuilders would descend on the Imperial shipyards in Ostia and Tergeste. Which had orders to be helpful and reveal all, including the water-powered sawmills. Which would have been invented in about a century, but without the millennia of refinements... windmills too, a thousand years ahead of schedule...

Helloooooo, profit! Mark thought. *Betcha the Germanii pick up the attitude fairly quick, too, now that they're Imperial subjects and can't cut the neighbors' throats for fun and... profit.*

"Not to mention the little firepower demonstration," Paula added.

Mark suppressed queasiness. "Yeah, bloodthirsty enthusiasm."

And the Roman navy was already planning expeditions to the North Sea and Baltic, as soon as the *topsail schooners*—about half this ship's size and shallow draught for inshore work—were ready, along with their broadsides of light cannon. A lot of German pirate raiders in big rowboats... who Romans called *Saxons* regardless of their actual origins, and who were sort of like early, low-tech proto-Vikings... were going to get very nasty surprises right at home. And learn that two could play at the rape-pillage-kidnap-kill-and-burn game.

"The Prof"—which was how the ex-graduate students referred to Artorius among themselves when they weren't annoyed with him—"says these two ships could sail around the *world* without much problem. A lot faster than the first guys to do it, too. Something about the *Roaring Forties*, whatever the Hell those are, and Australia and Tierra del Fuego, I think."

Paula nodded agreement. "Bigger and better... much, much better... than Columbus or da Gama or Magellan had," she said.

"Or even Captain Cook...and come to think of it, I don't think the Polynesians have gotten to Hawaii yet, have they?"

"Not for another eight hundred years at least," Mark said absently. "I read an archaeological paper about it when I was an undergrad. Three, four hundred years from now for the first humans on Madagascar, they were sort of distant Polynesian relatives. About a thousand for the Maori to arrive in New Zealand..."

Paula looked at him, brows rising: "And this morning you couldn't remember where you put your socks," she said in a tone of ongoing wonder. "Or whether you had a clean loincloth left."

"Hey, we all have our priorities. These ships could go there, right? Any of those places?"

She nodded. "They're about mid-Victorian level with some later tweaks. And we've got compasses now, and better maps, ones with the ocean currents and prevailing winds marked on 'em, those don't change on a historical time scale, and pretty soon sextants and chronometers and log lines to record distance traveled."

Then she went on with a grimace:

"I hope it's a bit easier on the places they'll be sailing *to* than the original version of the Age of Exploration, at least the ones that already have people now. Romans make Spanish *conquistadores* look...restrained and empathetic. *Some* Spaniards took the all-men-are-brothers-in-Jesus seriously. Mostly priests, but still."

He nodded. Both of them found the cheerful ruthlessness and lip-smacking bloodthirsty aggression of your average Roman a bit stressful, sometimes. Roman aristos and generals and for that matter rank-and-file legionnaires were mostly even more so than the commons. It simply never occurred to ninety-nine percent of them that you *shouldn't* conquer any place you *could* conquer, with the joys of rapine and plunder and slave-taking thrown in. Danger in itself didn't deter them much with a prospect of success luring them on, partly he thought because death by unspecified illness could strike anyone at any time, so why not take risks?

Marcus Aurelius is an empathetic softie by contemporary standards, and he'd be a notable hardcase as a head of state up in the twenty-first, Mark thought. *Well, in the First World, at least. He fights wars to establish peace...but he doesn't hesitate, and he never doubts Rome should rule everywhere forever.*

"Well, we're *working* on that," he said. "Making things less dog-eat-dog. You have to be able to *afford* to be un-ruthless. You can't do that here, not really. Which is why absolutely *everyone* is so . . . so hard-assed back here. You'd get eaten alive if you weren't."

Paula grinned. "Sarukê thinks *Fil* is sooooooo sweet and tenderhearted. It's a good thing Fil saved her life on that spying mission north of the Danube—that showed she was sweet and tenderhearted *and* brave as a lion, so she gets enough respect from her girlfriend. Heck, they're married now, more or less. Though they didn't get the ceremony the way we did . . . maybe we could do something about that?"

"Maybe we should! Nero did. Any excuse for a party. Though about the other stuff . . . *we* shock a lot less easily than we did when we arrived. Even if some of the Romans think we're sort of . . . wimpy."

He blinked at the memory of that blast of grape hitting the foredeck of the attacking galley. Nowadays that sort of thing didn't bother him nearly as much as it had at first . . . which itself bothered him at least a bit, when he thought about it.

Like ignoring the crippled beggars showing their sores, he thought. *You just have to.*

Paula sighed. "But being able to afford it doesn't mean you *will* be less hard-assed. I mean, look at the way Beijing treated the Uyghurs back uptime . . . and they didn't stop when Xi died, either. Sheer hate."

"Or what the Russians did when they could." He spread his hands. "But it does make it *possible.* That's . . . something. And with the Chinese here *now* . . ."

"Nothing wrong with Chinese *people*," she said.

"No, there isn't. Some of my best friends back up in the twenty-first, to coin a phrase. But the Chinese *government* . . . well . . . and they're the ones who would have picked their time travelers."

"There is that. Worse than the Romans—and without *any* of their excuses."

Their nursemaid Demetria came on deck with their daughter in hand. She was delighted with her job because she loved children and not only her own small son, and the pay was excellent by local standards and her treatment a dream come true. Which had produced an at-times embarrassing surplus of doglike devotion and a more welcome energetic willingness to learn.

Mark beamed as their daughter waved small hands, smiled

and displayed an uneven set of baby teeth, and showed hopping-crawling-dashing general enthusiasm; Demetria snatched her up before she careened face-first into the lashed-down breech of a cast-steel cannon.

They'd bought and emancipated Demetria's fourteen-year-old sister Metima too, to help with that exploring-toddler stage... when *someone* had to keep eyes on the toddler continuously, 24/7.

Four sets of eyes ought to do it. I hope. Oh, how I hope!

Metima appeared on deck, looking slightly guilty and brushing carrot-cake crumbs off her tunic, but with a bundle of fresh linen diapers in her hands.

Paula bustled over to check little Paula's diaper—getting across the *change 'em immediately when wet or soiled, plus a soap and water wash for the nethers* had taken a little work, but he thought they'd managed and Paula was going to reinforce the lesson until it well and truly stuck. Toilet training would be a relief by contrast...

Diapers wouldn't catch on outside aristo circles anytime soon, because cloth was so expensive...but they were working on that, too.

Thank goodness we've got all that selected food along. Keeping a check on her food sanitation...that's hard. At that age they cram anything they find into their mouths by reflex!

"This wouldn't be possible if the Romans weren't already good at what they do," Artorius said thoughtfully, eyeing the... reasonably...efficient bustle around them. "No, indeedy."

"Prof?" Jeremey said, frowning.

The ex-Americans were all standing in a clump near the wall of a warehouse down by the docks, amid a strong smell of stagnant water, sewage, and various exotic spicy goods in the warehouses combined with the more common scents of greasy baled wool and more pleasant stacked timber, salt fish and grain, and garum and wine and olive oil...the latter mainly from what happened when you tripped or slipped and dropped a clay amphorae you were carrying, and then the results got trodden into the street or floor and spoiled to rancidity.

There was a tub of a Roman merchantman of about two hundred tons tied up to the quay across from them, and Roman soldiers—from a regular legion—were filing down the gangplank, wearing their segmented armor which was polished to a gleam. But with their shields for those that still bore the scutum in leather covers and slung over their backs, all with helmets on their chests with the cheekpieces splayed open, and their gear over their shoulders on their furcae.

That was a carrying pole about six feet long with a crosspiece lashed on down a foot from the top, and the soldier's load in bags and nets and a leather satchel hanging beneath. *Furca* also meant "an instrument of judicial torture." Which made its name a mordant soldiers' joke; carrying fifty pounds over your shoulder on a stick all day *wasn't* a joke, even with the shoulder plates of a *lorica segmentata* to spread the weight.

A standard—a pole with a cast-bronze open hand at the summit, inside a bronze wreath, born by a man with a wolf's head on his helmet and its fur down his back—came first. The centurion followed it, with the transverse crest on *his* helmet leaving no doubt where he was.

That was the point of wearing it, though in the original history it had fallen out of use about now or in the immediate future.

Probably because it amounts to a kill me! *sign carried over your head with an arrow pointing down,* Artorius thought.

He spoke to the signaler beside him. The man blew a note on his curled *tubae* while the company commander stood by the base of the gangplank and tapped the gnarled end of his yard-long swagger stick into his left palm. It was made out of tough wood from a vinestock, and was a reminder that he could whack anyone under his command with it, too. Whenever he felt like it and with no formalities involved.

"The soldiers don't seem bothered," Mark murmured, dropping into English for a sentence and glancing the centurion's way. "*I'd* quail at that look. It could bore holes in granite!"

There was a story about a centurion who'd been nicknamed *Bring-Me-Another* by his men, because that was his cry when he broke a vinestock staff on someone's body or head.

As if the trumpet had played directly on their nervous systems, the men fell in, in a formation four across and twenty deep; half had rifles that were slung across their backs and their furca on the other shoulder. Another brief note and the whole formation marched off in hobnail-on-granite massed crunching step, without muss or fuss, and the *optio*—the second-in-command—following along behind, with a long staff topped by a brass ball in his hands. That was used for shoving and rapping noggins too, as well as being a rank marker.

Romans had a rather blunt approach to getting someone's attention, one that often involved hitting.

What did that orc sergeant say in Return of the King? Artorius thought. *Yeah, where there's a whip there's a will. Lots of agreement here. It's the Great Chain of Beating; starts with the Emperor, ends up with mine slaves and gladiators. People are... tougher grained here about that sort of thing. Muchly.*

A nervous-looking local was with the officer, to point the way to the city gates and the military campground in the fields outside it. Most of the Roman field force not based around here had set off to *march* here earlier via the Bosporus and Asia Minor, back in the spring.

All the cavalry lancer *alae* assigned here, and the new Sarmatian auxiliary horse-archer units, and the Ninth Claudian Legion and the Fourth Italica, for starters. Drilling as they came, and making fortified camps every night. They'd join the columns nearer the border.

"Imagine if we had to *teach* them how to move big units long distances," Artorius said. "They're damned good at it already, though. Especially considering what they had to work with."

"Well, there wouldn't be a great big Roman Empire if they couldn't do that, would there?" Fil said. "Though I admit, considering what their maths and accounting were like before we got here, it's surprising how well they handle the administrative side. They'll be absolute hell on wheels once they've really assimilated what we can tell them about that."

Classical technology, including the intellectual parts, had been her field of study. Paula snorted; she'd compared helping the Roman Empire unify the world to selling your soul to the Devil... preferable to global thermonuclear war, but not great in and of itself. Though since fate had added Chinese government agents to the classical stew, she'd modified that feeling a bit.

As she put it, the Chinese regime made nearly *everyone* else look good... even the second-century Roman Empire, which at least didn't have facial-recognition AI's keeping track of every word you spoke and every scrap you read and anything you typed and every time you stopped to pee and...

Jem had made a crack about crotch-recognition AI when she'd said that, and Mark had had to calm her down.

Jem can be seriously annoying.

Artorius nodded, but held out an open hand palm down, waggled it and said:

"Oh, you'd be surprised how many big... reasonably big... empires used to bungle things like that all the time. The British in the Crimea, for example—that's where Florence Nightingale got her start, cleaning up after official incompetence of the *haw-haw, bah Jove* Eton school and Sandhurst chinless wonder variety."

"Into the Valley of Death..." Jeremey said.

"Rode the screwed-over," Artorius said, completing a modified version of Tennyson's poem. "Or our Mexican War, a little earlier, when we took Texas and California and points between. My ancestors were involved with that—Texans were hot to trot on that one."

"We won the war," Jeremey pointed out. "And we *did* get California...and Texas...and the chunks in between."

Artorius nodded:

"We did, but only because Mexico under *el Presidente* Antonio López de Santa Anna was *even more* incompetent than we were under President Polk. Who at least had the sense not to fight the British over the Oregon country. Or the Spanish-American War at the end of the nineteenth century, you wouldn't believe what a mess *that* was. Teddy Roosevelt only got to Cuba for that charge up San Juan hill by outright *stealing* a ship for his Rough Riders, pretty much at gunpoint. And lying truth out of creation about it to boot."

"Teddy Roosevelt lied?" Paula said dryly. "What a surprise!"

Artorius grinned. "He was a writer, among other things, and they're professional liars, even more than politicians and lawyers."

"And he was a politician too," she said.

Artorius nodded. "From an early age, at that. Good thing we picked an elderly has-been armless, legless midget like Spain to beat on in that one. We'd have gotten our head handed to us if we'd gotten into a fight with someone who knew what they were doing. And we learned something from the embarrassment of our bungling, which was helpful, and Teddy became president, which was even more so. *He* knew what he was doing."

Fil was listening attentively enough, but her eye was on the

Imperium Romanum, several quays down, and she was smiling. Sarukê was overseeing getting their horses off, hoisted up from the hold with blindfolds on and broad bellybands beneath, attached to pulleys in the rigging. Then they were lowered to the deck and led down the ramps by grooms who saddled them up once they were ashore... and for a wonder, not one of them was having equine hysterics in the process. All of them were big, fifteen hands or better, and clean lined.

Horses generally did *not* like sea voyages, but the Sarmatian woman had an almost magical skill with them, and she'd spent part of every day in their section of the hold. Mostly singing to them in a pleasant soprano while she groomed them, ancient Sarmatian epic poetry for the most part. For some reason they found it soothing. Fil usually went with her...

"How's the SCPP going?" Paula asked her.

That stood for Sarmatian Cultural Preservation Project, a half-serious in-joke. Lately—as her Sarmatian improved—Fil had been transcribing the thousands of lines of epic poetry from her people's traditional stock that Sarukê had memorized. Writing it in Sarmatian, reading it back to her partner to check on it, and then translating it into Latin and Greek.

She'd found via their surviving computers that big chunks of the *Rig Veda* were surprisingly similar, and likewise bits and pieces of the *Avesta*.

And some stock phrases and combinations of lines from Homer as well, which meant that *those* probably dated all the way back to Proto-Indo-European. Marcus Aurelius had been fascinated when she pointed it out.

Sarukê had been astonished that you *could* write Sarmatian down. Nobody had ever tried before, as far as she knew, and she'd eagerly set out to learn how... and incidentally to write down her inimitable versions of Latin and Greek, too.

"Coming along, coming along nicely," Fil said, nodding. "Sarukê's enthusiastic. She's really bright, once you get to know her."

This section of the quay wasn't *too* crowded. Praetorian guardsmen were keeping bystanders and hawkers and hucksters and whores at bay, the stylized scorpions on their shields and stamped into low relief on the cheekpieces of their helmets more of a warning than the weapons in their hands.

Everything takes longer and costs more here, Artorius thought. *You get used to standing around and waiting... even more than in the US Army.*

Those carrying rifles were getting glances of awe and terror, after a little demonstration that an advance party had given. Which made those men preen and swagger. Things that shot an *invisible* projectile that could punch through any armor activated a lot of people's must-be-magic reflex around here, and being able to throw thunderbolts like Jupiter Greatest and Best... or Zeus... was serious ego-boo.

Other Praetorians would be escorting the Emperor to meet with the provincial governor—one Gaius Avidius Cassius—in the city's citadel.

Oddly enough, the name meant essentially Gaius the Greedy Helmet, or possibly Gaius the Greedy Iron-Head. Roman names were strange...

Cassius tried to usurp the purple in 175 CE, originally, in the history we learned, Artorius thought. *Though to be fair, that was only because he thought Marcus Aurelius had died fighting the Marcomanni up in Pannonia... news spreads slowly and gets distorted here, or it did... and* nobody *wanted Commodus.*

The Emperor had asked if history recorded anything about the governor. After an echoing silence, Artorius had told him the bare bones of it, and the response had been a frown, a sigh and silence.

Nobody wanted Commodus who knew *him, at least, unless they figured they could make a mint off him and to hell with the Empire. I think he's coming around to the notion that Commodus should be palmed off with money and meaningless rank if possible while Verus gets the actual power. Of course, Verus is still extremely young—too young to have a settled character... he's wild with glee at being brought along. Commodus turned the invitation down once it was clear he had a choice... he really doesn't like leaving Rome and vicinity. I don't think anything else is really real to him.*

There were plenty of spectators at a little distance, not too different in their looks from Romans though they'd be mostly Greeks here—you could see that from the one-shoulder fastening a lot of them used for their chitons, what Romans called a tunica, leaving the other bare.

There were plenty of Syrians proper around too; some in Greek dress but marked out by their longer hair and beards, others in their traditional vividly colored ankle-length striped robes and tall hats like tapering cylinders.

As far as complexions and features went, you couldn't really tell one from the other; there were plenty of big-nosed swarthy Greeks, after all, and some...a few...Levantines could have passed easily enough for locals in Germany. Populations living around the Middle Sea might differ enough that you could tell a *hundred* Syrians or Libyans from a *hundred* Epirot Greeks or Hispanians, but not any given individual.

You could also tell that thousands of years of the slave trade from sub-Saharan Africa hadn't happened here yet.

Hopefully, it won't.

The crew of the *Roman Empire*—which was what the name *Imperium Romanum* meant—had brought a carriage out of the hold with the same hoisting apparatus they'd used on the gee-gees. It was also new style, based on nineteenth-century models improved somewhat with steel leaf springs—courtesy of Colonia Ferramenta—in the suspension and shaped rather like a classical Western stagecoach. Except that it was covered in what Romans considered suitable decoration for an important person's personal transport.

That involved vivid paintings including Gods, Goddesses, winged cherubs, heroic warriors, famous women and similar busywork covering every square inch that wasn't decked in polished, gilded or silvered metal elaborately worked in repoussé.

Aesthetic restraint wasn't a notable Roman characteristic.

A Boer War-style transport wagon would follow it, also harnessed in the new way and drawn by a dozen locally sourced mules rather than oxen. It contained a fairly big mobile dome tent and nursery gear and carefully packaged foodstuffs for little Paula and the children of Jeremy's girlfriends, plus what the other Americans needed. Though it wouldn't be *quite* as gaudy.

Artorius laughed as the six-horse team was harnessed to the carriage and made a sweeping gesture with one hand and arm as he bowed.

"Lord Marcus, Lady Paula, your chariot awaits."

"Tasteful!" Jeremey added, with a grin.

As Sarukê led the grooms over with the riding horses the rest of them would be using, already fitted out with their very own new-style saddles, which had a modest amount of tooling and silver studs. A personalized saddle made long-distance riding a lot less wearing.

"Cool!" Jeremey went on. "Elegant! I saw an oxcart from Central America in a museum that looked a bit like that color scheme once...more abstract, though, not so many plump winged babies and nekkid goddesses rising from the foam and guys in armor striking heroic poses..."

Paula rolled her eyes. "We'd have had to stand over them with clubs and whips to get them to skip that, Jem," she said. "Have you *seen* the one the Empress Faustina has now? It makes this look like modernist minimalism, 1950s style. It's crusted with *jewels*; we drew the line at that, no point in putting temptation in everyone's face. You expect the Empress to get out wearing a magic glass slipper and the horses to turn into mice at midnight."

Jeremey's grin grew. "Or you could just *ride* horses..."

"*We* don't have a sexual fixation with getting on top of large animals, unlike some people I could name," Paula said, with a sniff...and then a hint of a wink.

Artorius hid his own smile.

The wink's relatively *new,* he thought. *We've discovered how much we depend on each other, over the years here.*

Paula and Mark had had six years of reluctant but steady equestrianism in their backgrounds now, and both were fairly... moderately, in Mark's case...competent in the saddle these days. Neither of them *liked* it, or horses for that matter, though Paula liked a slave-borne litter even less.

Jeremey and Fil had been horse enthusiasts in their teens, and Artorius had started riding himself on his family's West Texas ranch when he was about six.

Just something you do, he thought. *To Romans it's a fit gentleman's way of getting around.*

"Besides," Mark said, as the team was harnessed and the driver and guards maneuvered the carriage toward them, and Demetria and her sister came up with little Paula and her own four-year-old son in the background. "I have thinking to do about getting the medicos up to scratch. They know about bacteria now...but a lot of them haven't realized the implications. Thinking's much easier sitting down on something softer than a saddle."

"Depends on where you keep your brains," Jeremey said, and dodged a shin kick from Paula, laughing.

⮞ CHAPTER SEVENTEEN ⮜

Northern Mesopotamia
December 20th, 171 CE

The earth shook under the impact of thundering hooves as the Parthians charged, and even after yesterday's rain dust spurted up behind them, billowing up into the bright sky. The air smelled of sweat human and equine, horse by-products, the dry mealy-sandy scent of desert, and crushed herbs.

A roar of kettledrums accompanied the thudding of thousands of hooves—scores of them, huge things slung over horse's withers with one on either side, beaten enthusiastically and in unison with iron-headed sticks, a throbbing sound that carried over distance and vibrated in your teeth.

War with a musical score, Artorius thought ironically. *Doesn't make it any nicer. Not even on my birthday!*

Which this was; in Roman terms, he'd been born during Saturnalia, eighteen hundred and twenty-nine years from now . . .

He carefully examined the enemy force, then lowered his binoculars.

"I'd say about eight to ten thousand horse archers, and fifteen hundred to two thousand of their heavy-armed cataphracts there in the background, Legate Fronto," he said. "About a quarter more than our numbers."

The grass here was sparse, clumps separated by bare ground, but green right now, and the scattering of low bushes were green too . . . but both were a dusty, *dim* green. The air had been downright cold last night; now it was comfortable, somewhere in the low seventies...

Comfortable if you're not wearing a subarmalis *padded jerkin and a mail shirt,* Artorius thought.

Which he was, and sweat was running down his flanks and face and dripping off his nose, which was familiar enough from his home century and this one. Roman commanders couldn't count on being out of arrow range.

Or couldn't until now... we'll see.

"Yes, the horse archers to disorganize us... that's what they're planning when they get in range... and the cataphracts to charge home with their barge poles once they do," Fronto said.

Marcus Aurelius simply nodded after using his own telescope; he didn't joggle the elbows of his subordinates without a very good reason. His *Equites Singulares Augusti*—the Imperial Horse Guards—surrounded him at a slight distance. His son Verus was nearby on a pony, in a small mailcoat and helmet, and watching bright-eyed.

Could be worse, it could be July, Artorius thought—he'd *been* around here in July, in the US Army's 1st Ranger Battalion.

Everyone else here, many thousands of them, were sweating too and so were the horses. You got used to the massed smell of thousands packed densely together. Most Roman tribunes wore a cast-bronze muscled cuirass on campaign, or a leather imitation, but he'd avoided that—he had a reputation as a grimly antiflamboyant type and a bit of a dour killjoy.

More than one other tribune was imitating *him* now.

He *did* conform to the Roman custom of wearing your decorations in the field; a little replica of the Grass Crown was on a worked-leather strap over his chest. So far as he knew, he was the only person in the Roman army currently entitled to that. It was also the only decoration given *by* the men *to* an officer: the Tenth Legion had awarded it to him, for saving them in the first battle of the Marcomannic War.

And for killing Prince Ballomar and cutting off his head. They had a completely understandable major jones for him, Artorius thought. *Bastard started the war. What was that old Viking saying? Right:* He fell on his own deeds. *Straight up.*

Fronto grinned unpleasantly. From his point of view, the Parthians were doing *precisely* what he wanted them to do.

"They think a force as small as this is very vulnerable to massed arrow fire," the Roman general said. "Which it would have been, once. Of course, back then we wouldn't have *exposed* a force this size this way."

A sour chuckle, and he added: "Not after what happened to Crassus."

Marcus Aurelius leaned down and whispered in his son's ear. Verus nodded solemnly.

"Never hurts to have the enemy thinking you're stupid and make mistakes," Artorius observed. "Because that makes them more likely to take stupid chances themselves."

The military men—and the Emperor—all nodded.

The Parthian King of Kings, Vologases IV—or Shāhanshāh Walagaš, in his own East Iranian language—was probably, understandably, wroth that the Romans had attacked him out of the blue after nothing but a blunt demand for total and unconditional surrender.

After thoroughly thrashing him in the *last* war.

He wouldn't discount rumors of Roman magic because he *disbelieved* in sorcery. But as a hard-headed ruler, he would think magic was blamed because the Germanii were making excuses for their defeat, or the Romans were trying to terrify him, or both.

Then Fronto nodded thoughtfully as he trained his telescope on the enemy—it was a second-generation model.

"I agree on their numbers, Tribune," he added after a moment.

Then he nodded to the signalers. *Tubae* and *cornu* rang out, echoed by the signalers of each unit.

This Roman force was about fifteen thousand strong not counting the baggage train, two legions that were only moderately and normally understrength plus auxiliary bowmen and cavalry and the Praetorian cohorts. All three of the Imperial armies were all advancing in columns of about this size, deliberately offering the Parthians what they'd think were tempting targets.

And the massed attacks would likely begin as soon as the Romans crossed the frontier, which would be massively more convenient from a logistics standpoint. Every step after the border increased the cost and difficulty of bringing up supplies, and/or made you more dependent on what you could steal or barter from the locals.

Roman logistics here would be even more difficult considering the damage the unchecked plague of the new variety of smallpox had done east of the border, where it had already killed something between a tenth and a fifth of the population.

Everyone in the invading Roman army was vaccinated, of course, right down to the camp followers. Anyone who joined the Army on the road was too.

The Imperial front line was in cohort blocs...he mentally translated *cohort* as *battalion*...four men deep, deployed when cavalry scouts brought news of the Parthian force. That was a thinner formation than Romans had used in the past, but apparently it hadn't prompted any suspicion on the other side.

The last two ranks in each cohort had the new rifles; there were sixty of the improved *carroballistae* behind each legion, a hundred and twenty in all, ready to throw Jove's Balls; and the new *tormenta*, the bronze field guns, were massed on the flanks behind hastily dug ditches and low earth banks thrown up from their spoil, twenty-four of them on each side. From which positions they could enfilade the enemy—throw shot and then grapeshot if they got that close in overlapping oblique fans, rather like a squat X of death drawn on the map of reality.

Also behind the legionary infantry cohorts, between the *carroballistae* batteries, were blocs of foot-archer auxiliaries who'd mostly been recruited in Syria just west of here themselves. They were good solid professionals and they'd been very useful north of the Danube, but Artorius thought they were more enthusiastic about this campaign than they'd been about walloping the Germanii. They had personal reasons to fear and dislike the Parthians.

The cavalry was on the flanks, which was why cavalry regiments were called *alae*, "wings," in Latin. There were the new Sarmatian horse-archer regiments, and older auxiliary regiments with the lances the Americans had introduced. Both had been reequipped with modern saddles based on the ones in Fuchs's baggage, which had been traditional southern Spanish models. The nearly-as-new lancers were closer to the legions' ranks, and they had all been reequipped with *modern*—early medieval—armor and trained in how to use a ten-foot lance couched underarm.

Sarmatian and Parthian were related languages. That wasn't politically important since the Sarmatians were thoroughgoing tribalists, and cheerfully ready to cut the neighboring tribe's throats, when they weren't trading or intermarrying with them.

They were even more ready to kill weird-looking strangers from a thousand miles away who spoke something annoyingly *almost* comprehensible.

The lancers had traditional Roman cavalry helmets, domed and with broad hinged cheekpieces and flared neck guards, not all that different from what the legionaries wore though more fancifully decorated, and the long cavalry spatha at their belts. But their armor was different now. They wore knee-length mail hauberks made with riveted steel wire from Colonia Ferramenta, the skirts slit up before and behind to hang down when astride a horse and secured on the inside with straps, for starters.

It was based on what he remembered of European models from the eleventh century, and with elbow-length sleeves and plate reinforcement on the shoulders. Shins and forearms were covered in steel greaves and vambraces; round shields faced in steel with inside loops were on their left arms, and ten-foot lances rested with their lower thirds in tubular rests at the right rear of their saddles.

The long triangular-punch-shaped heads of the lances made a swaying glitter above them, and the pennants fluttered in the steady breeze above the Roman...which was to say Gaulish and Thracian and whatnot...heavy horse. The Parthians had a reasonable degree of respect for Roman cavalry, but they'd be counting on their substantial advantage in numbers of horsemen. This was ideal country for mounted men as far as tactics went.

There weren't many ordinary spear-equipped auxiliary infantry with this force. Those were mostly up north in what had *formerly* been the Barbaricum of Free Germany, where the heavy forest put a premium on their services.

Harder to see the enemy coming up there, Artorius thought. *Obvious here, at least in daylight. And managing cavalry at night...not really practical in these numbers. Plus if there's any substantial number of them you can hear them coming, and feel it if you put a palm to the ground.*

Aloud he went on:

"Open fire at three hundred yards, sir?"

"We can hit them further than that," Fronto observed. "Now we can, that is, Tribune. Four times as far! And better with the *tormenta!*"

"Yes, sir. But when they're that close they'll be committed to a charge into easy bow range, going to a flat-out gallop. They won't believe what's happening to them for . . . well, some crucial minutes . . . simply because it will be so unfamiliar. Then we can hit them at up to a mile while they run *away* from us. And *our* cavalry can counterattack while they're disorganized and on the run."

"Ah, excellent idea," Fronto said approvingly. "A very good thought, for the initial encounter when they've only got rumors to go on about our *new things* and probably discount them."

The Emperor leaned down to whisper to his son again; Artorius caught a little of it—something to the effect of always being ready to listen to advice from someone you respected.

A slight pause for thought, and Fronto went on:

"We may even get their cataphracts in range if we do that. Yes, yes indeed."

He gave the command, and messengers scattered out. Then he smiled in a way reminiscent of hyenas looking at an injured animal and chuckling while deciding what looked tastiest.

Hyena packs generally didn't bother actually *killing* their prey before tucking in to a nice family dinner, if they'd crippled them too badly to run away. They often pulled the guts out as an initial delicacy.

"If you only knew how intensely I'd been looking forward to this, Tribune . . . Oh, this is a *good* day. Mars is with us. *Mars Ultor.*"

That particular aspect of the war deity was God of *Vengeance*, too. To Romans, revenge wasn't a *guilty* pleasure. Most of them considered it a moral obligation, and most of them reveled in it, blood and screams and all. There were times you were forcefully reminded that they'd never been Christians.

"I think I can take a guess at how you've been anticipating this, sir," Artorius said soberly.

Damn, but can I ever, he reflected, as Fronto laughed, a sound as nasty as his tooth-baring smile.

Romans had sometimes been able to talk themselves into believing they didn't *want* the Barbaricum of northern and central and eastern Europe. Telling each other it was cold and poor, sterile and backward, swarming with filthy dumb-blond savages and covered in giant forests and endless prairies, not worth the trouble of conquering.

Until we *told them where the gold and silver were. But they* know *that Alexander's Greeks . . . well, his Macedonians and Greek merce-naries . . . conquered all the way to India and it smarts that they can't. They don't think of* Parthia *and* India *as poor and backward, not at all, it's* rich *territory by second-century standards and they'd like to get their hands on it. Oh,* how *it smarts that they can't. Well, they couldn't until now. . . . Damn the Chinese time travelers, they moved this war up by years! If we'd had more time, the Parthians might even have surrendered without a fight. A lot of brave men are going to die today and in the next year because of them. Not to mention lots of civilians who'll starve or get burnt out or marched off in chains.*

The Roman force waited impassively as the darting cloud of Parthian horse archers approached, their speed increasing until the dust cloud they raised towered above them and the pulsing roar of the kettledrums grew ever louder. The disciplined silence of the Roman ranks echoed loudly; nothing moved but an occasional horse stamping and tossing its head, or the slight sway of a standard in the wind.

"Eight hundred yards," Fil said quietly from behind Artorius.

He relayed it to Fronto. Who knew how good she was at quick estimates, but couldn't be *seen* taking advice on things military from a woman. Even one with a quasi-supernatural reputation; it might have been different if she'd been seen as a full-blown god-dess, of course. Sarukê was beside her and prudently silent, but her lips were curling in disdain at what she regarded as stupid Roman superstitions about the sexes.

The irony being Fil's a lot *better than I* am *at ranges, without lasers and built-in calculators,* Artorius thought, catching Verus looking at her speculatively.

The crews of the *tormenta* cannon and the *carroballistae* and the riflemen had already adjusted the elevation screws or sights of their weapons to three hundred and were standing by.

Sarukê was there because she wouldn't let Artorius go into battle without her, since he was her oath-sworn chief and lord, and a *good* lord deserving of the most loyal service. That was how she thought of her job as chief of his bodyguards, which she still technically was. She wouldn't let her sword-sister—effectively her spouse, by her tribe's customs—go somewhere dangerous alone either.

Right now she was whistling an oddly haunting minor-key tune and had her unhelmed head cocked to one side.

"A lot like us Aorsi," she said conversationally to Fil. "But not dressed quite same. Funny floppy hats, look like big loose foreskins on little, tiny dicks."

Fil chuckled and handed over her binoculars, and the Sarmatian used them with aplomb.

"And they small, dark," she added.

Her own tribe tended to have a lot of tall, hawk-faced, gray-eyed, reddish-blond types like her, though they also had a bit of an East Asian strain that cropped up sometimes, acquired long before they migrated west to Ukraine. Thus ending up where some of their very remote ancestors, the Proto-Indo-European speakers of the Yamnaya culture, had started out before moving *west*. And then *back* east through the forest-steppe zone, in the third millennium BCE. All of it making a gigantic, flattened circle across three-quarters of Eurasia, deeply imbued with bloodshed every step of the way.

The Aorsi are sort of like me, Artorius thought whimsically. *Except my eyes are blue, like Mom's. Apparently blue eyes started in the west of Europe and spread east, and pale skins and light hair and gray eyes started in the east and spread west. Except for redheads. Everyone on Earth is an ingredient in a stew...just with local variations in the ingredients.*

If he remembered correctly, archaeology and ancient DNA research had shown that the Proto-Indo-Iranians had originated just east of the Urals about twenty-five hundred years ago... back from 171 CE, that was...with an eastward migration of the Corded Ware culture, then through the Sintashta and Andronovo. The Corded Ware derived from some of the original Proto-Indo-European migrants from Ukraine into Europe who'd settled in what he thought of as western Poland and eastern Germany and expanded from there.

It had also been known as the *battle-axe culture*, from the characteristic grave goods buried with its chiefs: heavy stone tomahawks, more or less.

They'd interbred a bit with the locals they found there on the northern European plain, and then spread explosively east and west, and were the source population for northern Europe in general: Scandinavians and other Germanics and Slavs and

Balts and Celts. Ultimately, in the course of less than a thousand years, they'd spread from Ireland in the west to what had become Chelyabinsk Oblast thousands of miles to the east.

Their *farthest* eastward fringe had developed into the northern-steppe version of early Indo-Iranians on the eastern slopes of the Urals, where they invented the war chariot. And from there some of the Indo-Iranians had gone south into Central Asia, Iran and India. That subgroup had called themselves *Aryas*, meaning roughly *the noble free ones*.

Which was typical of self-bestowed ethnonyms.

I've yet to meet... or even hear about... a group who call themselves the "Wretched Gutless Scum Please Spit on Us We Do It Ourselves," he thought. *My tribe hot stuff, your tribe stinks, kill-kill-kill—a basic human instinct. And we do move around a lot.*

"*Usha*, not bad horses, though," Sarukê went on, adjusting the thumb screw of the binoculars. "No, not bad. We should get some, after battle, for our land place. They ride pretty good, too," she added with lordly condescension. "For peoples without stirrups."

As the enemy came to within six hundred yards, the long straight *tubae* and curled *cornua* sounded. The first two rows of infantry instantly went to one knee—the first rank propping their heavy scutum shields on the ground before them, and the second holding theirs up to present a smooth sloping surface to the enemy. Each of the second-rank shields rested on the upper corners of two of the ones in the front file, and together with the pilum points it ensured that no horse not terminally depressed and prey to suicidal ideation was going to ram into them.

The long pila javelins were grounded with their butts braced on the gritty earth beneath and their points in two bristling rows. Behind them both ranks of riflemen brought their weapons to port arms, muzzles pointing upward, and thumbs went to the hammers. The rifles were loaded, of course, but strict orders and drastic punishments kept the hammers down on an empty flash tube until the just-before-engagement order was given.

It had taken the troops a little while to realize just how deadly an unexpected shot could be and some hadn't fully grasped it yet. They weren't used to death being unleashed with the slip of a finger, except for catapult crews. You had to *intentionally* throw a javelin or cut and thrust with a sword for it to hurt someone, generally speaking.

CLICKCLICKCLICK—

A second or two of metallic noise as five thousand thumbs pulled back five thousand hammers in response to another set of calls from *tubae* and *cornu*. A *third* set of horn calls, and the first rank of riflemen levelled their weapons over the heads of the two rows kneeling before them.

"Three hundred . . . *now,*" Fil said.

Fronto had extended his right hand a moment before, with the fist clenched and his thumb upright—a rough-and-ready way of estimating ranges that Artorius had set out to learn himself. You could tell range more or less by how big a figure—man, or mounted man—looked next to the thumb with one eye closed.

Because it turns out I'm lousy at doing it instinctively, he thought.

The crews around the cannon and *carroballistae* stood ready, and the Syrian archers drew shafts from their belt quivers and nocked them to their powerful laminated-recurve bows. Those outranged horse-archer weapons, particularly Parthian ones; their Roman cavalry equivalents could use heavier draws nowadays, since stirrups let you use your legs and core to draw as well as arms and shoulders.

Pretty much as if you were standing on the ground. Not a massive advantage but it's there, Artorius thought.

The shrill whooping cries of the Parthian horse bowmen sounded through the eerie silence of the Roman ranks. Nothing moved in their formation, but for banners flapping or a horse tossing its head.

The golden Eagles reared above the ranks, their talons resting on silver thunderbolts . . .

"*Now!*" Fronto barked.

He called the command right on the heels of Fil's ranging estimate; this time he forgot to wait for Artorius to relay the data. Nobody would notice because . . .

The noise that followed his order and its—very loud—repeat by the horns was indescribable.

The *crack* of rifles multiplied by twenty-five hundred times, like a mile-long string of firecrackers going off in less than two seconds, the *BOOOOM!* of forty-eight cannon, and the multiple *tunnnng-WHACK* of the *carroballistae* throwing arms hitting the stops, all combined into one massive blow to the ears.

Seconds later came the *CRACKCRACKCRACK* of the hundred-odd bronze balls the catapults had cast as they exploded, like a single prolonged blast...with half a metric ton of gunpowder behind it.

At three hundred yards, the Parthian riders had just been setting their first arrows to the string. A massive cloud of dirty-white black-powder smoke from rifles and cannon hid the consequences for a moment, together with that from the scores upon scores of Jove's Balls and the powdered earth they'd thrown skyward too. Then it drifted back behind the Roman position—eastward—and sight cleared.

Tubae and *cornu* sounded again, and the second rank of Roman riflemen levelled their weapons while the first reloaded. The first rear-rank volley was very slightly ragged, because eyes had been caught by the spectacle ahead of them.

The wielders of the new weapons had expected them to be deadly...but not quite *that* deadly.

Twenty-five hundred rifles, Artorius thought, levelling his binoculars. *I'd say...oh, a third to a half of the bullets hit a man or a horse. Big, big target, not trying to hide, not very far away.*

In the century where he'd started his life, back before that day in June six years ago, it usually took hundreds or thousands of rounds on average to hit a living target. But that was a product of everyone dispersing, taking cover and camouflaging as hard as they could. You snap-shot at men in camo gear, ones you would only see for a fleeting instant in an environment where visibility very nearly equaled death.

Occasionally you caught them unawares and in the open, and then there was an ambush-slaughter.

That was all prompted by long painful experience, starting in the eighteenth century by light infantry skirmishers. Here soldiers didn't even *try* to hide, and their gear was bright, showy and intended to intimidate the enemy and buck up your own side as much as anything. So were the massed formations...which had abruptly become a bit suicidal.

Hmmm, second volley is doing even better. Damn, but point-blank volley fire on a massed target is deadly! They're even closer now—you can't pull a galloping horse up right away. Or it may just panic, and a panicked horse runs. I like horses, but they're not really very bright away from what they evolved for. Running is an instinctive solution to a problem for them and sometimes they just...run.

That first volley hadn't been bad at all...

Except from the recipients' point of view, he thought mordantly.

It was fairly close range and the target was at least six riders deep. And just preparing to turn right so that they could set up a circle of arrow fire, so if a shot missed the target the rifleman who was aiming for it had five more chances to do some damage.

A horse archer could shoot straight ahead, straight back, and anywhere between...as long as it was to their left.

Half or more of the Parthian front line were down from the rifle fire alone—men thrown by collapsing horses, or bucked off by wounded ones, or punched out of the saddle by the five-hundred-grain bullets which were about the size of a nine-year-old's thumb, still traveling at nearly a thousand feet per second when they struck. A scattering of casualties from the rifles extended right back to the rear of the horse archers.

The forty-two twelve-pounder cast-iron cannonballs had all done damage too. Each had hit between one and a dozen times as they struck diagonally across the Parthian formation. The ones that struck short on the hard desert ground and bounded forward had done nearly as much harm. Horse legs snapped like straws.

Even for an expert rider, coming off a damaged horse at high speed was very dangerous...starting with hitting the *ground* at high speed. And then the falling horse might land on you, or roll over on you, or just kick you in the head or ribs and shatter bone.

And there had been a hundred and twenty of Jupiter's Balls, from sixty launchers per legion. The carnage from those had been even worse than the small arms and cannon inflicted. Three hundred yards was medium-long range for the catapults, but a lot of the balls had rolled or bounced forward right under the hooves of the first two or three ranks of Parthian horsemen. Then the scores of lead bullets that lined each of them had blasted upward into the legs and bellies of horses and the legs of men gripping the beasts' bodies, punching into guts and groins, throats and heads, or snapping bones. When they hit at just the right angle it was like a long cleaver in the hands of a knacker, slicing open stomachs...

Artorius focused his binoculars. He saw one Parthian rider—he had a forward-slanting peaked cap of loose cloth on his head, with its strings dangling on either side of his black-bearded face—unhurt but splashed from head to toe with blood. His eyes were wide and his face slack in gaping motionless shock at the unseen death that had torn through his comrades, and then he frantically tried to turn his horse.

That failed because the animal was bolting in panic, and then two bullets from the third volley slammed him over the horse's rump and to the ground, about a hundred yards from the Roman front line. The horse galloped on, and Romans crowded to the side to let it through—someone would grab its reins when it was tired enough to slow down.

Fronto grinned like a happy wolf contemplating a crippled elk as the *carroballistae* reloaded—that was done by the six-horse hitches that hauled them, through pulleys built into their frames, and it only took about twenty seconds, slightly faster than the cannon. They weren't all that much bigger than traditional Roman field catapults, but they threw more weight a lot further.

Tunnnnggg-WHACK again, the noise going on longer as the crews had reloaded in not-quite-synchronization. Then a string of blasts as the Jove's Balls exploded, many of them in the air over the Parthians this time because the crews had lit the fuses closer to the bronze.

The cannon crews had been in their own ballet—pushing the guns back into battery, then a wet sponge down the barrel on one end of the ramming pole to quench any sparks, then a linen bag of powder with a wooden sabot on top, and this time a leather cylinder full of marble-sized iron grapeshot ahead of that instead of a single cannonball.

A man stepped up to each breech and ran a thin, pointed steel rod down the touchhole to poke a hole through the linen, then snapped a big percussion cap onto the raised rim of the redone touchhole, now a hollow steel bolt screwed into the bronze. A second and the big hammer was cocked, the gunner aimed, jumped aside and chopped his hand down, at which signal another crewman pulled the lanyard...

BOOOOM!

With a slightly different sound as the grapeshot fanned out before each gun, like a shotgun shell four inches across. Each cannon was skewed so the shot went *across* the Parthian formation, instead of just through it. That upped the probability of a hit considerably. The crews sprang back in, grabbing the wheels to run the guns forward again to their starting position where the rammers and ammo handlers began all over again.

And then the endless CRACKCRACKCRACK of the thunder-balls, and twenty-five-hundred rifles in each of the two ranks, each punching out a volley every twenty seconds...

More diffuse firepower than I was used to, but that's quite a punch *with the men all packed together like that. And we* never *got targets as big as what they're firing into. Nobody except ban-dits and skirmishers takes cover or spreads out here. They're used* to *seeing* what's coming at them, *too. From their point of view this is invisible death striking without any warning at all except a loud noise.*

"The Parthian cataphracts are moving forward," Fronto said, focusing his telescope past the carnage just to the Roman front.

"Won't do them any good," Artorius said judiciously; he wasn't looking at the massacre either once he'd gotten a good idea of the effect.

Why look? Won't make anything *any better if I get* more *nasty stuff in my head. God or the Gods know there's enough there already. Verus there... he's gulping a bit. Early exposure ought to case harden him more.*

"Yes, but I'm not surprised," Fronto said happily. "They're too far back to see what's happening very well... the smoke doesn't help..."

He tapped his telescope.

"... and they don't have these. Their cataphracts *always* move forward if their mounted archers get into trouble against us. Usually the threat's enough to rescue the light-armed horse so they can rally behind the heavy cavalry. If the cataphracts are in range for a charge, infantry facing them have to halt and close up. Often enough they don't have to *do* the charge, just *threaten* it. Which lets them choose when to have a battle."

He laughed aloud again, and his eyes were glittering. Fronto had been a general in the last war and had beaten Parthian armies.

Romans often did.

But then the Parthians simply rode off, regrouped, and the dance began again. Infantry armies couldn't force an all-mounted enemy to engage if they didn't want to, unless the infantry was heading for something the other side *had* to defend. Or had weeks to march the horses to death, and that only worked if they *didn't* have lots of remounts. Parthians usually had plenty. That mobility kept them from exhausting the grazing in any one spot, too.

"Or it *did* let them choose whether to engage and when to break off an engagement. Not anymore!" the Roman general from Asia Minor went on, gloating heavy in his tone. "Now they can't come anywhere near us! We're immune from their archery!"

Imperial armies hadn't often been in a position to *slaughter* their Parthian opposite numbers before this, and he was enjoying every moment of it. He went on:

"But the heavy horse... that's where their commander will be... don't realize they've *lost* more than half their mounted bowmen already! By the *Gods on Olympos* it's a pleasant change to be able to hit them from well beyond their range."

Chunks of the Parthian force had gotten to within a hundred yards or so of the Roman line and a spatter of arrows were going thunk into the row of shields; a few riflemen staggered as points bounced off their *lorica segmentata* armor or helmets. A few went down cursing or screaming or silent... dead silent... as the iron arrowheads bit flesh.

The wind bore the salt-metallic smell of blood now, as well as the burnt sulfur stink of black powder.

The Syrian auxiliary archers raised their bows and shot as their regimental signalers blew—there were several thousand of them, and the arrows descended in whistling clouds that sounded like distant wind through reeds. Into the ranks of the remaining unarmored Parthians and their even more vulnerable horses, dropping even more of them. There wasn't enough counterfire to throw the foot archers off their stride.

Probably they're enjoying this as much as Fronto is.

Then Fronto signaled to the trumpeters and *cease fire* rang out.

The surviving and still-mounted horse archers, about two thousand of them, were now bolting backward and away from each other in wild panic human and equine, scattering like beads of mercury dropped on a hot frying pan and no longer presenting a massed target.

Ones who'd lost their horses to death or uncontrollable bucking fits from wounds were running flat out on foot too, though much more slowly and with the waddling gait of those who spent most of their life on horseback.

Some others were limping, or just crawling on their bellies and leaving a trail of blood on the thirsty earth, some with arrows standing out of their backs, more with wounds from the firearms. Piles and drifts of bodies still or twitching or writhing in agony lay with their dead or dying horses, and a thread of shrill pain rose from them as the seriously wounded tried to staunch blood with their hands—or shove their guts back into blown-open stomachs, or gobbled with jaws shot off, or stared in disbelief for a few seconds at severed legs and arms before slumping in wide-eyed death.

A lot of newly dead men look surprised until their faces relax, he thought.

That hadn't changed, at all.

Norsirree, Bob, as grandpa used to say.

"Horsemeat stew for the men tonight," Fronto laughed. "Or roast horse. As much as they can eat! The meat won't keep in this warm desert weather! I'll order a double wine ration in celebration, too."

The Parthian cataphracts glittered as they moved up at a slow trot, a rippling sea of flashes of bright desert sun off polished metal. They were armored from head to foot, corselets of lamellar armor over their torsos, or tunics of scale mail, then more bands or mail or scale sleeves on their arms and legs, and veils of chain mail hiding their faces below the tall spired helmets with only the proud dark eyes showing. Even their boots were strapped with iron and brass.

Silver and gold glittered as well, inlaid on the armor and helmets, or shining from buckles and hilts elsewhere on their harness. Their big horses were covered too, sheathed from neck to rump with leather curtains sewn over with polished iron scales and fancifully decorated metal masks with grids for the eyes, leaving only the legs exposed from the knees or hocks down. Sunlight winked off the mounts too as they moved, and slobber drooled from the heavy bits as they tossed their heads. The horses didn't like the scent of horse blood, not at all.

Artorius knew a moment's melancholy; it was a stunning spectacle, beauty and dread combined... and one that wouldn't happen much anymore. Not in Parthia, at least.

They rode forward with arrogant self-confidence, their long *contus* spears gripped in both hands. The fate of the horse archers had been gruesome...but it had been fairly close to the Roman line, and they'd still be confident in their armor. Quite understandably; it meant they could stand up to arrows unless fired at close range, after all, unlike unarmored men. The horse archers hadn't been wearing any protection at all for the most part, only their normal riding clothes and an occasional helmet.

The cataphracts didn't *know* that the new Roman weapons could ignore any armor a man could carry. Nothing they knew about except catapult bolts did, and those weren't common.

They don't know yet. And they're landed aristos and their well-born relations and retainers, Artorius thought. *That gear costs the earth here and now, and horses big enough to carry it aren't cheap either, and they have to supply both themselves. The Parthians are closer to feudalism than to an empire like Rome with a real central government. Those men are used to being big fish in a small pond back home, and they've got elevated self-images. They probably listened to a lot of epic poetry about fearless heroes when they were kids as well.*

Fronto nodded when he mentioned that.

"They need taking down a peg," he said confidently. "Let's hope they're arrogant enough to think they're still invulnerable because of their ironmongery."

He paused, considered, and gave an order. Trumpets sounded in counterpoint, and the Roman cavalry moved forward and out, swinging wide as they rode forward.

"They'll stop," the Roman general said. "But they'll think they're safe enough at—"

"Five hundred yards," Fil said to Artorius as the cataphracts reined in, and he repeated it.

"Twice long bowshot...maybe bit less," Sarukê observed. "Good trick, let first ones get so close! Lord Artorius is war-wise, true and sure!"

She was relaxed and casual, armored like one of the Roman lancers save for the bowcase-quiver at her belt, but with the helmet slung at her saddlebow.

She nodded acknowledgment of the stratagem to Artorius. Death and mutilation simply didn't engage her emotions much one way or another, unless it was to her kin or friends: then it moved her to fury. Or if it happened to a personal enemy, in which case she actively enjoyed it. Otherwise dealing it out was simply one of the tasks of the warrior's trade, and being on the receiving end a known risk.

"Bad about hurt horses," she added casually.

She *liked* horses.

There was a paleness about Fil's clenched lips, though. To civilian twenty-first-century eyes this was like the biggest freeway pileup ever or some other bloody disaster; even a veteran like him wasn't used to so many dead in one spot.

Maybe in World War One, the opening day on the Somme? he thought. *Before people really grasped what machine guns and rapid-fire artillery could do to densely packed formations.*

"Fusion bombs," he murmured to Fil in English, and she nodded and relaxed a little.

That was what they were trying to save the world from, after all.

The Parthian cataphracts were drawing rein because they were cautious about being encircled. Though they still numbered more than the Roman horses, and more than twice the numbers of the Roman lancers. Cataphracts could ignore horse archers as long as they were moving en masse, at least for a while, and provided they were prepared to take *some* losses.

"Too flat here," Sarukê observed casually to Fil. "With *new things*, would need use fold in ground to get close. Then not get hit so much charging, maybe manage to get in sword distance."

She sighed and tapped her bow. "Rifles against bows, no use shooting arrows. Hmmm, I wonder . . . rifle could be used on horse? Maybe? Hard to load, though."

Nobody had ever said Parthian cataphracts weren't brave. If anything, they were reckless, as warrior elites obsessed with honor and reputation tended to be. By all their experience, they were also completely safe from Roman *infantry* at this distance, and from field catapults. Not even the fate of the mounted archers and the shattering noise of the new Roman weapons had disabused them of that notion.

After all, the archers *weren't* armored and they *had* been closer . . .

Not thinking it through yet, he thought. *Or they don't have enough evidence to do that. Let's see how quickly they learn.*

The *carroballistae* and archers stayed silent; five hundred yards was beyond their range, though only just for the field catapults. But the infantry leveled their rifles, and the gun crews of the cannon batteries were standing ready, each with its centurion waiting the order. The cannon could hit at up to a mile, and the rifles were effective on massed targets at more than half again this range.

Fronto laughed aloud as he chopped his hand downward; *gravitas* permitted that. Except for that expectation of emotional control that a Roman aristo had to show to maintain respect, Artorius wouldn't have been very much surprised if he'd started *rubbing* his hands together.

And slapping people on the back, and showing *the fig* to the enemy with both fists, the Roman equivalent of an elevated middle finger. Or getting down on the ground to dance a jig of sheer rampant glee, snapping his fingers over his head and clicking his heels.

Tubae and *cornu* sounded...

Cannon bellowed. Rifles crackled in stuttering volleys. The infantry reloaded quickly, and the gun crews danced their stylized rituals. The BOOM...BOOM of the guns was less synchronized now, but the volleys of rifle fire still slammed out with the regularity of a metronome to the trumpet calls. Hundreds of the cataphracts fell...

"There they go," Artorius observed; the Parthian heavy cavalry were turning about and trotting off.

Some turned in the saddle to make obscene gestures or shake their fists; distance swallowed their voices, but they were probably complaining about unfair tactics.

"Ah, they picked it up fairly quickly. But then, from where they stopped they could see what happened to the horse archers, too. And they got a quick lesson in how useless their armor is," Artorius observed.

Thousands of the horse-archers' bodies... and the bodies of their horses... littered the arid plain closer to the Roman line. The smell of blood was heavy, along with the fecal reek of ripped-open bodies; horse blood and human blood didn't have different scents to the nose, and even their opened guts weren't *very* different in the stink they made.

We're all just mammals in death, Artorius thought. *And retreating before deadly sorcery... that's different from running away from ordinary human beings with swords in their hands, too. That's what they'll be thinking, and praying to Mitra or Ahura Mazda to protect them.*

The screams of wounded horses were often loud, too, similar to but...

Bigger, he thought,

...than the cries of dying and mutilated humans. Fronto laughed again, and spoke to his signalers.

This time the sound sent the Roman cavalry forward; the mounted archers cantering further westward in two long arcs, and the lancers forming up in a block four *ala*—regiments—across, the heavy horse three deep.

The Roman horse archers could ignore the remnants of their Parthian equivalents, who probably wouldn't stop running until their horses dropped dead under them or they reached their home ranges, whichever came first. The Roman light horse were now better equipped, too; they all had short waist-length mail shirts with elbow-length sleeves, good helmets and round shields slung over their backs, besides the new saddles. Not enough gear to slow their horses perceptibly, but enough to make a difference in an exchange of arrows at a distance, and a really *big* difference for the lightly armed Parthians if they closed to sword range.

The Roman general waited—longer than Artorius would have—to sound the *cease fire* again. By then the Roman lancers were getting uncomfortably close to a few of the bounding or rolling cannonballs, and rifle fire kicked spurts of dust into the air only a few yards ahead of them. As if that had been a signal—which it had been—the far-off trumpets of the Roman lancers sounded the charge. The *ala* regiments sped up to a trot, then a canter, trailing a growing plume of dust.

A hundred yards from the Parthian cataphracts they spurred into an all-out rush but one that maintained their neat alignment, the lances going from a slant to the level in a long rippling fall as they were couched under right arms. That kept the advance to the pace of the slowest horses, but they'd been selected for speed and toughness and the riders thoroughly drilled.

Many of the Parthian cataphracts turned, welcoming a challenge they thought they understood. There were enough to outnumber the Roman cavalry by half, though their formation was more open because a fair number of the others had simply galloped off.

Fronto snickered again. "The ones running will be hunted down by *our* horse archers," he said.

Cataphracts in a mass could often stand off mounted bowmen

by threatening charges that the lightly armed horsemen couldn't match. Over a short to medium distance the heavy horse could move faster, too, since their mounts' legs were longer. Long bowshot was just about the distance charging long-legged horses could cover in a bit less than a minute at full speed.

But if the cataphracts scattered... then they were vulnerable. Very vulnerable. Particularly once their horses were tired, and that happened much more quickly with the weight of armor they carried. Then horse archers could swarm them, shooting from all directions at distances close enough to wound and kill.

It's a game of rock-scissors-paper, Artorius thought, *Or it was like that.*

Aloud he went on:

"The ones countercharging are braver, or better disciplined. But they're in for another—"

The two masses of fast-moving armored horsemen on big mounts collided. There was no unified crash; instead a multiple thudding with a metallic undertone as lance heads rammed into armor, beneath the massed, muffled drum of hooves. Horses collided shoulder to shoulder, and some of them went down—head over heels, or more commonly sideways, always with a surprised scream of equine terror.

"—nasty surprise," he said.

The Parthian heavy cavalry was moving at a fast canter or slow gallop, and they thrust their long spears two-handed like well-armored pikemen on horseback. The Roman lancers had their lances couched, held under their arms with three-quarters of the weapons' length ahead of them.

They weren't thrusting with their arms; they were just *holding* the lances, bracing themselves and letting the *horse* provide the punch behind the point. That meant an animal weighing around half a ton traveling at nearly thirty miles an hour and carrying a man wearing fifty or sixty pounds of gear... and when you were meeting a countercharge, the speed and weight of the *opposing* horse and rider got added in too.

All of it concentrated right behind the point of the lance.

Together the raised cantle, wooden frame and the stirrups of the new Roman saddles made that possible. Simple wood-framed saddles were already being used in what would have become Mongolia eventually, and would have spread. Stirrups would have been invented somewhere in East Asia about two or three hundred years from now, in the history Artorius had learned, and had arrived in Europe in the sixth century CE when the Avar nomads came careening in off the steppe and set up shop in what he thought of as Hungary. The couched-lance technique was much later than that, well into the early European medieval period, the eleventh century and after.

The Parthian cataphracts were meeting a full thousand years of shock-cavalry development all at once. It wasn't quite like cannon against men who'd never heard of gunpowder . . . but it wasn't absolutely different, either.

Nearly every lance struck home, and unlike the Romans, the Parthian cataphracts weren't carrying shields and . . . until now . . . hadn't needed them. Their gear made them invulnerable to arm-powered spear thrusts or sword cuts almost everywhere except the face and throat and possibly the hands and wrists.

The shields the Roman lancers carried turned most of the Parthian thrusts if the cataphracts got close enough, and their new-style armor most of the rest. The eastern cataphracts' heavy protective gear was *not* proof against the momentum of man and horse behind a hardened steel lance point shaped like an elongated metalworker's punch. Over half of the Roman lancers skewered their opponents right through their armor, killing them or wounding them badly, and letting the lance pivot in their hand to pull itself free. About half the remainder knocked their opponents off their horses and onto the ground where they lay stunned and immobile for long moments. Or longer, for those with broken bones or wrenched joints.

Fifteenth-century plate armor would have done a lot better, Artorius thought.

Because it was designed to shed lance points by sliding them off smooth steel plates . . . and would do the same to the point or edge of a sword. It would never get going here, of course, because it wouldn't keep out bullets.

We won't have a monopoly of gunpowder weapons much longer. We don't now . . . if you count China. Another generation or two, and body armor will be obsolete.

The Roman lancers swept through with light losses, rallied around their standards to the call of the trumpets a hundred and fifty yards beyond the Parthian mass, turned neatly and charged again. Those who'd lost or broken their lances, or more often had left them rammed through armored Parthian bodies, drew their long swords, or unhooked segmented maces and war hammers from their saddles, or in a few cases picked up a discarded Parthian *contus*. Those were about the right length.

A few of the Parthians simply fought to the death, and a few galloped away witlessly in panic.

Most of the cataphracts threw down their weapons after that second charge killed or unhorsed about a third as many as the first, bewildered, or tricked into thinking their foes protected by magic. They doffed their helmets, dropped their spears and raised their hands in the air.

Then they waited tensely to see if there would be mercy—no rule of war here and now said the Romans *had* to take prisoners. There was no point in trying to flee for those who hadn't given in to blind terror, not with the Imperial horse archers behind them and waiting with arrows on strings.

The Roman lancers had been instructed to take surrenders, orders that came from the Emperor himself. They brusquely ordered the armored Parthians down, to drop their weapons... including any concealed daggers, on pain of death...and kneel on the ground with their hands on their heads. Phrases like that were something most soldiers picked up quickly in the language of their enemies, and those who couldn't understand through the accents copied the ones who could.

Then the Roman troopers began to round up the big...and very valuable...horses. Off and spot-tiny in the distance the Imperial horse archers were taking prisoners too, or simply shooting the exhausted enemy down with bodkin-pointed shafts as they fled, and collecting their mounts. There was a quick, efficient flurry as the Parthian dead, wounded and prisoners were relieved of anything that looked small, portable and valuable including belt pouches stuffed with what these well-to-do fighters considered enough coin for day-to-day expenses. That was a perk of winning here.

"I'd advise we march on a mile or two and then make camp for the night, sir," Fronto said to the Emperor, glancing upward at the sky; it was well into the afternoon. "That'll give plenty of time for digging the ditches and building the earth berms... with the prisoners doing most of the work. And the new-style latrines, for that matter. They even make the camps smell better! If all of that's your will, sir?"

He added that to Marcus Aurelius, and the Emperor nodded agreement.

"Let it be so," Rome's ruler said in measured tones. "And the battle was brilliantly done, Legate Fronto."

Fronto laughed again, and waved a hand in Artorius' direction.

"Caesar Augustus, the real credit..." he said.

"Yes," the Emperor said. "The *new things* made this possible, but you *used* them very well, despite their novelty. That is to your credit; a bad commander can ruin even the best situation. And you not only took advice, you saw the reasoning behind it quickly. Obviously you had given the implications of the new weapons' capacities serious thought. Oh, and inform the troops that the Parthian prisoners won't be sold. Many of them may be ransomed; they're rich men, or rich men's sons and brothers and cousins. The cataphracts are, at least."

Fronto looked slightly alarmed; the sale price of prisoners was another valued side-benefit perk that Roman soldiers expected a share of after a victory. Slave traders usually accompanied the Army on campaign for exactly that reason. The troops would be seriously peeved if they were denied it.

Marcus Aurelius was very popular with the Army, more than any Emperors since Trajan and Hadrian and their regard for him hit a new peak after every victory, but...

The Emperor smiled. "No need for alarm, Legate Fronto. You may also inform the troops that they'll get a donative of the same value as the prisoners would have fetched, at the next pay day."

He looked over at his son, to see if the boy had gotten the point. The youngster pursed his lips and nodded, getting a slight smile from his father in return.

Roman troops were paid every three months, and most of them banked it with their unit's signaler, who in turn put it in the legion or cohort or *ala*'s strongbox, neatly labelled and duly recorded. Apart from a little carousing money and enough for the odd dice game, or rather more to hand over to their—unofficial— wives to support their equally unofficial families.

A good many of them had taken advantage of an offer to have some of their wages deducted and passed out to the wives back at their original bases, which Artorius had suggested. That was safer for the families and especially the children—every time you moved into a new watershed here the intestinal bacteria came in new varieties. As a bonus, it reduced the train of camp followers burdening the Army.

"The ransoms will be larger in any case," the Emperor went on. "Two or three times larger than the prisoners' sale price. Your campaigns in the north, Legate Fronto... and now those of Legate Bassus... have cut the price of slaves all over the Empire."

Which is a major reason why the rest of the Germanii up there are mostly surrendering on terms when Bassus' men arrive, Artorius thought. *Moderately generous terms by contemporary standards. Don't want to end up picking olives in Spain or tending sheep in Sicily... or spending a short, painful few years digging for silver and gold in ankle fetters and sleeping in caves on filthy straw and never seeing the sun again. It'll be a while before free labor comes out on top in the Imperial mines.*

Not least because *mining* was popularly associated with *agonizing death.*

The two Americans—and Sarukê—fell in behind Marcus Aurelius, along with a *turma* of his horse guards as the troops finished up the after-battle chores and went back into a column of march. The troops raised cheers and roaring cries of:

"Ave, Imperator! Roma! Roma!"

...as the Emperor passed. With an occasional good-natured:

"Ave Caesar Verus!" at which point the boy lost his peaked look, grinned and waved back.

The Emperor stopped occasionally to speak with an officer or man, who invariably glowed at the praise bestowed even if smarting from a bandaged wound (and the new doubled-superwine disinfectant slathered on it) that was too minor to send him back to the medicos. Marcus Aurelius would visit the seriously wounded later, when they'd made camp.

There were cries hailing Fronto too, and others for Artorius the War-Wise and his followers, often accompanied by slapping the barrels of cannon or the throwing troughs of new-style *carroballistae,* or shaking their rifle-muskets in the air or demonstratively kissing them. There had been hundreds of Romans killed and wounded, but very few compared to the enemy's losses, and the troops were fully aware of why. And who was responsible for the *new things,* and the way they'd inflicted one of the most crushing defeats the Parthians had ever suffered.

And Marcus Aurelius isn't the sort of Emperor who carries a grudge if someone else gets plaudits too. Thank you, God! If we'd landed in Nero's time... or Caligula's... Come to think of it, I don't envy whoever's in charge of the Chinese time travelers. Not with what history records about Emperor Ling. He makes Commodus look like a model head of state!

"Mark and Paula will be glad to hear that about not selling the prisoners as slaves," Fil said to Artorius—in English. "So am I, for that matter."

They'd come to terms with the ubiquity of slavery here, but it was still repulsive, the more so because of the universal flat, blank acceptance of its inevitability. *Everybody* and *everywhere* had slaves here, to a greater or lesser extent, from the northern barbarians on through Rome and east to China, where it was much more common now than it would be later in that nation's history.

Yeah, Han dynasty estate-farming manuals just presume labor forces at least partly of slaves, if I recall correctly, Artorius thought.

For that matter Australian hunter-gatherer Aboriginals had slaves too, mostly abducted women.

Nobody seriously tried to justify slavery here and now, because they didn't need to; it was just bad luck for the enslaved. Or as Romans put it, avoiding slavery was easy: all you had to know was how to die. And slavery wasn't ethnically selective here, with human chattels running the full range from coal-black Sudanese to pink-and-blond northerners. Even some Roman slaves owned slaves, and if as often happened a freed slave prospered, they were among the first thing he or she bought. Freed slaves were notoriously harsh owners, too.

Mark and Paula were back with the medical train, supervising and teaching along with Galen. The new field ambulances with springs were collecting the Roman wounded, with injections of more-or-less-morphine for the pain and disinfectant for the wounds. Roman surgical techniques had already been surprisingly good, and with antisepsis and painkillers and blood transfusions—only between living humans for the present—and fully accurate anatomy the rate of survival had zoomed skyward.

Galen had even been doing successful experimental appendectomies and removing inflamed tonsils.

And they were picking up those Parthian cataphracts who looked likely to recover enough to pay a ransom; the wounded horse archers were just finished off, along with horses too badly hurt to be useful. Many of the four-footed dead were roughly butchered and the meat tossed into carts for tonight's dinner issue. Romans didn't have any prejudices against eating horsemeat, and looks were cast that way and lips were smacked.

Fighting was very hard physical work, and it left you hungry just as surely as breaking rock or digging ditches. The emotional stress of mastering fear wore on you, too, and a full belly and a night's sleep became powerfully attractive. Roman discipline would see that the sleep took place behind the walls of a marching camp, though.

Fresh meat wasn't all that common on campaign, though the Americans had introduced modern...which was to say, nineteenth-century...style barreled salt pork and corned beef. And they'd introduced chuck-wagon style mobile field kitchens with cast-iron gear, which could trundle along with bread rising or baking and stew simmering.

Jeremey was helping manage the *remount* train and wagon teams, in a supervisory sort of way, helped by Sarukê and Fil much of the time; Fil and he had both been horse enthusiasts in their teens, and had worked closely with the veterinarians who visited. Jem had picked up a good deal about animals from the farmers his father sold seed, feed and gear to in the Wisconsin dairy country, as well. Study in the files and books in Fuchs's baggage had added to that for him and Fil both.

The remounts were much healthier than usual, because of the hints he dropped and immediate killing of any who showed signs of contagious disease, and not least because shod horses suffered far fewer problems with their feet on this rocky ground. It was also bigger than a Roman herd accompanying a field force would have been a few years ago, since the new harness made horses and mules more useful in any number of ways and let them pull about twice as much.

And anyone who saw the Roman military's new harness wanted the same. The horseleeches and blacksmiths would be busy shoeing and doctoring the thousands captured today.

Horse prices had gone up over ever-growing chunks of the Empire as the *new things* spread, simply because they were much more useful for ordinary work now...and so much faster than oxen. So had the cost of mules, and they weren't just used as pack animals anymore.

The procurators in charge of the *res privata*, the huge Imperial estates in each province, were passing the innovations along to the tenants of various sizes who actually cultivated that land as well. The captured horses from this battle were going to be a substantial profit center. So would imports of horses from Parthia, once it was *in* the Empire, since it contained huge herds and price signals operated whether people understood the concept or not.

"Was that your idea, not selling the prisoners, Prof?" Fil asked.

"No, the Emperor came up with that on his own," Artorius said. "He figures that the Parthian aristos need to be frightened until they wet their drawers...but not driven wild with anger."

"Killing a lot of them won't do that?"

"Oh, not much—they're warriors by occupation, that's a standard risk and dying bravely ensures a good afterlife. Selling them as slaves would add insult to injury, though. That'll help politically with the annexation, since it'll be a strong hint they won't suffer in their persons or in their pockets beyond bearing. And politics is the ultimate point of—"

He waved towards the battlefield the Roman army was leaving behind; various scavenger birds were overhead, or circling downward—they kept an eye on each other, and moved in when some started to descend. That could trigger chains hundreds of miles long. The flies that swarmed in deserts—he'd never understood why they were so big, obtrusive and ubiquitous in hot arid lands, but they were—were having a tasty banquet too. Fortunately that was growing more distant with every minute.

The Roman troops made a long column of bristling steel as they fell in, moving with a victorious swagger despite the dust and sporting items of bright plunder behind the spread-wing golden Eagles of the Legions and the standards of lesser units. Here a jewel-hilted dagger of fine Indian steel was tucked through a belt, or a belt with gold plaques hung from a furca, or cavalrymen trotted by with loops of plundered gold and silver rings on leather laces around their necks.

Marching songs broke out now and then, sung with gusto, and often promising actions that would have a war-crimes tribunal fainting with shock up in the twenty-first century.

The cavalry banners were dragons—serpents with gape-mouthed bronze heads with hidden flutelike inserts, and long fabric bodies sewn with glittering gold and silver scales. They hissed and moaned and shrilled and rustled as the troopers trotted behind them, throwing a network of scouts before, behind and to either side of the column of march. They were being careful about raiding parties, though after *that* battle it would probably be a long time before any showed up.

Good habits keep a soldier alive, Artorius thought. *Alive longer, at least. That hasn't changed either, just a few of the details.*

The Tigris river wasn't too far to their left as they headed south; you didn't go far from water here if you could help it.

Fil thought for a moment, then gave a long whistle and said in English:

"No flies on our glorious leader!"

"Not one, metaphorically speaking," Artorius agreed, in the same language. "One of the smartest men I've ever met—and that includes the faculty at Harvard. And unlike a lot of them... well, he's not just technically intelligent, he's *sensible* too. Prolonged contact with reality, I suppose."

"Sensible... related but distinct concept from IQ," she said, nodding.

Then she dropped back into Latin; they all used it, or Greek, these days when they didn't need strict privacy.

"That battle... well, it wasn't much of a fair fight, was it? I doubt we lost more than a hundred or two hundred men—"

"Two fifty-three dead or very seriously wounded and likely to die," Artorius said; he'd been listening to reports to the Emperor and Fronto. "About half-and-half cavalry and infantry. The cavalry were the ones who got up close and personal, even if they had better gear."

Fil nodded. "They lost... thousands. Half their men or better, not counting prisoners. And there were lots and lots of prisoners."

"Yeah, well, right now we're into partition-of-Africa-level tech gaps. For a while, until we meet someone the Chinese have armed. We don't have Maxim guns... yet... but the other side doesn't have any firearms at all. Or any concept of what they can do. Until they get an idea it'll be like Omdurman in 1898, when Kitchener conquered the Sudan."

She looked a question, and he went on: "British losses forty-eight, Sudanese Mahdist losses between fifteen and twenty thousand dead... counting wounded who died while they tried to crawl to water. Hopefully this war will be over fast enough that the Parthians won't get a *chance* to adapt."

The cataphracts had been stripped of their armor, which had been tossed into wagons for reuse as scrap. The captives who could walk were trudging along behind the Roman column, heads down and now and then encouraged by light cavalry with casual swings of bowstaves or the toe of a boot. They weren't *too* depressed, except those very, very unpopular with their kinfolk—they'd been told they could be ransomed, and bilingual clerks would be writing out letters.

"Even more one sided than that last big fight with the Marcomanni & Co.," she said. "Hardly seems fair..."

Artorius laughed, a short hard bark.

"Fair is for football," he said with the flat sincerity of bone-deep conviction. "A battle's far too serious for *fair*. The best battle is a totally one-sided massacre—and this one nearly fit the description. You're right, it was even more...decisive...than that last fight with the Marcomanni; we've got a lot more gunpowder weapons now, that was mostly the legionaries with short sword and shield at the end. I wish *all* battles were one-sided massacres, come to that. Then there wouldn't be nearly as many wars. Hell, before the...you-know-who...showed up, that was what I was hoping for. Enough *un*fair fights that everyone else would just give up and join up when Rome came knocking at the door."

"Rules for stick and ball," Sarukê said in basic agreement, naming the Sarmatian ancestor of polo.

Her folk had a brutally pragmatic attitude to war, rather similar to that of Romans, if less complex and sophisticated.

Unlike, say, the Germanii, Artorius thought. *Most of them think of battle as performing for the Gods to show you're brave enough for a good afterlife, when they're not totally focused on fun and plunder.*

Barbarian cultures differed from each other as much as civilized ones did.

Sarukê went on:

"War? War...you kill. Not give enemy chance to kill *you* unless have to do that. Good be brave, yes! Even better, not *need* to be."

The Parthians played the precursor of polo too, meaning it probably went back to the original Proto-Indo-Iranian migrations from the eastern flank of the Urals a long, long time ago.

A long time ago even from the 170s CE, Artorius thought. *About, oh, two thousand years, maybe a bit more.*

Fil nodded and sighed with a mixture of regret and acceptance.

She'd had a fair amount of experience with war as Classical antiquity waged it since they arrived . . . and the consequences of defeat *here* were far, far more drastic than was usual up in the twenty-first century.

Except with nukes, Artorius thought.

Carefully *not* thinking of the family he'd had uptime. They'd been in Amarillo the day he and the graduate students arrived in Vienna, visiting kinfolk. Amarillo was a remote small city . . . but it had a nuclear weapons assembly center and a factory making military tiltrotors. A strike there was a virtual certainty.

Nukes . . . that's drastic enough for Satan Himself.

⋙ CHAPTER EIGHTEEN ⋘

Ctesiphon
Western Capital of the Parthian Empire
January 20th, 172 CE

The walls of the Parthian capital city had been hastily repaired after the Roman sack six years ago, and they shone under the morning sun in a mixture of bright white—the original sections—and dull khaki in the mild winter sunlight, about six hundred yards away. The locals hadn't gotten around to stucco for the repaired bits yet.

The city was on the east bank of the Tigris river, around a mile south of the Roman pontoon bridge the military engineers had run up, which was routine for them and had been since before Julius Caesar's time.

And it was about twenty miles and a bit from the site of Baghdad-that-would-never-be northwest of here.

A town of which I have distinctly unfond memories, Artorius thought. *Always looking over your shoulder and waiting for the IED...*

Ctesiphon was also right across the river from the slightly smaller and considerably older Greek-dominated city of Seleucia, named for the Seleucid dynasty, Macedonian warlords who'd once ruled from Syria to what would have become Afghanistan. That had been before they were ground to dust between the Romans from the west and the Parthians from the east, but their capital had survived, albeit rather battered. Not least by the fact that it had been sacked too—and set on fire to a massive degree—by the Romans in the last war, the one the Parthians had started when Antoninus Pius died.

The smell of the town—human sewage, dung from oxen and milch cows, horses, pigs and sheep and goats, plus rotting garbage kicked into alleys or into heaps against walls, and everything else down to dead rats and cat piss—brought the memories back...

But to be this obvious at six hundred yards, it must be considerably stronger than anywhere in twenty-first-century Iraq. And considerably concentrated inside those massive walls; they were forty feet high, with round or octagonal towers at intervals higher still.

Roman cities are bad enough, and they mostly do *have sewers and aqueducts. This... God, what the smallpox plague must have been like inside! Whole families dead and rotting in their homes, thousands dying who might have lived if they'd just had someone to clean them up and bring food and water. And who weren't afraid of catching it themselves. It started around here, too, about the last time the Romans sacked it and Seleucia. Some mutation in the virus, here or further east... but that means there are probably a lot fewer people inside than there used to be, what with war and plague. What must it have smelled like* then? *And in summer?*

Smallpox wasn't a new disease here. It had jumped from cattle to humans... or possibly from dogs or some other beast... a long time ago. But it was usually fairly low level, sporadically killing a fair number every year, mostly children, and leaving more with terrible scars. Every now and then a new variety cropped up, and the result was disaster on an epic scale.

And populations were just getting dense enough for a disease to spread from here to eastern Asia and back.

The actual plague—the Black Death, *Yersinia pestis*, would have eventually done that. Probably starting with Central Asian equivalents of gophers or prairie dogs and spreading east and west, spreading with the increased mobility that the Mongol conquests and empire had brought, and usually killing half or more of the total when it first struck. Plus recurring from pockets every generation or two; he remembered reading that it wasn't until two or three hundred years later that England had as many people again as it did before June of 1348 CE.

Which pre-Black Death level had been roughly the same number of people as the late Roman province of Britannia.

That's what would *have happened, except that we came along!*

We stopped the smallpox epidemic cold, he thought with pride. *No reason it can't be eliminated completely, in the long run. And we can eliminate a lot of other diseases too, or keep them from growing into epidemics with sanitation and quarantines.*

Directly across from them four towers linked together made a rectangular fort and framed a huge gate, though by Roman standards the road leading to it would have been considered rough even in the wilds of Britannia. It crossed to the gate on a bridge with brick piles and a wooden arch structure of thick beams above that; a quick glance through his binoculars showed the wood slick with something black... probably petroleum-derived pitch, so it would go up with a whoosh if a torch were tossed down. There were plenty of natural seepages of oil in this general neighborhood.

There were some in Dacia too—what had been Romania in his time—and crude tube-well drilling rigs were now in use. That was making a killing for some landlords and merchants who were sort-of-basic-refining it for Roman Fire to sell to the government and a lamp oil resembling kerosene these days, which they sold to everyone for use in the new nineteenth-century-style lanterns. Roman glassblowing and brassworking was plenty good enough for those, they'd just needed the idea and some examples.

That was small scale... so far. Their equivalents would do even better here... with locations from Fuchs's helpful maps slipped to them, once Parthia had been incorporated into the Empire.

A deep ditch full of semistagnant water thick with rotting waste stood at the wall's base. Which would produce bottomless thick clayey mud for anyone attacking the wall. If you fell in wearing armor, you'd choke to death.

And would also ensure swarming mosquitoes to carry malaria, and lots and lots of flies with very dirty and infectious feet landing on people's food and faces and eyes and on their babies.

There were those gene-modified mosquitoes Fuchs packed in the baggage... couple of thousand of them... and we set 'em free the way the instructions said. They survived...

The way malaria had dropped off suddenly in Pannonia and adjacent provinces demonstrated that; mosquito generations were short. In this era, and up until the seventeenth or eighteenth century in the original history, malaria—*bad air* had been the original meaning—was endemic in Europe near marshy places as far north as Denmark.

He'd even gotten the credit for it going away on the Villa Lunae, though the estate workers and tenants thought it was beneficent magic. Functionally, gene-tailored bugs *were* magic here; it was going to be a long, long time before knowledge of genetics filtered down to ploughboys and vinedressers.

. . . but God knows if they'll ever get this far. The genes might, though . . . they were designed to spread and jump to different varieties of mosquito. And they'll take care of yellow fever too. Damn the little bloodsuckers anyway. That won't do anything about the flies and fleas and lice and rats, though.

There were scorch marks from multiple funeral pyres on an extensive ground near the river; that would have been the bodies from the previous Roman sack, and then the sickness. Plenty of Towers of Silence, too—Zoroastrians put out their dead for the birds of prey (and rats and bugs) atop tall structures, here made of mud-brick. Probably a lot of prayer was going on inside right now, and across the river in the Greek-founded city too.

And probably a lot of bodies from the lower classes just got dumped in the river to float, bloat, rot and spread disease downstream.

Both towns been sacked at the tail end of the Romano-Parthian War five years ago. *Sack* meant anything that really, really pissed-off soldiers felt like doing to the locals, combined with deliberate arson. Just *starting* with stealing everything that wasn't too heavy to carry in a wagon. Besiegers didn't enjoy sitting outside the walls and suffering from camp fevers much, to put it mildly, and were usually in a murderous frame of mind by the time they stormed the defenses.

Marcus Aurelius lowered his telescope. "They have repaired the walls quickly," he observed.

The Praetorian Prefect was with them, as he usually was when the Emperor was in the field—he was commander of the Imperial guards and a number of other functions that made him the closest thing Rome had to a Chief of the General Staff.

His name was Sextus Cornelius Repentinus, and he was from a landholding family whose estates were near Carthage, in the Province of Africa, what the Americans thought of as Tunisia. There was a very slight guttural accent to his fluent upper-class Latin, probably a legacy from Carthaginian—also known as Phoenician, a Semitic tongue and close relative of Aramaic, Canaanite and Hebrew. Carthage had originally been a colony sent out from Tyre on what he thought of as the Lebanese coast.

Many still spoke that language there around Carthage alongside Latin; it was only gradually giving way to the Empire's tongue, and Repentinus was probably bilingual. It would be useful for an aristo from that region, if only to give orders to subordinates who *weren't* bilingual.

Under his embossed armor—marked with the scorpion blazon of the Guard—his tunic would, like Artorius', have only the narrow stripes of an *eques*, a member of the Equestrian Order. The position of Guard commander was too sensitive, too close to the Imperial family, to let someone of senatorial rank have it... though the *children* of a Praetorian Prefect usually made the leap to the upper rank of Roman aristos.

Repentinus blinked, obviously consulting files in his head— Artorius had noticed that Romans generally had better memories than people in his own century. It was a lot harder to look up written records here and now; not just the lack of computers, or for that matter cheap paper, but filing systems in general had been primitive before the Americans arrived. Mostly based on *clerks'* memories and what they'd picked up from their predecessors. Big archives were forbidding warrens.

Better methods were spreading now, with hanging folders in file cabinets and alphabetization and cross-references and indexes and various other innovations, but it would be a while before they became general anywhere except in Pannonia and at the top of the Imperial tree in Rome. The Army would get them first, but that would help spread it since a lot of the administrative staff under governors were soldiers on detached duty.

An Army with an Empire attached... he thought.

Repentinus went on:

"The spies report that the walls were already under repair, from the moment our troops withdrew in the previous war. When King Vologases received your ultimatum, sir, he doubled the number of workmen so that they could labor all day and by torchlight after sundown."

One of the Praetorian Prefect's direct subordinates oversaw the *Frumentarii*, the Roman equivalent of a combined CIA and FBI. Repentinus would get daily briefings. He continued:

"And he ordered them to pay no attention to looks, just to getting the job done as fast as they could."

Marcus Aurelius nodded. "Sensible... given what he knows,

or knew at that point. Sieges endanger the besieging armies. He could always hope and pray to the Gods to smite us with plague if we were here sitting outside the walls for months."

Primarily sieges mean danger from disease, Artorius thought, or translated.

This Roman Army wouldn't be nearly as vulnerable as previous ones, but the combination of warm weather, stagnant water in irrigation canals and a dense population with little sense of personal hygiene here would still be a threat despite all the Americans had been able to do. It would be a considerable while before there was enough chlorine to make water-purification tablets general issue, or enough pyrethrum to damp down the disease-carrying insects in the enlisted ranks and camp followers.

"Not this time, sir," Repentinus said, and nodded to Artorius. "Thanks to you and your clients, Tribune."

The Prefect's voice was calm and detached, his dark-olive face carefully unexpressive behind raven-black beard and scars. As far as looks went, he could have been Sicilian...or Tunisian. You had to bear in mind that the *mind* behind the face came from a culture that was deeply alien.

Artorius was convinced that Repentinus didn't actually *like* him much, and spent a fair amount of time trying to figure out what his deep, devious game really was.

He probably suspects me of wanting to be Emperor. God forbid, but that's not a point of view easy to get across believably.

By second-century Roman standards the American was direct and blunt to a bad-mannered fault, he'd been an outsider to start with, and anybody with the man's job would suspect someone who'd suddenly...over the course of only seven years...acquired so much influence with the Emperor. It was his duty to safeguard Marcus Aurelius from *all* threats, and as far as Artorius could tell he took it seriously and was genuinely devoted to Rome's ruler.

Legate Fronto rode up and saluted the Emperor just in time to catch that last remark by the Prefect, and grinned with a remarkably sharklike expression.

"No, indeed, Prefect," he said jovially, after saluting the Emperor. "No sitting around getting camp fever or running out of food in *this* siege!"

But Repentinus respects me, I think...and he most certainly respects the new toys I've given the Roman military. I think Fronto does *like me, even if he's a…difficult acquired taste…from* my *point of view. Hell, even Julia was in some respects. But then, I've given his career a massive boost. And he appreciates the nonmilitary* new things *too, as well as the weapons.*

And Fronto had—originally—died as governor of Dacia, in battle with the Sarmatian tribes who'd joined in with the Marcomanni during the much longer—original—version of the Marcomannic Wars. Probably right about now. He'd never know that, of course.

He'll get another *set of* ornamenta triumphalia *out of this, and then probably retire and oversee his sons' careers and make matches for his daughters. Thinking of which, I do wish he'd stop dropping hints about how marriageable his eldest daughter is, though. I'm a one-woman man, and even if I weren't, the thought of marrying a sixteen-year-old girl at my age…seriously repulsive. Though not to Romans raised here, of course.*

A fair selection of the new equipment was in view right in front of them. A line of riflemen was in a set of slit trenches about three hundred yards from the wall; they stretched at intervals all the way around the great circuit of the city, which was large even by Roman standards. That was extreme arrow range, but they were safe enough with a four-foot pit and a heap of earth in front of them and they could reload without exposing themselves and rest their rifles on little wooden tripods.

The Parthians on the city wall were *not* safe, and the Roman soldiers had been sniping enthusiastically since dawn, hours ago. Shots crackled in the distance from the rest of the circuit. No Parthian troops showed anywhere on the wall or towers opposite them; they were probably still there, but keeping below the line of the crenelations. Splashes of lead showed on the stone there, if you looked closely. The downside of that was that the Parthian troops had probably figured out the rifle bullets were like shot from slings, just traveling too fast to see, rather than outright sorcery.

Occasionally an archer would stand and loose a shaft; usually a dozen rifles cracked when he did, and the bowman was punched backward by several hits. Men trying that had gotten less and less frequent as the day wore on and the Roman legionnaires got more comfortable with the distance and the mechanics of aiming up.

And I've heard them yelling bets to each other in those trenches...

There were catapults on the walls and towers too; they'd been riddled by multiple hits, and the enemy had given up any attempt to repair or man them.

Behind the riflemen were eight other weapons, four on either side of the road and facing the wall beside the gates. The crews had waited until the riflemen suppressed the opposition before they brought them forward behind two-horse teams, with their ammo wagons following behind with six hitch of horses or mules pulling *them*.

They were simple enough in themselves. The spoked wagon wheels they rolled on were unusual only in being made of iron, with a split trail behind and between them three superimposed rows of sheet-iron tubes, each row numbering eight across and each four inches in diameter on the inside. The whole could be elevated and traversed by screws with cranked handles on the end.

And finally I got around to this. Jem producing sugar was a goose up the ass, when I remembered what you can use it for besides cakes and pastries and rum, and got the news about our Chinese...co-exiles, I suppose. Were they volunteers, or shanghaied into it by lies like us? No way to know. Government agents, at least, but they'd have to be highly educated to be of any use. Just for starters, Old Chinese was even more different from the modern variety than Latin is from French or Romanian.

The crews were pulling the ammunition out of the wagons set up thirty yards behind the launchers, two men to each hundred-pound rocket. Each round was made from two tubes, the one that made the warhead bluntly pointed and four inches in diameter, the other three inches and considerably longer, ending in a circle of tilted fins inside an iron ring again four inches around. The soldiers slid each into a barrel in the launcher where a spring-loaded catch at the rear lip retained it. Then they uncoiled a long section of fuse—linen cord soaked in saltpeter—from each rocket. Those were tied together through a metal ring on top of a steel rod, adjusting the lengths to be roughly equal.

"Ah, those are the *rockets* you described to me," Marcus Aurelius said. "Propelled by that... *saccharo,* isn't it called?"

"Yes, sir, by sugar," Artorius said. "Mixed two-thirds to one-third with saltpeter, with a little powdered rust added, melted... sugar melts easily... and cast as a hollow tube. The larger tube at the head is filled with thunderpowder, or *Ignis Romanus*. Thunderpowder for the first volley."

Roman Fire was the closest he'd been able to get to napalm.

At least as good as Byzantine Greek Fire, he thought. *And very effective on a smashed-up large building.*

"Who would have thought there were so many uses for salt-peter?" the Emperor said, with a slight smile. "Besides treating plethora and curing sausage!"

Fronto grinned. "And every city that can is building leaching fields for their sewage, as soon as they realize what saltpeter is worth now."

He inclined his head to Artorius as he went on:

"Shit into gold—more magic!"

"Which cleans up the sewage, too," Artorius observed. "When combined with the artificial-swamp system."

And behind the rocket launchers and their ammo wagons, strad-dling the road and only ten yards ahead of the Emperor and his general and Guard commander, were the latest products of Colonia Ferramenta's foundries and—made with far more difficulty—boring machines. A single six-gun battery of twenty-four-pounder cast-steel cannon on wheels nearly as tall as an average Roman man, the plain gray tubes ten feet long and weighing just a hair over two tons.

Getting them here was a royal pain in the ass, Artorius thought. *Would have been worse if they'd been cast iron, of course. Heavier.*

He'd used special wagons with skeletal cradle frames, and they were put on the carriages with knock-down portable cranes only when use was imminent.

And making them was even more of a pain. But they ought to do the job.

"Shall we watch the siege guns at work, sir?" he asked the Emperor.

"By all means, Tribune," Marcus Aurelius said.

He looked genuinely interested; he was a philosopher as well as a ruler, after all, and philosophy had been his first love. And while his Stoic school was mainly concerned with morals and duties and emotional control, he'd studied what passed for sci-ence and mathematics here and now as well.

That curiosity had been sharpened quite considerably since the Americans' arrival and especially since he'd been let in on the secret of *when* they'd come from. He'd learned positional arithmetic from Fil, and was studying algebra too, and reading their new Latin and Greek manuals—laboriously translated—on biology and astronomy and physics, engineering and farming.

And historical linguistics, which fascinated him.

And he was going over a copy of his own philosophical *Meditations*, oddly enough, tweaking it a bit before it was published. He'd originally written it to focus his Stoic meditations during lulls in the fourteen-year span of the Marcomannic Wars, in a history now...somewhere else, or nonexistent except in five people's memories and as incorporated in the ton of goods that had arrived with them. The book had survived by multiple low-probability accidents...and now he'd read it himself.

Time travel be strange, Artorius thought, not for the first time.

They all heeled their horses into a slow walk—proceeded and followed by the Imperial Horse Guards, and various clerks, secretaries and messengers, the ones attached to the Imperial person and those of the two other Roman commanders as well.

Artorius led; he brought them off to one side, where they could rein around and watch without risking getting in the way, or in *front* of the cannon. A lot of Romans—not the Emperor or Fronto or Repentinus, but ones lower down the scale of rank—still didn't quite appreciate that the area in front of the muzzle of a firearm was to be avoided if you could. Particularly a *big* firearm like these, given the blast effect. Fortunately there was a warm, steady breeze from the north, which would disperse the smoke and the dust kicked up from the ground.

And we're about to demonstrate why *you shouldn't get in front of a cannon*, he thought dryly. *They'll get the idea, eventually. Though idiots will always manage something self-destructive. I met more than one in the US Army, come to that. Natural-born damn fools will always find a way to kill their own ass, as granddad used to say. And* yours, *if you're not careful.*

He handed out felt-and-leather earplugs, one on each end of a two-foot cord. The crews were already wearing them draped around their necks, ready to insert when the guns went to work.

"Ah, these do not shoot round balls of the new cast iron?" Marcus Aurelius said with interest as he watched the loading procedure.

"They can, sir; each of those would weigh about twenty-four pounds, which is why these guns are called twenty-four pounders. Those would knock down solid walls in a day or two or three, especially ones faced with stone but with a core of mud-brick or rammed earth."

Everyone nodded; that was how city walls were built here in Mesopotamia, where in the valleys of the great twin rivers mud was a lot more available than stone. Romans usually used stone rubble set in concrete for the cores of theirs.

"These loads ought to do it a...bit faster, shall we say."

There were wooden platforms about two feet high in front of each cannon's muzzle. Two men with a long wooden pole stood ready on each; it had an iron cup-disk on one end with the broad side out, and a built-up structure of sponges on the other, with a big barrel of water just to one side ready to soak it in. Another ramrod stood upright in a frame; it had something on one end like a giant corkscrew, to pick out any fragments of the last linen cartridge.

Since ramming that much black powder down on a burning fragment could have...

Unfortunate results, shall we say, Artorius thought grimly.

The centurion in charge of the six-gun battery turned and saluted as the Emperor rode near.

"Carry on," Marcus Aurelius said.

The man—he was the one who'd commanded the very first cannon battery in the final battle of the Marcomannic War more than half a decade ago now—looked uncannily like a thirty-something version of Antonio Banderas, and came from the Roman province of Hispania. He saluted again, arm vertical and palm out, then turned and barked more orders.

The crews were about twice what a field gun had, but they were thoroughly practiced—and they'd used veterans from field-gun crews to start with, in fact. Two ran up to the platform with the powder charge in a tube-shaped linen bag just under six inches in diameter, carried in a canvas sling with handles on either side. They stepped up and set it in the muzzle and hopped down.

The two rammers put the iron cup-disk against it and lunged in unison, continuing until it was firmly seated. Then they inserted a wooden sabot—a circle just a little smaller than the nearly six-inch bore of the weapon, with a disk of thin copper on its inner side; the copper was bent backward like a shallow cup. Meanwhile a man at the rear of the gun had run a steel spike down the touchhole to pierce the linen powder bag and snapped a big percussion cap on the touchhole's collar.

Artorius pointed to the sabot:

"That copper cup expands sharply when the thunderpowder is ignited, Caesar Augustus. It grips the walls of the barrel, and contains the hot gasses so that none leak forward and all of the force is used to push the projectile. Also it scrapes off much of the fouling that smoke and bits of unburnt powder deposits on the inside of the barrel."

"Ah," Marcus Aurelius said, nodding; he grasped things quickly. "Like the hollow at the base of the rifle bullets."

No flies on Our Glorious Leader, as Fil put it, Artorius thought, and said aloud:

"Just so, sir."

Now the loaders returned with the business part of the ammunition in their sling. It was an elongated, pointed teardrop of cast steel painted dull green to protect against rust, with a set of fins at the rear end held in a circle of thin steel plate.

"Why is this superior to a round ball, Tribune?" the Emperor asked.

Then he tossed his head before Artorius could answer: "Ah, the fins...they are like the feathers of an arrow, as with the *rockets.* They guide it on its passage through the air and make it more accurate."

"Yes, sir, they do. For the rest, it's bigger, to start with," Artorius said. "And its shape means that it loses speed less rapidly than a round ball."

"As an arrow pierces the air better than a rock," Repentinus said. "Or a ship with a sharp bow cleaves water."

No, they're not stupid, Artorius thought as the round was rammed home. *Once they've gotten the idea that air has weight and gets in the way.*

In fact he'd modeled it on a heavy mortar round of the sort he'd been familiar with in the US Army, scaled up to be just a hair under six inches in diameter. It was simpler and easier than building cannon-rifling gear, and nearly as accurate. Once they'd rammed it firmly home the men on the platform jumped down briskly and trotted behind the gun—but not directly behind.

"And inside the shell is a charge of thunderpowder. There is a *fuse—*"

All three of the Roman commanders nodded to show they were familiar with that concept now too.

"—that is armed only when the cannon is fired. When the

projectile strikes, there is a very slight delay—half a heartbeat, shall we say—before the thunderpowder explodes. That has a... substantial effect...on walls and towers. A heap of earth would be more effective as a defense—earth does not shatter as stone or brick or concrete does."

Fronto whistled. "Many of our forts have earth berms for a wall, topped with a palisade," he said.

Artorius nodded. *Starting with marching camps,* he thought but did not say: *that would occur to any Roman soldier.*

"But that is because it's easier to build them at first from turf and dirt and wood," the Roman general went on. "Now it will have to be done even when we could afford the time and money for stone and concrete! If *tormenta* become common...hmmm, but that shouldn't happen in the north for a long while. A long enough while that it'll *all* be well-settled Roman provinces by then. Even up to Thule."

"Or earth berms could be piled in *front* of the stone or concrete walls, to absorb such strikes," Repentinus said. "And—"

He frowned and continued:

"—perhaps a berm heaped up on the opposite, the *outer* side of the moat? That would reduce the area that *tormenta* like this could aim for easily. If the wall was low...low and thick. The walls of forts...or I suppose of cities...will not need to be so high, when they are defended by *tormenta* firing grapeshot..."

"Just so, Prefect," Artorius said respectfully.

That was an acute insight, the essence of the great military engineer Vauban's concept which had dominated fort-building for two centuries with its starlike layout and triangular bastions and low-slung appearance.

Another reminder that people aren't stupid *this far back,* he thought. *They just don't have as much* information. *Give them that, and a lot of them can quickly see the implications; especially since Roman aristos mostly get training in formal logic as teenagers.* Particularly *true around Marcus Aurelius. He doesn't tolerate dimwits in important positions, even if they* are *aristos from influential families. He tries to find the stupid ones something harmless and symbolic and sends them to do that instead, which keeps their relatives happy. Or less unhappy.*

The darkly handsome young centurion turned to face the commanders again. Marcus Aurelius nodded and pushed his earplugs home; the others did likewise. So did Artorius, and then he signaled to the battery commander.

The *optio* in charge of each cannon pulled the lanyard, all within a half-second of each other, and . . .

BOOOOOOM!

Some of the horses of the mounted command party shied at the sudden enormous noise. It was loud even through the felt and leather of the plugs, and horses had better hearing than humans.

Artorius had selected a horse with a stolid temperament for his mount today, since he'd be around cannon and other *new things* a good deal, and could watch unconcerned. Huge plumes of off-white, sulfur-stinking smoke shot forward from the muzzles of the siege cannon; he was conscious again of how different it smelled from the lighter, sharper scent of smokeless powder in his birth era.

More like fireworks on the Fourth, he thought whimsically.

The cannon recoiled sharply, but each had a thick cast-bronze brace behind both wheels, spiked down and secured with chains to the wheel. Each had an iron-shod curve on the forward-facing side that started slow and then turned sharply upward.

The wheels ran along it, and when they had to lift the whole multiton weight of the gun and carriage *upward,* the force of the recoil was quickly absorbed. The gun halted and then ran down again, to meet a similar arrangement on the other side. Which stopped it in its original position, after a few lurches back and forth.

All eight of the cannon shot hit; seven in the tower walls and one struck the gate itself, a huge thing of iron-strapped timbers whose wooden parts had been floated down the river from the mountain forests of the north. It was point-blank range for cannon of this size too, and the crews were well practiced by now, for all the quarter-masters' hand-wringing about the cost of the training ammunition.

A fractional instant after the booming thunder of the cannon came a set of hard ringing *ptank!* sounds as the pointed steel shot sank into the base of the tall walls. And right on the heels of *that* came the muffled thunder of nearly a hundred pounds of gunpowder exploding. The fabric of the wall did more than muffle the sound. The shells were completely surrounded by the enormous weight of stone and adobe by the time they went off.

And that means much less *of the force of the explosion is wasted on the air,* Artorius thought grimly.

Four shot hit the base of the tower to the left of the gate;

three went into the one to the right. The one that hit the gate itself blew a hole twice the size of a man in a shower of burning splinters. Then the gates sagged downwards...

That was scarcely noticed, as great plumes of powdered dirt and shattered stone shot out of the tower walls where the shells had struck. On the right a tall nearly-rectangular sheet of the tower's stone facing dropped straight down in a cloud of dust and smoke as the rows that had supported it were blasted to gravel and shot out into the moat.

Then the sheet of stones toppled forward into the great ditch too, mostly filling it amid plumes of splashing water, and exposing the great hole blasted in the adobe core of the wall. Several men were exposed too; three toppled after the stonework, screams abruptly cut short as they struck the fractured rock. More back-pedaled frantically or dove flat, and white puffs of smoke rose from the slit trenches as the Roman legionnaires opened fire on the suddenly exposed Parthian troops.

The same happened on the left...and then the tower itself seemed to shiver, sway...and the forward face of it, stone facing and adobe core and interior stonework as well slumped forward in an avalanche that only *appeared* to be slow. Rooms and chambers were exposed, mostly full of Parthians who'd been driven off the battlements by rifle fire.

They were staggering or fallen and clinging grimly as the timbers beneath the floors were twisted free of their outer anchors and slumped towards the moat. More of the men slid free and screamed—briefly—as they fell.

The Roman infantry happily opened fire, and their targets dashed or crawled on all fours for the interior exits.

Fronto laughed and slapped his thigh, and Repentinus grinned like something carnivorous and hungry from his native Africa. The Emperor's face was impassive as he watched through his telescope, then lowered it and nodded in somber satisfaction.

"There will be no long sieges," he said thoughtfully. "Not in this war. And the Parthian king is in Ctesiphon, I am told."

"Yes, sir, he is," Repentinus said. "He did not expect us to advance nearly so fast, my sources say. He was preparing to leave...with an extensive entourage and the royal treasury... when our cavalry arrived and set up patrols around his capital, and he is still in the winter palace here."

Parthian kings shifted with the season in peacetime. Winters were mild here in the Mesopotamian lowlands. In summertime when it was blazing hot they moved to the high Iranian plateau, usually somewhere south of the mountains that fringed the Caspian Sea, where the original Parthian tribe had settled when it came off the steppe.

Ironically close to the sites of Tehran and Qom, the governmental centers of Iran in Artorius' native century. In summertime the weather was fairly pleasant there.

"Now the *eruca iaculator*," Artorius said.

For some reason, most Latin speakers spontaneously thought rockets were like caterpillars once they'd seen them fired off, which was what *eruca* meant.

Possibly because of the smoke trail and the way it's ridged, you can't really see the rocket well in flight, it's a blur, he thought.

Iaculator just meant thrower or hurler: put them together and you had *rocket launcher*, pretty much.

Or *caterpillar thrower*, literally speaking.

The Romans in hearing mostly chuckled at that; even Marcus Aurelius smiled slightly.

Artorius signaled to the centurion who was battery commander of the rocket launchers—he was from Londinium in Britannia, originally—and eight men ran forward as he relayed the order. They each flicked a *Ronsonius*, touched the flame to the gathered fuses at the same instant, and ran back... much, much faster than they'd trotted forward. The rest of the crews hastily closed the iron-sheathed doors on the wagons carrying the ammunition.

A piercing fast-building scream sounded as the first fuse burned through to a charge of finely ground gunpowder at the rear of the de Laval-style nozzle of cast and machined steel. That flashed down the narrow hollow center of the sugar-saltpeter mixture and set it on fire. The inside-out combustion—with the area burning constantly increasing—kept the gas pressure building until the very moment the fuel was all gone.

You could have rockets without the nozzle, but *not* ones that usually went at least roughly where you wanted them. It kept the thrust evenly centered. That had taken considerable trial and error...

Long spears of fire shot out of the rear of the rockets, the scream grew to an ear-piercing shriek and then dense smoke hid everything. Shouts and prayers rose from the watching Roman troops...though they'd grown at least a little accustomed to signs and wonders from the *new things*.

Instants later the scores of rockets shot towards the city, each of the one hundred and ninety-two rising and leaving a trail of dense off-white smoke behind it. Those cut off at the peak of the missile's trajectory...except for one that went nearly straight up in a corkscrew and exploded.

Not bad, only one real malfunction, Artorius thought. *One hundred and ninety-one going downrange. Of course, they're not all that accurate, so anyone living near the king's palace is going to...well, collateral damage happens.*

That was just one of the many, many reasons war was not a good thing in itself. Just sometimes better than the alternatives.

Probably mostly Parthian nobles and their hangers-on, this time, which is...a little...comfort.

Some of the horses panicked at the sound and billowing smoke. It took a moment even for fine riders like Artorius and the three Romans to quiet their mounts. One of the Imperial Horse Guards was humiliatingly carried off across the green, irrigated market gardens and orchards and now Roman-occupied suburban villas that surrounded the Parthian capital, screaming curses in some Germanic dialect and hauling on the reins as his mount bolted.

By the time all was quiet again the last of the multiple thumps the rockets made when they landed behind the city wall was echoing off into comparative silence.

"All the...caterpillars...were aimed at the Parthian king's palace," Artorius said helpfully.

Repentinus' brows rose. "That is more than a mile from here!" he said.

Ctesiphon was a *big* city by second-century standards; bigger than Athens, though not as large as Alexandria's half million or so.

Artorius nodded. "Extreme range, but not *too* far," he said. "The next barrage bears *Ignis Romanus*, with small bursting charges to spread the gobbets of flame."

They all nodded in turn; smashing up a building exposed vulnerable wood and let uncontrollable fire take hold. Earthquakes and volcanic eruptions both did that too. Fronto punched his right fist into the palm of his other hand.

"The Parthian King of Kings will be receiving our gifts in

his throne room!" he said, at which Repentinus was startled into a chuckle.

"Then more thunderpowder and after that more Roman Fire," Artorius went on.

The crews of cannon and rocket launchers were reloading—the latter also had men beating with wet blankets at small areas of flame amid the scorch marks from the rockets, lest sparks set the fuses off prematurely. The booms of the cannon and high-pitched wailing, shrieking sound of the rockets were repeated, and the burnt-sugar-and-sulfur smell of gunpowder and rocket fuel overcame the city-stink.

It all went on and on. And then...

"Order the troops to cease throwing fire!" the Emperor of Rome said sharply.

His telescope was trained on the huge pile of smoldering rubble and shattered adobe brick that had been the gatehouse fortress. Which gap now offered a view of buildings within the city—mostly *burning* buildings, and pillars of smoke were rising and thickening behind the intact sections of city wall. Most of them were grouped around the area Repentinus' spies had put their thumb on as the Parthian shah's palace.

Fronto responded immediately to the Emperor's order, and the horn calls rang out. An echoing silence fell, though the crews kept reloading until all was in readiness. Some of them were scowling at the interruption to their fun; others, in old-soldier reflex, just took the opportunity to relax and rest. Artorius used his binoculars.

There, he thought.

A hand was waving a set of olive branches frantically back and forth from behind a heap of rubble. A Praetorian guardsman moved forward of the Roman position, waving a branch of olives himself—it was the equivalent of a white flag, and olive groves were common in the hilly country a bit further north, which had a winter-rainfall climate. Most formal gardens around here had small, irrigated olive groves too. In fact olives grew in warmer spots as far east as Afghanistan along with, in this era, even more extensive vineyards of wine grapes.

After a minute the Parthian rose and waved more vigorously; the Praetorian did too, and then made a beckoning gesture. That acceptance made the Parthian an envoy, protected and sacred until he returned home. Harming him would *really* offend the Gods, and locals would mostly believe bad, bad luck would pursue you for the rest of a short and miserable life if you harmed him. The technical term for behavior like that was hubris, here, and it was followed by nemesis.

Those who *didn't* believe that would be afraid of the majority who *did*. That pressure was about as effective as the more formal rules of Artorius' home century.

The man from the city walked forward, stumbling over the mounds of rubble. He was alone, and as he grew closer they could see he was middle-aged and slightly stout. A long, carefully curled black beard fell to his chest, and his hair was plaited in a sort of fan at the rear; he put a round, elaborately tasseled and sequined cylindrical hat on his head as he picked his way over the shifting wreckage that now filled the moat.

The gate and its bridge had gone up in flames some time before and were still smoldering and stinking beneath heaps of shattered stone and adobe littered with dismembered bodies. The smell of burning petroleum was oddly nostalgic to Artorius; it prompted memories of fighting in this general area...a long, long time from now, in a history that no longer existed.

The Parthian envoy was dressed in loose, pleated trousers tucked into strapped boots, a lap-over jacket secured by a belt encased in chased silver and gold plaques, and an elaborately embroidered cotton tunic-shirt below that. All the man's clothes had been of fine decorated fabric or soft-tanned leather with tooled gold plaques and silver studs...but now they were singed by scorch marks, stained by smoke and blood, and the cloth was torn in places.

As he grew closer a file of rifle-armed Praetorians dropped into place around him, their armor gleaming. So were their bayonets...

And that is a frightened man if I've ever seen one, Artorius thought as the Parthian came closer. *You can smell it in his sweat. Though he's controlling it, the more credit to him.*

Staring eyes, darting to the cannon and rocket launchers—apparently he'd seen them firing—and at the rifles too. A twitch jerked in one cheek as he watched. Lips peeling back from black-and-yellow teeth when his control slipped a bit, then back to a schooled calmness...

He recognized Marcus Aurelius as well, and managed to prostrate himself gracefully before the hooves of his horse.

If you knew the Emperor well you could see he found the gesture distasteful, though he kept most of that off his face. The Hellenistic kings who succeeded Alexander had taken up the Persian habit of *proskynesis*, subjects going down on their belly before a ruler.

Romans hadn't; it was reserved for some religious rites for them, something that was due to Gods and not men, even a quasi-divine living Emperor.

They haven't taken it up yet, Artorius thought. *They did take it up later, a century, century and a half from now. That may not happen in* this *history we're making.*

After the Parthian had kissed the dirt Marcus Aurelius gestured, one hand palm up and rising.

"Stand and name yourself and your rank," he said. "I presume you are an envoy from King Vologases?"

He said it in Greek, as something a Parthian courtier was more likely to understand than Latin. There were still Greek-speaking cities in this area, and for a considerable distance east of here, and it was the lingua franca of the educated and of large-scale trade hereabouts.

The man replied in the same language, fluent but accented:

"Yes, Great Lord, I am Barkāmak son of Spādēn, and I have the honor to be *marpet*—"

Which meant roughly *Steward of the Palace* in the Parthian dialect of Middle Persian, a fairly high official.

"—to *Shāhanshāh Walagaš*, may he live forever."

"Speak, then," the Emperor of Rome said.

The man glanced around at the arrayed Roman might, his eyes lingering again on cannon and rifles and rocket launchers, licked his lips and went on:

"My master, the King of Kings...he says that against men he can fight, but not against the weapons of Gods."

Barkāmak shuddered. "The...the screaming flail from the sky struck the very palace, the great White Hall itself, only last week fully repaired after the sack. Many died, many! The King of Kings was wounded himself, and only escaped the fires because he was carried by loyal guardsmen who leapt through the flames with their hair burning! The fires still rage! Nothing will be left!"

Fronto and Repentinus were smiling slightly, narrow-eyed and self-controlled in the fashion Roman aristos called *gravitas*, suitable for dealing with a foreign envoy. It was still roughly the expression that a sheep would get a glimpse of on the face of the very last wolf it ever saw. Marcus Aurelius' countenance was grave, even a little regretful, but stern with duty.

"Tell your master—" he began.

Then he frowned and modified the statement:

"—that my physician Galen shall treat your king's wounds immediately, when he ... gives himself into my care."

It would be highly inconvenient if the one man who could order a surrender died.

"And then—" the Emperor went on.

⋗ CHAPTER NINETEEN ⋖

Near Ctesiphon
Former Western Capital
Former Parthian Empire
January 23rd, 172 CE

Three days later the Americans and Jem's girlfriends and Sarukê were at dinner just after sundown in a...

Repurposed, Artorius thought. *Nice objective term.*

...a *repurposed* villa not far from Ctesiphon that he'd been assigned. They were all staying there and there was plenty of room, and he'd cemented his reputation for eccentricity by specifically asking for one quite a ways from the city.

Beyond infected-fly range, hopefully, he thought.

Nobody among the Americans wanted to sleep in the city itself, which had started out filthy and hadn't been improved by the widespread fires and rain of hundreds of rocket shells. And on their advice Marcus Aurelius hadn't either, giving the burning of the palaces as his excuse.

It turned out that they hadn't finished cleaning up the rotting bodies of the smallpox-plague victims, either. Repairing the city walls had taken priority.

This building was in the Greek style, roughly, paint and plaster and ornamental tile and stone over adobe, and a thick earth ceiling on the flat roof. There were paintings—of mythological scenes—on the plaster of the ceilings.

They were dining in the *andrōn*, the room the master used for entertaining guests at dinner, with a floor a step up from the tile-paved courtyard outside. You could see pruned bushes and flowers and fruit trees out there through the pillars, and a few tall palms for shade, with a brace of servants making a great show of diligence. They weren't quite as scared as they had been, but that was still plenty of terror. They'd picked up that these were the Romans' powerful wizards, who'd provided the sky-screaming weapons that had brought Parthia low.

Artorius was sitting upright on his reclining bench, but the others were prone; Fil and Sarukê were sharing theirs, and so were Mark and Paula, which was normal for married couples among Romans. Jem's girlfriends shared one beside his.

Fil and Sarukê are married, practically speaking, Artorius thought. *They're going to adopt each other's kids, when and if, too. Adoption's easy in Roman law, including for a* femme sole... *though that probably wasn't what the ones who made the laws were thinking of.*

Paula had brought the new-style lanterns they'd packed for their tent into the villa; pretty much like a classic kerosene lamp, and burning refined naptha—which *was* kerosene, or near enough. They were spreading rapidly since the light was so much better than the dim flickering of oil-soaked wicks, and cheaper than the new molded wax candles. The staff had come with the house and they were pathetically eager to please, though the Americans had managed to reassure them a little.

Not least by ensuring that they were well fed; a Roman army of fifty thousand sucked up a great deal of provender, and the country-folk were still hesitant about coming near though the Emperor had publicly forbidden plunder and mistreatment. Most of the troops would be moving on soon, and Artorius had successfully recommended that only a token garrison be kept within the actual walls of Ctesiphon...chunks of which weren't really walls anymore anyway, and they wouldn't be repaired for some time if ever. Prisoners of war were working at filling in the smelly moat with the rubble.

A hygienically arranged camp outside would be bad enough, though tolerable now that they'd drilled deep wells lined with cast-iron tubes.

The offer of top prices paid in cash for grain, vegetables and livestock—authenticated by actual, very public payouts in good silver coins—was bringing the farmers around, but slowly. Nobody on the Roman side objected, since the money was from the Parthian kings' own treasury.

The meal had been roughly Greek too, with Parthian touches. Mostly consisting of more meat than Hellenes below the upper-aristo level usually consumed, and deliberately slaughtered and skillfully butchered rather than random lumps from a sacrifice to the Gods.

There had been a good salad, dressed with olive oil and with vinegar too when they asked for it...

Though I miss tomatoes. It'll be a while before they get this far.

...and a main dish of marinated pork-loin kebabs with onions on a bed of spicy saffron rice, the latter something none of them had had since they arrived in 165 CE. Rice was still an expensive import west of here, and pretty well unknown in Pannonia. Right now taboos on pig meat around here were limited to Jews, and Mark wasn't religious and his parents hadn't been either.

From a few remarks he'd made, they were old-fashioned quasi-socialist *Nu Yawk* radicals and ostentatiously secular. He was too, though not exactly ostentatious about it. Artorius smiled to himself: twenty-first-century... or for that matter twentieth-century or nineteenth-century... politics were supremely irrelevant here, however important they'd seemed at the time.

Dessert was a cake dense with dates and almonds and walnuts, and a thick, sweet date wine.

Coffee, Artorius thought with an inner sigh. *I would* really *like a cup now.*

One thing he hadn't forgotten about being on campaign was how often you ended up sleep deprived. It was harder to take without caffeine and you couldn't get it in sodas here either.

Coffee started out in Ethiopia, and it grows wild there and the wild stuff is really good. Maybe someday... we could send an embassy to Axum, and ask about it? They could probably trade for it from the southern Rift.

"So the war's over?" Paula said hopefully as things turned to nibbling and sipping.

They'd all been hungry, after a strenuous day. She and Mark were trying to get some sanitation going in Ctesiphon to forestall plagues, and even with the locals falling over themselves to obey the dreaded Roman quasi-godlike supernaturals it was a struggle. Mostly because they had no idea *why* they were told to do what they were told to do. Less so even than in the Empire...

The older part of the now-greatly-enlarged Empire, Artorius thought.

...where Galen was spreading the doctrine of germs energetically.

Both of them also scrubbed down thoroughly with strong soap and boiled water and scrubbed their fingernails and changed their clothes before coming near their daughter here when they returned from work. They'd overseen a top-to-bottom scrubbing here in the villa too when the Americans arrived, and pyrethrum dusting, and a kitchen inspection and flat orders on covering food against flies at all stages of preparation, boiling all well water for baths or drinking...while a deep bore hole was put in as an offshoot of the program for the new Roman garrison fort...and handwashing with the new-style soap and so forth.

The staff here think it's religious taboos, or possibly just magic, but they're obeying. The SAT principle keeps them on their toes— Somebody Always Talks. Especially in a situation like this. Jem now, Jem simply avoids going inside the city wall and won't let his girls or kids go there either—he's out with the horse herds.

Sarukê snorted at Paula's hope that the war was over, and Fil winced slightly. Jeremey chuckled.

"You wish!" he said cheerfully. "The big *fights* are over. The war isn't, yet. Not quite, but who wins isn't in doubt anymore."

I think the lack of generalized empathy is something Jem finds comfortable about this period, Artorius mused. *Since pretending to have it must have been a bit of a strain for him back...or up... in the twenty-first. Not that he doesn't have any empathy—he's not a sociopath, he likes his girlfriends and he's fond of his kids, and I think he likes or at least values all four of us. But he doesn't give a damn for strangers, which fits right in here; he's not in the minority anymore. Congratulations, Jem—you have achieved neurotypicality through time travel!*

"Not quite," Artorius added in agreement, with a sigh.

"The Parthian king's surrendered," Mark pointed out.

And publicly kissed dirt at Marcus Aurelius' feet, Artorius thought.

"Yes, but Parthia's sort of...decentralized," he said aloud.

"Sort of feudal," Jeremey added. "Lots of big nobles with long trains of vassals and supporters, who have their *own* trains of vassals and supporters, and so on. Their King of Kings is just the biggest boss."

He paused for thought, and went on with one word:

"Theoretically."

Artorius nodded. "And there are other members of their royal family still at large who might proclaim themselves *Shāhanshāh* and fight on—they have a civil war here between branches of the King of King's kin every generation anyway. Which will stop once the annexation's in operation, thank the Gods. And we terrified the living Bejayzus out of everybody who was in any of the battles—"

There had been two others... three if you counted a large skirmish, four if you threw in the very, very brief siege of Ctesiphon... besides the one he'd been at with the Emperor. They'd all ended pretty much the same, differing only in degree. One of the Roman columns had let the Parthian mounted archers get within two hundred yards before cutting loose with Jove's Balls, which had taken nerve... and worked very, very well.

Parthian armies depended on a combination of mounted archery to whittle down and disrupt enemy ranks, and then shock action by their armored heavy cavalry to finish the foe off. They used foot soldiers only for defending cities and forts. Once the infantry they were fighting had distance weapons like rifles and cannon and Jove's Balls that simply didn't work anymore.

Neither did holding out behind high, brittle walls when cannon could knock them down with explosive shells, and rocket launchers could incinerate the city or anything else behind the defenses. They weren't really nomads anymore, not most of them, so they couldn't just ride away either.

And when we get enough rocket launchers to use them in the field... they're light, they move faster than twelve-pounders, and they can hit at well over a mile, Artorius mused. *That'll make dispersed formations catch on a lot quicker! And they terrify people on the receiving end with the noise they make, too.*

"—but not everyone who counts in Parthia *did* see our firepower," he continued aloud. "The Emperor is going to take Walagaš around so he can talk to holdouts, and make an example of anyone who isn't convinced. Before sending the ex-*Shāhanshāh* off into a comfortably subsidized exile in Hispania or Gaul. Or possibly Britannia, he hasn't decided yet, but they'll get a generous land grant for an estate. We captured the Parthian treasury here, by the way, about half their total precious-metal reserves—their shahs always kept it next to them. Everyone in the field army here will get a bonus, too—including us."

Jeremey smiled and held up his right hand, rubbing his thumb across his first two fingers, and his girlfriends giggled happily at the thought of the gifts he'd bestow. The Americans would all get a share of that, and the shares varied according to rank. The Americans' was...

Right up there. Not as big as Fronto's, or the legion command-ers, but big.

Artorius nodded. "Their treasury ought to pay the costs of this campaign too, comfortably."

Jem smiled again, Sarukê perked up at the thought of buying more breeding stock, Fil shrugged and Mark and Paula winced slightly.

"Making war support war, with a vengeance!" Jem said.

"More good stock," the Sarmatian woman added; plunder made her cheerful. "Get our hands on some of Walagaš' stud farms' best stallions, oh yes."

To her people, horses *were* money, much more real than gold.

"They're not going to keep Walagaš in Rome?" Jem said. "I'd think the Big Boss would want to show him off at the triumph."

"He will, but then he'll send him somewhere really obscure where he and his senior wives and their kids can gradually blend into provincial-gentry society. That'll go faster once they learn Latin. The King of Kings' grandkids... or great-grandkids... will be Romans. Just ones with an interesting ancestry they can trot out at parties."

"They'll be carefully watched by the *Frumentarii*," Jeremey observed. "Wait, don't the Romans strangle enemy leaders in a dungeon after they're shown off at a triumph?"

"They used to. Marcus Aurelius doesn't... do that sort of thing unless he has to. And we're going to be ransoming a lot of the prisoners. The cataphracts are mostly related to important people, sort of equivalent to the Roman Equestrian Order... or maybe closer to medieval knights and barons and their retinues. And they're going to be the best witnesses to—"

"*Resistance is futile*," Jem said solemnly; then his voice went cheerful. "My granddad was fond of that one."

He pumped a fist in the air and said:

"*Nos sumus Borg!*"

Then in English:

"*We de Borg!*"

Saruke and his concubines gave him an odd look; the Americans ignored him or winced a bit. Artorius went on:

"Yes, exactly. Some of them come from all the way east to the Kushan border."

"Well, then," Mark said.

Paula sighed and covered her eyes.

"That would be *well, then* if everyone in Parthia was *rational*, Mark, honey," she said, with her hand still across her eyes for the moment. "And made rational judgments on the basis of evidence."

"Right, Paula," Artorius said. "Without rejecting stories they don't want to believe. Or wishful thinking. Or both combined."

"Very philosophical!" Jeremey added.

Mark is irrationally rational, Artorius thought, knew the thought was shared fourfold, and went on aloud:

"But it will probably need another couple of . . . demonstrations . . . before *everyone* gives up. Everyone significant, at least. Tribal raiders and that sort of thing, that'll continue—but those will be the new provincial governors' problems now. Along with building roads and *mansio—*"

Which were official rest stops for government officials and messengers, spaced out along all the Roman highways. He'd talked Marcus Aurelius into making them the first element in a Roman postal system, complete with stamps and envelopes. Josephus thought it would even turn a profit for the Imperial government eventually, if well managed . . . and had recommended someone to do that.

A relative, but a competent one. That whole family are, or at least all the ones I've met are. Great Gods, but we were lucky we ran into Josephus! He's a good friend to have, doubly so since he's in on the truth about us.

"—and planting *colonia* and new cities and so forth. The Emperor is going to do a tour and appoint the governors in each new province on-site. And the old Syrian and Anatolian garrisons will mostly be relocated to the new frontiers. Going to be a *lot* of road construction here, too. And a new naval flotilla in the Persian Gulf. Topsail schooners at first. They'll sail rings around anything local and they'll have cannon, and they can show the flag as far as India."

"All of which will put the legionary garrisons further from Rome, always a good idea," Mark said.

Everyone nodded. Emperors were supreme...unless the Roman
Army turned on them. Which was an unpleasant fact. One not
usually mentioned in polite circles, and one that hadn't happened
since the Year of the Four Emperors a bit over a century ago in
69 CE, but a fact, nonetheless. There hadn't been any civil war
when Domitian was deposed in 96 CE, not openly...

Deposed by assassination, actually, he thought.

...three-quarters of a century ago, but it remained a pos-
sibility. Nerva had become Emperor after that...on the same
day...backed by the Senate, but he'd been elderly and childless
and had then adopted Trajan, a successful general and popular
with the military.

Fortunately the Army pretty much worshipped Marcus Aurelius now.

Literally worships *him, in many cases. If we can keep the
Army out of choosing the next Emperor for a while more, it may
stop it permanently.*

"Hmmm. The new Sarmatian auxiliaries...they'll be useful
out here, then," Mark mused. "Just as mobile as nomad raiders."

"And the Roman centurions who command them will have
sore asses," Jeremey said cheerfully.

Mark frowned and went on: "Because until recently they *were*
nomad raiders themselves. And the *old* frontier provinces won't
need big garrisons anymore," he noted. "Just some auxiliaries
for internal work."

He understood Roman politics and administration well enough,
as long as you could keep it abstract.

Artorius smiled. "But we're all going to go home with the
Emperor, soon, three to six months max—late next spring. Until
we get word of our Chinese friends, at least. All the Parthians
have heard is rumors of powerful magicians at the Chinese court,
and those are garbled and passed hand to hand, like a game of
telephone. They get knocked down to the general noise level."

He raised his cup. "I've written to Julia about it and we plan
to celebrate! And here's to Jeremey for seeing that Parthia was
crucial! If our Chinese friends—"

Fil muttered something in Korean, and Sarukê put a soothing hand on the back of her neck and got a grateful look and a
pat. If there was one thing Sarukê understood down to her very
bones, it was a long-lasting grudge against an enemy.

And Fil's feuds were now hers, too.

"—try distracting the Empire, they're going to have to start with the Kushans. Further from Rome, nearer to them. Easier for them, but better for us too—Parthia was far too close to really significant Roman assets. Syria and Anatolia are some of the richest parts of the Empire. Chunks of Parthia will be, but not yet... need to get the roads built and so forth. Barrages on the rivers, too... there's a set of plans in the *baggage*."

Which was how they referred to the stuff... and even more crucially, the information... that Fuchs had sent back with them.

"Far too close to significant Roman assets when there *was* a Parthia," Jeremey said cheerfully.

Artorius sighed and stretched. "And we can go home in the meantime."

Julia, I'm coming! Back to see you and Claudia and the kids.

Sogdiana, Kushan Empire
October 18th, 173 CE

I wish, I wish, I truly *wish* I didn't have to come along on this trip, Black Jade thought. *For one thing, I've got lice. Again! And going back before the spring would be dangerous. Really dangerous, as in freeze to death on the steppes or in the mountains dangerous.*

She restrained herself from scratching; they weren't *head* lice. The itching at least distracted her from the risks... for a moment, before her unfortunately very good memory recalled:

Let's see... she thought as the encyclopedia entry tolled through her head. *Pubic pruritus... body lice can transmit a great variety of diseases, such as epidemic typhus, louse-borne relapsing fever or trench fever...*

You just couldn't trust blankets or cushions here to be free of indwelling life that was interested in sinking its miniscule but sharp mouth parts into your nethers, especially when you were traveling. Though Bingwen was growing a flower that could be made into a potent insecticide; evidently it did well in high-altitude places in central and southern China. The authorities were distributing the seeds and offering good prices for the resulting powder.

She had some of that powder with her from the first experimental batches, and intended to...

S.M. Stirling

Dust myself, she thought. *How I wish I could just roll in heaps of it and rub it all over me like lotion, but...*

The problem was she didn't have *much* of it, so had to save it for situations where all else had failed.

After the bath I hope *I can have tonight. Fortunately there were Greeks here not so long ago and they took baths so they've still got tubs and such. And this...castlelike thing...gets its water from artesian springs out of naked rock through stone channels. Probably safe enough, no nausea or runs.*

Colonel Liu was talking with the group of Kushan nobles in a corner of their banqueting hall. Torches flared against the interior walls, casting shadows up into the rafters above, moving like ghosts. A fire trench held a long stretch of glowing coals, which made the temperature not...

Too bad, she thought. *Back home...in the Eastern Capital, I suppose it's home now...in a way...I actually have central heating now. And hot and cold running water. I've even made some friends, despite how weird the people are. And...I really wish I wasn't here. Or with the colonel. He's been fine with me, but I can't help remembering what he probably did uptime. And the others just refuse to discuss what happened to the man I replaced. Did Liu execute him?*

Liu talking meant she was translating. Into Greek, which many of the Kushan aristocrats spoke, albeit a rather eccentric dialect of Greek, and with a strong accent from their native—East Iranian—tongue added in. Which she was learning as fast as she could, mainly from the *maidservants* they'd been assigned.

Some of whom, she thought, were rather piqued at being used solely for language instruction and tidying up, and they were undoubtedly reporting to *someone* on everything they observed. And unhappy that they didn't have all that much to report.

I think that at least two of them speak Old Chinese, they're probably from Xinjiang...the Tarim Basin, they look like it too... but we can just talk in Mandarin. Absolutely nobody *except the five of us speak that!*

She'd gotten the basics of Kushan but couldn't follow everything in that formerly steppe tongue.

Not yet.

She did pick up a bit, and she whispered what she could to Colonel Liu in the intervals when the Kushans were talking among themselves. Probably they'd overestimate her command of the tongue and guard *their* tongues. The Kushan Empire was dotted with Greek towns but otherwise a maze of East-Iranian dialects anyway, with Indo-Aryan ones—Prakrits—in its southeastern parts.

They all had a strong basic similarity this far back, but that didn't mean they were fully mutually comprehensible; they just merged into their neighbors in overlapping dialect chains. It had been a good two thousand years since their original source started splitting up. The fact that Turkic languages hadn't started spreading yet—probably never would, in this history—did reduce the complexity a bit.

For what it's worth, if you subtract some sound shifts, they're not all that different from classical Greek and Latin.

A little exercise from her undergraduate years ran through her mind in scholar's reflex—comparing a sentence, "God gave teeth; God will give bread" in different Indo-European languages.

In Latin it was:

Deus dedit dentes; Deus dabit et panem.

In classical Greek:

Theōs dédoke ódontas, Theòs dōsei kaì artón.

And in Sanskrit it was:

Devas adadāt datas; Devas dāt api dhānās.

In most of the languages around here it was recognizably similar to that last and not too far from Latin and Greek. Subtracting around two thousand years put you more than halfway back to their common ancestor.

The Kushans were talking among themselves again, now. She was the only female actually eating—mostly garlic-heavy grilled mutton and flatbread at this time of year, with some fresh and dried fruit to follow. The other females in the room were servants serving food, or had been dancers earlier, in nothing much but silk loincloths and jewelry...

And goosebumps from the chill, she thought sardonically. *These Kushans make the Old Chinese look like paragons of enlightenment.*

Her nose made it also painfully apparent that a lot of the nobles here didn't wash very often, doubtless an unfortunate inheritance from the steppe nomads who made up a lot of their ancestry. Even after years in this period it was obvious. A few seemed to have picked up the habit of washing occasionally, at least...

S.M. Stirling

But if her political antennae were at all sensitive ... these *particular* nobles were part of a conservative faction who didn't like the current Kushan emperor's pacific disposition ... probably derived from his Buddhism, at least a bit ... and longed for the endemic bloodthirstiness of their steppe ancestors.

And to be uniformly filthy is also *the habit of their Noble Nomadic Ancestors, whatever other things they are,* she thought dismally. *Huns, Hsiong-nu, Saka, all caked in* filth. *I couldn't eat much of dinner. Just thinking of what their kitchens are like ... we have medications, but ...*

The local nobles *looked* roughly like Tadjiks and so did the commoners she'd glimpsed around here. There had been students from Tajikistan at Beijing University during her undergraduate years, and she was reminded of them.

Olive-skinned to pink European types with bold boney faces, in other words, mostly with dark hair and eyes. They could have been Italians or Greeks, but a few of them could have been Swiss or Germans or English. That was more common here west of the Tien Shan than in her day, since the steppe migrations from east of the mountains had only just begun here, and would ...

Would have, she corrected herself, and added dutifully: *Of course, eventually China will incorporate this area too.*

... would have eventually culminated in the campaigns of Genghis Khan a thousand years from now.

In ancestry the Kushan nobles were obviously a mixed lot. A core of Yuezhi, steppe Iranians driven out of western China—mainly Gansu—by the Xiongnu several centuries ago. They'd moved west of the mountains, and then down south to Bactria and into India later, overthrowing the Bactrian Greek kingdoms in the process.

With a strong dash of local Bactrians, more or less similar to Pushtu Afghans, she judged, some South Asians of the northwestern varieties, a little of something related to *her* physical type which they'd probably picked up *in* Gansu. And another strong dash of Tocharian from the Tarim Basin.

That showed in occasional light-colored eyes, and two blonds and a red mane among the dozen or more dark heads. Parts of their trip through the Tarim to get here had been like an excursion through a very dry preindustrial Sweden where everyone dressed like an elf in that American TV series based on Tolkien's books. The Uyghur migration to that desert basin wasn't due for another seven hundred years and wouldn't happen now anyway.

But much more ragged and dirty, except for nobles and rich merchants, she thought. *Much, much more.*

Smuggled copies of that series had circulated at Beijing University.

The clothes right around here...for men...were long caftan-like lap-over robes cinched with leather belts and baggy trousers and tooled-leather boots. That gear was as filthy as their bodies, but of fine fabrics, woven from thread vivid in bright colors and with a plethora of gold and silver embroidery and ornaments; they were even wearing earrings and necklaces. Some of the decoration on those looked classical Greek, others sinuous and stylized.

The head Kushan was middle-aged, with gray in his thick black beard and longish hair that was done up in a topknot. Above very cold brown eyes ringed with kohl makeup and more gold and jewels than any of his compatriots, a long dagger with a fancy gold-and-jewels hilt shoved through his sash; his silk coat was now stained with mutton juice. A long, straight single-edged sword in a tooled scabbard leaned against his couch.

Coat not stained for the first time, she noted; the Han dynasty types back east were bad enough, but this...

Oh, please let hygiene spread fast! It's catching on at court in the Eastern Capital, at least, and they were better...somewhat... than these ex-nomads to start with.

"We appreciate those new things you have brought us from your country of Han," the Kushan noble said. "We know what has happened in Parthia—those fleeing from the Romans have told us enough, besides our spies and merchants. With their new weapons the Romans have done in a year and a half what they could not for centuries before. But we would appreciate it even more if we could *make* these new things for ourselves."

Liu smiled and spread his hands. "I see your point, but that is a matter you must take up with my superiors," he said—in passable Old Chinese—and lying with convincing fluency. "I am merely following my orders; I do not know how to make the...thunderpowder. You can see that it would be unwise to send anyone who *did* know how. *Some* of our...novelties...you can make immediately."

And you were scornful of how the Americans in the Roman Empire were not keeping the gunpowder formula secret, she thought.

They seem ... to be academics led *by an academic, oddly enough. Instead of academics commanded by a secret policeman.*

Black Jade translated his remarks into Greek. One of the Kushans murmured in their leader's ear; they had someone who could speak the Han tongue, then. She glanced aside and Liu gave her a very slight nod, so he'd seen that too. They'd come with an escort of Xiongnu cavalry in the Han empire's service and under Han officers ...

The Huns are possibly the source *of my lice, damn them!*

... and *they* were all using the new framed saddles with stirrups. The Kushans could copy that easily enough—they'd probably bribed the guards to tell them the details. The guards had been instructed to *take* bribes about that, since that wasn't a secret that could be kept once you'd taken a look and thought about it.

"Some of them," the Kushan leader said dryly. "Yes, you now have better saddles and we will copy them. The Romans have similar ones now; the Parthian refugees we took in have brought a few."

A couple of the older Kushans stirred at that; probably traditionalists who scorned easier riding. From his taut smile Liu had caught the implications of the Kushan noble's words.

Which amounted to: *Thank you for nothing in particular, you tightwad bastards. You want to shove us face-first into the Roman guns to buy yourselves time.*

"But what matters ... really matters ... is the thunderpowder," the Kushan leader went on. "You offer us muskets; you offer us cannon; you offer us thunderpowder. But the muskets and cannon are useless without the thunderpowder ... which we can only get from *you.* Through the Tarim by camel caravan ... which is a long, long way from your Eastern Capital."

"I am told," Liu said smoothly, "that the thunderpowder is often made closer than the Eastern Capital."

Which was true. They'd set up four plants, north and south, east and west, each staffed with well-paid men pledged to silence ... and all watching each other for *very* generous rewards if anyone was caught out in treason.

What was that American science-fiction book ... she thought.

Science fiction was a guilty pleasure of hers, and some of it had proven surprisingly useful here. She'd gotten credit from the colonel for ideas she'd stolen from those tales.

Yes! Lord Kalvan of Otherwhen! Where a religious cult had

the secret of gunpowder under its control in an alternate universe! We're doing that... for now. But it's not a difficult formula, and it will escape our control in a while. Or people will learn it from the Romans.

The senior Kushan had a musket they'd brought by his side, and a flintlock pistol a third of a meter long tucked through his sash across from the glittering dagger hilt. Both were gifts, carefully tooled and engraved and inlaid with precious metals by artisans at court. Giving lavish gifts to foreign chieftains was an old-established diplomatic method for China.

Now he nodded to a guard by the door; the man leaned his spear against the brightly colored tile of the wall and returned with a four-foot bundle and handed it to the man giving the orders. His master unwrapped it. It was a musket too, but different in its details, and severely plain.

The Kushan inclined the weapon so that the lamplight caught what was engraved on the lock plate behind the hammer: in the Roman alphabet, *Leg. III Ital.*

And under it *cohors septima, prima centuria.*

And under that *A-17723.*

For a moment she simply read it: Liu sighed. Then she blinked herself—those were Arabic numerals in what must be a serial number, and the name of a legion in the Roman Empire's service—the 3rd Italian. And the letters weren't all in *capitalis quadrata,* either.

Upper and lower case, she thought. *Modern Western printing conventions, like that piece of paper the colonel showed us.*

She sighed. An older friend of hers had managed to get to the United States, via Mexico, before they clamped down on that. She'd never dared to think seriously about it. Plus it would have rebounded on her parents, while they were alive.

Liu hissed slightly; he must have been noticing the same things. He extended his hand and the Kushan noble tossed the weapon; it smacked into his palm, and he brought it closer.

"Percussion lock," the colonel said in Mandarin, pulling back the hammer; she saw it was different from the flintlocks they'd introduced. "More nearly waterproof."

He brought it close to his eyes; the light wasn't very good, since they were using the old style of oil lamp.

Liu's finger flipped open a circular lid on a shallow cylinder in front of the base of the hammer.

"Tape primer—metal, I would guess, from the design of the rear of the hammer, paper would not be practical, too prone to swell and tear if it is wet. They probably did that...the Americans...because northern Europe is so wet, as opposed to the steppes north of China. Lead, pewter, or some other soft metal in a narrow strip with percussion material at set intervals. It runs up this slope and over the touchhole mounting."

He worked the hammer again, and a few of the Kushans flinched away.

"Yes, when you draw it back it turns the central rod inside this circular magazine at the same time as it cocks the mainspring. Thirty to forty caps in the metal tape. It's better than the ones we've introduced...well, we didn't think anyone else would have *any* firearms, so why get fancy? There are some worthwhile ideas here."

Oh, wonderful, Black Jade thought. *An arms race...then fusion bombs, eventually...I thought we were going to make this age* better *than it was.*

He put it butt down and ran a little finger into the muzzle.

"Rifled, too. Probably with expanding-base bullets, the Minié system. We weren't going to bother with that for a few years..."

The Kushan who spoke Old Chinese was looking baffled at the Mandarin, and Liu smiled thinly.

"Thank you for your gift, noble sir," Liu said—in Old Chinese.

Black Jade translated it into Greek...

When they were walking back to their quarters, Liu spoke casually to her in Mandarin:

"Oh, Dr. Yuè...about those bodyguards you hired in the Tarim."

"Yes, sir?" she said, concealing a sudden tautness...though she couldn't be sure it *was* concealed from someone as sharp as the colonel. "I didn't want to bother you with trivialities."

"Thank you, but the security of our mission is my business. When we return, please discharge them in the Tarim, near to their birthplaces. I will furnish you with a bodyguard detail recruited in China proper."

"Yes, of course, sir, if you think that advisable," Black Jade said.

Which means I have to make up my mind about what I've been trying to decide to do...or not do. Soon!

⇒ CHAPTER TWENTY ⇐

Rome, Palatine Hill
May 17th, 173 CE

"And in the history from which you came, I would be in Pannonia now, fighting an interminable war against the Germanii and Sarmatians. And winning it, but my...successor...would give up all that I devoted fourteen years to winning," Marcus Aurelius said.

My son, Commodus, he thought. *I had to push Artorius into telling me what came of his accession...do I wish I had not done so? No: Truth must be confronted and understood, at any cost.*

It brought a spike of inward pain that his Stoic training let him...not ignore, but disregard.

Artorius bowed his head slightly. "But that will not happen now, sir," he said calmly. "Germania is now a set of Roman provinces, right up to the German Sea...what we called the *Baltic*. So is Parthia, and so are the former kingdoms of the Caucasus on both sides of the mountains...and *they* surrendered without fighting after they saw what happened to the Parthians."

He is a Stoic too, the Emperor of Rome thought ironically. *And brought to it by reading my* Meditations, *at that! And he and I agree that being Emperor is a burden, not something for which a sensible, self-controlled man would strive! Unless duty compelled, of course.*

They were alone save for Galen in the conference room...

"It was here in this room that I decided to go to Pannonia after the news of the Tenth's victory...your victory...over the

Marcomanni," Marcus Aurelius said. "Somewhat ironic! From that . . . a great deal sprang."

"Indeed, sir," Artorius said.

He looked at the murals and grinned.

"Though that depiction of Cleopatra . . . that *is* meant to be Cleopatra, there? It is not . . . completely accurate, shall we say."

The Emperor of Rome laughed aloud. "Exactly my thought at the time!" he said. "But doubtless Octavian . . . the first Augustus . . . thought it more dramatic to defeat a powerful Egyptian sorceress . . ."

"Rather than a highly intelligent Macedonian Greek woman with a big nose," Artorius said. "And the memory of his propaganda survived."

Galen laughed aloud as well, and Marcus Aurelius felt his smile expand . . . slightly . . . as he let the ache of Commodus recede.

The others would be arriving shortly; the air was mild, and only a little city smell came up from the lower parts of the Roman capital to war with incense and the early cherry blossoms. It would be milder even in summer this year. After he and Galen . . .

Inspired by our travelers in time, the Emperor thought.

. . . had grasped the relationship between filth and disease . . . and how insects could carry the miniscule parasites that got into your blood and organs on their feet and mouths . . . they had tightened up the sanitary regulations of the City greatly. Via the *praefectus urbi,* what the Americans called the urban prefect, whose authority extended downriver to Ostia and around Rome for a hundred miles.

And the saltpeter leached from the sewage pays for it, he thought. *Now that the leeching beds and artificial swamps are in operation and the sewers redirected. Even the Tiber stinks much less! Already deaths have declined somewhat, I am told, and there will be more.*

That had started in conjunction with the vaccination campaign that had stopped the plague from the east. Marcus Aurelius flattered himself that had reduced resistance overt and passive to the new sanitary regulations. Cities throughout the Empire would compete to emulate Rome, too, of course. Galen's reputation was godlike, now . . . and that rebounded to the Emperor's credit as well.

If only all my problems could be solved by such a stroke of cleverness! he thought.

There was a clank of segmented armor as the two Praetorian guardsmen by the outer side of the door drew themselves up—but no clatter of shields, since both of them were carrying rifles these days, and of the latest make at that. They raised them vertically before their faces in both hands, and set their right heel slightly backwards, what Artorius called *presenting arms*.

The imperial *comites*, his closest advisors and heads of various parts of the government, came in and bowed; Galen and Artorius rose and did likewise.

My cabinet, *Artorius calls it,* he thought. *An interesting concept—perhaps I will bend this toward that institution he has described. It seems of much practical use! With regular meetings, at which each is informed of the other's deeds and problems... very convenient for mutual help. And a* General Staff *for the Army...*

When everyone was seated... Marcus Aurelius first, of course... Artorius received a number of glances. Some friendly, like that from Legate Fronto, some impressed by his reputation, a few annoyed by his rapid rise. This wasn't the first such meeting he'd attended, though. The Emperor spoke:

"Gentlemen, I have two announcements to make."

Everyone looked at him. He was conscious of how those looks had changed, over the past... it was nearly eight years now.

He wasn't just a well-thought-of successor to his uncle... and adoptive father... Antoninus Pius anymore. He was the conqueror of Germania and Parthia, voted the names *Germanicus* and *Parthicus* as triumphant titles by the Senate.

The Emperor who'd added nearly a million square miles and ten or fifteen million more subjects to the Empire.

Not to mention more provincial governorships to hand out as patronage; the senatorial families nearly all approve of that, at least. And everyone is relieved that the Army garrisons are further from the City.

And he was more deserving of those titles than previous holders, who'd simply won victories against those folk. *He* had outdone even the accomplishments of the first Augustus... and without the necessary but unpleasant fighting against fellow Romans that then-Octavian had waged.

The first Emperor had conquered widely, but he had also presided over the disaster of Varus' defeat in the Teutoberger Wald and the loss of newly conquered Germania, and had merely negotiated the return of the Roman legionary eagles the Parthians had captured from Crassus and implied that it was an act of submission to bolster his reputation.

Whereas I had the Parthian King of Kings carried behind my chariot in the triumph.

"The first concerns the narrow-stripe Tribune Lucius Triarius Artorius," he said.

More glances at Artorius, who was looking surprised and a little alarmed.

"In consideration of his great services to the State, I have decided to elevate him to the rank of Imperial Quaestor," he said.

Artorius started a little in astonishment, though he tried to conceal it.

"He is a freeborn citizen," Marcus Aurelius said. "He meets the property qualification for the rank—"

Which meant he had a minimum of one million sesterces in property, which Artorius did—many times over, though he'd have to buy land in Italy as well. There were dozens of senators who had less than he. Artorius seemed a man of very limited covetousness, indifferent to wealth beyond a reasonable minimum save as it made other things possible, but his innovations had increased it willy-nilly.

"And he has rendered invaluable services to the *Res Publica Romana*."

There were nods at that, some friendly, others grudging... but nobody was going to deny that the *new things* had indeed strengthened the Roman state!

Not to mention the other, nonmilitary things which were spreading rapidly and making the Empire richer, as well as greater and more powerful. More concretely, they had made almost everyone in the room—except the clerks—richer by considerable amounts too.

Even the clerks would be eating better and at less risk of sickness, and doing their writing on paper and their figuring with the new mathematics. And for a sestertius to buy the stamp, they could send a letter anywhere in the Empire now.

Even I am richer, the Emperor thought. *The revenues from the* res privata *have grown considerably as the* new things *are applied there, and bid fair to increase even more. I can compel a more rapid change on the Emperor's estates... which example makes them spread more quickly elsewhere, too. Egypt now makes cotton cloth as fine as what we bought from India at great trouble and expense. All the* saccharo *anyone makes sells at high prices. That and the new mines and the revenues of the former Parthian territories means that ordinary taxes bear less heavily on everyone. And so strange, to think of famine as something no one need fear! Soon that will be true for the whole Empire, with the new crops and methods.*

"Accordingly, he shall now be a broad-stripe man," the Emperor said; that was the colloquial phrase for elevation to the upper senatorial caste of the Roman aristocracy.

A quaestorship in Rome made you presumptively a member of the Senate, and Artorius' square, bluntly handsome face was briefly fluid with shock as he remembered that, and his slightly tilted blue eyes blinked. Marcus Artorius smiled a little at that, and at the glances from the others. Which showed they realized that this was a surprise to Artorius, too. Few men without keen perception reached this level of the Imperial government.

Not if I can prevent it! the Emperor thought. *The danger to the Empire of stupidity in high places more than outbalances the danger to* me *of keen wits.*

There was a murmur of congratulations, more or less sincere... and Repentinus, the Praetorian Prefect, followed suit grudgingly.

Artorius himself rose and bowed. "I pledge my gratitude and loyalty to you, Augustus Caesar," he said. "But...ah..."

Marcus Aurelius waved a hand. "Please, no false modesty, excellent Artorius," he said. "I consider this to be necessary for reasons of State, as well as abundantly deserved."

He gave another slight smile. "And you may tell your lady wife Julia that you and she are bidden to dine with me and the Empress tomorrow, with a select circle of mutual friends, in celebration."

Artorius bowed his head, this time in acceptance.

His wife will be pleased for him. And his brother-in-law will be transported with delight, the Emperor thought. *But Artorius... he is genuinely uninterested in rank for its own sake. An unusual man. He values it only for what be done with it, as he does with money. He labors ceaselessly for Rome, as I strive to do.*

"The second matter is that of our relations with the Kushan kingdom, to the east and northeast of our new provinces in what was formerly eastern Parthia," he said. "I will let the *Tribunus laticlavius* Lucius Triarius Artorius explain the details."

Well, damn, Artorius thought. *Come on, man, get it together! It won't make all that much difference if you have senatorial rank.*

"Ah..." He cleared his throat. "As you know, I and my clients... former students of mine... arrived here nearly eight years ago from a realm in the western ocean called *America*. A country not unlike Rome, if not so great, and with a system of government based on Roman precedents, ruled by a Senate and a single chosen ruler. One which was destroyed in a terrible war, fought with weapons far more powerful than those I have provided here. More powerful than those I *could* introduce here."

There were grave nods. Nobody doubted the story now... or that weapons of terrible power had been used. Not after what he *had* introduced had wrought such destruction, and expanded the Empire beyond the set bounds that had endured for nearly a century.

"My clients and I thought that my former nation's enemies... the *Zhōnghuá rénmín gònghéguó* in their tongue, a powerful but wicked empire... had wholly perished in that war. Recently—"

A couple of years ago, he thought. *No need to be too detailed about it.*

"—Caesar Augustus became aware that as I and my four clients survived to seek refuge in the welcoming arms of glorious Rome, so five from the *Zhōnghuá* sought refuge in the Empire of Han, which is on the other side of this—"

He tapped the marble-topped table with his knuckles.

"—great continent."

Eyes went to the map board standing on a set of tripods at the foot of the table, opposite the slightly raised dais and back-and-arm bearing chair where the Emperor sat. It showed Eurasia, with the borders of the realms—and it showed it from Hibernia/Ireland to as far as China and Japan. The Han Empire was outlined in black, and Rome in red.

And everyone can understand at a gut level how big Eurasia is, because they know how long it takes to get from Britannia to the other side of ex-Parthia, Artorius thought. *And we've put up metal maps in every provincial capital, too, and anyone can buy paper ones. It gives the merchants ideas, just for starters.*

"The Empire of Han is the only state comparable in size and numbers of people to Rome in all the world. Well, comparable to Rome before the recent annexations. And there these refugees have done as I and mine have here—introduced much the same in the way of *new things*."

There were hissed curses, and expressions of shock and fear, swiftly tamped down by *gravitas*.

Fronto frowned and measured the distance with his eyes.

"But...that is too far for active hostilities," he said. "Especially since so much of the distance is desert, or frozen mountains, or both," he pointed out. "Even when our roadbuilding is completed...which is proceeding rapidly...it would be *difficult*. Not impossible, but difficult...and slow."

Artorius nodded. "Indeed, though once the new ships are numerous enough... But...it has recently been revealed that they are providing thunderpowder weapons to the Kingdom of the Kushans, who are on our new eastern border. And their previous, peaceful king has been overthrown..."

A muttered growling sound came from the Romans.

Artorius sighed inwardly. *And so the game commences,* he thought. *God dammit.*

"Congratulations," Legate Fronto said to Artorius, and they shook hands.

"You just made me a hundred aurei and bragging rights," the Roman general added.

The meeting had split up into twos and threes, gradually drifting toward the door, after the Emperor left. Artorius let his brows rise. The Roman from the east...

No, from the center *of the Roman Empire, nowadays!*

...grinned and went on:

"I had a bet on how soon you'd be a broad-stripe man with Legate Bassus, Lucius," Fronto said easily.

And now he's addressing me by my praenomen, Artorius thought; *it wasn't* Tribune *anymore. Do they ever have a sense of social gradations here! Fiddle-de-de, as Scarlett O'Hara would say.*

"*He* thought it would take another two years...though I have the advantage of knowing more details of the situation on the new border."

Another grin. "And don't worry, I'm not going to drop hints

about my daughter again. She's betrothed to someone else now, and she'll be married in two months."

Artorius frowned. "She's...what...eighteen years old now? Nineteen?"

Which is rather old for a Roman aristo's daughter to marry, he thought. *Weird, but there you are.*

"Ah, yes. You might think it rather late, but I've been listening to Galen. He says...now...that the risk of death in childbirth is much greater if a girl marries less than four years after her first menses. Flora wasn't happy about waiting—she wanted badly to be mistress of her own household, for which I don't blame her—but I insisted. I'm not going to let my other daughters marry before they're eighteen or nineteen, either."

Artorius smiled and spread his hands. "You are a good father, then. By the way, Julia is expecting again," he said...not quite changing the subject.

"That'll be your...fourth, yes? And all flourishing? You're a lucky man."

"Yes, the first three are all thriving...Marcus."

Fronto gave a half wink and laughed, shaking his head.

"Also a *new thing,*" he said. "I've secured a graduate of the Galen Medical Institute for my household too...a woman, who's fast friends with my wife now. *And* she speaks Greek—from Neapolis, originally. Many senators have. That will make a difference."

Childhood mortality had taken a nosedive among those who'd listened to Galen's advice...and since he was the Imperial physician and widely rumored to be the son of the God of healing, Asclepias, many had, especially at first among the upper class. His stopping the plague in its tracks had elevated him to the point where some were making sacrifices to his name.

They'd been walking over slowly to the door while they chatted.

"Ah, the new rifle!" Fronto said, as they passed through the doorway.

Both the Praetorian guardsmen there carried them. They *looked* very much like the first iteration...except that there was a brass strip down the back of the sloped grip, with a knob on the end. One of them handed his weapon over to Fronto at a brisk command. The general tugged at that knurled brass rod.

The brass strip came up; it was hinged at the forward end. That exposed the breech end of the barrel, with its bottom end machined down into a cone. On the underside of the sturdy strip of brass was a rectangular steel block, with a corresponding cone shape inset on its forward face.

"Hmmm. I wouldn't have thought that that would contain the hot gasses by itself," he said thoughtfully. "And they wear away metal if they escape, I'm told."

"It wouldn't on its own...Marcus," Artorius said, switching to the praenomen instead of *sir* at the last instant.

I'm not as sensitive to rank as a proper Roman aristo, he thought.

He extended his hand, and spoke to the guardsman: "A round."

"Sir!"

The Praetorian dropped one from the right-hand ammo pouch into his palm, and Artorius showed the bottom of the paper cylinder to Fronto.

"It's stained...that's grease, from the smell..."

Artorius nodded. "There's an inch-thick wad of greased felt there at the base," he said. "It gets shoved back against the join between the cone and the negative of it in the block by the explosion and seals it against the gasses. And it only has to work once. You shove the next round against it and it goes out ahead of the bullet, helping to keep the barrel clean."

Thank you, Westley Richards of Birmingham, he thought.

That British firm had invented the system in the 1850s. It wasn't as good as a drawn-brass centerfire cartridge...but it was quite workable, and mass-producing precision brass on that scale wasn't going to be possible for quite a few years.

"Ten or twelve rounds a minute with this, Marcus. Four or five times the rate of fire we had with the first model. We should have them all rebuilt by the end of the year...it takes only a few hours to do it for each, so we're rotating them through the workshops at Colonia Ferramenta and Colonia Chalybe as well as producing new ones to this pattern. The first legion turned over their old models for the new, the old ones were refitted and issued, and so on."

"Ah, as many shots per minute as a bow!" Fronto said. "And nine-tenths of the legions have rifles now. Even many of the auxiliaries."

Artorius nodded. "And it can be loaded lying down, or on horseback," he said.

Fronto's eyebrows went up. "Lying down?" he said, sounding slightly scandalized.

Artorius smiled and shook his head.

"Marcus, when the other side has rifles too, you *want* to have your men lying down to shoot. And running forward...or back, if they're retreating...from one piece of cover to another. Hopefully, the other side will be idiots and stand in plain sight to be killed, but you can't count on it. Idiocy like that tends to diminish over time, because it gets you killed. Or your side defeated. Or both."

Fronto's mouth quirked; that changed to a frown of distaste as he thought.

"That grates a bit...but I can see why," he said.

Artorius nodded again. "Bravery comes in different types, different ways. Roman soldiers are brave—they stand up and meet the enemy head on, shoulder to shoulder with their comrades."

Fronto nodded proudly. "They certainly do!"

Artorius sighed. "But with weapons like this—"

He tapped the rifle and with the knuckles of his right hand and handed it and the round back to the guardsman, and went on as they walked between him and his comrade and into the corridor with its polished marble floor:

"—you need a different type of courage. One that doesn't depend on having a comrade within three feet of you each way. One that will keep you moving forward from rock to rock, aiming and shooting, with invisible death always waiting. You only glimpse the man you kill; the one who kills you is usually invisible."

Fronto began to speak, then shook his head. "That is...different indeed," he said, casting a look over his shoulder at the door to the meeting chamber. "Quite different."

No, he's not a fool, Artorius thought. *But the implications... those are a different matter. You don't naturally see them before they kick your balls up around your ears. Repeatedly. Fortunately, they don't have to come up with them on their own as a fruit of terrible experience. We...me, specifically...know that history and the solutions to the problems. No need to repeat Pickett's Charge or Mons and Passchendaele.*

Then he looked eastward, his mind traveling six thousand miles.

Unfortunately, that's something the other side knows too. So, what do you do when you don't have an advantage? You figure out a way to cheat, *is what you do!*

⇒ CHAPTER TWENTY-ONE ⇐

Near Rome
April 25th, 173 CE

Josephus ben Matthias looked at his nephew Simonides across the marble-topped table in the courtyard of his uncle's suburban country villa. The smell of cherry blossom was strong in the air, and a fountain cooled the air behind him with its spray.

The younger man—his eldest brother's youngest son—was just turned twenty-five now. He'd lost the gawky shooting-up look he'd had when...

When we discovered Artorius and the others unconscious next to their... baggage... in that field in Pannonia, he thought. *In normal times it would be time and past time to arrange his marriage.*

Josephus paused for a long minute, amid the sound of birds singing and the scent of blossom, and the murmuring plash of the fountain. Then he went on aloud:

"Your Persian is much improved," he said.

He could see the younger man suppressing a smile; the improvement had come via a Persian-speaking slave... a girl, and a very comely one. She had been freed just recently, and given a pension... or dowry. And she'd also converted to their religion. It wasn't totally dissimilar to the Zoroastrian faith that some in Persia followed; they believed in One God too, even if they made far too much of His opponent.

"Nobody would mistake you for someone who grew up speaking it," he went on. "But anyone who speaks it could understand you. And it will work... more or less... for several related tongues

335

east of Persia itself. East of the former Parthian eastern border...
which is now *our* eastern border."

Now Simonides was a young man in truth in the flower of
his strength; about his uncle's five-foot-six, slimly muscular and
trim, his dense curly black beard and hair cut fairly close. Josephus examined him critically...

*Yes, he could pass for a local anywhere from Hispania to north-
ern India, he thought. For a Greek, for instance... his Greek is
obviously a native language for him... or for a Syrian, his Aramaic
is very good too. Or for a Roman, come to that, he has a native
accent in Latin nowadays... well, he is a Roman in a way, born
a citizen to citizen parents. His accent is from the City, at that.
Young people are more flexible that way.*

He sighed; in a year he'd turn forty himself. He still felt
strong, but you slowed down a little every year, and hardships a
young man could shrug off... well, time passed for every man.
Such was the will of HaShem.

At least my teeth are sound and white, he thought. *Another
gift from Artorius!*

Then he went on aloud:

"Have you considered this... this task seriously?"

His nephew grinned.

Was I ever that brash? Josephus thought.

Then: *Well, yes, when I was his age! Though by then I was
married and a father, which sobers you.*

"Certainly, my uncle," the younger man said... in Persian.
Then in Latin: "And I have considered the rewards, as well."

Simonides had done well managing the family's paper factory
here in Rome and the relentless expansion of its water-powered
pulping mills and presses; it employed two hundred men now,
slave and free, and Simonides owned a third of it himself through
the new limited-liability shares arrangement.

That share made him quite affluent, if not quite *rich* by the
standards Josephus used nowadays. The rewards for taking this
mission... they *would* make him rich. Enough to be eligible for
the Equestrian Order as soon as he returned, courtesy of the
Imperial *fiscus.*

If he returned. Josephus judged the odds of that as no better
than even.

Then the younger man's grin died.

"And we owe Artorius a great deal," he said soberly. "Further, we owe the *Emperor* a great deal—and not just our family, but all Jews. He has made himself *our* ruler, rather than merely a ruler over us. As Cyrus was, who ended the Babylonian Captivity."

Josephus nodded with a slight smile. Just this month, Marcus Aurelius had abolished the *fiscus Judaicus*, the special tax that had been levied on all Jews after the revolt of a hundred years ago... and which had been tightened up after the Bar Kokhba rebellion. And he had abolished the law forbidding Jews to enter the city of Aelia Capitolina, the Roman colony founded on Jerusalem's ruins a long lifetime ago by the Emperor Hadrian.

Not quite permission to restore the Temple, but the next thing to it, he thought.

There had been grumbling in the Senate, which the Emperor had simply ignored. Perhaps Artorius had suggested it... but while he was a very powerful man, a friend to Josephus and a benefactor to his people, the Emperor was more powerful still. And did not *have* to listen to any advice, even from a man he knew came from the remote future.

Simonides didn't know *that*, of course. He simply thought that Artorius came from a land now destroyed—perhaps sunken beneath the ocean. That was enough.

And in a way, even true... and very convenient, now that the Renewal *and the* Roman Empire *are back from their voyage over the western ocean. Strange lands, savage peoples, without even knowledge of bronze, much less of iron... the world is so vast! And thanks to Artorius, I know of the things of note there. And I am building similar ships. For our family... and more immediately, for my sons...*

"You speak the truth," Josephus said to his nephew. "The Emperor is righteous, even if a gentile, and he has treated us with more justice than any Roman ruler did before him. So is Artorius righteous... more so... and he is our benefactor—of our people, and more particularly of our family. Helping him... and Rome's ruler... is an honorable thing to do, and if you are determined to do this, I will not attempt to dissuade you."

Simonides smile returned. "Unlike my mother!" he said, with a chuckle. "She is horrified. But she will keep silent, knowing it helps keep me safe." He paused and went in: "Well, a *bit* safer."

The older man pointed a finger. "But you must take great care! Every detail of the pretense you will undertake you must commit to memory! I will grill you concerning it...and I warn you, I will be merciless!"

"I'm not a fool, my uncle," the younger man said. "Of course you will. I welcome your help *and* your grilling. My life will depend upon it."

Josephus sighed, stood and extended his hand. His nephew knelt, and he placed his palm on the young man's head.

"Then my blessing upon this, and I ask that of the Most High as well. *Baruch HaShem.*"

Hopefully, he added to himself. *But His will be done.*

Eight months later, Simonides looked behind him at the string of camels, squinting against the westering sun. There were forty of them, mostly laden with paper, superwine disinfectant, and crates of the new leaded glass, so clear as to be almost invisible. The handlers, servants and roustabouts were mounted on camels themselves, unlike himself and the guards, who were riding horses...ones carefully habituated and trained to tolerate camels.

Not to like *them,* Simonides thought. *Who does? Even male camels only like females during the mating season! They spit and gargle curses upon each other when that is over! And the guards respect me and will probably be...reasonably...honest. Even a false merchant journey requires endless juggling! If you want to be convincing.*

The deserts of eastern Parthia were behind them now, and the mountains of Bactria, and the winding mountain pass that led into this valley—that had been a bit nerve-wracking, despite the frequent forts and patrols, because the mountain tribes were notoriously cruel bandits.

You could see rocky hills from here, but the plain around them was rich farmland irrigated by canals from the river, reaped stubble and sprouting new-sown grain and deep-green alfalfa pasture and orchards; like the road, the waterways usually had trees planted by their sides.

He cast an eye on the fields. Further from the city they'd been mostly in wheat and barley—or rather, in stubble or newly plowed and planted grain. With patches of cotton, and the sweet reed the people here made sugar from though it was not as white or as sweet as that made from beets in Pannonia and the greatly expanded Dacia.

This close to the great city of Pushkalavati—for some reason Artorius had called it Peshawar occasionally, though the Greek name for it was Peucelaitis—vegetables were encroaching.

They were in commercial fields rather than truck for the villagers, sure sign of a city nearby. And there were extensive orchards of fruits—apricots, pears, pomegranates, quinces, peaches and figs, with wine vineyards and the courtyard-centered houses of grandees set in walled gardens here and there.

Now and then one rode by, gorgeously robed, with an escort of mounted spearmen.

Peasants, slaves and hired workers labored, picking and planting. The air smelled of greenery, water, manure, and a growing hint of the city-stink, stronger even than the smell of his camels. Traffic had been getting steadily heavier, as well; everything from two-wheeled oxcarts heading in with loads of produce and out with iron tools and bar stock and other household goods, to long trains of camels like his, to pack mules and throngs of travelers on foot, often bent under burdens of their own.

And not far from the rough, bumpy road...

No Roman highways here! he thought, with a hint of condescension. *Not even the old style, much less the new ones of macadam.*

...was a caravanserai, a complex of mud-brick stables, pens, rooms, and a central hall where food and drink and charcoal and firewood were sold. He nodded—his information was spot-on; and what could be a more natural enquiry for a merchant?

He was just about to retire for the night when the soldiers came. The messenger came into the big room the same instant as they did, with drawn swords.

Simonides shouted and threw himself at the armed men. It was totally futile...except that the messenger turned on his heel and left in the same instant. He would *probably* escape and *probably* make it back to Roman territory with a tale to tell...

That's something, *at least,* he thought, as the shields clubbed him down.

⇒ CHAPTER TWENTY-TWO ⇐

Gandhara Province
City of Pushkalavati
Western Capital
Kushan Empire
January 1st, 174 CE

The dark cell stank, of fear and feces. Simonides rattled the chains that held his arms up in a Y above his head; less in the hope of weakening them than to keep his arms from cramping. So far there had only been beatings...except for the little finger of his left hand, which was now missing its fingernail. And throbbing painfully and swollen.

Something scuttled in the darkness; almost certainly a rat. The young Jew grinned tautly to himself, feeling the hurtful flex of his swollen lips. That was more frightening because he now knew that rats...and their fleas...carried diseases that could kill him.

Not that they will likely have the opportunity, he thought. *The Kushans will do it first. Or those mysterious strangers from the east! The enemies of Artorius' homeland...and now, of Rome.* Baruch HaShem...

The older man among them had called him by his name and his father's name, too. Obviously that was how they'd known he was spying; some spy of *theirs* further west, perhaps in Rome itself, or Antioch, had marked him down as a member of the Jewish family who were close to Artorius.

And perhaps he sent a letter by the new post to someone in the new eastern provinces, who went across the border and informed them, Simonides thought. *That would be bitter irony—a second cousin of mine commands the new postal service! May HaShem send me courage! Let me not disgrace Rome or our family and faith.*

He was carefully *not* thinking of what they'd do to make him talk. Sufficient unto the day was the evil thereof. Still, his head whipped up when the iron-shod door clanked.

"Here he is, great lady," the jailer said... in vile Greek. "The stinking Roman spy."

He laughed, hawked and spat on Simonides feet, and prodded him with a club, grinning with blackened gap-toothed relish. The younger man could see that clearly, because one of the woman's attendants had a lantern—of the new type—in his hand, and set it on a shelf in the rocky wall of the cell. There was a squeaking and chittering as he did, and Simonides could see a gnawed skull resting in one corner of the little room.

He looked at the woman's attendants... then looked again. They weren't Kushans. Their belt-cinched lap-over jackets were shorter, and not as dirty, though they were rough everyday working garments. And they didn't look quite the same... though both were alike enough to be brothers, both with weathered skins, brown hair and greenish-hazel eyes...

They look more like native Pannonians, in fact, he thought. *They say the Tocharians who dwell east of here in the Tarim deserts look like that. And their jackets... that is what Pannonian Gauls call a* plaid *fabric.*

His gaze sharpened on the woman. He'd seen her before; she'd been present as an interpreter at his first questioning. Now she spoke... in Latin. It was oddly *accented* Latin, but comprehensible enough if he concentrated.

"Jailer, you are the bastard son of a perverted whore who fucked donkeys," she said.

The jailer kept grinning... and didn't even blink. From what Simonides had seen and heard, people hereabouts were even more sensitive about insults to their mothers than they were where he'd been born.

Either he has magnificent self-control, or he just doesn't speak Latin... and I would not bet on his self-control.

The woman went on to Simonides:

"You are from Artorius," she said, also in Latin... which they now knew the jail guard very probably didn't speak.

It wasn't a question.

Well, technically I'm working for the Frumentarii. *But Artorius... yes, more or less. He oversaw this project, with the Praetorian Prefect.*

"Would he welcome me? If I go over to him?"

Simonides licked his lips. The question was a jolt... but was it sincere? Or a trap?

My life depends on my answers, he suddenly realized. *But I don't know what answers she wants! I don't know enough to lie... best the truth, then.*

"Yes, lady, he would. He is a merciful man, and only kills when he considers it inescapable. A great warrior, but not a lover of war. I have heard him say that even victory in war only creates possibilities, for peace, for prosperity through the *new things* he has introduced."

"Yet he attacked Parthia," she said. "Or rather, the Romans did at his urging."

Simonides nodded. "But he... and his... in his language I have heard him say *graduate students...*"

She looked at him blankly, then blinked. Evidently she spoke the English the Americans used among themselves, though it had taken her a moment to penetrate his accent.

"Ah, students," she said in Latin. "He was a teacher?"

"A soldier at first he says, and then a scholar and teacher after he retired with serious wounds. The other Americans were his students—now his clients and helpers, two women and two men. I have heard him say that the war which destroyed his homeland was probably started by the government of... of *Zhōngguó.* But that the ordinary people there were not to blame, for they had no say in the direction of the State."

She closed her eyes. The moment stretched, and then she opened her eyes and sighed... and said something in a language that had a haunting pseudofamiliarity. Not Greek or Latin or Persian, but one that had something in common with all three.

Her two attendants moved in swift unison. One pulled a cord out of his sash and whipped it around the jailer's neck; the man goggled and grabbed at it as it came tight. The other drew a long straight dagger and stabbed up under the man's ribs... which showed why the cord had been used. There was nothing but a breathy grunt from the local man. That and a smell as of bowels and bladder released, and the iron scent of blood as the man collapsed and the killer withdrew his knife and wiped it on the man's clothes.

And nobody will be surprised at such smells in a dungeon for enemies of the Kushan emperor...the new Kushan emperor.

Blood flowed, into the crude drain in the floor and toward the exit. Things rustled in the darkness there, beneath the filthy straw.

The wrist manacles holding his arms above his head were fastened with soft-iron pins hammered closed and peened over. One of the attendants went out into the corridor, and returned with a stool and a hammer and chisel, both probably the dead jailer's; a few strokes freed him. The woman...

"What is your name, lady?" he said, careful to be respectful as he rubbed his wrists.

"Daiyu. In Latin...it means black...jewel. *Yù*, in my tongue... it refers to a precious stone that isn't known here. No matter."

"Lady Daiyu," he said, inclining his head.

She produced a pair of manacles, and snapped them open and closed. "Wear these. They will not be locked, but discard them only if we are in great danger or I tell you so. And look..."

"Frightened, lady?" he said quietly. "That will not be hard!"

"Well-concealed fear would be better, *Domine* Simonides," she said. "You did an admirable job of that earlier."

One of the attendants picked up the lantern, and jerked his head for Simonides. The Roman hung his head a little, forcing his steps to drag a bit, and took up a position between the two men with the eastern woman behind them. They both had long straight swords with cross guards and ring hilts at their belts in scabbards with square tips, and knives in smaller versions of the same.

She's armed too, he thought. *That thing at her waist is a* pistul. *It holds the death of a dozen men, from what Lord Artorius said.*

It was still very hard not to swing along with a smile. *Not doomed to death by torture!* he thought, deliberately darting his eyes about.

Blessed be HaShem!

Simonides' arms hurt, of course, and his wrists were badly chafed. He flexed them inconspicuously, working out the stiffness and ignoring that in his neck and back for now. Daiyu followed along behind him, and as they walked up the corridor and out of the dungeon gate the Kushan soldiers there made obeisance to her, bowing deeply...though from the sidelong glances some of them resented it.

The attendants...her bodyguards, he supposed...ignored them. They climbed more stairs, the corridors and rooms about them growing less Spartan as they did. When they emerged into a torch-lit courtyard he looked up at the sky in reflex; by the stars and moon, it was past midnight. The city-stink wafted over them, not as strong as the pong of the dungeons, but *deeper* and *wider* somehow.

Another man like the first two...and a similar-looking woman dressed in the same clothing...waited there, by a string of horses. They were armed as the first pair had been, and all the saddled horses save two had combined quiver-bowcase sets before the right knee, of a pattern he'd have called Sarmatian, differing only in details.

Some of the other mounts bore packs, five had saddles, and a round dozen were apparently just remounts.

Good horses, he noted. *All over fourteen hands, and they look strong and well cared for.*

His mind was calm, after an intense effort; he tried to keep it receptive, drinking in sight and smell and sounds, making only obvious judgments.

New-style saddles...different in a few details from ours in the Empire, but not in essence.

One of the two original guards jerked a thumb at a horse... one that did *not* have a bowcase. He made a performance of mounting it slowly, moving awkwardly and groaning a little, sitting slumped over with his chained hands on the pommel. Daiyu mounted her horse with ease, but he noticed a sheen of sweat on her face as she turned her beast.

She's afraid too, but keeps it controlled well, he noted.

The Kushans opened a gate—a narrow one, not the broader main entrance which was closed for the night, and they all had to duck their heads as they went out in single file. The street outside had a semicircle of light on the—roughly cobbled—street; and the dungeons had been below the citadel, so they had a view over the rooftops. Most of them were flat, and here and there a light flickered. This time of year was too cold for people to sleep on their roofs, of course. The streets were in deep shadow, and few showed the moving lights of lanterns.

Nothing so black as a city after nightfall, Simonides thought. *Or as dangerous if you're alone. Though the Americans say that can change . . .*

They rode silently save for the clop of hooves on stone—he noticed from the sound that these were *shod* horses, with the nailed-on horseshoes that Artorius had introduced.

And these . . . Chinese, was the word he used . . . did likewise, Simonides thought.

They spent half an hour in the darkened streets, mostly moving at a fast walk; occasionally one of the bodyguards held a shuttered lamp above a map Daiyu held across her saddlebow and clicked it open for a heartbeat or two. At last they came to a gate—not the main one on the road that led down from the mountain pass to the western side of the city wall, but a smaller secondary one.

A soldier came out and hailed them. Daiyu rode forward and bent in the saddle to talk to the man; she reached down, and something passed from hand to hand—something that chinked.

Coin, Simonides thought, as he fought to keep the bubbling joy from taking him over. *A bribe!*

A postern gate was opened—one of the narrow ones to the side that many forts had, used in war for spies and scouts and sudden attacks on a force trying to overrun the main gate.

And sometimes opened with bribes! he thought.

They rode through, stepping up the pace. After a few minutes they drew rein in the shelter of a copse of woodland, and she dropped back to sit her horse beside them. The man with the shuttered lantern leaned closer and opened it, yellow light spilling out.

"Show me your left hand," she said—in Greek.

She speaks many languages, like my uncle Josephus, he thought.

He held out the hand; she took it and turned it so that the light fell full upon the wounded finger, which brought a hiss of pain.

"This is infected," she said. "You know about—"

Then a word in English: *bacteria.*

He nodded. "Yes. Artorius . . . and the Emperor's physician, Galenos—has told me of them. Me and many others, now."

"We can't have you slowing us down," she said, then applied something she took from a saddlebag.

It was cool and soothing, without the biting pain of the redoubled superwine now used further west to prevent infection. She wrapped a bandage around the little finger and the one next to it, and the chafed wrists, and then shook some pills out of a bottle—of some very smooth white stuff, not glass or pottery, that he could not put a name to.

"Swallow these," she said, offering him the pills and her canteen. "We can't have you down with illness, there will be a pursuit—a relentless one."

He did, reflecting that she had something else in common with Artorius—a no-nonsense bluntness not hidden in a mantle of false concern.

He took the pills without hesitation. Josephus had sworn him to secrecy, when he saw *him* giving pills from Artorius to his dying son, and he had kept that oath... but he'd also noticed how the boy rallied and steadily healed when he'd been on the verge of death. The canteen held water cut with local wine. He supposed the feeling of relief was illusion—not even American medicines could heal him in an instant. But it wasn't just his own hopes that buoyed him. The knowledge he held would have strengthened the enemy, strengthened them greatly.

One of the bodyguards came up—the woman. She handed him something he recognized, a tunic jacket from his baggage that he pulled over his head against the suddenly apparent chill. And something else he recognized from the gear he'd brought, that had been hidden in a false bottom beneath a crate of glassware wrapped in cloth.

It was a rifle; of the new sort that loaded from the breech. With it was a leather bandolier on a strap, holding forty rounds. He checked the roll of pewter caps on the lock, then raised the lever and pushed a paper cartridge into the breech and snapped it shut. Now it would fire as soon as he pulled the hammer back and squeezed the trigger. Artorius had taken him aside on an Imperial estate in the suburbs and trained him personally before he left Rome.

There was a clatter as one of the bodyguards came down from a ridge and spoke urgently. Everyone reined around.

Daiyu smiled grimly. "Lights and noise from the gate we left," she said. "Now we ride!"

They did. The horses were fresh...and when they weren't, they'd have remounts who hadn't been carrying weight.

He spoke to Daiyu—in Latin, this time; there was little chance anyone else here would understand it.

"Your guards—" he said.

Daiyu shook her head. "Brothers and a sister," she said. "Their father was killed by the Han governor of their town in the eastern Tarim. They can't go home and have sworn loyalty to me; I kept them alive."

Simonides hoped that was enough...enough to counterbalance the reward the pursuers would doubtless dangle.

A week later the urgent, soft call of the bodyguard on watch brought them all starting up out of their bedrolls and reaching for weapons.

They were on the western flank of a range of hills, hidden under a cleft in the rock.

"Men approaching," he said—in Greek, for economy of time; they all spoke it at least a little, and it was Simonides' native tongue. "From the northeast, two dozen at least, all mounted."

It was dawn, with a dry, dusty freshness to the chilly air. They all swung their saddles onto the day's first mounts and led them quickly down the little defile that led out onto the rolling plain to the east...

To find two dozen riders barring the way. Their horses were ponies, and they were sitting simple pad saddles or bareback, but half of them had recurve bows with arrows on the strings, and the other half had bundles of javelins slung over their mounts' withers. And they all had swords, or at least long knives. Their beaky hook-nosed faces had unpleasant expressions that their straggling black beards did not conceal.

"Well, well," their leader—he was the oldest, looking a hardworn forty or so, with one of the odd round, raised caps on his head. "Strangers on our clan's land without our leave."

He grinned. "We'll take your horses and the two whores, and then we'll sell you. Throw down your weapons."

Simonides could follow it, with a bit of strain. Apparently they'd never seen a rifle before, but the leader frowned as his thumb moved the hammer back.

Daiyu sighed.

"Utpalavarṇā," she said.

That was the name of the Tocharian woman.

"You take left," she went on in Greek. "I'll take right. Everyone ready."

"You all of you—throw down steel," the leader of the ... bandits, Simonides decided ... said in atrocious Greek.

"*Nûn!*" Daiyu said ... and he thought he heard a tinge of regret in the word, which was odd.

That was Greek for *now!*

Simonides had the rifle to his shoulder before the word was finished. It was only fifteen feet; his finger *squeezed* the trigger without jerking it as he'd been taught, with the bead of the foresight on the bandit leader's chest through the little circle of the backsight.

Bang!

The horse beneath him moved at the last instant before the plume of stinking off-white smoke jetted out of the muzzle.

Instead of striking the man's chest, the bullet punched into his face just above the bridge of his commanding nose. It was a length of soft lead the size of a child's thumb, half an inch across, and moving very, very fast. The puff of smoke hid the target for an instant, and then he saw the man sliding out of the saddle in a sideways-to-the-rear lurch with his robes fluttering and a round blue hold in his forehead ...

... and a hole the size of two smallish fists in the back of his head, and a spray of blood and brains and splintered bone catching the two behind him across *their* faces, dripping and clumping across almost comical astonishment.

His hands reloaded automatically. It was fortunate that he didn't need conscious attention for that, because—

Beside him Daiyu had her *pistul* in both hands. It went *crack-crack-crack-crack-crack-crack-crack-crack-crack-crack-crack-crack*, a rapid sharp-edged stutter unlike anything he'd heard before. There was no smoke, but half a dozen of the bandits were dead or wounded ...

Utpalavarṇā had drawn something from beneath her coat. He knew roughly what it was—Artorius and his clients were working on something similar. He called it a thing-that-revolves, and apparently the Chinese were ahead with that. She held it in her hands in the same grip Daiyu was using, and it went *bang!* ... six times.

It jetted smoke too, like his rifle but less.

Three more of the bandits went down, amid a fair cloud of thunderpowder smoke. By the time she shoved it back into her jacket and drew her sword, he had the rifle reloaded: when he brought it up, all the living bandits were riding away in a spray like an opening fan. He brought the sights down on the rear of a galloping horse and fired.

Bang!

Another puff of smoke, and the horse went down with a scream of equine pain and terror. The rider bent over its neck was thrown free, came down with his head striking a jagged rock...and didn't get up. The male Tocharians had used their bows to some effect too.

Daiyu's hands had been moving as well, snapping a little rectangular metal box out of the grip of her *pistul*, and shoving in another with a *click*. Utpalavarṇā had snapped the revolving part of her weapon out, and shoved in another...also with several clicks.

"Ride!" she said. "They'll be back with more, probably!"

Then she stopped, said something in a totally unfamiliar language that sounded like a *sung* curse, and levelled her binoculars to the west.

"More!" she said, well-concealed fear in her voice.

"Let me have them!" Simonides said, reaching out.

She did. He focused them—it was the same arrangement of a central screw you moved with your thumb as the instruments Artorius had brought from America. The line of riders was suspiciously neat for a gang of hill-country raiders...

They sprang closer through the binoculars. Simonides started to grin; the lead rider had a helmet with a transverse crest, and was shouting something over his shoulder and gesturing with his spatha.

"Romans!" the Jew shouted, his voice cracking with incredulous joy. "*Romans!*"

⇒ EPILOGUE ⇐

The cavalry *ala* was making camp. It was the First Victorious Thracians, a veteran unit, and they were laying out their bedrolls and picketing their horses with efficient dispatch. On a reconnaissance mission like this they didn't have wagons and tents along, of course. They'd be on hardtack, cured sausage and cheese tonight; a few packhorses had cracked barley for their mounts, since the grazing was sparse here.

A screen of sentries was at some distance, dismounted and with their rifles out—each man in this unit had one of the new single-shot breechloaders. Usually carried in a scabbard strapped to the saddle in front of the right knee, as well as a ten-foot lance in a tube behind the right hip. Their dark-gray mail was covered by camouflage-patterned surcoats, and their swords were hung from their saddles—dismounted action didn't use them, under the new regulations.

Artorius stood beside his own mount, looking at Simonides and...

Yuè Daiyu, he thought.

The young Jew was looking rather battered, hair and beard dusty and disheveled, and a bandage on his left pinkie and around both wrists. He was also grinning convulsively, which wasn't surprising.

"You did right distracting the men who arrested you," he said to his friend's nephew. "The messenger got out... and I was out here on a tour and heard what he had to say. I decided to ride with one of the scouting *alae* we sent out."

"HaShem inspired your thought!" Simonides said. "That... simplified matters considerably!"

"You are...Artorius?" the Chinese woman said...in good but accented English. And she'd apparently learned it from someone who spoke the British variety.

Subtract the stress and dirt, and she's about thirty, maybe a little more, Artorius decided.

It had been eight years since their joint arrival. So much had changed...

Competent in a whole bunch of ways, from what Simonides says. Well, you wouldn't expect otherwise!

"Arthur Vandenberg, history professor at Harvard, until eight... nine years ago in June," he said easily in the same language. "Before that I was a soldier, until I took some bad wounds and retired. Now I'm Artorius. And you're...an academic, if I've ever seen one, Ms. Yuè?"

"Doctorate in historical linguistics, from Beijing University," she said, nodding. "Before I was...well, conscripted, more or less, for this—"

She waved a hand around. "—thing. An emergency replacement; the man who had the...mmmm, spot before me...failed somehow. I don't know what happened to him. Though I *suspect* I know."

Artorius nodded. "And you want to defect?"

Daiyu nodded back. "You accept that?" she said...as if she was having difficulty believing it.

Don't blame her. She'd doubt her own shadow, if it could talk, Artorius thought. *Growing up in the world's finest surveillance state.*

"Provisionally." He smiled again. "It's not your innocent face, Ms. Yuè. It's just the fact that I don't think your...Colonel Liu?"

"Yes. I think...Ministry of State Security, but I'm not sure."

"Probably State Security," he nodded. "I don't think he'd risk a quarter of his uptime assets on this...particularly since there was no guarantee you'd reach us alive. It's Afghanistan, after all, even if they call it Bactria! I don't think he'd have let Simonides go, either—too valuable an intelligence asset, and I believed him when he said he hadn't spilled his guts yet. But you realize we'll have to keep an eye on you for a while?"

"Yes," she said, and almost visibly slumped in relief. "Of course."

"But you'll be valuable to *us*," the American...

He could see her switch gears to: *Roman-American.*

...went on. "We'll give you protection and as much property

as you can use. You realize that your colonel will try to have you scragged...killed, that is?"

"Yes," Daiyu said. "But...I was helping ensure another nuclear war. Before we realized you were here, I was helping to *stop* one. And what Colonel Liu would like to build in the Han Empire...I was not...favorable to our government, shall we say. To prevent the nuclear war...well, I could not do you any substantial harm. I *could* do Colonel Liu harm...and I wanted to because I hate him."

At his raised brows she went on:

"Two of my grandparents were at Tienamin Square in 1989," she said bluntly. "They escaped...and did not leave their names on any official list, or I would not be a graduate...but—"

Artorius nodded. "Well, there's no reason you should have been happy with your government; that's credible."

He chuckled. "There were times I wasn't all that happy with *our* government, but you had more reasons and better ones. Tomorrow we'll head west, and we'll do our best to keep you safe."

⋙ AFTERWORD ⋘

FOR NERDS LIKE ME:
CONCERNING TECHNOLOGICAL
INNOVATIONS AND TIME TRAVEL

PART DEUX

If you've endured to the end of this book, you'll have noticed that the pace of innovation my time travelers have introduced has sped up a bit.

Partly this is simple addition: some innovations help make other innovations possible. Partly it's that they've gotten the Imperial government (in the person of Marcus Aurelius) on their side and have more resources to draw on.

My primary protagonist, Artorius, classified the tech stuff he and the other time travelers could introduce into two categories in the first book: Type A, and Type B. Type A are those where only the idea, the *concept*, was new, and existing—second-century Roman—materials and craft skills could make them. Examples were a wheelbarrow, a cradle scythe, and, oddly enough, black gunpowder.

All three were easily within the skill sets of Romans of the time...and all would be significant. Gunpowder is obvious enough; wheelbarrows would make moving heavy loads short distances much more efficient; and the cradle scythe would increase harvesting productivity for small grains (wheat, barley, oats, rye) by up to eight times. Other examples of Type A included wood-framed saddles with stirrups, windmills (wooden gearing was not a mystery to Romans) and fuller's earth and mechanical fulling.

You could add, for example, macadamized road surfaces to the Type A catalogue. Romans built good roads, but they built them with layers of stone and concrete five feet deep when they could. With McAdam's early-nineteenth-century technique, you can get very similar results with simple crushed rock, in a layer about a foot deep, on heaped-up and well-drained dirt tamped firmly down. Much faster, much less labor intensive, and oddly needing much less *skilled* labor than the Roman style. Romans tended to over-build; their motto was that if some is good, more is better, which is an important reason we have a lot of their ruins about us still.

Then there were things like potatoes and maize/corn, or cotton seed (which they sent to Egypt with a hope and a prayer). Those would have massive consequences, but growing crops from seed was not a new concept for Romans, to say the least.

Slightly more difficult items like late-model spinning wheels and treadle looms with flying shuttles would be a bit more difficult, even with the diagrams and miniature models the time travelers have along, courtesy of Dr. Fuchs... who didn't survive the transition, but had planned to. Those were made mostly of wood, by hand, and would be at least ten times more productive per labor hour than the drop spindles and much more primitive looms the Romans used.

There are whole rafts of things like that, and their cumulative impact would be massive. Paper, printing—and ideational technologies like germ theory, accurate anatomy, positional arithmetic and algebra. Medical knowledge would revolutionize demographics; for example, you could have cities that didn't kill more people than were born, and infant mortality would be reduced by nine-tenths. Fairly simple lens grinding would do amazing things too, once you delivered new formulas for glass. So would better hull forms and sails and rudders for ships.

However, you'd run up against some of the limits of classical-era technology fairly soon in other fields.

The example I'll use here (and used in the book, too) is iron.

The Romans were a thousand years into the Iron Age, which began around 1000 BCE and spread rapidly. Not least because iron is so much more *common* than the copper and tin used to make bronze. The problem there would be that the Roman methods of producing iron (and still more, steel) were insanely low productivity and weren't really very hot quality-wise either.

At the time of my story, the Chinese had early, rather primitive blast furnaces producing liquid cast iron.

The Romans didn't. They were still using bloomeries—furnaces about the size of a tall man that produced a "bloom" of iron mixed with semiliquid slag. This lump—rarely more than a few pounds—then had to be heated and hammered over and over to get the slag out. The iron was mostly "wrought" iron, low carbon and soft; but it varied widely, some being steel of sorts.

Producing steel usually required heating iron in contact with carbon, then doing...extremely labor-intensive...things with it. The quality was extremely variable and couldn't really be controlled well; you had to take your chances and it was ultraexpensive.

The Roman Empire in the 160s CE had somewhere between 50–80 million people in it; it produced somewhere around (no exact figures are available!) 80–85,000 tons of iron a year. It probably used several hundred thousand people to do that, counting part-timers. Most iron production was in small, artisanal bloomeries; the Imperial government had much bigger ones of its own for the armed forces, but they used the same techniques, just many more of the same small clay furnaces. Oh, and the air draught for the bloomeries was slaves or other workers with a hide bellows, and the ore was hauled in in baskets on the workers' backs, like the charcoal.

By way of comparison, in 1776 the United-States-To-Be had around 2.5 million people...and it produced 30,000 tons of iron. That was around the same as Great Britain did, and it was in eighty or more widely dispersed blast furnaces. The total labor force was probably about 20–30,000, again including part-timers. The power for draught and other purposes was supplied by water wheels.

So the American colonies, at the end of the colonial period, produced nearly half as much iron as the whole Roman Empire, with a population that was something like one-thirtieth the size. The iron was vastly cheaper, much better quality, and used for vastly more things than the Romans had done. That was done with charcoal-fired blast furnaces; the British had invented coke-fired ones as the Chinese had long before (coke is to coal as charcoal is to wood) but they hadn't spread far yet. American furnaces didn't generally switch over to coal until the decades leading up to 1850...by which time the US, with a population of

23 million was producing a bit over half a million tons of iron. In other words, ten times the Roman Empire's peak production with a third or less of the population.

So, what are Artorius & Co. to do vis-à-vis iron? Well, he knows where the iron ore is, courtesy of Dr. Fuchs's maps—there's a big source in what was then the Roman province of Noricum, not far from Pannonia; it's called the Erzberg, the "Mountain of Ore."

And he knows what to do—the books and records Dr. Fuchs sent back include detailed plans. Could he do it?

Yes, probably... provided he had lots of money and much the same thing, government backing.

The Romans built big stone structures all the time and had good concrete; the shell for a blast furnace wouldn't be difficult for them. The lining of firebrick would be a little harder... but they did make brick. Making firebrick would be a *bit* more complicated but not beyond them, once the ingredients had been pointed out and the kilns given mechanical draught. And they did use water mills already, though almost all just for grinding grain.

Improved models would be simple enough—mostly Type A. Ones driving wooden piston bellows could be done. Crankshafts hadn't been invented yet, but they soon would be and could be made from beams of wood at first.

Steel... ah, that's a bit different.

Bessemer or open-hearth converters wouldn't really be practical, not for a long while. But there was a technique (discovered much earlier by the Chinese, naturally) and developed in the West about the same time as the Bessemer converter: the Heaton process.

Basically, this involved pouring molten iron (from the blast furnaces) into a crucible containing... saltpeter. That reacted with the carbon, there was a dazzling bit of a display of sparks, and, with care about the amount used, you got steel. You could consolidate and homogenize that by pouring the still-molten steel into larger crucibles.

That would be more expensive than Bessemer or open-hearth steel... but vastly easier and vastly cheaper and vastly better (in that the quality was more consistent) than the Roman methods of making steel.

So Artorius makes, over the course of about a year, a "modern" iron and steel plant... modern as of the 1830s, as he says, with an excursion to the 1850s in the form of Heaton steel.

And that would have massive, massive downstream effects. It would make metal tools of all types vastly cheaper, with knock-on effects in virtually every sort of handicraft—just for starters, it would make iron cheap enough that everyone could use horseshoes.

It would introduce *cast* iron and *cast* steel, neither of which the Romans had...and which could be used for everything from cooking pots to stoves. And one such plant could produce about one-tenth of the entire Roman Empire's iron production, with far, far fewer workers, and including products they just couldn't make before.

For example, cannon made from cast steel...much stronger than bronze, much lighter than cast iron. The real problem there would be boring out the barrels, but that wouldn't be impossible given detailed plans and models and a fair amount of trial and error. That's easier if you know it eventually *will* work.

Boring engines would be very useful later, for example for cylinders for steam engines. Cannon-boring machines were what James Watt used in our history, initially!

Ten such plants could double the Roman Empire's iron production, and push steel production much further than that (so it would be far less expensive and used for far more in the way of tools). After a short working-in period they'd also make the Imperial government a *lot* of money. You wouldn't need to run them with maximum efficiency to undercut the production costs of everyone else; the tech gap is that big.

Twenty plants—about a quarter of what the US-to-be had in 1776—would double Rome's iron production at a fraction of the cost.

With unpredictable consequences! For instance, what would the suddenly unemployed bloomery workers do? Possibly...many different things.